A hippo-size foot caught Ryan in the side

The kick seemed to be almost in slow motion, yet was monstrously powerful. It threw him out of the water and onto his back on the wet grass.

He heard screams, shots. Shaking his head to clear his eye of water, he saw an unbelievable sight: a man as tall as himself, with a trim waist, powerful chest, bare from the waist up, his skin and long flying hair as albino-white as Jak Lauren's, swinging a pair of swords at a group of swampies while other men surged out of the wind-whipped brush, holding spears, cutlasses and longblasters.

Then a pale fist the size of Ryan's head slammed into his solar plexus, doubling him like a dying caterpillar. The air erupted out of him, and he passed out.

Other titles in the Deathlands saga:

JAMES AXLER

DEATH LANDS®

Haven's Blight

A GOLD EAGLE BOOK FROM

W✺RLDWIDE®

TORONTO • NEW YORK • LONDON
AMSTERDAM • PARIS • SYDNEY • HAMBURG
STOCKHOLM • ATHENS • TOKYO • MILAN
MADRID • WARSAW • BUDAPEST • AUCKLAND

Recycling programs
for this product may
not exist in your area.

First edition January 2012

ISBN-13: 978-0-373-62612-0

HAVEN'S BLIGHT

Oh, Creator! Can monsters exist in the sight of him who alone knows how they were invented, how they invented themselves, and how they might not have invented themselves?

—Charles Baudelaire
1821–1867

THE DEATHLANDS SAGA

This world is their legacy, a world born in the violent nuclear spasm of 2001 that was the bitter outcome of a struggle for global dominance.

There is no real escape from this shockscape where life always hangs in the balance, vulnerable to newly demonic nature, barbarism, lawlessness.

But they are the warrior survivalists, and they endure—in the way of the lion, the hawk and the tiger, true to nature's heart despite its ruination.

Ryan Cawdor: The privileged son of an East Coast baron. Acquainted with betrayal from a tender age, he is a master of the hard realities.

Krysty Wroth: Harmony ville's own Titian-haired beauty, a woman with the strength of tempered steel. Her premonitions and Gaia powers have been fostered by her Mother Sonja.

J. B. Dix, the Armorer: Weapons master and Ryan's close ally, he, too, honed his skills traversing the Deathlands with the legendary Trader.

Doctor Theophilus Tanner: Torn from his family and a gentler life in 1896, Doc has been thrown into a future he couldn't have imagined.

Dr. Mildred Wyeth: Her father was killed by the Ku Klux Klan, but her fate is not much lighter. Restored from predark cryogenic suspension, she brings twentieth-century healing skills to a nightmare.

Jak Lauren: A true child of the wastelands, reared on adversity, loss and danger, the albino teenager is a fierce fighter and loyal friend.

Dean Cawdor: Ryan's young son by Sharona accepts the only world he knows, and yet he is the seedling bearing the promise of tomorrow.

In a world where all was lost, they are humanity's last hope....

Chapter One

With a loud splash, something huge flew out of the black bayou water and smashed to pieces the water-strider boat pedal-driven by the gangly young Tech-nomad called Scooter. The motion of the dark form breaking the surface had caught Krysty Wroth's eye as she stood in the stinging sun by the rail of the yacht *Snowy Egret* talking with Mildred Wyeth. Now she stared horrorstruck as the enormous shape slid back below the surface as if being absorbed into the thick water. Her long red hair stirred around her shoulders, although there wasn't a breath of wind on the bayou.

A cry of fury and despair came from *New Hope,* the lead ship of the Tech-nomad convoy. Krysty looked that way to see a woman built not that much differently than she was, buxom and broad-shouldered, standing in the prow shouting for someone to do something. She had a brush of russet hair, and was dressed in a dark green tank top and baggy camou cargo pants with lots of pockets, clothing the Tech-nomads seemed to like.

"That's Jenn," Mildred said. "The poor bastard's woman."

The group's healer, Mildred was shorter than Krysty and stockier. A fairly light-skinned black woman, she, like Krysty, wore a long-sleeved shirt. And like the ivory-skinned Krysty, she had a tendency to burn in the harsh Gulf of Mexico sunlight. Her hair, braided into beaded plaits, was covered by a floppy canvas hat.

"They're all around us!" a voice shouted. Krysty looked

around to see mounds resembling living hills of water rolling on all sides of the little fleet. The other water-striders were fleeing as fast as their pilots' legs could drive them. Their function was to scout out danger.

They had.

Krysty saw Ryan, the companions' nominal leader, up on the *Hope*'s bow beside Jenn, forward of the first of its three weird cylindrical rotor sails. The tall and rangy man, his long black hair tossed by the stiff breeze, shouldered his Steyr sniper rifle, bringing the eyepiece of its telescopic sight to his single piercing blue eye. Despite the danger of the vast dark plunging forms surrounding him, Krysty's heart thrilled to the sight of him. To her he epitomized everything good about a man in a desolate world.

Beside Ryan the slim form of Jak Lauren crouched on the rail, clutching a guyline in one hand. His big .357 Magnum Colt Python revolver glinted in the other. Krysty thought the albino team resembled an updated version of a typical pirate from one of the few picture books she'd read as a girl. Which was ironic, in that pirates were a major reason the normally pacific—and reclusive—Tech-nomads had hired the six companions onto the convoy. The companions and Tech-nomads had a history.

In general Ryan and his companions were aboard to provide protection against nautical dangers. Such as seaborne raiders—and whatever the gray shapes were, easily the size of land wags, humping the dark water all around and vanishing beneath.

"These people are pretty well-heeled for pacifists," Mildred muttered, unslinging the weapon their employers had lent her to augment her favored ZKR 551 target revolver. It was an M-1 Garand semiautomatic military rifle that had been elderly when Mildred herself was born, decades before the skydark. Longblasters were also coming into view up on the white rotor-ship ahead of them. Jenn waved bare sun-browned arms, shouting at people not to shoot for fear of hitting Scooter.

To Krysty's distress she could see no sign of the pilot of the stricken scout boat. Just a few long splinters of wreckage bobbing near a green bank of the broad pool the convoy was crossing, between stands of cypress hung with Spanish moss.

"Whatever these creatures are, they must weigh tons," Krysty said.

"Not much hope for that poor man," Mildred agreed. "Damn thing looked as if it came down right on top of him."

Shots cracked from the *Hope*. Jenn screamed. Ryan lowered his SSG to grab her upper arm and give her a good shake.

The *Egret* lurched below Krysty's feet and she lost her balance. Mildred's hand clamping on the woman's arm saved her from slamming her ribs against the sailboat's lovingly polished brass rail. She smiled and nodded her gratitude.

The ship's captain strode up to them with long strides of her long slim legs. Her name was Isis. She had long silver hair caught in a topknot that hung far down her slim back. Her complexion was dark olive, her face narrow, high-cheek-boned, with dark eyes set on a slant and showing distinct epicanthic folds. She was a tall woman, and was ignoring a little grubby hairy guy in shorts whose splayed bare feet were padding on the deck, taking two steps to her one to keep up.

"I told you, Ice," he was saying. "I told you and told you. These things *hate* power craft. It's in their genes from predark."

"It's dead calm here, Jammer," she said without urgency. "If we spend too much time sitting like logs in one place, the Black Gang'll be all over us."

Stopping by Krysty, she held out a long, dark object with one bare arm.

"Here," she said. "That thump was one of these mutie monsters trying to stave in our hull. My sailing master's right. They hate us. And they're big enough to take us down if they get a good run."

Despite her own substantial strength, Krysty almost dropped the object when she accepted it in both hands. It was a Browning Automatic Rifle; she knew it weighed upward of twenty pounds.

"Time to earn your keep," Isis said. Her disreputable-looking companion, Jammer, dropped a canvas bag full of loaded 20-round magazines at her feet. The heavy BAR, actually a light machine gun—*light* being a relative term—shot the same ammo as Mildred's Garand, .30-06. It was potent enough that both women, neither of whom was shy about firearms or afraid of a little recoil, were glad their longblasters were both on the hefty side. Especially since they didn't have to carry the things.

That was the sweetest part of this gig: they didn't have to hump it at all. They had ridden a hundred miles of Gulf Coast with no more effort than it took to get along with their employers. They admittedly could be a prickly bunch, although as Mildred said they preferred to avoid conflict rather than to seek it out.

And now conflict had sought them out.

"What *are* those things?" Mildred called after the captain as she moved on, snapping orders to her crew in a voice that cracked like a whip without being raised.

"Big and pissed," Isis said without turning her head. "Shoot them."

With a loud, meaty thump the *Egret* heeled hard to starboard, throwing Krysty and Mildred against the port rail. Krysty set her butt on the low rounded housing of a gangway that led below and swung her legs across. Her companion putted around abaft the housing, clutching her beefy rifle and muttering.

The corrugated rubber soles of the red-haired beauty's boots thumped the deck. The far rail was still angled up against the sky. Peering over, she saw a vast gray shape rolling in the thick, murky water alongside the *Egret*'s sleek hull.

"Crap!" Mildred exclaimed, joining Krysty and peering over. The gray mound disappeared, then came back with another shuddering impact, trying to capsize the seventy-foot yacht and making a good go of it. "Whatever those things are, you shoot them and they find out, there's gonna be trouble!"

"One way to find out," Krysty said grimly. She shouldered her heavy weapon, hung it over the rail with the muzzle not three feet from the heaving gray back, and fired.

She took no pleasure in harming any of Gaia's creatures, but Krysty was no more a vegetarian than she was a pacifist. She respected, indeed in effect worshipped, the natural cycle of life. It had amused her once, when Mildred told her an activist of her own childhood years had recorded a song called, "I Don't Eat Animals and They Don't Eat Me."

"They did, though, when her time came," Krysty had observed.

Mildred had just stared at her, then broke up laughing.

The Browning roared. Its steel-shod butt jackhammered Krysty's shoulder even though she was snugging it in firmly, the way the shooter of a longblaster should. A yellow-and-blue flame jetted from the black barrel and almost licked the gray wet hide. An arc of shiny brass casings spurted away to one side, twinkling in the sun, looking incongruously like droplets from a seaman pissing over the rail.

Holes appeared in what had to be immensely thick hide, and black blood spurted. Chunks of blubber and hide were blasted away.

Though its head was under water, the creature uttered a roar of pain and outrage. It bubbled up around the great shape as it vanished hurriedly and with amazing smoothness into the black water. Its vehemence rocked the boat.

"Did you kill it?" Mildred asked, peering doubtfully at the roil of water. Then she ducked back as a big fleshy fluke sent a parting shot of water geysering up at the women. Mildred jumped back with a yell.

Krysty just turned to shield her blaster from the bulk of the water. The slog of swamp water against the back of her head and shoulders was neither cool nor refreshing. It would take forever to dry in air that seemed scarcely less wet than the bayou itself, and would stink while it was doing it. But that, too, was part of Nature.

"Doubt it," she said.

BOTH RYAN'S GROUP and the Tech-nomad squadron under the guidance of a long drink of water called Long Tom had happened to fetch up in a little trading post called Port Landrieu at the same time. The companions were looking for work. The Tech-nomads had it: delivering a load of meds and medical equipment to a healer in the ville of Haven to the east, far enough up an estuary to have at least a little protection from the savage storms that rolled in from the Lantic.

For two days the three-boat convoy hugged the coast, slipping inland when the ever-shifting interconnections of the confusing skein of bayous and ponds made it possible to move laterally that way. Ryan and his friends were dubious about the densely grown swamp country. Jak had grown up in it and knew it well enough to know just how unwelcoming it was—although he had also, as a mere boy, proved to be among its most dangerous predators. Their employers, though, assured them that as bad as the bayous were, the open Gulf was worse.

The friends had enough experience of the Gulf and its special terrors not to doubt that.

But the trip had proved uneventful, even though the Technomads were vocally uneasy about the depredations of a particularly potent and nasty band of pirates calling themselves the Black Gang. Sight of a number of unfamiliar sails just on the horizon to the southeast had sent the convoy ducking up a stream late the evening before.

The companions had breathed a collective sigh of relief when the three ships, accompanied by a cloud of half a dozen surprisingly fast little pedal-powered scout boats, had embarked onto what looked like a small, placid, green-scummed lake. Some of the bayous they'd negotiated that very morning were narrow enough for a coldheart to step right aboard from the bank. Or even for some poisonous snake, a water moc or a copperhead, to drop from a dangling tree limb right onto the deck. Or onto an unsuspecting crew person's head.

Then the big angry whatever had smashed Scooter and his water-striding scout boat to splinters.

WITH SURPRISING ALACRITY Mildred whipped up her heavy Garand and fired. She was a stocky woman, and after years tramping the Deathlands with her newfound friends not much of it was fat. The rifle roared, and Mildred yelped and dropped it. Only the fact she had the sling wrapped around her arm kept it from dropping into the tea-colored water.

Twenty yards from the *Egret* a big, bulky, smoothed-off shape plunged back under water as fast as it had appeared, leaving a loud snort and a plume of vented air hanging above where it had been. Just before it vanished, Krysty caught a glimpse of a blunt muzzle and a glaring red-rimmed eye. Mildred was grimacing and holding her wrist with her left hand.

Quickly slinging her own massive weapon, Krysty

grabbed the longblaster, eased the strap free of the wounded woman and lowered it to the deck.

"What happened?" she asked, disengaging Mildred's wounded right hand. The doctor seemed disinclined to let go. Without even thinking about it, Krysty pulled the hand free.

"You've skinned your thumb pretty badly," she said.

"Sprained it, too," Mildred grumbled. "Now I know what the phrase 'M-1 thumb' means."

Krysty shook her head. "The Tech-nomads warned you. The bolt slams right back on you."

"Tell me about it. I'm not used to a rifle anyway. And it doesn't feel natural to keep my thumb on the same side as the fingers, instead of grasping the rifle like I would a pistol grip."

"We need to get this cleaned up and bound."

"Screw that! Screw the damn rifle, too." With her left hand she reached around and grabbed the blocky black revolver from the holster on her right hip. "This may not do much when I hit, but at least I *can* hit something with it!"

"And shoot one-handed," Krysty said. She unslung her BAR and started looked around for targets.

Its steam engine pounding furiously, *Finagle's First Law,* the squadron's third major vessel, churned past the *Egret* at about the same spot the great creature Mildred had messed up her thumb shooting at had vanished. Although he was out of sight on the far side of the main cabin, Krysty heard Jammer screech in outrage at the black pall of smoke it trailed from its doubled stack. The Tech-nomads' time-honored philosophy of avoiding confrontation only applied outside the family— as the companions had learned abundantly the past couple of days.

Above the engine's rhythmic thud rose a sharp-edged snarl. A cloud of white steam puffed away from the steamboat's prow. Krysty saw the skinny bare shoulders of a Tech-nomad named Stork turned toward her, pressed against the mesh back of a recumbent seat as his gangly pallid legs ped-aled wildly. His pedaling turned the six barrels of a Steam Gatling powered by the *Finagle*'s boiler. It was hurling .450-caliber lead slugs at targets on the far side of the tubby craft.

"Oh, shit, Krysty!" Mildred called. "Look at the *Hope!*"

The redhead turned to look past the *Egret*'s own prow, so much narrower and more graceful than the *Finagle*'s. Beyond the bowsprit she could see at least half a dozen water mounds churning around the rotor-ship.

Whatever these angry aquatic monsters were, a whole pod of them appeared to be on the attack.

As the two women watched, a creature erupted from the water to the *Hope*'s starboard. Its elephantine bulk crashed down across the ship's bow in an explosion of brown water.

Chapter Two

"Ryan!" Krysty screamed. She raced toward the *Egret*'s bow, holding her BAR at port arms. She heard Mildred's boots thumping after her.

A knot of *Egret* crew had gathered at the bow. A few held blasters or crossbows. The others were mostly pointing and shouting contradictory advice.

Krysty shouldered them roughly aside. She wasn't shy about using the Browning's butt or even its muzzle, still warm from the burst she'd fired at the one creature, to clear a path. The Tech-nomads yelped but gave way, seeming if anything more shocked and hurt than resentful.

As she came up to the rail she saw a slim pale figure, white hair streaming, leap from the rail onto the broad gray back of the monster draped across the *Hope*'s bow. With feet splayed on the tough hide, Jak pointed his Colt Python at the back of the oil-barrel-size head and fired.

A second man charged forward to hack at the monster's bristly snout with a long, broad-bladed knife.

"It's Ryan!" Mildred exclaimed, coming up beside her. "He's all right!"

But how long he'd stay that way remained an open question. Even as he slashed the beast with his panga, its companions began to ram the *Hope* with impacts Krysty could feel through the *Egret*'s hull. The rotor-ship no longer moved. The creature draped across the bow had stalled it. With the wind calm, its mass was apparently too great for the vessel's auxiliary electric motor to move.

Krysty raised the Browning. "Careful where you shoot!" a man nearby said. "Those're our friends up there."

"That's my man up there," she snarled. "And I know how to shoot."

She aimed at the nearest monster, a mound twenty feet long and almost ten broad, heading toward the port stern of the stalled *Hope*. She triggered a short blast. Spray flashed from the wide back. Another burst. With a steam-whistle wail the monster slid below the pool's greasy surface.

Bleeding from deep gashes generated by Ryan's panga, the first monster reared up from the *Hope*'s bow. The movement tossed Jak away like a watermelon seed. But the albino youth had sensed its muscles bunching and read the beast's intent. As it snapped its vast bulk up he sprang, using its motion to hurl himself up into the rigging of the *Hope*'s foremast. He caught the mast one-handed, like a monkey on one guyline, then planted his feet on another.

Ryan had stuck his big knife back in its sheath and was retrieving his Steyr rifle from the deck where he'd laid it. As lethal as the big scoped bolt-action was at range, it was a liability in a close-in fight.

Krysty fired another burst at a monster closing in on the *Hope*'s midship from the left. As her ears rang from the Browning's roar, she heard a snarl and a curtain of pink-tinged spray shot upward from the beast's back. Stork had apparently hand-cranked his Gatling around to bear.

He also got a touch too enthusiastic. Krysty's heart leaped into her throat as Ryan dived aft to avoid the burst of bullets that raked across the *Hope*'s prow. She heard Smoker, the *Finagle*'s black, burly and bearded captain, roaring angrily at the Gatling gunner as the squat steamboat passed between *Egret* and her stricken comrade.

A multichambered thunderclap from right behind Krysty made her duck her head instinctively. She spun to see Isis three feet behind her, a thin trail of blue smoke unspoiled from the muzzle brake of the BAR she'd just fired. Another fat tail like a giant beaver's paddle was just vanishing into a roil of water.

"Don't forget it's this ship you're mainly supposed to be protecting," the long, lean woman said. She sounded neither reproachful nor excited, just matter-of-fact, as always. There was a reason her crew called her "Ice."

Krysty nodded. For a few moments she concentrated wholly on shooting at any of the great gray shapes that presented itself, always keeping mindful of what lay behind them, as Ryan had taught her. No point in trying to help your friends if you chilled them yourself with your own blaster-fire.

She burned through three of the 20-round magazines so fast they might have been strings of firecrackers. Though she also knew to shoot in short bursts the long black barrel quickly grew so hot the heat shimmer interfered with her sighting. Even on such gigantic targets.

"Give it a rest," Isis suggested from right beside her. So focused had she become on her own shooting Krysty had been all but oblivious to the roar of the tall, lean woman's own big Browning, and the muzzle-blasts that buffeted her like a stiff wind. "We don't want to burn out the barrel. Or even have to take time to swap it out."

Krysty nodded. She looked around. The *Finagle* was running back on a reciprocal course along their starboard side. Before view of any of the steam craft but its stacks and radio masts vanished behind the *Egret*'s cabin, Krysty saw Stork with his Gatling swiveling and blasting away as fast as his long, wiry legs could revolve the barrels.

Beyond the wake the steam boat left in the black water,

topped with yellow foam, an object like an overturned whaleboat floated to the surface near the reeds of the far bank of the little lake. Red streamed down its blubbery sides. It was clearly dead.

But the death of one of their own only redoubled the aquatic muties' fury. The *Egret* was suddenly torqued counterclockwise by simultaneous impacts at bow and stern.

Krysty heard Isis's teeth grind. "Dammit!" the captain groaned as if in sympathy to the noises of the tortured hull. "Even if we wound the monsters fatally, most won't die quick enough to help."

Despite the fact she could still feel the heat from her BAR barrel on her skin, Krysty had to shoulder the heavy longblaster and open up again. She fired toward the port quarter, where a monster was charging, attempting to ram again. Some of the *Egret*'s crew joined in with fancy compound bows and crossbows, feathering the animal's back like an elongated seagoing porcupine. Krysty's powerful .30-06 slugs literally ripped bloody chunks out of the broad back.

The creature submerged before it struck, and Krysty staggered as the deck lurched beneath her bootsoles. The beast had clearly slammed against the keel in passing below, trying to break *Egret*'s back or turn her turtle.

Instead a huge basso roar of agony vibrated up through the very timbers of the former yacht. The mutie had succeeded in driving some of the arrows stuck in its hide deeper by hitting the boat. It was clearly in great pain.

As she popped another empty magazine from the BAR's well and stooped to grab a new one from the rapidly dwindling stock in the messenger bag Isis had dropped at her feet, Krysty grimaced.

"I hate the thought of wounding them without killing them." She was untroubled by killing when it was needful.

To eat, or to prevent whatever you were chilling from chilling *you*—man or beast. But she deplored wanton killing.

And she abhorred cruelty. She'd seen more than enough of it, known her share of it. That was one of the reasons she loved Ryan as she did: he was never cruel, never inflicted pain for its own sake.

"Me, too," Mildred said.

She had gone green. Despite the blood dripping from the gauze she'd hastily tied around her wounded thumb, she had kept up the fight. She was clumsily jamming a fresh 8-round spring clip into the top of her M-1 receiver, impaired by her wound.

"The Deathlands just seem to find something awful to throw at you every single day."

A shout from the bow made Krysty look. The water around the *Hope* seemed to boil. As she watched in horror a mutie with a good head start rammed its blunt head into the rotor-ship's hull just aft of the bowsprit.

She heard the crunch as wooden planks gave way.

Then she tensed as Ryan went over the rail, right on top of the gray back.

But the man hadn't been knocked overboard to his death. Or at least he wasn't giving in to Death. In an instant he had jumped up to stand with boots planted wide on the monstrous back, holding the panga with its long, heavy blade downward, both hands wrapped around the grip.

An enormous single-fluked tail whipped up out of the water as he plunged the blade almost to his hands in the creature's flesh. A cascade of water surged over Ryan, momentarily hiding him from sight. Krysty's heart almost stopped beating.

But the waters receded and she saw him still there, ripping his panga free, leaving a trail of gore in the heavy humid air as he cocked the weapon over his head again. She realized the splash had been produced by a reflex reaction to the pain of having the knife bite deep, more than any attempt to wash him off. Though she could barely believe it hadn't, so violent had the wash of stinking dark-stained water been.

Three times more Ryan plunged his panga into the horror's back. The beast backed away from the hole it had stove in the *Hope*'s hull. Its big blunt head snapped up, venting a squealing roar of pain and fury.

It dived with breathtaking speed. But like Jak, Ryan felt the creature's muscles bunch in preparation. Clutching the panga in his teeth, he threw himself toward the rail of the damaged boat, flinging out a hand.

His fingers reached just short of the rail. Then a bone-white hand gripped his wrist, his other hand clamping on Jak's wrist. Ryan's boots thumped into the white hull. A moment later he was clambering over the rail, helped by a dozen hands, which shortly were clapping him on the back.

"Whew," Mildred said explosively.

Krysty let loose the breath she'd unconsciously been holding, as well. "That man just doesn't do anything that isn't heart-stopping, does he?"

But Ryan was brushing off the Tech-nomads' congratulations. He gestured angrily. From her vantage point on the ship, trailing the other now by no more than forty yards, Krysty could see what he meant with painful clarity.

A dozen or more of the monsters still beset the squadron. No matter how dramatic, everything the defenders had done had amounted to a pinprick. Nothing more.

With a snarl of disgust Isis threw down her own BAR. Its barrel was glowing red now. It was almost certainly ruined, burned out. More to the point the heat would have warped the barrel, which could trap a bullet before it reached the muzzle. That meant there would be nowhere for the expanding gases of the next fired cartridge to go, except by blowing the receiver apart in the captain's face.

If she was lucky, that would chill her.

"This isn't working," she said. "If there was some way to discourage the bastards…"

Mildred hauled up her longblaster and cranked out all eight shots at a mutie making right for them. The empty 8-round steel clip flipped free with a ching. Krysty saw red streamers in the water before the humped form vanished again.

"Oww," Mildred moaned. "I feel like a mule's kicked my shoulder. With sharpened shoes on. Do you have any explosives? They might not kill the things, but—"

A roar made all three women turn to look aft. The *Finagle* was crossing *Egret*'s stern. A geyser of water, dark with a white crown, erupted from the bayou close beside the steamboat's starboard hull. Behind Stork the equally storklike figure of Doc Tanner wound up, raising his left leg and cocking his right arm way back, then hurling an object at an angle off the *Finagle*'s stubby bow. It splashed among at least a quartet of the huge forms. A moment later another waterspout blasted upward.

"What was that?" Isis exclaimed, shading her eyes with her hand.

"Bombs!" Mildred replied. "J.B.'s making up bundles of some kind of explosive and passing them off to Doc!"

"Son of a—" the captain said.

"We got dynamite, too," Jammer said from right behind her. Krysty could barely hear for the ringing in her ears. "Waterproof fuse. Whole nine yards."

The sailing master showed his brown gap-toothed grin. "Never know when you might need to shoot a channel to clear passage."

Another dirty fountain erupted, then another. The waters

around *Hope* churned white with the furious efforts of the giant aquatic muties.

But Krysty quickly saw the water was being churned by the creatures' frenzy to escape. A dead monster floated to the surface, belly up, distended and already turning blue from internal organs ruptured by shock waves transmitted much better through water than mere air. The rest seemed to be protected by the thickness of their hides, along with muscle and blubber and whatever else lay beneath. Judging by the speed they made, they weren't hurt badly.

"I hope they're not permanently injured," Krysty said. "Now that they no longer threaten us."

"Yeah," Isis said. "So long as they keep running They don't like the shock waves much."

Mildred sighed heavily. "So, what the hell were those things, anyway? They looked familiar, somehow."

Isis turned toward her. "Manatee."

"You're telling me we've just been attacked by giant mutant sea cows?" Mildred exclaimed.

Jammer grinned at her. "Huge mutie sea cows."

Chapter Three

Somewhere in the gathering dusk a bittern boomed. A flight of herons rose up from the dense woods northeast of the little island in the middle of a relatively broad bayou where the Tech-nomad squadron had anchored for the night. The bugs swarmed around the companions in jittery clouds, biting lustily despite the smoky driftwood fire that was burning in a pit that had been scraped clear.

Mildred stood with her companions by a small driftwood fire near the widening of the bayou, watching the herons winging majestically into a sky blazing red and orange with sunset. She felt bone-weary. She had helped the Tech-nomads tend their injured, including poor Scooter. The mutie manatee had broken almost all of his bones and torn most of his tendons free of the bone.

Three Tech-nomads had died: one strider-boat pilot drowned, a crew woman on the *New Hope* had fallen and broken her neck when a mutie manatee rammed the ship, and Scooter had succumbed to his horrendous injuries.

Another dozen were hurt badly enough to require treatment. That meant about a quarter of the squadron's people had wound up as casualties. Four of their eight pedal-powered scout boats had been smashed beyond repair. Of the three large craft only the *New Hope* had been seriously damaged. She now lay with a third of her length grounded on a little island down the sluggish stream. The starboard bow had been holed; some seams had been started on the portside.

These had been patched up to what the chief shipwright, a short-haired, hard-faced woman named Vonda, claimed was as good as new. Mildred had thought she heard doubt in the woman's voice, though.

The human toll affected her more than the material. But she was acutely aware the damage the Tech-nomad craft had incurred could come back later and bite somebody in the ass.

Even her friends or her.

Now she watched the big birds fly over, their white feathers turned to flames by the sunset, and sighed deeply.

"That's one way these swamps are better than most of the Deathlands, anyway," she said. "Sometimes it doesn't look at all as if the nuke war and skydark even happened."

"The waters have tended to obviate the scars left behind by the conflagration and its sequelae," Dr. Theophilus Tanner said. He was a tall and skinny man with pale blue eyes and a long, hard-worn face framed with lank, gray hair.

Although he looked decades older than any of his companions, he was really about Mildred's age, mid- to late thirties—if you stacked the years he'd actually lived through together. Like the physician, he was chronically displaced. He had been time-trawled from his own epoch, the late nineteenth century, by late twentieth-century whitecoats working for an ultrasecret project. Doc proved to be difficult. Tired of his antics, his captors sent him hurtling through time into the Deathlands. His time-trawling experiences had aged him so much that he looked to be in his sixties.

He and Mildred were by far the most extensively educated members of the party, in a formal sense—by Deathlands standards, almost ludicrously overeducated. His well-bred manners and pedantic manner sometimes irritated Mildred, as did his holding forth on a vast array of subjects. She considered his knowledge hopelessly out of date. Yet a lot of what he knew of history and natural sciences hadn't been superseded by time, and he had learned a great deal unknown to his own period during his torment by the whitecoats of Operation Chronos.

Mildred flipped him an annoyed glance and turned her attention to the fire. "Sometimes I think some of the wild things have done better after skydark," she said.

J.B. chuckled. "Like the killer sea cows," he said. "Getting turned mutie and all giant and everything seems to have turned the tables for them."

"GOT VID," JAK SAID. "Tech-nomads."

In his economical way the albino teen sounded as if he'd said all that needed saying.

Mebbe he did, Ryan reflected. True to their name the Tech-nomads lived and all but worshipped technology: a combination of tech preserved from the world right before the skydark, low-technology gleaned from millennia before even that, and the results of research and development they'd continued in their own secretive and eccentric way. They mostly tended to avoid contact with outsiders—as in, the rest of the world.

Which made this current gig the more a mystery. Ryan and his friends had brushed up against the Tech-nomads a few times before. The dealings had been peaceable: Tech-nomads avoided conflict. But as the crew had seen this day, they fought fiercely and with some skill when pressed.

"Wonder what they're up to over there," J.B. said. He jerked his chin toward the woods. Leaving only a couple sentries on each big vessel the Tech-nomads had trooped deep into a stand of live oak on the stream's south bank. Glancing that way, Ryan could just make out the odd orange gleam of firelight through the trees and undergrowth.

"They said they were 'sharing the water' of their dead brothers and sister," Mildred said. "Whatever that means."

"Not want find out," Jak muttered. He hunkered down by the fire, where the flamelight danced in his ruby eyes. He wore his customary camou jacket with jagged bits of metal and glass sewn into the fabric to discourage people, or other things, from grappling with him.

"They neglected to invite us," Ryan said. "Just as glad, myself."

"Look on the bright side, Ryan," J.B. said. Ryan cocked an eyebrow at him. His old friend wasn't known for looking on the bright side of anything. He was an ace armorer and tinker, though, and Ryan Cawdor's best friend in this whole treacherous world. "At least they aren't blaming us for the damage they took."

"In fairness, they could scarcely do so, John Barrymore," Doc said. "They knew when they engaged our services we lacked heavy weaponry."

Darkness had settled in. The only thing left of day was a sour yellow glow in the western sky, shading quickly to blue and indigo overhead. The crickets began their nightly commentary. The tree frogs trilled rebuttal.

J.B. showed the old man a rare grin. "But you more than made up for that in the end, didn't you?" He shook his head in admiration. "Thinking of using explosives to drive off the muties was pure genius."

"You did your customary splendid job fabricating the bombs."

"Not much doing, there. Mostly chopping up blocks of C-4, sticking in initiators, adding some short pieces of safety fuse, then lighting them and giving them to you to toss."

"Don't downplay your contribution, John," Mildred said reprovingly. "I've tried patching back together the hands of farmers who got careless trying to stick blasting caps in dynamite to blow up stumps."

J.B. shrugged. "Part of my job."

"We all did well today," Krysty said. She looked at Ryan, her green eyes gleaming. "I'm proud of you, the way you jumped on that mutie's back, though I wish you wouldn't do that sort of thing."

"Do I do it if I don't have to?" he asked.

He saw her ivory-skinned brow furrow, then realized he'd spoken a bit gruffly.

"Sorry," he said. "Guess I'm still on edge. I only did what looked to me needed doing."

Her smile dazzled him.

"Anyway," he said, "Jak did it first."

He slapped palms on the grimy thighs of his jeans and rose.

"I hope the Tech-nomads get their funeral ritual done with soon," he said. "I could use some food."

RYAN'S EYE snapped open. He was surrounded by darkness as tangible as a blanket with humidity and heat. He knew where he was at once—lying in his bedroll by the embers of their campfire, with Krysty's comforting presence peacefully by his side.

Something had tapped lightly on his right upper arm. It was uppermost as he lay with his head cradled on his rucksack. He happened to be facing west; the stars were invisible for a third of the way up the sky above the blackness of the forests.

"Know awake," Jak said softly. "Heard breathing change."

Ryan sat up, scratching his scalp on the right rear of his head.

"Can't get a pinch of powder past you, Jak," he said. He realized the albino youth had awakened him by tossing pebbles at him from a safe distance. A wise idea for one so young. When awakened too suddenly people had a reflex to lash out.

Beside him Krysty grumbled and sat up. "What?" she demanded.

"We have to move on," Mildred said grumpily. Her voice wasn't fuzzed with sleep. The night's rotation had her paired with Jak on sentry-duty.

"Why?" Krysty muttered. She could come awake with feline suddenness when danger loomed. But this night she was letting go of sleep's shelter only reluctantly.

"Tech-nomads say there's a big hurricane coming. We need to get out to the open water and beat feet east if we want to miss it. And we do."

"Now, how do the Techs know a thing like that, Millie?" the Armorer asked, sitting up and reaching around for his glasses. "Sky's scarcely cloudy."

"Not a clue."

"They're the bosses," Ryan said, standing. "If they say saddle up and go, we saddle up and go."

Chapter Four

As the hot sun poured from the blue Gulf sky, the Tech-no-mads and the companions raced east before the storm. The clouds began to pile up the sky behind them, black and ominous.

The companions had gathered on the lead ship, the *New Hope,* in the bow, sitting on the hot wood deck or leaning against the rail, talking with Long Tom, who was the squadron commander, though neither he nor any other Tech-nomad would use the term, and some of his crew. Ryan squatted in front of the cabin, admiring the curve of Krysty's buttocks as she stood in the prow gazing forward. The movement of her long red hair wasn't altogether in tune with the stiff wind blowing from their starboard quarter.

"So how did you know the hurricane was coming?" Mildred asked.

"Well, duh," said Highwire, an overly wound Asian techie with prominent ears and horn-rimmed glasses. He was shorter than J.B. and wispier. "We talked to them others of our group by phone."

J.B.'s own face tightened up a bit. It wasn't a respectful way to talk to his friend, much less his woman. Ryan shot his friend a deceptively lazy look. These people were their paymasters, not to mention the fact they outnumbered the companions enough they could just pitch them over the rail for the sharks if they got pissed off, despite the companions' weapons and proficiency at using them. And it wasn't exactly a surprise when Tech-nomads showed bad manners, even by rough and ready Deathlands standards.

"So, do you use surviving communications satellites?" Mildred asked.

"Nope," Sparks said. A wiry black kid—almost all the Tech-nomads were on the lean side—he wore shorts and a loose jersey, and his hair in dreads. "Use meteor-skip transmission. Bounce the signal off the ionized trails they leave. Reliable and easy. Don't have to wait on satellite coverage. Which is pretty scant these days."

"Meteors," Krysty said. "But they're not all that common except when the showers happen a few times a year, are they?"

"Always meteors falling," said Randy, the fleet's electronics ace. He was another black man, but big and powerfully built, with a shaved head and a surprisingly high-pitched voice. He always seemed pissed off about something and spoke in aggressive, staccato bursts. Dark lenses covered his eyes as if they were part of his face. That creeped Ryan out slightly, although he suspected that was the intent. "Whether you see them or not."

"Who'd you get the word from?" J.B. asked.

"The Tech-nomad flotilla," Long Tom said.

Ryan scratched at an earlobe. "What's that mean, exactly?"

The captain shrugged. He lived up to his name. He was a long lean drink of water with muscles like cables strung along bone, a long narrow head with ginger beard and receding hair both shaved to a sort of plush.

"Lot of things," he said. "It can refer to the seaborne Tech-nomad contingent, or even all Tech-nomads worldwide. In this case it refers to a group of seacraft passing across the mouth of the Gulf."

"Tom," said Great Scott, an overtly gay guy in a loose

canvas shirt and shorts, who shaved his head and wore a tiny little soul patch. His voice had a warning tone.

He was another technical wizard of some sort Ryan didn't even understand. Then again, that pretty much defined any random Tech-nomad. Even when they had some kind of readily defined and comprehensible specialty—like Sparks, the commo guy, or Jenn, who kept the *Hope*'s unconventional power train turning smoothly and was keeping to her cabin today, unfortunately incapacitated by grief at having watched her lover die the previous day—they usually had a raft of other skills. Almost always including ones Mildred and even Doc Tanner strained to grasp, and which went right by Ryan.

The captain scowled. "Blind Norad, Scott. They're two hundred miles away. It's not like these people know where they're heading, or could pass along any information to anybody. And besides, they're on our side. Remember?"

Long Tom smiled. He had what amounted to extraordinary diplomatic skills for a Tech-nomad. Ryan reckoned it had a lot to do with why he was boss of this traveling freakshow.

Great Scott just glowered. Ryan reckoned he could read that pretty clearly, too. There were Tech-nomads, and there were outsiders. Never the twain should meet.

And he could understand that, at least. It was the same way he felt about the little group of survivors he'd gathered around him, who'd become his family in a deeper and truer way than any blood kin ever had.

Voices pulled his attention aft. Doc was walking toward them talking animatedly with the squadron's chief engineer, a pretty woman named Katie who wore incredibly baggy khaki coveralls with only a green sports bra beneath them. She had her brown hair covered by a red bandanna. Her normal gig was boss wrench on Smoker's *Finagle's First Law*. But her skipper had virtually built the ship's steam-powered engines with his own hands, Ryan had been told. He could keep them turning smoothly while his mechanic spent much of her time doctoring up the eccentric and cranky rotor-sail-driven system onboard *New Hope*.

Doc and Katie were just passing the foremost of the three rotor-sails: tall white cylinders pierced with spiral whirls of holes that apparently could catch wind from any angle to turn the rotors. These in turn could either act somehow like sails, or drive propellers. They also turned generators to store power in batteries for when the winds died down. It was a mystery to Ryan, and it was fine with him if it stayed that way.

The sails tended to creak shrilly and annoyingly when a stiff wind turned them rapidly, as it did now. Everybody had to raise their voices to make themselves heard.

"What I'm endeavoring to understand, dear lady," said Doc, who was in his shirtsleeves, the height of informality for him, "is, why do you not share the gifts of your wondrous technology with the world at large? It sorely needs them."

The group of Tech-nomads at the bow went silently tense. "What do you mean by that?" Randy barked.

"Why, nothing deprecatory, friend," Doc said, blinking like a big confused bird. "I merely…wondered. Oh, dear."

Doc's experiences being yanked back and forth through time had had effects other than prematurely aging him. They had fuddled his mind. It didn't keep him from being brilliant, nor functioning at a very high level. For periods ranging from minutes to months at a time. And sometimes he was easily confused.

"I've been wondering the same thing, too," Mildred said. "I mean, no offense or anything. But why don't you share more of your knowledge with people? You could make a big difference."

"You think we haven't tried?" Katie asked with unlooked-for ferocity. Normally the wrench was among the most approachable of Tech-nomads, would've been considered affable by the standards of normal people. To the extent anybody in the Deathlands could be considered normal.

The others tossed a look around like it was something hot.

"Uh-oh," J.B. said to Ryan under his breath. "We stepped on some toes, here."

Ryan shrugged. However spiky the Tech-nomads could be, no one had ever called them quick on the trigger. While he was never going to take for granted they could never get pissed off enough to chuck him and his friends over the rail and tell them to walk from here, a Tech-nomad was more likely to get spit on your shirt screaming into your face than take a shot at you.

Long Tom wrinkled up his bearded face. "Don't think we haven't tried," he said. "The problem is, people aren't willing to listen."

"Tom," Great Scott began. "Are you sure—?"

"No," Tom said. "It's been a long time since I was sure of anything. But if we're going to trust these people to have our backs in a fight I think we can open up a little with them."

"Good thing we had them in that fight with the mutie sea cows," Sparks said. "Without Ryan and the kid they'd've sunk us for sure yesterday."

Jak looked fierce at being called a "kid," but he didn't say anything.

"Problem is," Sparks said, "most people don't want to know. Or the barons won't let them learn. And we *never* teach to barons."

"You don't believe in law and order?" J.B. asked.

Sparks shrugged. "Mostly we don't believe in rule."

"When we give common people what I like to call tech-knowledge-y," Styg said, "the barons steal it, suppress it, or both."

Styg was a stocky Tech-nomad with curly brown hair, who carried a number of pens and mechanical pencils in an ancient, cracked, yellowed protector in the pocket of the long-sleeved blue, white and black plaid flannel shirt he wore despite the humid heat. He'd been introduced to the companions as, "Styg, short for Stygimoloch. Don't ask." Nobody had.

"When we give it to barons the barons use it to strengthen their iron grip on the people. So I say, fuck barons, and fuck people who won't help themselves."

That got a murmur of assent, although Long Tom looked pained. To Ryan the Tech-nomads sounded frustrated.

"What if they grab you and try to make you teach them?" Ryan asked.

Long Tom chuckled humorlessly. "That'd be a triple-poor idea, friend. We make real bad captives and hostages, and even worse slaves."

"We got measures," Randy said with a nasty grin.

"What ones?" Jak asked.

"Pray you never find out."

"Wait," Krysty said. "There's something here I don't understand."

"What's that?" Long Tom asked. Like all the men except Great Scott, he was especially attentive to Krysty. Mostly it amused Ryan.

"Isn't the cargo we're guarding Tech-nomad tech for the baron of Haven?"

Everybody spoke denial at once. "It's not the *baron*," Long Tom managed to say over the others. "It's his chief healer and whitecoat, Mercier."

"But he works for the baron," J.B. said. "What's the difference?"

"She," Katie said.

"Huh?" J.B. said.

"Mercier," Long Tom said. "She's a she."

"Don't you think a woman can be a whitecoat?" asked Katie, who seemed to still be in defensive mode.

J.B. shrugged. "Man, woman, doesn't matter to me. At least, not that I'd ever let on, or Mildred'd yank a knot in my…tail."

"Damn straight," Mildred said, crossing her arms beneath her breasts.

"Question stands, though," Ryan said. "Baron, baron's healer, whitecoat, whatever."

"She's different," Great Scott said. "She's a great whitecoat, very dedicated. Just like her father."

"We've got total respect for the late Lucien Mercier," Sparks said. "Even if he did go to work for that shitheel Baron Dornan."

"Maybe Dornan wasn't such a total shitheel after all," Long Tom said. "He hired Lucien."

"Gimme a break," Randy snorted. "His own kids had to chill him."

"So he wasn't Father of the Year," Long Tom said. "He still had the welfare of his people at heart."

"Except for the ones he worked to death, tortured, or just plain murdered," Randy said. "He was a tyrant motherfucker."

"Now, Randy, you know a lot of that's down to his sec boss Dupree," Long Tom said.

"He hired the man. He kept him on. You met Baron Dornan. He didn't like a mosquito to fart in his ville without his by-your-leave. Dupree did nothing Dornan didn't sign off on."

"Baron Tobias is different," Katie said firmly. "He's not like his father at all. Except he supports Amélie in her work the way his father did hers."

Ryan perked his ears up. The *Finagle* wrench had changed

her tone again. She sounded distinctly fond of Baron Tobias of Haven.

"And his sister," Great Scott said with a certain bitchy relish. "She rules as his co-baron. She's a big supporter to Amélie, too."

"Because she keeps her alive!" Katie said.

"Elizabeth Blackwood has some kind of wasting disease from childhood," Long Tom explained. "Amélie has managed to slow its progress. Now she's working on a cure."

Krysty caught Ryan's eye. He could tell she was wondering the same thing he was: was that the cargo they were guarding? The cure for the life-threatening illness?

In one way it didn't matter: the gig was the gig. They'd given their bond to do the job. They'd do it as best they could. But Ryan's mind couldn't help calculating in the background: could they turn this to some kind of lasting advantage in Haven?

Isis HAD TURNED UP. Ryan had noticed that except during emergencies or special maneuvers, the captains and even crews of the three vessels tended to circulate among the ships at whim. He guessed there wasn't much reason not to.

Now the tall, silver-haired woman said, "I still think it's a mistake dealing with a baron at all. Even if it's through a trusted servitor."

Long Tom shot her a pained look. "Isis, we've been through all this—"

"There's still time to come to our senses."

"But, Ice," Katie said, "it's Baron Tobias."

She cocked a thin-plucked brow at the other woman. "And that matters how?"

"Well, he's hardly a typical baron. He really tries to help his people."

"So did the old baron, Dornan—in his way," Randy said.

"He got the same concern for the people a rancher has for his cows. It profits him to keep the livestock healthy as possible. Nothing more."

"Oh-hh," Katie said in exasperation. "You people."

"If we judge people by actions and not what we imagine their motivations are," Long Tom said, with an air that made Ryan sure he was invoking some long-held principle of Tech-nomad life, "then Tobias is a pretty right guy. He hasn't shown any of his father's hard-ass tendencies so far."

"He certainly has a fondness for leading the troops into battle," Great Scott said. "Not one to lead from behind."

"You people aren't exactly backward when it come to a fight," Mildred said.

Ryan frowned at her. He didn't want to get into any debates with these people. Anyway, they seemed to do ace at arguing without any help from outsiders.

But instead of snapping at Mildred the shaven-headed man just shrugged. "Well, true enough. When we have to."

"Beside the point, anyway," Isis said. "Power corrupts. If Tobias isn't objectively bad now, he'll go bad. And he'll have more of our tech to help him."

"Fine grasp of cliché, Isis," Great Scott said, sneering. "But does power really corrupt, or do only the corrupt seek power?"

"Tobias Blackwood had power pretty much thrust on him," Long Tom said. "He was born to it."

"Aside from the killing his dad part," Randy said.

They started an increasingly savage wrangle. More crew were drifting over to join in, not all of them from *New Hope*'s contingent. Apparently word a juicy argument was on had spread among the squadron.

Ryan quickly caught the eye of each of his companions in turn and jerked his head, slightly but emphatically, aft. Moving softly so as not to attract attention, he headed amidships himself. When he turned his back to the rail near where one of the water-strider pedal-craft was strapped to the hull and leaned back, he saw the others drifting after.

"'Bout time," Jak said. "Bored."

"I think it's their favorite sport, arguing," Mildred said, shaking her head.

"Indeed," Doc agreed.

"Speaking of which, Mildred," Krysty said with a smile, "do we really want to wade into the middle of it ourselves? These people have spent years roaming the Deathlands in each other's company. The whole wide world, as far as we know. They've got a whole complicated spider's web of relationships spun together. Do we want to get tangled in that, especially with emotions involved?"

Ryan raised a brow at that statement. He'd been about to raise that very issue with Mildred himself.

Mildred sighed. "Yeah. Sorry. I realized what I was doing the moment I opened my mouth. I guess I'm as bored and stir crazy as Jak, here."

Krysty caught Ryan's eye behind the other woman's back and winked. He grinned.

"Trader used to say when minds and hands were idle the Devil'd find a use for 'em," J.B. said. "Like most everything Trader said, that proves out true. Except when he was trying to pull a fast one, of course."

"What do?" Jak demanded. "Stuck on boat."

"Well," Ryan said slowly, "as to that, we can always clean and oil our weapons again. The spray and salt air can eat a barrel from inside like belly worms. And we never know when trouble's going to hit. Only that it's going to, sure as the sun rises in the east."

A patter of bare feet on the deck brought everybody's head around. Katie was running toward them, her hazel eyes wide.

"Why, Katie, dear child," Doc said. "Whatever has put you in such a state?"

Ryan caught the eye of a wolf-grinning J.B. and shook his head. Slick old bastard, he thought.

"Long Tom wants you up front," she said breathlessly. "There's a fleet lying just over the horizon, off the entry to the estuary where Haven is. Tom thinks they're Black Gang pirates!"

Ryan nodded briskly. "Saddle up, everybody. Break time's over. And the last easy day was yesterday."

Chapter Five

"For what we are about to receive," Doc murmured, "dear Lord, make us thankful."

Ryan smiled a tight smile. Engines thumping like a giant's heart, the tubby steamship tossed on a rising storm swell. The sky was gray and rapidly being overtaken with black from the west, just as the little fleet was rapidly being overtaken from the east by at least a dozen pirate craft their own size or larger.

They were splitting the difference and running for the coast. A little inlet gave onto the bayou network. There they hoped to lose the pirates and shelter from the storm. Or at least make it harder for the pirate ships to come at them all at once.

J.B. and Jak were riding on the rotor-ship in the middle of the convoy. In the urgent calm following news of the Black Gang Ryan had dispatched Mildred and Krysty to the *Snowy Egret*. They couldn't object; they were leading the way, after all. The fact that they were running for safety didn't matter. If safety existed on this planet in this century, their best efforts hadn't turned it up so far.

Of course the fact was the *Finagle's First Law* was closest to the pursuing foe, and the most likely to be able to intercept enemies going after her two sisters. The risk was overwhelmingly greater here. But the two women never said a word to show they realized they were being protected.

While the six companions had talked among themselves

amidships of the *New Hope,* the Tech-nomads had a lookout mounted atop the mast of the rotating sail sixty or seventy feet over their heads. Along with all their fancy detector gear, radar and lasers and who knew what, the thing the Tech-nomads relied on most to keep their convoy safe was a keen pair of basic-issue human eyeballs and a good pair of binoculars.

And the lookout had seen something that made him lose his mind in buckets: the Black Gang pirate fleet, standing right over the horizon, dead between them and their goal. But that was where their ways diverged from the old days, at least as they were portrayed in the storybooks it had been Ryan's privilege, as a baron's son, to read growing up in Front Royal. Instead of cupping hands over his bearded mouth and hollering "Sail ho!," he quietly but frantically conveyed the word to squadron boss Long Tom via the Tech-nomad commo system. Which Ryan knew entailed headsets that basically passed for fanciful and not very large items of jewelry.

"We seem to find ourselves caught between Scylla and Charybdis," Doc said. He stood in the bow with his foot up on a bollard, gazing toward the nearest enemy craft. With his unassisted eye Ryan could see the railings were crowded with scrubby-looking pirates.

"Care to translate that into English for me, Doc?" he asked, as he shouldered his Steyr. He had to adjust his scope to its greatest magnification. The lead ship was a yacht not unlike the *Snowy Egret.* The pirates were running right into the teeth of a rising wind blown before the storm out of the southwest. The masts were bare. Like the *Egret,* it was using some kind of engine.

"Scylla and Charybdis were a many-headed monster and a giant whirlpool that mythology claimed guarded the Strait of Messina," the professor explained. "The great heroes Odysseus and Jason were both forced to pass between them in their respective epics. The phrase, 'between a rock and a hard place' conveys much the same import."

"Or 'between hammer and firing pin,'" Ryan grunted, his good eye pressed to the eyepiece of his scope.

"Indeed. Are you seeing anything of interest, my dear Ryan?"

"No good news," Ryan said, reluctantly lowering the rifle. "They're still over a thousand yards off. If we were both standing still, on a surface that stood still, I'd probably take the shot."

He stood scowling toward the approaching fleet. The waves were nasty, at least by the standards of a man who spent most of his life with his boot soles planted firmly on dry land: ten to twelve feet high and breaking higher, with the wind ripping pennons of foams from their tips. Despite that the pirates were pulling boats alongside the bigger vessels that had them under tow and loading crewmen bristling with arms off all varieties into them.

"Whoever's in charge of that boat's keeping inside the cabin," Ryan said, "although when the taints get a little closer I'll put a couple through their windscreen on general principles."

"Do you think the commodore of yon pirate fleet rides the leading vessel?"

"Not a chance. Black Mask is supposed to be a smart operator, and he's brushed up against the Tech-nomads before. He knows they got some nasty tricks up their sleeves."

"But don't men of the class you so colorfully describe as 'coldhearts' usually consent to obey only a commander who leads from the front?"

"Depends," Ryan said. *Something* was happening on the bow of that nearest ship. He didn't like it and started to raise the rifle again. "If he's got some bully-boys to whip the troops on, he doesn't have to expose his own precious carcass, any more than any other baron. Plus I reckon he makes plentiful use of Sergeant Jolt and Sergeant Shine to keep the boys leaning forward. *Shit!*"

"What do you see that so displeases you, my dear Ryan?"

His answer was loud and brief. The SSG roared and bucked its steel-plated butt against Ryan's shoulder. The heavy copper-jacketed 7.62 mm slug it launched at a thousand yards a second streaked invisibly toward its target.

And as Ryan feared, the motion of the boat beneath him, or the one his target rode, threw off his shot—the windage wasn't much consideration with the gale blowing from almost right behind him. A pirate standing next to the crew of three or four who were busy setting up a heavy machine gun on some kind of mounting in the bow jerked as a dark spray appeared from his black-clad right upper arm. He grabbed himself and fell.

The machine gun belched yellow flame as big as a land wag. It was bright as the sun in the gloom of the rising storm. A line of water spurts higher than Ryan's head shot up astern of *Finagle,* cutting dead cross its wake.

"Shit," Ryan said again as he cranked the bolt. The multiple thunder of the burst buffeted his eardrums. "Big-ass machine gun."

He aimed hastily, fired again. But even for a primo marksman with finely tuned tools a thousand-yard shot was near impossible. Especially under conditions like these. Ryan missed his target, the huge bearded man in the black bandanna who stood behind the .50-caliber Browning hanging on to its spade grips. Grimly the one-eyed man worked the bolt yet again and drew breath for another desperate long shot.

"Ryan," Doc said with quiet intensity.

A savage command not to disturb him at a moment like this flashed through Ryan's brain. But something at a deeper level than his conscious mind made him break his fierce blue eye away from the eyepiece of his telescopic sight and look left.

Lines of fire lanced away from the *Snowy Egret* on a rising course as bright against the lead-hued sky. Their trails formed a fiery rainbow of afterimage on Ryan's pupils as they arced down to strike the lead pirate ship and the sea around it.

Orange fire billowed from the pirate yacht. It rolled forward across the bow, enveloping the heavy machine gun and its crew. Blazing men danced on deck or threw themselves over the water. Hell glows of muted orange from within the waves showed even the ocean provided little shelter from the hideous flesh-consuming flames.

"Nape rockets?" Ryan said in wonder.

"Indeed, it is as you said, my dear Ryan," Doc said. "The Tech-nomads tend to pack a mighty sting."

A burst of machine-gun fire from another pirate craft raked *Finagle*'s stern. A woman's scream was cut off, and a man began to moan in a voice that sounded as if it was being crushed out of him by giant boulders.

A sudden curtain of dirty brown smoke appeared in front of Ryan's and Doc's eyes, cutting off all view of the pirate fleet.

"RYAN!" KRYSTY clutched at *Egret*'s rail as brown smoke enveloped *Finagle*'s *First Law*. The little squadron was staggered so that the middle ship, the *New Hope,* was out of line upwind of *Egret*. Before the smoke she'd had a clear view of the trail ship.

Isis laughed. She stood on the rail beside the two women. BARs awaited them in closed boxes, waterproofed against the ceaseless spray that soaked their clothes and made their hair hang like seaweed, dripping clammily down their backs.

Mildred glared at her. "They're your friends on that burning ship, too," she declared.

"The *Finagle* isn't burning," Isis said. "That's a smoke screen."

She gave no signal or command that Krysty could identify. But suddenly from the water churning not ten feet from the *Egret*'s hull, a wall of smoke erupted. It was the same dirty brown as that which hid the *Finagle* from their sight.

Both Mildred and Krysty jumped back from the rail. "Whoa!" Mildred said. "Don't startle a body like that!"

"Smoke screen?" Krysty asked.

"Uh-huh," the captain said. "With the wind blowing it right up the pirates' unwashed snouts."

Krysty felt the slim and graceful yacht heel to starboard as she tacked a few points into the wind's teeth.

"Changing our vectors a little," Isis said, as a burst of machine-gun fire sent up a line of waterspouts fifty yards ahead of them and slightly to the right. "Spoil their tracking solutions."

"What if they have radar?" Mildred asked worriedly. "Marine radar was pretty common once upon a time. I'm sure if they wanted they could cobble a working unit or two together."

Isis smiled. "They may *think* they have a working radar," she said. "Imagine their surprise."

"What do you mean?" Krysty asked.

"The smoke contains a biodegradable, nontoxic aerosol that masks conventional radar wavelengths like old-time chaff," Isis said. "It also blocks infrared pretty effectively."

Mildred gestured helplessly at the metal crates containing their own longblasters. "So now we can't shoot at them, either," she said sourly.

"There are more of them than there are of us," Krysty said, as ahead of them the *New Hope* let loose its own smoke screen and was instantly lost to view. "Even though our friends have some pretty potent weapons, if neither side can see to shoot the other I judge we got the better end of the deal."

"Long as my friends and I aren't getting shot at," Mildred said, "I'm okay. *Hey!*"

The last was accompanied by a defensive duck as a burst of automatic fire cracked overhead.

"They're shooting blind," Krysty said. She wasn't sure which woman she was trying to reassure, Mildred, or herself. Isis as usual seemed to cool.

The long, lean, exotic captain had opened the lockers and was pulling something out. Before Krysty could tell what it was a whooshing roar drew her attention forward. Even through the dense concealing fog she could see the glows of rocket engines arcing away from the *New Hope*'s launch racks toward the enemy fleet.

"I guess we are, too," Mildred said. A heartbeat later an orange glow flared like the sun behind the vivid clouds of an incoming acid-rain storm.

"Not at all," Isis said, smiling. She held a pair of bulky dark goggles toward the women. "Try these."

From *Finagle's First Law,* the distinctive moan of Stork's bow-mounted Gatling began to rise above the storm howl. Krysty hesitated momentarily, then pulled the goggles over her eyes and the strap to the back of her head.

Immediately the pirate fleet appeared. It seemed all shades of gray, the hulls brightest, almost silver, as were the blasters in pirate hands. The pirates themselves were duller gray, the ocean a strange liquid construct of endlessly shifting panes in tones of slate and gunmetal, like stained glass robbed of color and rendered somehow fluid. Everything was overlaid with a rainbow shimmer, almost like the sheen of oil on water, except jittery instead of fluid.

"What *is* this?" Mildred demanded at her side. "I've looked through Starlight scopes and IR goggles. I've never seen anything like this before."

"Millimeter wave radar," Isis said. "Much, *much* shorter wave than conventional radar. It gets translated into visual imagery by the ship's computers, then broadcast to these headsets."

The magical eye of the goggles wouldn't see through the waves, apparently. Because just then a shift in the shimmery planescape revealed something Krysty hadn't noticed before. A swarm of small motor craft was forging toward the Technomad squadron, packed dangerously full with pirates wearing black clothes or armbands.

Just how dangerously overloaded they were was proved a few heartbeats later when Krysty saw the bow of a whaleboat plunge into a wave—and keep going until the water swallowed it and the crew whole. Another wave surge, its top torn ragged by the fierce insistent wind, hid where it had vanished from sight. When it subsided, she saw a few heads bobbing and arms flailing futilely above the churning water. She never saw the boat itself again.

A roar of gunfire assaulted Krysty's eardrums. Through the ringing it left in her ears she heard Isis say, "Hard to hit the buggers in this sea. But at least it's just as hard for them, plus they're shooting blind."

Krysty pulled down her goggles and looked at the approaching swarm of boats. Flashes told her some of the pirates were shooting into the dense brown bank, now rolling toward them like a fog. She heard a few stray shots crack overhead.

She aimed and fired at the nearest boat. As far as she could tell, she missed it cleanly. She heard Mildred fire a burst, then curse. Evidently she'd whiffed as well.

The *Egret* pitched so vigorously in the waves Krysty was finding it hard to keep her feet. Her stomach, normally as

strong as cast iron, was starting to weaken from the complicated motion induced by the storm. But she willed herself
to keep her feet, ripping burst after burst at the pirates. Her
shoulder started to ache from the relentless pounding of the
Browning's recoil.

"Where do they get all these suckers?" Mildred asked as
she bent to grab a fresh magazine.

"From the poor souls downtrodden in the baronies," Isis
said. "From the hopeless trying to scratch a living among
the islands, or up the fever-swamp bayous. From the crews
of craft they've captured."

She fired a burst. "From other pirate bands they've absorbed. They get the same choice as other captives—join or
die."

"They must be doing mighty well," Mildred said. "Ha,
except for you!" Apparently she'd seen a target go overboard.
The range was close enough now Krysty was able to bring
punishing bursts on targets, spatter boat crews with bullets.
Even if the pitching of the sea was so savage that she could
only hit one or two at a time before *Egret*'s motion threw her
aim totally off.

It also meant the range was short enough for the pirates'
blind-fired blasters to have effect, as well. Krysty heard a
grunt from the rail aft, where other goggled Tech-nomads
were shooting with a bizarre assortment of weapons, from
M-16s to crossbows. She didn't look that way as she clawed
an empty magazine from the well of her longblaster. Its receiver and barrel cast heat like a midwinter stove.

"To have that many predators hunting together," Mildred
said, "they must eat well."

Isis was momentarily distracted. She lowered her BAR
and moved her lips soundlessly. Krysty guessed that somehow she was still speaking to her crew.

"Dammit," the captain said, shaking her head. "Another one lost."

She snapped back into focus, looking at Mildred with her startling blue eyes. "Yes, they eat well," she said. "And the fattest feast for a hundred miles of this coast is Haven. But so far that shell's too tough for them to crack."

"And that's part of the reason they're attacking so furiously now, despite the storm and the damage we're doing," Krysty said. "Just the value of the Tech-nomads' own equipment, like these goggles. Let alone whatever cargo we're carrying."

"And that's a big reason we seldom deal with outsiders," Isis said. "Even the ones who aren't out-and-out pirates can usually resist anything but temptation."

A commotion from astern made itself heard even over the noise of blasterfire and the approaching hurricane. "Krysty, look!" Mildred called. "Some of the boats have broken through *Finagle*'s smoke screen."

Krysty's heart lurched with an adrenal shock of fear for Ryan. Not that he was in any greater danger now than a thousand times before, she told herself. And yet despite herself her mind framed the words, Mother Gaia, please, keep him safe.

And Isis cried out, "Here come the bastards!"

Chapter Six

Using his iron sights and the goggles Smoker had provided him and J.B., Ryan snapshot the man steering a twenty-foot boat as it started to slide down the face of a wave toward them. As a vagary of the storm sea pushed the unguided boat past the *Finagle's First Law,* Ryan saw Doc leaning out to fire his bulky LeMat into the craft.

Whether by the blast of the big gun or the lurch of the ship, Doc was pitched over the brass rail. Gripping the longblaster in his left hand, Ryan lunged. He managed to tangle his right fist in the long flapping tail of Doc's frockcoat.

As skeletal-thin as the old man was, he weighed enough to slam Ryan face-first into the rail. The one-eyed man tasted blood. Shaking off the momentary wooziness, Ryan slung his rifle hastily, then got hold of the other man's coat with his other hand.

The LeMat roared again. By chance he saw the head of a pirate who stood in the stern of the little boat, grinning and aiming some kind of handblaster improvised from a piece of pipe, snap back as the .44 caliber round hit him over the right eye. A piece of his skull came off, taking with it the filthy pink bandanna wrapped around the pirate's head. He toppled back among his fellows, who were all more interested in scrambling toward the tiller to try to regain control of the wildly tossing little craft than fighting.

The *Finagle* heeled well over toward the starboard side. Ryan looked down to see Doc's head and shoulders fully submerged in foam-shot green water. One big bony-knuckled hand held the huge blaster that would normally be down by his thigh—and was now up, out of the water.

Ryan hauled hard. Doc's head broke free of the waves, streaming and sputtering. As Ryan straightened his legs in a sort of dead lift, a line slithered over the rail toward the fallen man. Doc's free hand caught the blue-and-white nylon rope and he was able to help haul himself to safety.

"Pretty hard core, aiming and shooting while you were upside down like that," Ryan said as Doc scrambled inboard with alacrity surprising for one who generally looked as if he weren't just at Death's door, but walking on through it. "Triple hard."

"It was the danger I could do something about, Ryan," Doc said. He coughed violently, spewing up a torrent.

"Thank you," he said, recovering quickly. "As well as to my other benefactor."

"Yeah." Ryan turned to see the ship's owner and commander himself, the burly grizzle-bearded black man called Smoker, standing there with his oil-stained coveralls soaked through. He had a big long-barreled Smith & Wesson double-action blaster holstered on one hip and a cutlass with an eighteen-inch blade and a vicious knuckle-duster handguard thrust through his belt at the other. "Thanks, Captain."

"Least I could do." From the bow came the weird grinding roar of Stork's pedals turned, steam-powered Gatling. "Need all the fighters I can get today. Pretty impressive presence of mind, there, Doc, holding that handblaster free of the water even when your head was under."

Doc smiled. "Though the LeMat isn't what it once was, the workings must be kept dry."

"What was the blast?" Ryan asked. He scanned the moving hills of water but saw no immediate danger this side of the smoke screen, which was beginning to fray and come apart under the wind's increasingly savage onslaught.

"RPG," Smoker said around the stub of cigar clamped unlit between his teeth. Like all Tech-nomads except a few apparent eccentrics, he had teeth in perfect condition, almost blinding in their whiteness.

"Hit the stern. The nuke-suckers were trying either to take out the prop or the steering. Didn't make either. Didn't hurt anybody, beyond a few scorch marks and scrapes. Won't be so lucky long."

A hefty thump forward, accompanied by another quick violent vibration of the planks beneath his boots, made Ryan turn.

"There's our luck running out," Smoker said as grappling hooks thumped on the deck. He drew his weapons. "All hands stand by to repel boarders."

As a pair of hooks slithered backward to catch on the rail, Ryan followed his example. He ran forward, drawing his SIG-Sauer with his left hand and his panga with his right.

Men swarmed up both ropes. Ryan was still raising his handblaster when the captain's blaster cracked off behind him. A dark-skinned head with a black do-rag wrapped around it, which had just appeared above the nearer rope, snapped back. The pirate fell away, carrying at least a couple of his mates with him, to judge by the shouts. Ryan heard a body splash into the water.

As another pirate swarmed over the rail, Ryan took him out. Struck through the left shoulder the man reeled back, but got hold of the rail with a black-nailed left hand. A shot through the body sealed his fate.

As the second pirate fell, the one-eyed man hacked through the rope closer to him with a single stroke of his panga. That elicited more yells as bodies thumped back into the whaleboat and others splashed into the raging sea, hopefully never to be seen again.

Ryan heard shots and screams behind him. Putting his back against the cabin, he risked a quick glance that way.

Pirates were swarming up over the stern of the steamer. Two raced toward Doc, one armed with what looked like a short spear, the other with a fire ax.

Doc had emptied the fat cylinder of his LeMat, but he had a nasty surprise in store. There was a single stub of shotgun barrel mounted beneath the revolver's cylinder. Doc took the ax-man's face off with a charge of double-00 buckshot.

A four-foot adjustable boiler wrench smashed the skull of the guy with the short spear. A following pirate shot the crewman who'd swung the massive wrench off the housing with some kind of one-shot homemade blaster. The lower half of the face of the guy with the pipe-gun blew out over the rail in a shower of red liquid as another Tech-nomad inside the cabin shot him out a port with a crossbow, the heavy quarrel going sideways through his mouth and tearing his teeth out. As the pirate gurgled and choked on his own blood, Smoker, roaring, grappled him and threw him bodily into the sea. Cackling with manic glee, Doc put away his giant handblaster and pulled his swordstick from his belt. Pulling the slim blade from within, he began to duel a pirate armed with a machete, using the ebony cane sheath as a parrying weapon.

A flicker of motion in Ryan's peripheral vision snapped his head back around. A hand grabbed his wrist as he tried to raise his SIG-Sauer. A blast of foul breath hit him in the face as he turned toward his bearded, sunburned attacker. The pirate held a two-foot length of pipe with a heavy join on the business end cocked back over his left shoulder, intending to bust open Ryan's head.

To discourage the move, Ryan jammed the panga into the

man's swag gut almost to the grip and twisted. The man bellowed in pain, then sagged, letting go of Ryan's gun wrist.

The one-eyed man promptly raised his left hand and shot a second charging pirate over the shoulder of the man he'd stabbed. Then he put his boot against the breastbone of his first attacker and kicked the man off his blade. Howling in agony, the pirate fell backward, trailing a loop of gut like a strand of greasy purple-gray sausage.

This is going to be a long day, Ryan thought, as the sound of clashing weapons and angry voices broke out from the cabin roof above his head.

WITH A LOUD CHUNK the ax that had been swung at Jak's face sank into the bulkhead of the *New Hope*'s main cabin. As the nicked blade, crusted with old brown blood, descended toward his face, the albino youth had bobbed the upper half of his body aside. He felt a slight tug as a lock of his long white hair was severed by the cut.

He finished the act of holstering his now empty Colt Python. With the enemy on top of him there was no time to reload the big blaster.

That suited Jak fine.

With a quick wrist-flipping flourish Jak drew and opened his current favorite knives, a pair of balisongs with matching ironwood hilts. With his left hand he slashed the ax man across his eyes as his attacker, at least twice the boy's size, wrenched and grunted in frenzied desperation to yank his weapon free.

The man squealed like a scorched pig as the tip of Jak's butterfly knife raked across both eyeballs. A hot jet of blood and aqueous fluid hit Jak in the face as he sliced the blinded pirates face and throat to blood-gouting ribbons.

Shrieking in fury a second pirate lunged for Jak, raising a four-foot-length of pipe with six-inch spikes welded to the

head to smash the albino teen. Instead his sallow face contorted more as a shotgun discharged into his temple from no
more than a foot away. Jak saw yellow muzzle-flash lick the
side of the long, scarred countenance, which twisted into the
most surprised look the teen had ever seen.

Then it seemed to collapse back and in on itself like a
rubber mask stretched over a deflating balloon as the shot
column took away most of the skull and facial bones that gave
it structure from behind, right out the right side of the head.

"Rad-blast it, Jak!" J.B. shouted, stepping up and jacking
the action of his Smith & Wesson M-4000. "Quit screwing
around."

Jak grinned. "Okay, let's fight!"

A WHALER CHURNED past the rounded prow of *Finagle's First
Law.* The muzzle-flashes of the score of pirates crammed
board were bright despite the fact the air was full of rain
and spray.

Ryan's rifle slammed his shoulder and cracked. A pirate
fell over the rail. The one-eyed man slung his Steyr and drew
his handblaster. Holding it in both hands he popped rounds
furiously at the craft as it curved around toward the stern.

His 9 mm bullets either had more effect than he saw, injur-
ing or unnerving the man at the tiller, or the pirate steering
the thirty-foot boat got careless. Or maybe the unpredictable
thrashing of the sea betrayed it. The vessel swung far enough
wide of the *Finagle* that Stork could depress his multibarreled
steam-powered blaster to bear on them.

The Gatling set up its terrible grinding moan. The heavy
slugs sent up a geyser of water in front of the launch, and the
boat powered right into the lead spray.

It was as if a giant invisible butcher began chopping at the
pirates with a giant cleaver. Heads blew apart like ripe watermelons dropped on boulders from a great height. Arms

and legs flew free, cartwheeling through the water-heavy air like pinwheels spraying blood sparks. Splinters snapped up from the thin hull. Greenish-brown water surged in around the pirates' legs, some of which stood without the benefits of torsos above the waists. It instantly turned a tainted maroon.

The boat turned sideways; its bow swamped.

The roar of the Gatling stopped. For a moment, as the only sound seemed to be the descending whine as the six barrels gradually slowed their spin, Ryan thought Stork had stopped firing for lack of targets.

Then he saw what looked like a thin red hose hooked from the gangly man's throat to the deck, which rose and fell rhythmically.

Chapter Seven

Stork's beaky, wildly hair-fringed face took on a look of almost clinical curiosity. He brought walking-stick fingers to the bullet hole. He pressed the fingertips against it.

Blood squirted out to the sides, down his T-shirt and up into his beard, to the decreasing rhythm of his heart. He toppled from the mesh sling seat.

Wildly Ryan looked around. The smoke screens had turned into a few random brown wisps twisting in the wind. Ahead of the convoy's lead ship, the *Snowy Egret,* he could see a break in the waving green wall of the mangrove swamp that made up the shoreline. It was sanctuary of a sort, offered by a bayou mouth: tantalizingly close, yet perhaps an infinity away—because the bigger pirate ships were fast approaching, and the survivors of their swarm of smaller boats, sensing opportunity now that the terrible Gatling had quit ripping at them, were closing in like a pod of killer whales on the *Egret* and the *New Hope.* Meanwhile the *Hope* was no longer sending out a volley of its terrible rockets. Ryan didn't know whether they were out, or the launcher was out of service, or whether the rocket crew was dead or injured. It didn't matter.

The sound of rotating barrels got sharper, higher. Ryan spun.

Grinning, coattails flapping behind him like storm-crow's wings, Doc sat in the recumbent seat of the steam gun. His feet pumped the pedals furiously spinning up the barrels.

once more. His hands worked the crank to swing the bizarre weapon to bear on fresh targets.

"Have no fear, Ryan!" he sang out over the howl and smash of wind and battle. "I am on it!"

TEETH SHATTERED as Krysty whipped the heavy butt of her BAR across the face of a pirate with long greasy locks and a pale scar running down his face over a dead eye like a cruel parody of her own lover. A long black mustache contradicted the impression until it vanished in the general eruption of blood from his smashed nose and upper jaw.

"Krysty! Behind you!" Mildred yelled.

Half by reflex, half instinct she kicked hard, straight back. Before her leg fully extended, her boot heel contacted hard flesh. She heard a cough of exhalation and the person she kicked fell away.

She spun, bringing the muzzle of the Browning around level with her narrow waist. A wiry little pirate, shirtless to reveal a sunken chest spiderwebbed with crude tattoos, had reeled back against a man twice his size with a gold ring hanging from a much-mashed nose. He had a fat bean-shaped face, steel-wool hair and sideburns poking out to the sides as if he had hedgehogs glued to his cheeks. The big man grabbed his comrade in one hand and pointed a sawed-off double-barrel shotgun at Krysty over his shoulder with the other.

She triggered a quick burst. The smaller man jerked as dark holes appeared like flies caught in the webs of his chest tats. The other man's tiny bloodshot blue eyes stood suddenly out of their sockets as the jacketed .30-06 slugs, barely slowed by blasting through the lights and heart of his smaller pal, ripped through his belly.

Judging by the way his bandy legs folded one had to have smashed through his spine and cut the cord.

Explosions were blasting off all around. Waves crashed over the rail. The ship rocked through a complex three-dimensional pattern that was ever-changing and totally disorienting.

Smoke obscured Krysty's vision aft, from where the most recent two attackers had come. She wasn't sure what was burning. The sharp stink of wood combusting blended with the sweetish barbecue smell of roasting human flesh singed the roof of her mouth and tormented a stomach already disordered by the unpredictable motion of the ship. The smells had to be strong to be detectable at all through the rain and spray, so dense and fierce she couldn't tell them apart.

On all sides people shouted and screamed. A ferocious tumult rose from the stern, beyond the wall of smoke. Fighting raged there.

She turned the other way to see Mildred caught from behind in a bear hug by a big Latino-looking pirate with his back to a ladder coaming. A smaller man cocked back his arm to drive a long narrow rod with the tip ground to a point into the woman's belly.

Krysty pointed the BAR at what she hoped was a safe angle clear of Mildred and held back the trigger. The blaster barked and bucked twice, and the heavy receiver locked open. One bullet hit the pirate with the spike on the hip and passed through him, smashing his narrow pelvis. He fell screaming, the needle-like weapon falling from his hands and washed out instantly through the scuppers by a backwash tendrilled with his own blood.

Mildred smashed her head back into the face of the man who held her. He grunted in unexpected pain. Blood squirted from his smashed nose.

The unexpected turn of events made him loosen the grip of his big bare arms. Mildred kicked back just beneath his right knee with her bootheel, then scraped it down his shin. He moaned and she broke free.

As the pirate pawed at her, she brought her knee up hard into his groin. His eyes bugged out and he doubled over.

As his big shaggy head descended, she jammed the muzzle of her ZKR 551 target pistol into his open mouth. Teeth broke. Blood streamed freely where the big sharp-edged front site tore the roof of his mouth. So furious was the sturdily built black woman, the force of it straightened him back up.

Fear of what was coming overcame even the agony and airlessness of smashed balls. His eyes flew wide. Pleading.

"Fuck you," Mildred shouted, and pulled the trigger. There was a short, sharp bark. His eyes bulged out farther, impossibly far, until one popped from its orbit and fell to bounce off a filthy cheek, staring crazily around. He sank to the deck. A clot of hair and brains remained on the housing. A slug trail of blood ran down beneath it.

Caught in the midst of kneeling to discover there were no more magazines in the satchel Isis had provided, Krysty saw an ax handle fast descending toward Mildred's skull. She dropped the empty longblaster with a clunk and grabbed for her own snub-nosed .38 revolver. But her warning only gave her friend enough time to begin to dodge, so that she took a glancing blow to the side of her head rather than taking the whole sickening force full on the cranium.

She slumped against the housing next to the man whose brains she'd blown all over it. Her new attacker cocked his leg to put the boot in. Crouching, off balance on the dizzily tilting deck, Krysty knew she would never get her blaster in action in time to keep him from stomping Mildred's skull in.

"Here, catch!" a voice cried from above. Krysty looked up to see Isis standing atop the front of the cabin. She lobbed a head-size dark object right at the pirate's face, turned upward like Krysty's to see who had called out.

Reflex betrayed him. He dropped the ax handle to whip up both hands to protect himself. The pirate fielded a package of what looked like gray clay blocks taped together.

Krysty launched herself between the pirate and his intended victim, with sufficient power and the proper angle to bodycheck him clean over the side.

A moment after his wildly kicking cowboy boots vanished from sight, the boat shuddered. A column of water shot skyward twenty feet, shot through with red and body parts. Krysty just recognized a single pointy-toed boot before the sea swallowed the whole mess.

Mildred picked herself up. She looked up at Isis. "Kinda took a chance there, didn't you?"

"Life is taking a chance," the captain said. "Anyway, I had faith in your resourcefulness. There were reasons we hired you."

Krysty found time to wonder fleetingly what those reasons were. The mouth of the stream the fleet had been making for beckoned welcomingly not fifty yards from the lead ship's graceful prow. It wasn't much: it looked like a mere hole, scarcely wider than the narrow sailing yacht herself, hacked in a wall of green that would've looked brick-solid if it weren't waving like grass in the gale.

The rain wasn't currently heavy, but the drops hit like ice bullets. Raising a big pale wave of water before its bow, a big launch roared in from starboard, trying to cut the yacht off from entering the bayou's sanctuary. Blasterfire flashed. Bullets cracked by Krysty's head. She heard a despairing cry as one found a target. From the direction she knew at least it was neither her friend Mildred nor the exotic and coolly competent ship's captain. Knowing it would be ineffectual, she held out her Smith & Wesson with one hand wrapped over her blaster hand to brace and emptied its 5-shot cylinder.

Then it was as if an invisible circular saw ripped diagonally across the rear third of the intercepting pirate launch. Blood fountained as jeering men were ripped apart. Both sides of the hull shattered.

A wave carried the stricken launch up onto its frothy peak. The engine's weight promptly snapped off the stern. By the time the wave plunged into the trough, all that remained above the water surface was bobbing debris. Including half a dozen heads, with faces that gazed up at Krysty with despair and desperate imploring.

"I never thought I'd be happy to see people doomed to drown like rats," Mildred said. "I hate even being happy seeing rats drown. I hate what this world has done to me."

"Well, you can be grateful to Stork in *Finagle* for clearing the way for us," Krysty said, meaning it to help. She often was unsure how to deal with her friend's occasional episodes of remorse, despair and homesickness.

Isis stood atop the cabin, shooting a gigantic pristine Desert Eagle handblaster at the pirate boats that still sought to overtake them. Looking toward the enemy flotilla, Krysty saw a long black yacht, its masts bare like *Egret*'s, bearing down on them. Where *Egret* was spotless white, this vessel was painted black on every visible surface, hull, superstructure, even mast. A black-clad figure stood in the bow as if its feet were bolted to the deck, apparently unaffected by the violence of the waves. Its features were obscured by blackness as featureless at several hundred yards as the hull.

"Damn!" Isis exclaimed from overhead. "That ship's the *Black Joke,* and there stands Black Mask his evil self. If only I had a decent fucking blaster!"

Krysty knew the rare handblaster was well-made, as such things went. She also knew what the Tech-nomad captain meant. No matter how good a handblaster it was, to reach out and have any chance at all of touching the pirate overlord, she needed range.

Mildred looked up from rummaging through the debris strewed about the deck for loaded BAR magazines. Krysty noted that not even pounding rain and the waves that broke over the railing with increasing frequency could wash all the spilled blood away.

"Speaking of blasters," the physician said, "what's that next to Black Mask?"

Krysty realized he stood beside a long tube laid horizontally on some kind of mount. It flared to a wider diameter at the after end. A wide steel sheet stood angled back behind it.

"Some kind of cannon—" Krysty began.

"Recoilless rifle," Isis said.

Yellow flame and white smoke erupted out the rear of the tube to splash against the steel plate and boil out to all sides.

A blinding flash lit the thrashing cypress trees. A shock wave planed off the wavetops for fifty yards around.

Krysty's breath solidified in her throat. *Finagle's First Law* had blown up.

Chapter Eight

Someone was shaking Ryan by his shoulder. He wagged his head to clear the cotton that filled it. His hair slapped his cheeks and forehead like wads of seaweed freshly hauled from the sea. His knees were pressing down hard on something hard, and his face felt sunburned.

Also his head rang like an anvil, which was currently in use to forge red-hot iron.

"Ryan!" a voice called from the distance. He shook himself again. His sensory impressions, his very thoughts, whirled around him like shoals of little fish. Little flickering fish, their sides flashing silver in the yellow sunlight—

"Dear boy, please! The ship's sinking. We have got to act upon the instant, or most assuredly perish!"

Whatever else could be said about Ryan, he was a survivor. He gave his head a final shake, short and sharp, and shook all those little vagrant fishes back into place.

He looked up to see Doc's long face, streaming water, with raindrops exploding in little bursts all over it. His usually lank hair was plastered right down both sides of his head, making his skull look narrower than usual.

"Get up," the old man urged. His words still seemed to cross some vast distance, although his bloodless lips moved barely the length of his long outstretched fingers from Ryan's nose. "We must be taking our leave, and quickly."

"Right." Ryan gripped the other man's forearm, and was glad of the unlooked-for strength with which Doc pulled him to his feet. He reeled, first from dizziness, then a second time because the deck was doing its level best to pitch him into waves that leaped up on all sides as if eager to receive him. Then he shook off his friend's helping hand.

"What happened?" he asked, his voice a bone-dry croak without the water that covered every external inch of him.

"Boiler explosion," Doc shouted. "A cannon shot from the *Black Joke* struck home. The steam Gatling has lost all power."

It came back to Ryan, then: the flash and smoke as the recoilless rifle fired. The brilliant blue-white spot streaking like a renegade star toward *Finagle*'s fat stern. The flash and eardrum-torturing crack of a shaped-charge warhead going off. The answering yellow flash, followed by a sudden explosion of steam so hot it was initially invisible, and made the falling rain and spray sizzle as it expanded.

Then a scalding hot pressure wave had picked him up and slammed him down. Pain had shot through his head, accompanied by purple-white lightning. And then the world had gone out of focus.

"Didn't lose consciousness," he muttered. He tasted salt and copper. He'd cracked his head open on something, probably a metal bollard. "So mebbe my brain isn't going to swell up until the inside of my skull implodes it."

"Ryan…" Doc said.

Ryan became aware the deck was tilting sharply. He looked aft. A huge white cloud covered the whole rear half of the steamship, apparently proof against the efforts of wind and water to disperse it.

A figure walked out of the cloud. At first Ryan thought its clothes were hanging off it in rags, then he realized similar rags were dangling from its chin.

Even Ryan's cast-iron stomach clenched in nausea and

horror. The rags weren't the man's clothes at all. They were his skin, flash-boiled off him by live steam.

The man's eyes met his. For a moment he thought the man was imploring him. Then he realized the other couldn't possibly see him. The eyes were white, parched like eggs, sightless from the blast.

Ryan realized he still had a reassuringly familiar hardness gripped in his right hand. He did the only thing he could do: raised the SIG-Sauer P-226 smoothly in both hands, acquired his target, then squeezed his finger into a compressed surprise break. The handblaster cracked and jumped.

A dark hole appeared in the cooked red mess of that forehead. The scalded Tech-nomad folded to the deck. He had received the only relief possible.

The burly figure of Smoker, the ship's captain, next appeared from the artificial fogbank that still hid the after half of *Finagle's First Law*. The big black man didn't look as if he'd gotten burned. But he was hurt, and badly, if Ryan was any judge—which he was. The right side of the big man's coveralls were a darker shade than usual from midchest down. He clutched his right side and limped on his right leg.

But whatever had wounded him hadn't damaged his voice any. "Abandon ship!" he bellowed like an enraged bull elephant. "All hands—we're going down!"

A sudden line of bullets stitched fore-to-aft along the side of the cabin. Its path intersected the captain. He jerked, then sagged. Finally he collapsed to the deck of his sinking ship, where an outward roll of the hull sent him limply into the scuppers.

"Shit," Ryan said.

"We had better seek out boats," Doc said.

"Do you see any?" Ryan demanded. The two men had to hang on to lines against the ship's heaving. "The lifeboats I remember were carried back by the stern. We may have to swim for it."

"In this sea? That would be madness!"

"Mebbe," Ryan said. They were shouting at each other to make themselves heard over the howl of the storm and the drumming of the rain. "Mebbe triple-stupe. But the way I calculate, if we swim, we may drown. We stay on this tub, we *will* drown."

Another blast rocked ship. A yellow fireball rolled upward from the midst of the steam cloud that enveloped the stern. Black smoke poured after. Yellow licks of flame began to dart out the sides of the steam cloud.

"Or burn," Ryan added.

Doc clutched his arm. "Perhaps there is another choice."

It was on Ryan's tongue to say he didn't see it. Instead he looked where Doc pointed.

The *New Hope,* rotors spinning furiously in the wind, backed toward the sinking *Finagle's First Law.* A small pirate boat tried for some unknown reason to dart between the ships and was crunched as the steamer rode it down. Ryan couldn't see the impact of *Finagle*'s up-angled bow, but heard the screams of men being crushed.

Jak stood on the slippery brass railing of the rotor-sailer's stern, his hair hanging down his face and shoulders like spilled milk. He held on to a guyline, riding the wildly pitching and rolling and yawing craft like some Western cowboy taming a bronco. He laughed into the face of the storm. J.B. stood beside him on the deck, preparing to throw over a rope in a very business-like manner.

"You know," Ryan said as Jak threw back his head and uttered a panther-scream of exaltation, "that boy's just having himself way too much fun."

THE WIND DIMINISHED when they entered the river mouth, which wasn't to say it cut off. Nor did the rain slacken. Rather it grew even fiercer, and lightning veined the sky in bluish white in an almost continuous pulsation. The thunder was one loud roar, competing with all the other noise.

One noise it wasn't competing with was blasterfire, Ryan was pleased to note as he stood in the stern with his Steyr ready. The small pirate craft had pulled back and were being laboriously recovered by the larger vessels of the fleet. The ones that survived. It didn't seem to him there were that many.

"Hard to imagine they'll keep coming," Ryan said, "after taking losses like that."

Cold as the hearts of coldhearts were, they were, after all, mainly predators. And predators tended to seek easy prey. Or they didn't survive to pass on their genes to baby predators.

"I don't know," Long Tom said worriedly. He stood in the stern with them, more concerned with pursuit than with the dangers of navigating a narrow, relatively shallow passage in a hurricane. Clearly he trusted Micro, his sailing master. "Once Black Mask catches the scent of a rich prize, he doesn't like to let it go. He's not a man who deals well with disappointment."

On their last sight of the *Black Joke,* it had been tossed on massive waves five hundred or so yards astern. Perhaps half a dozen other large craft still clustered around it. That was less than half the fleet that first hove into view over the horizon.

Ryan was pretty sure the *Hope*'s rocket racks had only accounted for two or three of the enemy ships. If the Technomad squadron boasted any other weapons able to sink a ship of that size, he hadn't seen them used in the fight. More likely the other captains had chosen to cut and run, from the battle or from the storm.

"He doesn't much care about losses," Randy said. "Easy

come, easy go. And the more casualties he takes, the fewer pieces the pie has to be cut into."

J.B. had his hat off and was wringing water out of it. "Not the kind of employer I'd like to work for," he said, clapping the fedora back on his head. Ryan couldn't see it was an ounce less soaked than before he'd wrung it out.

"How does he get anybody to sign on with him, got an attitude like that?"

Randy shrugged. "As we told you, there's no shortage of men without much other choice live along this coast. Not to mention the ones he signs on at blasterpoint. Anyway, he's free with the jolt and red-eye. And with the women, they say, when they make landfall. Lotta men reckon a fast death with the Black Gang beats a slow death ashore."

"Cast in those terms," Doc said, "the attraction of his employ becomes, at least, more readily comprehensible."

Randy nodded. Despite their circumstances, Ryan felt brief amusement. The black Tech-nomad himself was pretty plainspoken. But by and large the Tech-nomads were about the only people left on Earth who didn't think Doc talked funny.

"Looks as if the *Black Joke* is making for the inlet," a voice called from midships as the *Hope* fully entered the river. "Pursuing."

Long Tom winced. "Great. Just what we need. Even with the real storm about to land on us like as asteroid from fucking space."

"Thought you were the one pointed out this Black Mask slagger didn't like to let go the trail of fat prey," Ryan said.

"Doesn't mean I can't hope," Long Tom said.

DESPITE THE LASHING of wind and rain, Ryan stood in the bow of the *New Hope* at him. J.B. stood by his side, hands in the pockets of his leather jacket. His hat was somehow crammed so hard down on his head the 60 mph winds couldn't dislodge it. Their two other friends were inside the cabin.

"You know, this is crazy, Ryan," he said. Actually, he hollered. It was the only way to make himself heard. "You know, when nature gets too much for even Jak to handle, it's probably time to pack it in."

"You head inside if you want to."

The Armorer lifted his face to the rain. Ryan wondered how he could see a blessed thing. Even if the rain didn't totally obscure his glasses, the round lenses were fogged white as Jak's hair.

"Reckon I'll stay with you a spell," the little man said.

This bayou wove a tangled skein of waterways, ever-changing—and never changing faster nor more decisively than when a brutal storm blew in off the Gulf. Ryan had hoped the surviving craft could power directly upriver, put some quick distance between them and the Gulf. Hurricane winds were bad, but water was the big killer.

But they weren't having that kind of luck. The channel here all but paralleled the coast; from time to time Ryan could see gray waves whipped frighteningly high by the storm through the trees. Sooner or later the water would rise and surge right over the trees at them. And what happened next he didn't care to speculate about.

"Anyway," J.B. said, "could be worse."

"How do you reckon that?"

"We could be out there in one a them little bicycle boats."

One of them had just appeared off the port bow, surging ahead of the *New Hope* along the landward bank. Normally the *Hope*'s wind-augmented electric motors would drive her faster than the water-strider boaters could pedal. But they were moving against the current here. Like their namesakes, the little outrigger-equipped craft skimmed the water. The current bothered them lots less than the bigger ships, shallow draft though they were.

The four surviving water-strider riders had all volunteered to go out despite the wind and the waves it drove up the bayou. They were hunting for some kind of side channel or passage that would allow *New Hope* and *Snowy Egret* to sail inland to a place offering better shelter.

"Got that right," Ryan said. "These Tech-nomads are triple weird, but they've got balls, got to give them that."

J.B. stiffened by his side. "Wait," he said. "We're comin' up on the *Egret*'s backside mighty quick."

Ryan looked. The Armorer was right. They were closing quickly on the yacht's taffrail.

"Shit," he yelled. "They're aground!"

Chapter Nine

Tech-nomads swarmed around the grounded yacht like ants. Ryan and the companions stood in a group on a patch of ground high enough not to be boggy, although the way the rain was coming down the ground was getting soft anyway despite the roots of the tough grass that grew there holding it together.

Their packs lay nearby, covered in tarps held down by the packs' own weight. Their weapons were wrapped in plastic that seemed to be of Tech-nomad manufacture. The companions themselves made no attempt to shelter from the rain. They weren't going to be anything but soaked for the foreseeable future. As for the wind, they'd seen too many trees blown over in the half hour since a sudden shift in the wind had run *Snowy Egret* up onto the shallowly submerged bank to want to get too close to any of those. So they stood in an open area and let the hurricane's rising fury beat on them.

It made it easier to do their job of keeping lookout, anyway.

"I almost feel like helping them," Mildred shouted. "Feel guilty about not, anyway."

A mob of Tech-nomads worked in the water up to their waists, hauling on ropes; others pushed against the hull of the grounded ship from land. The *New Hope* had bent on a cable and was trying to tow her sister ship free, although the channel's narrowness meant she had to pull at an angle. They worked with a fierce singleness of purpose, with none of the parrot chatter that often characterized the Tech-nomads when they were among themselves.

Not that they could've heard one another.

"Don't," J.B. yelled. "Didn't they teach you to never volunteer back in your time?"

"But maybe if we helped we could speed things along."

"We're not going to escape the hurricane," Krysty called. "This is it."

"The Tech-nomads hired us to guard their fleet," Ryan said. He stood watching the rescue operation with arms folded. He willed himself not to feel the wind's hammering. Compared to controlling the atavistic, instinctive fear of the storm's awful power, that was a breeze.

"They could ask us to help if they wanted. They told us to keep an eye out. So that's what we do."

"Good," Jak said. Though the albino teen was willing to work like a slave on his own account, and for his friends, he had a reluctance to work on a stranger's behalf.

"More than you know, my lad," Doc shouted. "Unless you believe that's an innocent oceanic wayfarer seeking shelter from the storm coming around that bend downstream?"

The others saw the high prow of a sturdy little vessel that looked like an old shrimp boat, just poking around a stand of black mangrove.

"Wouldn't you know it," J.B. said.

An ear-tormenting rattle pierced the storm's howl. Ryan saw Kayley, a female Tech-nomad rescued from the sinking *Finagle's First Law,* spin and fall into thigh-deep water. He looked up.

Across the river men and muzzle-flashes appeared among wind-lashed trees. They were shooting at the Tech-nomads trying to rescue *Egret.* From the big clouds of smoke produced by most of the weapons, visible for an instant before the wind whipped them away into curling threads that quickly vanished in the rain, Ryan guessed most of the pirates were firing black powder blasters.

"Good luck to them reloading if the smoke poles're muzzle-loaders," J.B. remarked unconcernedly. He yanked the plastic wrap off his Smith & Wesson M-4000 shotgun and began ejecting buckshot shells into his hand. Feeding those into a cargo pocket of his baggy pants, he produced a box of rifle slugs and loaded those in their place.

Mildred sat, fastidiously managing to get a piece of the waterproof material to hold still long enough for her to plant her behind on it. As if it could make any possible difference, given how skin-soaked they all were. She took out her ZKR target pistol and propped her elbows just inside her knees.

Ryan unwrapped his own sniper rifle. He wiped condensation off the outsides of both lenses of his scope with a handkerchief from his pocket. Raising the longblaster to his shoulder, he confirmed the insides of the lenses were clear. The scope remained waterproof after all the years and abuse it had been through.

He wondered how long that would last, as nothing lasted forever.

A nearer rattle of blasterfire told him the Tech-nomads had begun returning fire at the pirates who had infiltrated through the trees on the far bank. He swung his scope down along the river. He didn't have the option a normal shooter did, of using his other eye to discover where to point the much more restricted vision field of the telescopic sight. But he had a lot of practice with pointing toward the last place he'd looked.

And the shrimp boat wasn't a small target. He picked it up right away. It was stained white and sun-faded blue, the paint peeling badly from long exposure to sun and weather. The name *Mary Sue* was painted on the bow.

He lined up the post of the telescopic sight on a man hun-

kered behind a battered M-60 machine gun laid across the
shrimper's bow rail. These pirates had some serious armament. Then again he'd noticed both the Tech-nomads and
the pirates tended to use only heavy full-automatic weapons,
like the M-60 or the BARs Isis favored. Support weapons.
For personal arms both sides stuck to semiauto, conventional
repeaters, or even black powder and non-firearms. He knew
why: ammo. It was expensive, hard to come by, heavy. Even
though he was pretty sure the Tech-nomads reloaded, and
maybe manufactured some of their own, full-auto fire was a
pretty wasteful way to go.

It was a long shot at the machine gunner, especially in
these conditions, at least five hundred yards. The only thing
going for Ryan was that the wind trying too hard to knock
him on his rear was blowing almost right into the teeth of the
shot. It wasn't going to deflect the hefty 180-grain copper-
jacketed traveling about 2800 feet per second bullet much.
He took a deep breath and started to let about half of it out.

Ryan's field of view filled with yellow fire. He jerked his
head back, completely surprised. The shrimp boat was awash
with flame. The gunner in the bow, completely wrapped in
flames, let the heavy black blaster fall overboard. An instant later he followed, flapping his arms like firebird wings.
Crewmates were doing likewise. The lucky ones weren't on
fire. Although luck in this case might just mean a chance to
drown in the raging river, rather than burn.

"It would seem the *New Hope* got her rocket rack re-
paired," Doc said into Ryan's ear. The one-eyed man hadn't
even heard the multimissile launch for the storm.

"Oh, no," Mildred said in disgust after triggering a shot
across the river. "Hell no. I can't hit anything in this cross-
wind."

She got up to fetch one of the extra longblasters the Tech-
nomads had lent them. A bullet kicked up sand from where

she had been sitting an eyeblink after the wind plucked away
the black plastic groundsheet she'd been sitting on.

"Get to cover," Ryan shouted. "Bastards are shooting at
us."

"But the wind—" Krysty said.

"Find a tree that looks like it'll stay put," Ryan shouted.
A bullet cracked past his ear. *"Move!"*

They did, scrambling back among the gnarled cypress
roots on the relatively high ground behind them. Ryan moved
quickly to take his own advice. He kept his eye on his companions to make sure they all did likewise.

When everybody had put a bole between him or her and
the pirate blasters, he took stock of the tactical situation
again. Most of the Tech-nomads trying to free the trapped
yacht kept at it, trusting in their comrades aboard *Hope* to
deal with the pirates. Once again Ryan admired their grit, as
he did that of the three remaining water-striders. The riders
kept zipping in close to the bank to shoot at the pirates before
scooting away again.

The wind had grown truly monstrous. Pirates were getting
knocked over by it as well as Tech-nomad bullets, and more.
Ryan saw arrows standing from the front of a body bobbing
on its back in the water on the far side. Though *New Hope*
was still rolling and surging, her motion was nowhere as violent or radical as it had been in open water, with not even
the insufficient coverage of the dense woods to cut the wind.
The Tech-nomads aboard seemed to be compensating for it
just fine.

From their new positions, relatively secure against both
blasterfire and the wind that sought to pluck them away like
leaves, the companions added their fire. Mildred had a Mini-
14, Krysty a lever-action .44 Magnum carbine. Doc used the
same weapon with a longer barrel. J.B.'s rifled slugs gave his

scattergun range and accuracy enough to have a chance of hitting across the water.

And a chance was all you could hope for. Ryan lined up his scope dead on the center of a hairy bare chest and fired. The guy was scarcely sixty yards away; normally Ryan would've used iron sights. But the pirate was still standing there, blasting away with some kind of revolver, when he brought the longblaster back down from its recoil rise.

Saving the breath it took to curse, Ryan swung his rifle into the wind, so that the aim point was a few fingers left of the flabby, dark-furred rib cage. This time he saw the man was dropping even before the Steyr kicked up far enough. He vanished from the scope.

Ryan was swinging around, waiting for another target to jump out at him, when Mildred shouted, "Folks, we got more trouble!"

A crack cut across the storm roar. Dark water fountained from midstream. Two Tech-nomads pulling the grounded ship with ropes went down.

Ryan looked downriver. A sleekly sinister black shape was just nosing past the shrimp boat, which was now basically a bonfire sitting inexplicably atop the churning river with no visible boat about it.

"The *Black Joke,* I presume?" Doc asked.

"I sure hope Long Tom got his rocket launcher reloaded," Mildred said.

"Rad-blast it." Ryan raised his rifle. Through the scope he saw men working frantically at the rear of the long tube of the recoilless weapon. Next to it stood a man dressed completely in black.

Ryan lined up a shot on the black-clad chest. The recoilless rifle was a major threat, but Ryan reckoned if he took down the pirate boss, the rest would stand down. As raindrops spattered on the objective lens, he pulled the trigger.

He knew even as the Steyr kicked up he'd missed. When he brought it down again, cranking another cartridge into the breech, he saw Black Mask hustling aft. A pirate was in the process of falling backward over the railing behind where he'd stood a moment before. Ryan hadn't missed completely, but this shooting match gave out no second prizes.

Ryan's next shot took down the man reloading the recoilless. By the time he brought his longblaster back down another was stepping up to take the dead man's place. He had to pause, then, to reload.

"Come *on*," Mildred as saying. "Doesn't *New Hope* have any more rockets?"

"That black ship don't seem to be having such an easy time getting past the wreck," J.B. said, thumbing more solid-shot shells into the tubular mag of his scattergun.

"Indeed not!" Doc shouted.

It was true. The channel was narrow, and flames continued to billow from the wreck despite the rain. The *Black Joke* seemed to be trying to work past its stricken sibling without taking light herself.

The recoilless fired. The shell went off somewhere in the woods inland of Ryan's party. Leaning into the tree for added stability, the one-eyed man managed to drop the new gunner. When the pirates seemed a little reluctant to make a conspicuous target of themselves, he looked around at the battle closer to hand.

A brisk firefight was in progress between the pirates and the Tech-nomads. The defenders had finally given up trying to free the *Snowy Egret* for the moment and sought cover—and weapons to shoot from it.

The *New Hope* still wasn't launching any more of its incendiary rockets. Ryan dropped a couple of the pirates attacking overland. Then he heard the recoilless go off again. This time the shell threw up a fountain thirty yards upstream of *New Hope.* An answering snarl came from close by. Isis had apparently found some more .30-06 ammo for her BAR. She lay atop *Egret*'s cabin, firing back at the pirate flagship.

She didn't manage to suppress the enemy gun crew. But Ryan did, on his third shot.

Isis began to spray the pirates on the far bank with quick savage bursts. The other Tech-nomads added their shots to hers from crossbows and blasters. The pirates fell back.

"Listen," Jak called. "Black ship guns engines double-hard."

Ryan gave up looking for targets to do as the albino teen said. Downwind he could hear the higher-pitched knocking of *Black Joke*'s engines, distinct even through the bellowing wind.

"Running!" Jak shouted triumphantly.

It was true. The black ship backed away and quickly vanished behind the subsiding flames of the derelict. Ryan could actually see her mainmast above wind-bent trees as she fled downstream.

"That's how they knew how to cut us off," Ryan said. "Their lookouts saw our masts over the trees. They knew where the channel we were following had us headed and put men ashore to bushwhack us."

"They're cutting stick and running now," J.B. said.

The shooting dwindled and died. The pirates who had attacked through the trees now seemed interested only in retreating as rapidly as the wind and mucky footing would allow. Those who were in condition to. Ryan didn't notice anyone wasting time trying to help the wounded get away.

"Why is the river dropping?" Mildred said.

Everybody looked. It was true. The level of the water was falling perceptibly. Ryan noticed it was taking on the black-ish tinge of tannin from rotting vegetation a channel like this usually showed, rather than the dirty brownish-gray appearance it had before.

"The wind's not dying," Krysty said. "Why isn't it still driving the seawater upriver against the flow?"

"Perhaps the tide recedes?" Doc suggested in a voice that didn't display much confidence despite the fact he, like everybody, was bellowing against the hurricane roar. The wind lashed them like invisible whips now.

Ryan shook his head. "Don't know," he said. "But the damned *Egret*'s stuck harder aground than she was before."

And then Isis, who had slithered over the downstream side of the cabin when the shooting ceased, fired a shattering burst in the air.

"Everybody, get aboard ship!" she screamed. *"Suckout!"*

Chapter Ten

"What the blazing nuke death's a suckout?" Ryan demanded.

Isis looked toward them and waved the twenty-pound BAR one-handed as if it were a willow wand. "You! Grab your traps and get your asses aboard! Do it now!"

After an instant's frozen hesitation, the Tech-nomads—who now stood in water a good two feet shallower than they had moments ago—boiled into action. Some splashed out toward the *New Hope* and scrambled aboard. Others piled back onto the *Egret*.

"What good getting onboard stuck ship?" Jak shouted. He was clinging to the tree he'd taken cover behind with one white hand. His long white hair was blowing almost straight out to the side. The wind was threatening to toss his skinny body through the air.

"You got me," Ryan said. "But the lady sounds like she means it."

"Hurry!" Isis shouted. She fired another shot from her BAR. "You! Outlanders! Get your asses on board now if you want a chance to live!"

"She does mean it, Ryan," Krysty said. "We need to do it."

Bent low to reduce her cross-section to the now brutal wind she scuttled from the shelter of her tree to plop down next to her pack. She yanked the tarp off. The wind grabbed it from her and whirled it away out of sight up the once-more sluggish river before she'd got it all the way clear. Her hair was blown in front of her face, the scarlet tendrils, their colors muted by the dim gray light, twisting like a ball of agitated snakes.

"It appears our friend the Black Mask is retreating out to sea at a goodly clip," Doc shouted. He pointed a long skinny arm. Ryan could see the mainmast of the *Black Joke* dwindling rapidly to become lost in the trees.

"May not be all under his own power," J.B. said.

"Let's go," Ryan said. Krysty's move had sealed his decision.

Following Ryan, the others made their way against the force of the wind to recover their packs. A tree thirty yards downstream tore loose. It flew up the channel, its roots shedding mud, right between *Egret*'s stern and *New Hope*'s bow. Somehow it missed both ships, and didn't even tangle the taut tow line before splashing into the river.

Ryan stood with his pack on his back and his rifle slung. He had to lean hard into the wind to keep it from doing to him what it had just done to the big cypress tree. Onboard *Hope* Long Tom stood gesturing excitedly at Randy in the lee of the cabin, pointing toward the fallen tree, which now lay in the middle of the channel with half its dark foliage above water. Apparently they were discussing whether it blocked their passage or not.

"Everybody grab on to somebody," Ryan yelled. He reached out blindly as he did, found himself holding on to Doc's skinny biceps. The old man hastily grabbed Ryan's arm in reply.

Stumbling, staggering, blinking in a mostly futile attempt to clear raindrops driven hard as bullets out of their eyes, the six made their way to the stern of the *Snowy Egret*. Half the ship's gleaming white keel was now fully exposed.

Ryan just had presence of mind to lead his people around the grounded ship's downwind side. It was as if a giant hand pressing against him had been swatted away. He almost toppled into the hull from leaning hard into a relentless pressure that was suddenly no longer there.

Isis herself helped hand him up. Her grip was strong, as if her muscles were steel cables. Her exotic face was set hard as an ivory statue's. Some of the Tech-nomads who had gotten aboard disappeared below.

"No room left belowdecks," she shouted. "Grab on to something. Do it now. Hang on as if your life depends on it, 'cause it does!"

Ryan had let go of Doc to clamber aboard the Tech-nomad yacht. Now he looked around and hurriedly found Krysty. She came to him at once. Putting an arm around each other, they grabbed on to a railing that ran along the top of the cabin.

Ryan looked around. He could only see J.B. and Mildred, doing the same thing he and Krysty were a few feet toward the bow. "Sound off!" he roared. "Everybody secure?"

Through the storm howl he couldn't hear the response from Doc and Jak. But J.B. yelled, "Other two are locked down, too."

Isis stood braced in the hatchway to the main cabin a few feet astern of Ryan. "What're we waiting for?" he yelled.

"You'll see."

He noticed that the wind had blown the *Egret* against the slow current so that she now lay almost at a right angle to the bank. It had to have happened before the water level dropped; he'd been too buried in the scope to notice. He figured it had to be a good sign.

"There goes the *Hope!*" J.B. called. The rotor-ship was powering upstream away from *Egret,* severed tow rope trailing into the water off her stern. She literally scraped between the fallen tree and the seaward bank.

"Friends running out on you?" he shouted to Isis.

The wind made her topknot stick straight out like a silver pennon. "Nothing more they can do for us," she shouted. "Might as well save themselves if they can."

Before he had a chance to say more, a shout was raised from somewhere on the far side of the boat. "Here it comes!"

"What?" Mildred shouted back.

"The Gulf of Mexico," Isis said.

A porthole opened into the cabin right next to where Ryan and Krysty stood clinging for dear life against some as-yet-unknown threat. He couldn't resist leaning forward and peering through.

By chance it gave an unobstructed view out the port on the far side. And what he saw through the rain-streaked polycarbonate was—

"Glowing night shit!" he yelled. *"Tsunami!"*

Isis about had it right. The Gulf was coming back, with a vengeance, piling up into dirty gray-foaming waves so high he could see them rise right up above the trees of the seaward bank.

"Storm surge," the captain yelled back.

The rolling water wall blasted through and over the trees. Ryan turned away and he and Krysty huddled against each other for all they were worth.

Then with a mighty roar, the wave hit *Snowy Egret* and kicked her hard up into the air.

The sea boiled all around them. The yacht spun counterclockwise as it was hurled inland. Ryan felt the impacts and scrapes as her hull pushed through the treetops, now submerged beneath the enormous, irresistible churning flow of the storm surge. He caught a glimpse of the *New Hope* whirling away to the east like a dune buggy doing doughnuts on a salt flat. He saw a water-strider boat riding the foamscummed crest of a wave, its rider pedaling furiously, miraculously afloat and intact. Then they spun out of sight.

The *Egret* was now being flung bodily inland, stern first. Ryan and company were exposed to the full force of the wind. The good news was that it pressed them against the cabin, rather than try to pluck them away. The bad news was that the triple-digit wind speed made it hard to breathe, as if a giant anaconda had thrown its coils around Ryan's chest and was constricting.

Lightning lanced across the sky. Thunder cracked so loud he thought the *Egret* was breaking up. But the ship didn't break into pieces beneath and around them.

Not yet. But no matter how fiercely driven by the monster storm, no matter how far the water had been sucked out to sea, no matter how flat the land beneath for that matter, there was a limit to how far inland the wave could carry them. Sooner or later they'd come back to Earth. Odds against a soft landing were good.

And as he thought that the surge began to fail.

With a splintering crash the *Egret* hit exposed treetops. Ryan's grip was broken and he started to tumble sternward. But Krysty's strength held. For a moment he was stretched horizontally in the air, his heels toward the stern, Krysty's hand locked like an iron band around his wrist.

Then something knocked the *Egret* spinning again. The side of the cabin slammed against Ryan's left side. He felt one of his boots slam into Isis, braced in the doorway, felt her break free and tumble inside.

Then there was nothing but the roaring and the darkness and the water that slammed over the bow and rushed over the deck. And through it all, somehow, the grip on his wrist, warm and solid, maintained.

Something banged into Ryan's head. He didn't black out, not wholly, but he lost track....

"RYAN," A VOICE was calling. "Ryan!"

His awareness, which had been a roaring redness, began to resolve into bright sun and heat.

"Ryan, you got to pull yourself together in a hurry." He recognized J.B.'s voice, coming as if from a great distance.

But it wasn't competing with the roar of the wind. It seemed that had been his entire being for an eternity. That and then a wild whirling ride. Then multiple impacts and... confusion.

Something pressed his right cheek, soft and plaint, then tickled his right ear.

His lone eye came all the way open. Krysty leaned over him, her red hair haloed by sunlight. He couldn't see her face for shadow but from her silhouette and smell and the sheer feel of her he knew it was her, and knew she was smiling from the kiss. Her sentient red hair caressed his face like feathers.

He saw the paleness of her smile in her shadowed face. "I thought that was a better way to call you back to this world, lover," she said. "And I thought you'd wouldn't react so violently as you otherwise might."

"I'd rather you rouse me by kissing my cheek than J.B.," he said, his voice a frog croak.

"That's both of us, partner," came the Armorer's dry voice. "Now get up and get a move on."

Ryan sat up, realizing he did so against gravity. That was strange. As was the realization that the surface he sat on was tilted to at least thirty degrees.

"Did I sleep through the hurricane?" he asked.

"Nope," J.B. said. "Welcome to the eye."

"Oh, shit," Ryan said.

He got hastily to his feet. Immediately he swayed. He was looking back at the stern, which was crazily framed against the empty sky. His head swam and his gut churned.

The steadying grip on his biceps was strong and sure. This time he could see Krysty's smiling face perfectly. He gave her a quick, tight grin.

"Status?" he asked.

"Heard the old expression 'up shit creek without a paddle'?" J.B. asked. "Well, we made it come true. Also we're up a tree."

"Several trees, actually," Krysty said. "We need to get down in a hurry."

"The rest?"

"The Tech-nomads have lowered a rope, and some of them have climbed down. So has Doc. He's reloading his LeMat."

"Keep him out of trouble for a while. You both fit to fight?"

"Never better, Ryan," J.B. said laconically. "You're the one took a hit to the head."

"Jak? Mildred?"

"Hurt his arm," Krysty said. "So did Isis, but she told Mildred to look Jak over first and slid down the rope to take stock on the ground."

Ryan nodded. He was glad she'd come through. "What about the rest?"

"Of the Tech-nomads?" Krysty asked. She shook her head. "I don't know where *New Hope* is, or whether she even survived. Communication's out. Of the people who got onto the *Egret* before the wave hit, there's mebbe ten alive. Some of them are hurt pretty bad."

Ryan looked around. At the bow, which was tilted down toward a disarmingly placid black bayou, Jak was sitting on a jumble of gear as Mildred examined him. His face looked paler than usual, somehow. His narrow jaw was set.

"How is he?" Ryan called.

"Not so good. His arm's dislocated."

"Oh," Krysty said, "is that all?" She strode purposefully aft.

"Is that all?" Mildred repeated. "Okay, well, I suppose there's one way to deal with it."

The redhead had walked up to the albino teen. "You ready?" she asked.

He nodded.

Mildred was shaking her head. "Go for it."

Krysty had grabbed Jak's limply hanging right arm. Bracing the sole of a boot against his rib cage, she pulled.

Even Ryan winced at the ensuing crunching sound. From a corner of his eye he saw the usually unflappable Armorer do likewise.

Jak grunted stoically.

"Better?" Krysty said.

Experimentally the albino teen raised his arm. "Yeah."

Chapter Eleven

"So what now, Ryan?" Doc asked when they were all on relatively dry, or at least not currently flooded, ground.

It was a grassy patch far enough away from where the *Snowy Egret* hung improbably suspended twenty feet in the air that if gravity caught up with the yacht it wasn't likely to land on their heads.

Not far away Isis, her broken arm hastily set, bandaged and looped in a sling by Mildred, stood beneath the hulk supervising the extraction of the last wounded member of her crew: a bearded young man named Freebo, whose back seemed to be broken. They were bringing him down strapped to a door—or hatch, as they insisted on calling it because it was on a ship. Mildred was helping tend to the other wounded who had already been brought down.

Isis had directed them to keep watch again. She assessed threat levels as low even though the trees cut off view in a hundred yards in all directions. She explained that while the sight of the *Egret* perched high up in a tree would normally bring swampies running from miles around greedy for loot, muties hereabouts were familiar with the behavior of hurricanes. No matter how hard up they were, they weren't about to risk getting hit by the full force of the storm while plucking the marooned *Egret* of her booty.

Ryan hoped she was right. He'd seen desperation drive people to do some stupe things. He'd seen muties do crazy shit for no reason he could conceive.

Norms, too, now that he thought about it.

Already the wind was picking up. "We don't have long, do we?" Ryan asked.

Doc shook his head. "Soon the eye will have passed. We are in the proverbial calm before the storm."

"The eye-wall winds are the fiercest in a hurricane." Her injured shipmate safely on the ground, Isis had walked up to the group. "What do you intend to do, Cawdor?"

Everybody always asked him that. The thought grimly amused him. "Don't have much experience with hurricanes in these kinds of circumstances. I'd say we should find as dry and sheltered a spot as we can, mebbe tie ourselves to some trees that don't look like they'll blow over easily, and try triple-hard not to die."

The exotic woman's silver topknot bobbed as she nodded. "Sounds like as good a plan as any. But I was curious what you and your companions had in mind."

He scratched his eyebrow with his thumbnail. "We still work for you, far as I know."

"Your contract was with Long Tom."

"He don't seem to be around," J.B. said, "so looks like you're the boss now."

"We signed on to protect you," Ryan said. "Don't know how good a job I can say we've done so far. But once we take a job, we see it through."

The captain showed gleaming white teeth. "If you people knew a way to defend against a hurricane, you'd be the bosses of everything. You've fought alongside us and done what you could. Only problem is, paying you could be a problem. No way we get poor *Egret* unloaded before the eye passes and the hammer comes down."

"We'll see the storm out," Ryan said. "Then if we live, we can work out the details."

"Our best bet's sticking together anyway, right now," Krysty said. "We should be finding a lie-up."

Isis nodded. "See to that then. We'll—"

Ryan heard a hard thunk. Mildred cursed, and Isis glanced back toward where her surviving comrades were gathered.

"Looks like Freebo decided he didn't like his chances and opted to catch the last train for the coast," she said.

"Poor Mildred," Krysty said. "She takes losing a patient that way hard."

"Forget her for now," Ryan said. "You heard the lady. Let's find cover and get ourselves stuck into it."

"WATER RISING," Jak said.

"Oh, dear," Mildred said.

Silently, Krysty echoed the sentiment. Then the physician gave voice to Krysty's own fear, which she hoped no one would voice.

"Do the eye-wall winds drive a second storm surge?" Mildred asked, her voice rising and taking on an edge that bespoke the nearness of panic. "If another tsunami like the last one hits us here, we're toast. Um, soggy toast."

"Easy, Mildred," Ryan said, his voice calm.

"Nothing we can do about it, anyway."

They had found a clearing in a cypress grove whose floor Isis estimated rose four feet about the current level of the nameless bayou chance and the tsunami had dumped them on. It was the best shelter anyone had been able to find in a fast recce. Doc and Jak had inspected the trees, one using his antique science, the other his intimate knowledge of nature and swamp terrain, and pronounced their roots sound and liable to hold. Krysty had no way of knowing if either had the faintest notion of what he was talking about. But the roots seemed sound to her, too, and anyway, it wasn't as if they had a lot of choice.

The most important thing was that the survivors of the *Egret* could all clump together in the little clear space without being too crowded, yet able to grab one another and the trees if threatened with being swept away by wind and water.

After a hurried consultation out of earshot of the rest, Ryan and Isis had agreed they wouldn't try lashing themselves to the trees. They had enough forest around them to damp the effects of the wind. And if the waters did get too high, being tangled in rope was the last thing anyone would need—it could shave the slimmest chance of survival down to none.

"It shouldn't be as bad," Isis said over a rising whine of gale winds. "Bad as the eye-wall winds are, they don't have time or space to build a really wicked surge."

Then the wind hit like a hammer.

It was as if a vacuum was sucking the very breath from Krysty's lungs. She battled to breathe as the wind beat at her face with the bruising impact of fists. She groped blindly, found Ryan's strong grip with one hand and Mildred's with the other.

It was bad. Worse than before. Their mad whirling trip across the storm-surge wave had terrified Krysty, but it had also distracted from the wind's brutal impact.

And they had ridden above the water, at least. The winds of the eye wall, which had to have greatly exceeded a hundred miles an hour, didn't create a second tsunami-like surge. But they did drive the waters ahead of them, piling the salt waters of the Gulf on the "fresh" water of the river, driving all in front of them with the force of a great pump.

The tea-colored water frothed yellow and rose around them. It felt as warm as blood as it lapped against Krysty's legs.

"Forget me, girl!" Mildred hollered. "Grab a piece of tree!"

The sturdily built black woman followed her own advice. Ryan caught Jak by the hair as a sudden rush of green water knocked the youth off his feet, and dragged him to where he could clutch another bole like a half-drowned kitten. Not far away J.B. and Doc stood on opposite sides of the same bole, hanging on as if holding the tree up.

Krysty saw animals whirl around them on the raging river. Snakes wriggled. A beaver tumbled over and over, slapping the water with its broad tail in a desperate attempt to right itself and regain control. Alligators were launched against what was usually the bayou flow like dark brown lumpy torpedoes. Off in the distance, largely obscured by the rain that suddenly fell in gray sheets, Krysty saw a vast dark shape fighting the water that swept it along. It might have been a bear, but she had a crazy impression it sported a short horn from its flat, broad head.

The Tech-nomads raised a clamor like frightened shore birds. Krysty looked around to see Freebo's door whirled away. Isis made a one-handed grab and fell on her face with a mighty splash. Jammer dived after her, grabbing her by her long, slim legs. Both were reeled back to safety by their surviving comrades.

The storm seemed more savage than before. Krysty had to press her face against the rough bole of the cypress tree to protect her eyes from raindrops that stung like hail and random bits of debris propelled by the awful wind. The wind beat on her shoulders and back and head like hard fists. She clung with all her strength to keep from being ripped away, and could only pray to the Earth Mother that if one of her companions was torn loose, she'd learn of it in time to help.

The water rose to midthigh and began to recede again. The wind continued to scream. Its efforts to pluck Krysty loose from her hold diminished, though she still had to hold on hard. Relief flooded her like mother's love. The eye wall had passed us by!

Then the sound of human voices screaming nearby forced

her to expose her face to the wind and open her emerald eyes. A squat dough-colored shape had a struggling Isis gripped in arms like huge uncooked sausages. The Tech-nomad thrashed furiously in its grip, unable to break free, trying to reach behind her with her one good hand to get a thumb in her attacker's eye.

"Swampies!" Krysty shouted.

Jammer threw himself on the mutie. Both were a good head shorter than Isis, but the swampie was so broad it likely outweighed both the humans together and more besides. Jammer stabbed furiously with a hunting knife at the arm pinioning his captain. Blood spurted black in the gloom. From somewhere another swampie appeared and sank an ax into his back. He slumped into the water, which had changed direction again, and was swept, facedown, past Krysty downstream.

Ryan let go and slogged through the water toward the swampie who held Isis. He had his SIG-Sauer P-226 out at arm's length and was shooting as he splashed forward. Krysty wondered at the risk he was taking of hitting the captive.

Then the second swampie, who had struck down Jammer with the ax, pitched forward to land with a huge splash in the water. The muties were notoriously hard to kill, but one of Ryan's 9 mm slugs had penetrated the back of its head.

Ryan ran up to the swampie that held Isis. He bobbed away from a clumsy swipe that for all its almost comic effect could easily have broken its neck if it had caught him in the side of the head as intended. Then he pressed the muzzle of his SIG into the rolls of fat around the mutie's right eye and fired.

A gush of liquid spewed out the right side of the mutie's head: brain matter flash-heated and overpressurized by both the 147-grain bullet and the gases that propelled it. The swampie emitted a shrill steam-whistle squeal and collapsed. Isis splashed into the water.

Krysty saw no more of what happened there because Mildred started screaming closer at hand. Her hair twisting like a mass of frightened snakes, Krysty whipped her head around to see a swampie had caught Mildred by one wrist and was trying to drag her away. The creature wasn't bright. It seemed to be trying to pull the black woman through the tree, allowing her to hang on tight with her other arm and keep her face and body pressed against the trunk. Stymied despite the fact his strength was many times hers, the only thing the swampie could think to do was to pull harder.

Krysty ripped her knife out and began slashing at the doughy forearm. Past the squat dirty-white mass she saw J.B. trying to maneuver to get a shot with his shotgun that wouldn't endanger either Krysty or his woman.

Then pain like lightning shot up Krysty's right thigh, through her belly to her spine to explode in her brain. At the same instant she felt a strange sick edge to the blinding agony and knew she had been poisoned.

She looked down. A long narrow sinuous body a good four feet long, green and brown, writhed in the water right beside her. Its jaws gaped flat open. It had sunk its two forward-extended fangs into her leg like spears.

She heard Mildred scream her name.

"Gaia, give me strength." Krysty saw a glittering arc descend and chop the snake in half as Ryan struck with his panga.

And then the darkness enveloped her and bore her down.

"WHAT IS THIS?" Ryan shouted, holding up the snake that had bitten Krysty. He had chopped it in half a foot and a half down from the head. He held it near the stump. The head itself still waved, jaws opened menacingly.

"I think it's a water moccasin," Mildred said. Cradling her freed wrist, she half waded, half swam to where Krysty floated on her back in the water. Her eyes were closed. Her hair spread out about her like a halo, framing a face still as ivory that seemed calm and composed.

J.B.'s shotgun roared again. He had blown part of the head off the swampie who had held Mildred's wrist. That hadn't been enough to kill the mutie. He was finishing the job now. Around them the surviving Tech-nomads were battling more muties who had come out of the storm to catch their prey unsuspecting and nearly helpless.

"I never saw a snakebite victim react like this," Mildred said, grabbing Krysty's wrist. "She's alive. I—"

"Ryan," he heard Doc shout. "Watch out!"

Before he could react Ryan was picked up out of the water and hurled through the air. He flew a dozen feet and landed sideways against a tree trunk. Pain shot through his side and turned his vision momentarily red.

A terrific blow caught him on the side of the head, and he slipped into the water. For a moment he saw beneath the surface: yellowish light, swirling motes, waving submerged grass. Then he got his hands under him and pushed himself up out of the water, heaving and gagging.

A hippo-size foot caught him in the side. The kick was in slow motion yet monstrously powerful. It threw him up out of the water and onto his back on wet grass and hard dirt.

He heard bellowing, screams, shots. Shaking his head to clear his eye of water, he saw an unbelievable sight: a man as tall as himself, with a trim waist, powerful chest, bare from the waist up, his skin and long flying hair as albino-white as Jak Lauren's, swinging a pair of swords at a group of swampies while other men surged out of the wind-whipped brush, holding spears, cutlasses and longblasters.

Then a pale fist the size of his head slammed into Ryan's solar plexus. It doubled him like a dying caterpillar. The air erupted out of him, and he passed out.

Chapter Twelve

Ryan became aware of the world again. More precisely he became aware of pain: a dull ache that throbbed constantly in what seemed like every molecule of his body.

A deeper pain throbbed in his heart and soul: Krysty!

He felt as if he were swaddled in wet blankets. He could force his eyelids open no more than a slit. It seemed he saw an angel sitting beside the place where he lay, hair gleaming as black as obsidian surrounded by a halo, oval face pale and perfect.

"You're beautiful," he dreamed he heard the apparition say. "Perhaps you bring hope."

Fade to black.

Sometime later, it seemed to Ryan that he dreamed of a second presence. Through slits, filtered by his eyelashes, he seemed to see a feminine figure, more substantial-seeming than the first ethereal angel, yet still slim: sitting primly upright, with dark brown hair drawn up into a severe bun. As with the first, he could open his eyes no more, nor make out more detail.

"You are beautiful," this apparition said, in a voice tinged with French accent. "Yet I fear you bring chaos and confusion."

That seemed a harsh thing for an angel to say about Ryan Cawdor, and him defenseless and all. But before he could work up any kind of heat about it, he went black again.

"OKAY, RYAN," a familiar voice said, "you've been doing your malingering act long enough. Time to rouse your lazy ass out of bed."

"Fuck you, J.B.," he said, stubbornly refusing to open his eye. "And the wag you rode in on."

He heard a grumpy throat-clearing he quickly identified as belonging to Mildred Wyeth. "We have company here, Ryan," the physician said.

"Or to put it with considerably more precision," Doc said, "we are the company, in the presence of our most generous host and hostess."

Ryan heard a growl from Mildred, followed by a snicker that could only spring from the slender throat of Jak Lauren. Well, he thought with a relief that spread through him like the warmth of a good bed in wintertime, my friends are okay.

And then an ice spear shot right through his bowels into his vitals. Krysty!

He found himself sitting bolt upright. The name of his beloved still echoed in his ears. He had cried it aloud without meaning to. It made him feel naked, vulnerable. They were two feelings he scarcely knew.

He didn't want to get better acquainted.

Looking rather wildly around, he noted that he was in a small, neat room, with cream-colored paper pinstriped in green, and little pictures of old-time people riding on horseback with dogs on the walls. His eye chose to fix and focus on the first human shape it hit.

"Jak?" he said. "Why're you dressed up like that?"

As he spoke he realized it wasn't his companion. It was a young man with the same milk-white skin, the almost silver-sheened hair hanging to his shoulders, the ruby eyes. But he was obviously older, bulked out from Jak's adolescent leanness. Possibly Jak would look like that when he was twice as old as he was now. But even sitting it was obvious Jak would never be as tall as this man. Nor could Ryan easily wrap his mind around the notion of Jak dressed like that, in a dark suit pinstriped pale lavender, with a spray of lace at the throat.

Ryan would've thought the man somewhat soft, sitting with one slim leg crossed over the other, if it wasn't for the width of the shoulders in that fine silk coat, the air of controlled panther power the man gave off even sitting smilingly relaxed. And the fact that Ryan was sure he'd seen the albino wading hip-deep through storm waters and a pack of pissed-off swampies, swinging a pair of broadswords like they were willow withes.

"Guess we owe you a debt for saving us," Ryan said. His voice rasped as if the box was a gate grown rusty from disuse and in need of a good oiling. "I'm Ryan Cawdor."

"Your friends have apprised me," the man said in a startling deep baritone voice. "You are welcome, as they are.

"And it seems we owe you a debt as well, Mr. Cawdor."

His gaze tracked to the other side of the bed. There was a table, on which stood a porcelain water pitcher with water droplets condensed on its fluted white sides, and a vase of purple glass with a spray of lilac blooms. A second figure sat beside the table: a woman, with jet-black hair held back by a brooch from a pale face with a widow's peak. The face was achingly beautiful, the eyes big, a striking dark violet, and haunting. She wore a black dress, simple yet elegant, which emphasized both the narrowness of her waist and the thrust of her bosom. An air of fragile sadness seemed to hang around her, though her smile was as beautiful as any he had ever seen.

Even Krysty's. His gut spasmed again.

"What about Krysty?" he asked.

"She's…alive," the woman said. Her voice seemed somehow familiar, but he couldn't place it. "Please, lie back down."

He started to get out of bed. "Take me to her," he insisted.

"Lie the hell back down, Ryan," Mildred ordered. "Or we'll tackle you and tie you down. Krysty's condition is stable. She's in some kind of coma. I'd be more precise if I knew what was going on with her. And there's nothing more certain on this godforsaken Earth than that there is nothing you can do to help her."

His head started to spin. He found himself lying back to save himself the indignity of collapsing.

The humid heat didn't help. He felt sweat sliming his face and his bare upper torso. The lilacs didn't mask the smells of vinegar and ammonia used to clean the room, and those smells failed to hide the odors of mildew and old sweat.

At least his other four friends were present and not looking too badly dinged or scraped.

"How long have I been out?" he asked. "What the nuking hell was wrong with me?"

"You were, to put it technical-like, all beat to shit," J.B. said. "Please pardon my language, ma'am," he added to the raven-haired woman, who nodded.

"You suffered massive bruises and contusions, as well as several sprains," Mildred said to Ryan in her precise clinician's voice. "You also got some cracked ribs."

"They're still barking at me," he acknowledged ruefully. He still hurt all over, for a fact. But the pain from his left side was sharper and more insistent.

"The ville healer, Dr. Mercier, kept you sedated."

"Say what? I've been drugged all this time?" Outraged, he started to sit up again.

"*Lie down,*" Mildred ordered.

"Dr. Mercier advised it on the grounds that you wouldn't otherwise permit your body the rest it required to heal rapidly. Despite the fact she is primarily a researcher and not a clinician, I was forced to agree."

"She read you like a bill of sale, Ryan," J.B. said.

"Forgive me," the albino man said. "I forget my manners. I am Tobias Blackwood, baron of Haven. This is my sister, Elizabeth."

Ryan nodded.

"You and your friends have rendered a signal service both to my ville and to me personally," Tobias Blackwood said. "We would be honored if you were to remain as guests for as long as you care to."

"It's on the level, Ryan," J.B. said. "They've been treating us right."

"Exceptionally well, in fact," Doc said.

"Not bad," Jak said.

"Young Master Lauren has been availing himself of the fine hunting in the woods outside the ville," Tobias said. "A compensation for the terrors they too often conceal."

Ryan chuckled, despite the stab in the side it cost from his cracked ribs. "Even if it's full of muties and monsters, the biggest danger you're likely to find in the woods is Jak."

"If only that were so, my friend," Blackwood said. "If only that were so."

He uncrossed his legs and rose, as supple as a dancer. "If you will excuse us, my sister and I have matters to attend to before dinner. At which I trust you will join us?"

"He says yes," Mildred said. Both the baron and Ryan looked at her in surprise.

She shrugged. "With Krysty down I'm taking over temporarily as Ryan's keeper," she said. "I'll make sure he acts civilized."

Ryan scowled. J.B. laughed again. "It's what Krysty would want, Ryan," the Armorer said. "And you know it."

"Yeah," Ryan grunted. Cautiously he sat up again, as Tobias walked around the bed and gave his arm to his sister. She seemed to need his help to rise from the chair. She bestowed another sunrise-bright smile and let her brother squire her out of the room, subtly leaning against him for support.

"What's wrong with her?" Ryan asked when he was sure they were out of earshot. "She sick or something?"

"'Or something,'" Mildred said. "She has some kind of condition that weakens her. It's apparently come and gone since childhood. It seems to be in an especially debilitating phase now."

He took in a deep breath. "So what the hell happened?"

"I think you already know the high points," J.B. said. "The storm and the swampies were kickin' our asses. Then the baron led some of his sec men to the rescue. I think you saw that part, even though you were guest of honor at a swampie-stompin' party at the time."

"What about our Tech-nomad pals?"

"The good baron informs us his people believe several of them got away," Doc said.

"They ran out on us, you mean?" Ryan said.

"Well," J.B. replied, dragging out the word, "that's certainly one way of looking at it. Another's that we woulda done the same."

"Didn't we?" Mildred said. "When the hammer came down, the Tech-nomads stuck by their own. And so did we."

"In the event it made little difference," Doc said. "We would have been overwhelmed regardless. We *were* overwhelmed, but for the timely arrival of Baron Blackwood and his people."

"Yeah," Ryan said. He'd lost interest in this discussion. He seldom had much patience with words. At least not when he itched with the urgency to see Krysty for himself, see how she really was. He felt the irrational conviction that because he knew her better than anybody he might know something that would bring her back from…wherever she was.

He struggled out of bed. Doc grabbed an arm to steady

him with his surprisingly strong grip. Mildred, scowling with disapproval, took his other arm.

"Thanks," he said, nodding. He just stood for the space of three deep breaths, getting used to having his legs under him again.

Then he nodded briskly and pulled away from his friends. "I'm okay now," he said. "Take me to see Krysty."

"Your funeral," Mildred said.

"KRYS—" HE SAID. His voice cracked like a dry stick in his own ears.

He had made it by himself, down the hallway to the room farthest from the stairs where Krysty lay alone on a bed. Once he saw her, he sagged against the door frame for support.

The others knew better than to try to help him.

In a moment he'd recovered his iron self-control and willed himself to stand upright again. No matter how much effort it cost him to resist the jelly-like weakness in his legs. Then he walked to her side and gazed down.

She looked beautiful. Not that that was anything unusual for her. In his experience it sure was unusual for someone suffering the effects of a serious dose of snake venom. Her cheeks were perhaps paler than usual, her breathing shallower as she lay on her back beneath a white coverlet with little purple flowers embroidered on it, and her hair spilling across the pillow like blood. Her eyes were closed. Her full lips were set as if in effort.

"What's the matter with her?" he rasped. "This isn't like any snakebite I've ever seen."

"Me neither," Mildred said. "You killed the snake that bit her. What kind would you say it was?"

"Water moc," he said. "Sure as slow rad death."

She shook her head. "Could you be mistaken?"

"Don't think so. Then again I'm no snake expert. Why?"

"A water moccasin is a pit viper," she said. "Like rattle-snakes. They produce predominantly proteolytic venom. That means it destroys proteins—makes cells, including red blood cells, explode, basically. It's associated with severe initial pain and massive tissue damage."

Ryan frowned at Krysty's leg, hidden beneath the flower coverlet. The idea of that flawless ivory flesh corrupted and decayed tore at him like wolf teeth. But she was his life's partner, he thought fiercely. No matter what.

"The baron's men were able to extract some of the poison," Mildred said. "They told me later—none of us in much better shape than you. We'd all been running on adrenaline too long, plus getting beat on by weather and bad guys. But she seemed to instantly lose consciousness when she was bitten. And she's been this way since."

"So what's the bottom line?"

Mildred shrugged. "I'm no snake expert, but I'd say the symptoms more resemble neurotoxin-heavy venom. Which is characteristic of elapids."

"Meaning what?"

"They are the other major kind of poisonous serpent," Doc said. "As opposed to the vipers, among whom the water moc-casins are numbered."

"The ville actually has some antivenin," Mildred said. "Mainly for cottonmouth bites. But Dr. Mercier refused to administer it because Krysty doesn't show any of the usual viper-bite symptoms."

Ryan shook his head. "I'm confused."

"As are we all, Mr. Cawdor," a voice said from behind. Its feminine lilt struck him as oddly familiar. As Elizabeth Blackwood's had.

Yet he could never remember hearing it before in his life.

Chapter Thirteen

Ryan turned. As if through some protective instinct, his friends had moved into the room to surround the bed—the pack shielding and caring for an injured member. The voice, soft and feminine and delicately accented, had come from the open door.

A woman stood in the door. She was of medium height, about the same as Elizabeth Blackwood, willow-branch slender in her black jacket and slacks. Skinnier even than the baron's sister, in fact, although she gave an impression of wiry solidity, as opposed to the other woman's wispiness. Her face was a long oval, her nose pert, her mouth pursed, her brown hair drawn back into a severe bun. The eyes that peered at him over the tops of her square-framed spectacles were large and liquid-brown.

"Ryan, this is Dr. Amélie Mercier," Mildred said. "She oversaw our medical treatment after they carried us back here. She's ville healer."

Mercier smiled with thin lips. It looked like a perfunctory, professional smile, of the sort Ryan had seen on plenty of whitecoats who appeared a good deal less benign than this one did. Did he also note a flash of shyness to the expression, as if in her case the austere professionalism masked a lack of confidence dealing with others?

Mentally, Ryan shrugged off such speculation. He didn't know what made people tick, though he'd learned it could be important to have some understanding of what made people do what they did.

"If I may?" Mercier said. Without waiting for a reply she glided past Ryan and gave Krysty a brisk, thorough examination. "Her condition seems stable. As to whether or not that's an altogether good thing, I'm not prepared to say."

"There're worse alternatives," Ryan said.

She looked at him with her thin-plucked eyebrows raised into arches of comic surprise. Interesting note of vanity, he thought, that she plucked her brows. "How do you mean?"

"She could die."

"Ah. Yes. So she could. Unfortunately, until and unless I am better able to understand her state I'm in no position to define the relative likelihood of whether she dies, spontaneously awakens, or continues in this condition. Oddly, and fortunately, I'm seeing no signs of the usual deterioration that affects patients in a comatose state, even after relatively short periods."

"What, in your studied opinion, is the cause of her state, Doctor?" Doc asked in his courtly way.

"You mean, this curious…suspension? As to that, I have no hypothesis as yet."

"What about what kind of snake that bit her?" Ryan asked.

"As your own healer no doubt told you, her symptoms are highly anomalous for the dominant species of poisonous snakes who inhabit this region."

She paused, biting a pale lower lip with neat, gleaming white teeth. It struck Ryan she could be a good-looking woman, if she bothered to take trouble with her appearance.

"There are rumors among the people, especially the ones well back up Blackwood Bayou," she said. "The backwoods folk tell of something they call a Dream Snake, whose bite induces not tissue rot and painful death, but a strange dream-like state. Some victims simply die. Some experience terrible nightmares from which they can't awaken. Others sleep for a time and then wake up with no ill effects."

"That doesn't sound like any snake I ever heard of," Mildred said.

"It could conceivably be a mutation," Doc said.

Mercier shrugged her thin shoulders. "I can't attest to the truth of that. I've never seen even an alleged victim of this Dream Snake's bite, much less examined or treated one. I'm a person of science, trained to trust only what experiment and reason show me. These rumors may be nothing more than folk tales. And yet, I must admit, sometimes the wildest of backwater stories proves to contain a grain or more of truth. My father and I have uncovered herbs with medicinal properties unknown to the surviving literature by pursuing certain such tales."

"Your father..." Mildred began.

"My late father," Mercier said.

"I'm sorry."

The healer shrugged again. "Even as we seek to prolong and enhance life, do we not learn the inevitability of death, Dr. Wyeth? I have...come to terms with my father's death. And now I fear I must return to my lab. There is much work that needs doing. I'm still inventorying the materials recovered from the Tech-nomad ship. They might hold the key to various breakthroughs which would significantly affect the people of this ville."

"Krysty—" Ryan said.

"I will do what I can for her, Mr. Cawdor," she said. "That is all I can do. In the meantime Dr. Wyeth can see to her day-to-day care. Good afternoon."

She walked out. The others looked after her for a moment. Ryan stood with chin sunk to clavicle, gazing at Krysty.

"Strange bird," J.B. said, taking off his round-lensed spectacles and cleaning them with a handkerchief.

"She seems competent," Doc observed.

"Ice queen to the max," Mildred said. "Still, yeah, she does seem to know her stuff. To a surprising degree, actually."

"One surmises her father handed down to her a tradition of scientific training and the spirit of inquiry that proceeds from before the Apocalypse."

"Yeah, and we haven't had luck with those kinds in the past," J.B. said. "You neither, come to think about it."

Doc turned his palms upward. "Yet I myself was schooled in the scientific tradition."

"Gaia," Jak said.

The albino youth had been perched on a sill of an open window, covered against insects that had begun to really rise and swarm in the late afternoon, with a screen that had to be premium predark salvage. He had been sitting with his arms crossed in his usual attitude for such discussions: bored half to death but realizing he had to endure the conversation.

J.B. cocked an eyebrow at Jak. "You comin' late to religion, Jak? You don't seem the type."

Jak dropped noiselessly to the hardwood floor. "Krysty talk about Gaia powers," he said. "Calls on in emergency. Mebbe Gaia power helps fight poison, whatever kind snake bite?"

"Mebbe," J.B. said. "Got no way to know, do we?"

"Pardon, *messieurs, madame,*" a timid female voice said from the door.

A small, plainly dressed young black woman in an apron stood there. "The baron and Lady Elizabeth request that you join them for the dinner now, *s'il vous plâit.*"

"Yeah," Ryan said. He realized he was ravenously hungry. "We'll be there."

The servant curtsied and went away. Ryan turned back and looked down at Krysty again. He longed to somehow absorb

her through his good eye, as if somehow that might mean he
would never lose her.

He bent and kissed her cheek. It was cool. He straightened,
frowning.

"She's cold," he said. "What does that mean, Mildred?"

"That she's not suffering fever," Mildred stated flatly. He
turned a hot blue glare on her, but she didn't flinch.

"We don't know anything about her condition, Ryan.
Except that Krysty's stable and doesn't seem in any danger.
We need to let time, and hopefully Mercier, do their work."

"Will we get time?" he asked.

She shook her head. "I'm a doctor, not a doomie."

He felt J.B. grip him firmly by the upper arm. "Come on,
Ryan," he said. "Let's go get some food before we turn inside
out. I could eat a week-dead skunk myself."

Mildred gave him a sour smile. "That's my man," she said.
"Always knows how to whet a woman's appetite."

He tipped his fedora to her. "Part of my natural charm."

STERLING SILVER SERVICE tinkled against white porcelain as
thin as a sec man's mercy. The dining room was long and not
very wide. The off-white walls were hung with dark portraits
of pale-skinned, gloomy-looking men and women in old-days
dress. Baron Blackwood sat at table's head with Elizabeth,
looking radiant and sad in a dark yellow dress, on his right.
Ryan sat at his left.

Looking entirely uncomfortable, Jak perched on a chair
beside Elizabeth. Across from him, at Ryan's left elbow, sat
Doc. Next to the professor sat J.B., and across from him Mildred. They were all dressed in their usual garb. Although like
Ryan's own clothes, it was unusually clean.

At the foot of the table sat Hal Barton, a man of middle
age and middle height, plump-cheeked and decidedly stocky,
with blue eyes bright behind glasses with rectangular wire

rims, a shiny head bald and pink as a baby's bottom fringed with wisps of prematurely white hair that continued down his cheeks in the form of extravagant muttonchops. He had been introduced as the baron's secretary. He mostly sat and listened, using his mouth mainly to eat.

"—radios powered by a few generators adapted to run on kerosene, fish or palm oil, or even shine," the baron was saying. He wore a deep scarlet tailcoat that made his feral eyes glow like rubies. The outfit had to be hot as hell despite the fan circling overhead. Yet Blackwood's manner was as refined as Doc's at his most courtly.

"We obtained them from the Tech-nomads," Elizabeth said. Despite her sickly appearance, she seemed animated and happy.

"Do much trade with the Spookies, ma'am?" J.B. asked, spooning up some of the rich, creamy green soup. "Er, Tech-nomads."

Elizabeth turned her lovely smile on him. It wasn't so much sexy as it made a person feel warm from the pit of the stomach to the tips of his toes. Ryan had experienced it a few times himself since they'd sat to supper.

"Much is a relative term, Mr. Dix," she said, sipping from a glass of tea with a slice of locally grown lime in it. "They may visit us twice in a five-year period."

She turned her head. "But I don't want to interrupt my dear brother's explanation."

The baron drank red wine. Ryan had a glass of that himself; he was no connoisseur, but this was good stuff. Even his jaded palate could tell that.

Blackwood sipped and smiled back. "An illustration is never an interruption, Elizabeth dear. We communicated with Long Tom's fleet, although somewhat sporadically, given the interference from the storm. Which prevented us from warning them in timely wise that the pirate Black Mask was blockading the mouth to Blackwood Bayou."

"How'd you know that?" Mildred asked.

"Very little happens in the ville's environs that Baron Tobias doesn't know about," Barton said from the end of the table. His voice came low and slow in a Southern drawl with no hint of French.

"Good spy network, huh?" J.B. said.

"The people of the ville," Barton said. "They have the 'swamp telegraph,' a rumor network almost as fast as radio. And in its way more reliable."

"And they share that info with you, Baron?" Mildred asked in surprise.

Savoring another big spoonful of that rich-flavored soup, with yellow liquid fat floating on the top, Ryan understood her astonishment.

"Why wouldn't they tell us?" Elizabeth asked.

"Most villes we been through," Ryan said, "people're usually more concerned the baron, or anyway his sec boss, *not* overhear things they say."

He caught a look from Mildred, despite her own startled question. Well, fuck me, he thought, I guess I was too blunt again. He needed Krysty around, if not to smooth his own rough edges, at least to smooth the feathers he sometimes ruffled.

And for a wagload of other reasons, besides.

But neither the baron nor his sister took visible offense. "That's not how we do things here," Blackwood said matter-of-factly.

"At least not since Father died," Elizabeth said.

For the first time Blackwood's red eyes were briefly hooded. Then he smiled and nodded and went back to being his genial self.

"We managed to figure out where the Tech-nomad squadron entered the bayou system from such scattered communications as we were able to receive," he said. "I summoned the sec men and set out immediately. Fortunately, we encountered some of our people who reside in the region, who were able to give us a solid notion of where your vessel had wound up. Less fortunately we proved unable to arrive in time to keep you and the Tech-nomads from being assailed by those mutant barbarians."

His manner became intense. His features seemed to sharpen, become feral and wolflike, and his eyes glittered like drops of fresh blood. His sister patted the slim white hand that gripped the stem of his wineglass as if to strangle it.

"Tobias, please, don't exert yourself."

He relaxed with visible effort, then laughed. "You're the one who needs to watch her overexertion, sister dear," he said, sitting back in his red-velvet upholstered chair. "But as always you're right—it does me no good to grow overexcited and dismay our guests. It's just that the swampies give us so little rest. They constantly ambush our hunters and parties extracting pine sap for turpentine, plunder wags bringing lumber and produce to Haven ville from the countryside, raid isolated dwellings and butcher the hapless inhabitants."

"Some say they eat their victims, as well," said a mellifluous voice from behind Ryan. It drawled like a Southerner's, and was touched with a French accent, as well.

Ryan half turned in his chair to see a man in a ruffled white shirt and black trousers, carrying a decanter of wine. He was tall and skinny, skinnier than Doc even, with an exquisitely trimmed black beard that came to a point beneath his narrow chin, slicked-back hair and eyes that glittered like black glass beads.

"Ah, St. Vincent," Blackwood said. "I see you've come to refresh our guests' beverages."

"Always eager to serve the baron's guests," the man said with a smile.

"St. Vincent is our chief steward and majordomo," Tobias said. "Don't know what we'd do without him."

"That's just a wild story, you know," Barton said. "About the swampies eating people. Their actions are bad enough on the face without making them out as cannibals."

"Ah, Mr. Barton," St. Vincent said. "A fine gentleman such as yourself would perhaps not spend enough time among the common people to learn to trust them."

Barton's pink face went purple. But he said nothing, glaring down at his soup bowl and lapsing into stubborn silence.

"This soup is delicious, Mr. St. Vincent," Mildred said as he bent to refresh her own glass, trying to paper over the uncomfortable gap in the conversation. Ryan noticed she still wore a bandage for her "M-1 thumb" incurred during the fight with the Black Gang. "What is it?"

"Sea turtle, *mademoiselle.*"

Mildred twinkled—the other staff all insisted on calling her "Madame" or "Mrs.", it seemed—for just a moment before her eyes got wide and her cheeks went pink with outrage.

"Sea turtles? But they're—they're endangered!"

He arched a brow. "One wouldn't care to contradict a lady such as yourself…"

He glanced toward the baron. "Actually the waters offshore teem with them, as well as with all manner of marine life," Blackwood said. "The old sunken oil rigs harbor an abundance of edible sea creatures. They're a main source of our sustenance."

Mildred looked confused. Doc blinked indulgently at her.

"We need to learn, you and I," he said softly, and half dreamily, "that in this sorrowful day and age, the only endangered species is Man."

St. Vincent went out, presumably to oversee readying of the next course. As servants entered bearing salads of greens and chopped peppers and tomatoes, "Don't mind St. Vincent, Hal," Elizabeth said to Barton. "He means well."

"As you say, Lady Elizabeth," Barton said without looking up from his place at the table.

"He practically raised us, you know," Elizabeth said to their guests. "He's an old dear, really. If a bit of a fussbudget."

She looked to her brother. "I believe you were rather circumspectly preparing to tell them about salvaging the cargo?"

"Yes," Blackwood said. "Sorry. I tend to get distracted these days. After we tended your wounds as best we could and got you on boats headed for more settled surroundings, we waited for the winds to subside enough that we felt safe enough going inside the marooned vessel—the *Snowy Egret,* by the name painted on the bow?"

"That's the name," Ryan said, munching salad. He wasn't big on rabbit food, but even after a big bowl of that turtle soup he felt as if he could start in on the stuffing of the chair backs for a second course. Briefly he wondered what had gotten Mildred's back up about the fact the soup was made of turtles. She'd eaten worse things since they'd thawed her out. If not always knowingly at the time.

"Sadly, we found no surviving Tech-nomads aboard. But we did find a substantial portion of the cargo consigned for us, which I surmise was divided among the three vessels."

He beamed at Elizabeth. "We don't know for sure yet, but Amélie—Dr. Mercier—tells us that both the medications and paraphernalia aboard give us great hope in the constant war we wage against disease here in Haven. Including a possible cure for Elizabeth's condition."

She smiled back. "We have every faith in Amélie," she said. "We grew up with her, just about. She knows what she's doing."

"Her father, Lucien Mercier, wasn't always the easiest man to get along with," Blackwood said. "Perhaps that's why he and our father got on so well. But he taught his daughter well."

"Have you any knowledge of the fate of the surviving Tech-nomads, Baron?" Doc asked, sopping up the last remnants of vinegar and oil dressing from his plate with a chunk of flavorful, tough-crusted white bread.

Blackwood shook his head. "Several appear to have escaped alive from the fight with the swampies. The storm was fierce enough not even our local denizens proved able to track them. The *New Hope* survived the storm, but was blown far east and south out into the Gulf."

"They did?" Mildred said. "Glad to hear it. Will they come back and deliver the rest of the cargo?"

"Not to mention our payment," J.B. said dryly.

"It's not like we succeeded at protecting them," Ryan said.

"You did what you could," Blackwood said earnestly. "Before we lost touch with them, the Tech-nomads mentioned how bravely you fought against the giant sea cows."

"I doubt we'll see the Tech-nomads again for some time," Elizabeth said sadly. "They tend to react to tragedy by withdrawing. Tech-nomads believe the mundane world, as they call it, is in league against them. And they suffered most cruelly from both the pirates and the hurricane."

Her fine features had grown sad. It made her cheeks seem hollow and gave her pale skin a sort of parchment texture. Then she brightened again.

"At any rate we can hope the pirates suffered so much damage they won't trouble us again for a great long time," she said.

"I don't think the Black Gang are as skittish as the Tech-nomads, Lady Elizabeth," Barton said. "Black Mask isn't."

"The pirates have been another terrible burden on our

people," Blackwood said. "Any respite we can get from them will be most welcome. And that brings me back to the matter of your payment. The Tech-nomads are in no position to provide it, but we are. And we're most grateful for what you were able to help bring us, aren't we?"

"We are indeed," Elizabeth said.

"We shall see you well rewarded. Haven may not be rich, but neither are we on the ragged edge. And, as I've said before, we hope you'll consent to stay with us as long—"

"A moment, Baron, if you please?" the silken voice of St. Vincent interrupted.

"Yes?" Blackwood said, turning.

"I fear your security chief, Mr. Guerrero, has news for you."

The majordomo faded from the doorway. A dark, burly, swag-bellied man with a beard straggling like Spanish moss down his several chins clumped in on heavy boots. He wore a 1911-style .45 blaster in a holster on his right hip, hammer back, secured with a thumb strap. This was at least a familiar type to Ryan: your basic ville sec boss.

In a way it was almost reassuring, after all this niceness and reasonableness from the ville's ruling siblings, which for all that it worked much to his and his friends' advantage struck Ryan as almost against nature. Guerrero's straightforward thug appearance suggested the world was secure in its orbit, somehow.

"Sorry to bother you, Baron," Guerrero said. His round face seemed to be sweating more than even the oppressive humid heat could account for. "It's the Beast. It's struck again."

Chapter Fourteen

Great gaping holes had been smashed in the walls of the shack. Planks had been torn loose with such force that they snapped away, leaving jagged scars of ends, bright in comparison to the weather-faded wood. In the yellow light of the lantern the baron held in a white hand, the inside looked as if somebody had splashed buckets of blood around the cramped interior. Loops of intestines, greasy and marbled purple-gray, hung from sagging rafters like strings of sausages in the Devil's butcher shop. Pale arms and legs, ruptured chests and half faces, eyes staring through blood masks in paroxysms of agony and terror, were strewed like chunks of broken meat furniture through the chaos.

The buzzing of flies almost drowned out the sounds of the creatures in the dark bayou night all around. The smell brought a curl to even Ryan's lips. The gibbous moon leered down at the party like a pockmarked yellow idiot face through black treetops.

"Fairly fresh," the Baron said grimly. The sleeves of his fine white shirt were rolled up his arms. His white hair was tied back with a black ribbon. He carried two swords strapped in scabbards across his back, the hilts protruding above his shoulders. His two Smith & Wesson revolvers were holstered butt-forward at angles in front of either hip, cross-draw style.

Jak sniffed, oblivious to foulness so strong it made Ryan's cheeks tighten and his eye narrow. "Day old, mebbe."

Mildred was frowning past the baron's wide shoulder into

the chamber of charnel horrors illuminated from without by the yellow light of several lanterns. "I think he's right," she said. "Blood's congealed. And the bodies look rigored. Uh, parts."

Her normally healthy light-brown complexion looked as if it had been dusted over with fine wood ash.

"How many?" the baron asked his sec boss. Out in the night a dog barked. Blackwood had experienced handlers with bloodhounds out following the Beast's track.

Guerrero carried a Mossberg 500 Marine pump shotgun with an 8-round magazine in a big, hairy hand. He and Blackwood sported the only repeating smokeless-powder blasters Ryan had seen in the ville. The other dozen or so sec men and ville inhabitants who accompanied them carried black powder blasters or crossbows, if they had projectile weapons at all. Several carried no more than big knives or machetes. None Ryan had noticed failed to bear arms of some sort.

That said something about Haven. Most barons Ryan had encountered were careful to try to keep weapons out of the hands of their subjects. Other than their sec force, of course.

The sec boss shook his head. Sweat flew from the tips of his greasy long black locks. "No idea, Baron."

"For cases like this," Mildred said, "the EMTs used to joke they counted feet and divided by two."

Blackwood raised a brow at her. "Who were these people to joke at such things?"

"Men and women who dealt with violent death every day," Mildred said. "Sorry. it wasn't a very appropriate thing to say. I'm trying to cover for my own uneasiness, I guess."

"Five people lived in the shack," a local with a gray-stubbled, uneven jaw said, scratching an open sore on the side of his skinny neck. "Old Bluie McCall, his wife Charice, two daughters and a granddaughter. Annabelle, her name was."

"Mebbeso Luc and Ed Guillebeau was visitin', and some of their kin," Carbo, another local said.

"We count six heads, Baron," a black sec man said, coming around the side of the shack.

"Including that one stuck up there on the stove chimney pipe?" J.B. asked, pointing with his scattergun.

The sec man looked up and visibly paled. "Um. Seven. Sorry, Baron. This is the worst attack yet."

"So much for poor Bluie," Carbo said. "Bon voyage, Bluie. You was a crusty-ass ol' bastard and your feet stank like billy hell, but you deserved better'n you got."

"Don't worry about getting the count wrong." The baron shook his head. "A man or woman who could remain unmoved by a spectacle such as this is not to be trusted, Augusto, my friend. Even in such a world as ours."

"Something I don't quite track, begging your pardon, Baron," J.B. said, then paused. The Armorer, Ryan knew, feared no man nor mutie. But he was practical, which meant he exercised the same sort of caution handling barons as he would room-temperature nitroglycerine. For much the same reasons.

"You have it," Blackwood said. "Please speak freely. Honeyed words and soft gloves won't change this horror. Nor help us combat it."

J.B. nodded. "Yeah, well. You mentioned at dinner how nothing much happens here in Haven without you hearing about it pronto. But that big, fine house of yours is only an hour from here."

"Easily explained," Barton said. "This house is isolated. Nearest neighbor's a quarter-mile away. And they reported they were playing loud fiddle music and drinking shine all last night."

The baron's stout aide looked as if he'd have trouble mounting a flight of stairs without stopping to rest. But while his round, cheerful face—considerably less cheerful now—was sheened with sweat, so was everybody's. He seemed not at all winded from hiking in darkness on treacherous trails of slick black mud, some little more than game tracks, clambering over deadfalls, struggling through low-hanging branches already dripping with dew, and hopping over tiny creeks with the rest. Somewhere along the way, Ryan realized he wasn't as old as he looked: he was middle-aged, sure, but the white hair made him seem much older. The man wore knee-high boots and carried a pair of cap-and-ball dueling pistols stuck through his belt beneath his paunch. He also carried a stout stick that looked to be meant for busting heads as much as helping him walk.

"We only get reports if someone lives to tell the tale," Guerrero said. "And the Beast don't leave nobody alive when he hits."

"I apologize if I gave you all a false impression at Blackwood House," the baron said. "Yes, our 'swamp telegraph' extends throughout the ville, and even beyond the fringes of region we claim, in places. But its coverage is far from complete. Our people have lived here for generations, since skydark. But even to us this remains in many ways a land of mystery."

"Ace in the line," J.B. muttered to Ryan.

"What do you want," Ryan asked in the same undertone, "egg in your brew?"

"A break every now and then would be nice," the Armorer replied, "if only to break the monopoly." He took off his glasses and rubbed off the condensation with a hankie.

With a soft boom something white unfurled above their heads. Most of the men ducked; some cursed. Crossbows and single-shot blasters were raised at the pale winged shape that swept over their heads with a soft, strange, mournful cry.

"Don't shoot!" someone yelled. "It's a demon! You'll only make it angry!"

"Not demon," Jak said in evident disgust. "Owl."

"So it is," Blackwood said.

But some of the ville folk muttered darkly among themselves. They seemed to be speaking a blend of French and English, with a liberal dose of Spanish stirred in. Ryan couldn't understand more than every fourth or fifth word.

Jak sneered. "Triple stupes think owls spirits of dead. Just owls!"

J.B. scratched his stubbled cheeks. "I'm not a superstitious man, but dark woods and a bloody massacree like that got me in a mind to see ghosts."

"As long as you don't waste cartridges on ghosts," Ryan said. "Or owls, either."

The Armorer chuckled. "No worries, Ryan. You know me better."

And he did. An expert using weapons as well as tinkering with and repairing them, J. B. Dix knew the value of a blaster cartridge as well as any man in the Deathlands and better than most.

Lights bobbed in the woods nearby. The baron's retinue tensed and started to raise blasters and crossbows. Ryan's little group grew closer by sheer reflex, although none made to draw a weapon.

"Don't shoot, *chers,*" a voice called out. "It's only us."

The Havenites recognized the voice and relaxed. Ryan and company didn't. They'd seen people gulled before by clever enemies pretending to be friends.

But it was only the dog handlers and a couple of sec man escorts, their bloodhounds' eyes gleaming in the orange light, veined with black smoke from the resinous pinewood-splinter torches the trackers carried.

"Sorry, Baron," they said. "Dogs lost the track."

"Again," Barton said in disgust.

Guerrero started to sputter, half apology, half outrage. "But mebbe the monster swims! We don't know. No one can track it far. It's like it vanishes into thin air."

Blackwood held up a deceptively slim white hand. "Peace," he said. "We know that."

He hadn't cut off the sec boss's blubbering quite soon enough, Ryan judged, by the way eyes rolled in the light of torch and lantern.

"These people're seriously spooked," he said quietly.

Holding a turpentine-soaked rag in front of her nose, Mildred ventured into the shack with a kerosene lantern to examine the human wreckage. Not even Ryan envied her. She moved gingerly around, occasionally prodding at a detached organ or limb with a stick.

A few locals objected to that as disrespectful treatment of the dead. Guerrero barked at them to go stand guard somewhere else. They did. The swag-bellied sec boss might have seemed more clown than brute, but he still commanded respect. Or at least fear.

The Baron stood to one side, his long, handsome, lupine face drawn into a mask of pain. Barton stood beside him like a stanchion.

After a few minutes Mildred came out shaking her head.

"Sorry," she said. "I can't tell anything that might be of actual use. Like I told you, I'm not an expert on examining murder victims to see what killed them."

"Please, Dr. Wyeth," the baron urged. "Tell us what you can. Who knows what might prove valuable?"

Though she had to sit on an old stump near the door of the shack, Mildred cast a sly glance and a wisp of a grin Ryan's way. "See how a gentleman talks to a lady, Ryan? You might learn a lesson or two."

"If I ever decide to become a gentleman," Ryan said, "I'll keep it in mind."

Shaking her head, Mildred looked at the tall and pallid baron. "Everything seems consistent with some kind of big animal doing the damage. Bodies are torn up as if by teeth and claws. Not sliced up cleanly the way a blade would do. The killer must've been fast, to incapacitate so many people. There's even a longblaster of some kind in there with its stock all busted and the barrel bent almost double."

"So it's strong, too, you might say?" J.B. said.

She shrugged. "I found what I think might be the torso belonging to that head up there. By the look of the neck the head was just twisted off like a chicken's."

A gasp ran through the crowd.

"Could it've been a bear?" Ryan asked.

"You'd know better than I would. I'm not Marion freaking Perkins, either."

"Who?" Ryan said.

"Never mind. Sorry. I— This has got to me, all right? Even after all my years of training. And years of—this world."

"*Mort vivants* coulda done it," Jim-Jack said.

"Swampies aren't generally the swiftest of muties," J.B. said. The companions knew people in the southern swamps often called the short muties by that name. It was French for the living dead.

"The Beast is a pale creature," an oldie's cracked voice said, quavering from the darkness. "Not much bigger'n a man. With a mane of dark hair, like a lion from a picture book. And eyes that shine back light like a animal's."

That roused Doc from the meditative funk he'd been in since arriving at the shack. "Have you seen the creature yourself, then, my good man?"

"Not I. But I heard tell."

"I thought you said the Beast left no witnesses alive," Ryan said sourly to Guerrero.

The sec man glowered and jutted his fleshy underlip in an almost comical pout. "It leaves none of its intended victims alive," the baron said, "as far as we have learned. Others, though, claim to have glimpsed it hunting by night."

"Only time he comes out to hunt," Guerrero said.

Ryan scratched the top of his head. It felt like a swamp up there. He was used to killer heat or so he thought. But the humidity here in this swamp was like living under water.

"Does anyone believe we have any more to learn here?" the baron asked the group in general.

"What about tracks, Jak?" Mildred asked.

The albino youth shook his head. "Not see."

"And the dogs came up dry," Ryan said. "So, no, Baron. Not as far as we can see."

"Anyone?" the baron asked. No one else spoke. Guerrero only shook his head. His eyes glistened as if he were near to tears. Ryan guessed he was in a fright about letting his baron down once again. Blackwood seemed forbearing for a baron—what another baron would likely call ridiculously soft. But even the kindest baron had his limits.

Yet what could even the most squared away of sec men do against a pale phantom that struck from the darkness and then just dissolved back into it? Ryan shook his head. He was rad-blasted if he knew himself, and no man had ever judged him a slouch and lived to profit from that miscall.

"What about identifying the casualties?" Doc asked.

Mildred shook her head. "I think their own mothers would have a hard time recognizing them at this stage. Even if the raccoons haven't yet started chewing on their faces." It was as if scavengers and predators larger than insects were wary of the place as humans were.

"We can talk to people in the area and find out who's gone missing," Barton said.

"Right." Blackwood nodded decisively at the cabin. "Burn it."

As THEY BEGAN the long, treacherous trudge back to the ville proper, and Blackwood House, Ryan glanced back once at Bluie's shack, which was now the pyre for him, his family and so-far-undetermined others.

The yellow flames had already eaten through the shake roof to dance high into the starry sky. The householder's detached head stared out from the brightness, its features beginning to soften and sag in the heat.

Ryan got the eerie sense it would've welcomed the fire instead of what it got.

Nuke shit to that, he told himself savagely. He turned his back and marched into the darkness without another backward glance.

Chapter Fifteen

"A word with you, Mr. Cawdor?" Baron Blackwood said as they stood in the foyer of the big house.

Despite not having been awake and on his legs more than eight or ten hours, Ryan felt so weary that his bones seemed to sag. But like J.B. he had learned to use a certain circumspection in dealing with barons. After all, he'd been brought up the youngest son of one—and had lost his eye, and almost his young life, to the treachery of a close family member.

"Sure," he said. The others had already trooped off to the guest rooms they'd occupied since being brought to Haven.

He followed the tall, graceful form down a corridor and into what proved to be a study. Books lined the walls, ancient volumes with dark, cracked spines behind glass. A silent servant woman lit a pair of lamps. Kerosene, by the smell, not the fish oil the poorer people used for much of their illumination and cooking. He based that on the smells they'd encountered walking back through the cluster of a hundred or so dwellings that constituted the ville of Haven proper.

"We manage to produce a certain amount of kerosene from crude oil seeps, both inshore and off," the baron said. "It provides one of our most reliable trade items, along with turpentine distilled from pine resin. Brandy?"

"Thanks."

"Take a seat, if you will." The baron himself went to a cabinet and brought out a dark glass bottle and glasses. Ryan did his best not to collapse into a comfortable leather-covered chair.

Blackwood set the glasses on a table and poured a couple of fingers of dark liquid into them. "It's not salvage, you know," he said. "There's a clan of crazy French-speakers east along the coast who make it from a mixture of fruits, according to some recipe they keep secret with fanatic determination."

He brought a glass to Ryan before settling himself in a chair covered in soft green velvet with a grateful and weary sigh. He sipped.

"It's surprisingly smooth and flavorful," he said. "Try it."

Ryan did. From his youth in Front Royal he knew a bit about liqueurs, for all that his tastes had roughened since leaving there. This brandy had a smoky, slightly sweet taste that concealed a definite burn on the tongue that only kicked in after he swallowed.

"Goes down smooth, bit of a kick after," he said. "I'd say they're on to a thing or two."

"As we are here in Haven, I hope. Cigar?"

"Never had a taste for tobacco, but go ahead."

Blackwood rose and removed a cigar from a humidor, snipped the end and lit the smoke with a complicated and compact little flint-and-steel striker. Ryan reckoned J.B. would like to have a look at it; he loved little gadgets like that when they came across them.

"Ah." The Baron sighed, settling back in the chair and letting loose a dragon puff of smoke.

"I try night and day to do my best by the people of this ville," he said at length. "My sister's calm, cool intellect is an invaluable aid. It wounds my heart to see how hard she works for us all. I fear so desperately for her health. But despite all we do, Haven is sorely beset."

"The Beast's that big a problem, huh?"

"You saw that frightfulness. If that was the first and only time that happened, it would pose a major problem. But sadly it's not. Yet the Beast is far from the only of our challenges. It may not even be the worst."

Ryan grunted. "That'd take some doing, to be worse than having something does that on the loose."

"Listen and judge. Our trade is ravaged by a cruel pirate gang—you made their acquaintance, to your sorrow. They raid our coastal dwellings and even up the rivers, raping, robbing, torturing, enslaving, burning and killing. And we wage constant war with the swampies who live deep in the moss-hung cypress woods inland of Haven.

"Some people even whisper that the Beast is a demon summoned to afflict them by Papa Dough, the swampies' voodoo king. Absurd, of course—although the indisputable existence of a creature capable of such atrocities makes it hard to sneer too hard at the thought of demons existing."

"I've seen a lot of things as bad, I have to tell you. Worse, even. And not a bit supernatural about what did any of it—some done by muties, some by regular folk," Ryan replied.

"Indeed. And then, of course, there are the more mundane threats—the storms, failed crops, disease, attacks by terrible animals that are nonetheless less frightful and…mysterious than the Beast. The people of Haven have struggled long and hard to make this place a haven in more than just name. And we've achieved much. But there's so much more to do. Always there's always the risk some disaster, or concatenation of disasters, could bring it all crashing into ruin."

He sat a moment holding his hand up, elbow propped on the arm of his chair, cigar an ember in the dim lamplight against the blackness of a window. Smoke trailed out the screened but otherwise open window. Blackwood's chin had sunk to his clavicle.

"We still dwell in the shadow of my late father, Baron

Dornan. No doubt you heard stories of him on your journey here?"

After a moment's hesitation Ryan said, "Yeah."

"He was a larger-than-life figure, no question of that. In ability, and depravity, as well as physical size. A blue-eyed, black-bearded giant of a man, prone to rages that got worse when he drank, which was all the time. He ruled with an iron fist—with the aid of his sociopathic security chief, Dupree. Yet the people were convinced he was what they needed to protect them from the horrors of Deathlands life. Especially the swampies. The war with them started after Dornan took power from his own father. Dupree encouraged the people to believe they were cannibalistic although whether they'd really be cannibals if they ate our kind but not their own is a fine question for debate."

"I take it you don't believe that."

Blackwood shook his head. "I've seen no evidence to support it. The situation is bad enough without that. They are a cruel and wily foe. Fortunately they show no inclination to wage large-scale warfare against us, but the constant threat of their depredations is bad enough. In any event, my father and Dupree were glad enough to use the swampie threat as a pretext for even sterner and more cruel repression of the people."

Ryan didn't know what to say, so he remained silent. It sounded as if Tobias and Elizabeth's father was more the sort of baron he was familiar with.

"I killed him, you know."

That brought Ryan's head up sharply. He looked at Blackwood to see the baron regarding him calmly with those blood-colored eyes.

"I challenged him as he challenged his own father. He had flown into one of his rages—goaded, I think, by Dupree—

and was threatening to murder Elizabeth. That was the final straw for me. I killed my father, then.

"Dupree tried to kill Elizabeth himself. She defended herself stoutly, gashed his face with a knife. I turned on him, but he escaped out into the swamps, and he hasn't been seen since. I hope that the alligators got him. But I doubt that the world would be that kind."

Ryan had to chuckle at that description of kindness, but he saw it, too. "I know what you mean," he said.

"Despite all, the people of Haven seemed to breathe a sigh of relief at my father's death. After they had supported him before because of his very harshness. Does that seem odd to you?"

"Lots of people think they need an iron hand to rule them," Ryan said, choosing his words with more care than usual. "At least, till it clamps on their necks. Then they commonly change their mind. When it's too late."

"Do you think I'm too soft, Ryan?"

"Nobody who ever saw you wade into the swampies with two swords through sixty-mile-an-hour winds would ever call you soft, Baron. And you fought like a man who was used to doing it. I saw that much at least before them stumpy bastards stomped my lights out. One thing I try not to do is mistake cruelty for strength. Or kindness for weakness."

His laugh this time was like pebbles shaken in a can. "In this world, only the strongest can afford to *be* kind."

He looked up at the baron. The lid of his lone eye was starting to droop despite his titanium-steel self-control. "You got a reason for telling me this, Baron?"

"I feel you should know these things before I ask you and your friends to sign on with us here."

"Sign on? As mercies?"

"As whatever you can be or do. Certainly, to fight. But you seem to have many remarkable skills encompassed in your band. Dr. Wyeth, the healer. Dr. Tanner, the man of science. Jak, the consummate hunter and tracker. Mr. Dix, tinker and weaponsmith. You, the ultimate survivor, strategist, leader."

"And Krysty."

Blackwood nodded. "I've not yet had a chance to learn her strengths. I assume they must be extraordinary, for her to travel in such company."

"In a lot of ways," Ryan said slowly, "she's best of all of us." He frowned. "You got me at a disadvantage, here, Baron. Not that I can hold your using a strong bargaining position against you."

Fiercely the baron shook his head.

"*Mais non!* Not at all! I have told you—you and your friends are the guests of the ville—of the House of Blackwood. For as long as you wish to stay. We shall continue to bend every effort to finding a cure for your Krysty, and to sustain her as best we can until we do. This is a separate proposition. I ask that you and your companions join us. Help us. For the short term or the long."

He calmed himself with visible effort, smiled, then sat back in his wing-backed chair. "Perhaps I offer you a less advantageous arrangement than you currently enjoy. I would work you very hard indeed. Still, while we are not rich, we would compensate you well."

"I can't commit to anything like that without talking to my friends, Baron," Ryan said, "including Krysty. Especially her. It's an attractive deal.

"But for now—until Krysty comes out of it—we will stay here, since you offer. And we'll do what we can to help you in the meantime. If that means fighting muties, marauders, or monsters, well, that's what we'll do."

Blackwood started to protest. Hoping he'd judged the man right, Ryan cut him off. "Hospitality works both ways, Baron."

The baron's broad shoulders heaved in a sigh. "Very well." He grinned and stood. "Good to have you with us, then, Ryan. For as long as you stay."

Ryan rose. The two men shook on it. Tobias's slim pale hand felt as if it was wound with steel cable. Ryan was unsurprised.

"If you'll excuse me," the baron said, "I'm going to turn in. I'll have a servant see you to your room."

"Actually, could I trouble you for a bedroll?"

"Bedroll?"

"Yeah. For Krysty's room. Reckon I'll stay by her side."

Blackwood smiled. "I'll have a cot set up beside her bed. Your loyalty does you credit, Ryan."

"Like hospitality," Ryan said, "it's a stream that runs both ways."

A STIR OF MOVEMENT brought Ryan awake in an instant. He sat up. Fortunately some residual body memory kept him from causing the cot to fold up beneath him.

Amélie Mercier stood in the doorway with a lantern in her hand. Its flame was turned down to a low blue and amber mutter of light.

"What are you doing here?" she demanded.

"I might ask you the same question."

"Why, I'm tending to this woman, of course."

"Me, too."

The healer sniffed. She had a long, fine nose to do the job with.

"Don't let me get in your way," he said.

But Mercier shook her head. "I've seen quite enough. Her condition remains unchanged. I will leave you two alone."

"What if she needs something?"

"Then I'm quite certain I can trust you, the loving partner, to notify me." She turned and disappeared from the doorway.

Ryan sat watching as the amber light of her lantern dwindled and dimmed to nothing on the far wall of the highway. When there was again darkness but for the cold light of the stars outside the open window he shook his head.

"That was strange," he said softly. "Wonder what it was all about."

He looked again at Krysty. Her upturned face was still, pale in the faint gleam of stars. He tried not to think how dead she looked.

Ryan made himself break the lock of his gaze. He lay back down on the cot. He was asleep as soon as his head hit the pillow.

Chapter Sixteen

Although Blackwood House was shaded by ancient weeping willows, the air in the front foyer was as flat-iron hot as that outside. The windows and curtains all stood wide open to admit any breath of breeze.

Unfortunately there wasn't any.

Closing the big door behind him, Ryan padded inside. Flowers sprayed in frozen explosions of color and scent from vases set on tables, beneath ancient faded oil paintings of people riding horses in front of what looked like the house itself. Along with their delicate odors he noted the harsher smells of varnish and ammonia.

He wore the white cotton shirt that had been awaiting him when he awakened. Its weave was a bit coarse and irregular, enough to convince him it wasn't predark salvage. It was good cloth; it was light, as cool as possible and didn't itch his skin. The shirt was well made. It was a big improvement on the shirt he'd been wearing when they carried him here, which even before the fight with the swampies was in bad shape.

He wore the same baggy, many-pocketed camou pants he'd worn then. The many rips and tears had been neatly mended while he recuperated. And each and every night his and his friends' garments were gently but insistently confiscated for washing by the quietly efficient house staff. Ryan gathered the baron, or perhaps his sister, didn't want their guests, esteemed or not, stinking up the house with dirty clothes. Although apparently Jak had needed some persuading, which Ryan understood from the others had been provided by the soft-voiced and achingly beautiful Elizabeth Blackwood herself, the procedure didn't bother Ryan much. Fresh clothing was always provided in exchange.

One thing: the baronial siblings believed in a soft touch and soothing ways, and it seemed to work well enough for them. But their chief steward, St. Vincent, was cut from different metal entirely. For all his soft voice and snooty accent, he had shown himself a martinet who cut none of his subordinates slack.

St. Vincent, at the moment, stood inside the dining room, polishing silver at a sideboard. Despite heat more stirred than alleviated by the generator-powered ceiling fan, he was impeccable and crisp in his high-collared white shirt and black trousers. He never seemed to sweat. Looking at him made Ryan feel shapeless and grubby, which wasn't anything that bothered him much before.

"Ah, Master Cawdor," the majordomo said with a smile as professional as a gaudy slut's. "May I help you, sir?"

Ryan didn't hold the smile's likely falsity against the man, any more than he would a gaudy slut. It was equally a part of St. Vincent's job. And if you were boss servant for a baron, whether a stoneheart like Dornan or relatively benign like Tobias—if his words and, so far, actions were to be believed—only death was surer than that you'd have to act like you liked some people you didn't.

"I was wondering if any of my friends were here?" Ryan said. "I was out for a walk in the woods to stretch my legs."

"Alas, Master Cawdor, I fear not. J. B. Dix is, I believe, touring the Hadid family metalworking shop. Young Master Lauren went out before dawn with some of his friends to practice crossbow hunting up Breakleg Creek. Mildred Wyeth assists Miz Mercier with her researches in the laboratory. And Dr. Tanner appears content to…wander our fair ville, no doubt absorbed in his own thoughts."

"Yeah."

The little pause seemed to confirm what Ryan had feared—Doc's mind had decided to wander, and it wasn't necessarily taking the same route his body did. It didn't surprise him much. They'd been wound to near the breaking point for days. Now the inevitable letdown of what was, at least for now, a literal Haven of peace and safety had no doubt caused his fragile grip on reality to slip. Ryan could never help wondering: might Doc someday stray so far from the real world he'd never find his way back?

"Thanks," he said. "I, uh, I think I'll just head upstairs, look in on Krysty."

"Of course," St. Vincent said.

Ryan turned to head to the stairs. The majordomo called him back.

"Master Cawdor?"

"Yeah."

"I hope I don't speak out of turn when I say, I hope that you'll choose to stay here and work with us."

"At least till Krysty's up and around. After that we'll have to see."

"It would be immensely beneficial were you to remain with us long term. Our baron could use a strong hand at his side."

"Baron Blackwood seems to have a plenty strong hand of his own."

St. Vincent's smile was as thin as a razor cut. "A ville can't have too much strength at its head, Master Cawdor. Don't you agree?"

"Strength is good," he said, and moved on.

"RYAN," MILDRED shouted, "what the hell do you think you're doing barging in here like that?"

The workroom was dim after the hot light of morning. It smelled of chemicals.

Ryan made a fist of his forehead and jutted his jaw, which was shadowed blue despite the fact he'd shaved it himself with a straight razor and soap lather that morning. It was the only graceful way to escape from one of St. Vincent's staffers doing the job him or herself. They were persistent as stickies, those Blackwood House servants. Except covered in nice instead of mucus.

"I want to see what's being done for Krysty," he said stubbornly. "You two have been thick as thieves in here since I woke up."

"We're doing the same thing we were doing last time," Mildred said furiously. "And the time before that, and all the other times—trying to work out how to cure Krysty and wake her up, which we aren't doing right this minute because you're back here pestering us again!"

Amélie Mercier stood to one side, her expression cool and detached. She made no effort either to rein Mildred in or to support her. She seemed more to be observing the interaction as though under a microscope. As when he'd first seen her, once again was forcibly reminded that she was a very handsome woman despite her almost deliberate plainness.

Ryan, feeling a tad traitorous because of his attraction to the woman, cast his gaze around the room. It was an actual bunker with concrete walls inside and out. J.B. had told him with some admiration how it had been built during Mercier's father's—and Dornan's—time first with stout hardwood logs, which were then covered and reinforced with concrete and rendered as waterproof as anything could be in this climate where the difference between the blackish bayou water, the ground, and even the air was largely a matter of degree. If not opinion.

The room was lit with some kind of panels that gave off a steady white light. Since the house had artificial electric power, it was small surprise Mercier's facility should. Nonetheless Ryan was impressed with both the size and completeness of the workroom. To his eye, of course, it was all gleaming polished steel and glass, with some ceramics thrown in and no purpose his brain could calculate. Mildred assured him it was wonderful.

Mostly what it did was put Ryan on edge. It reminded him too much of predark laboratories they'd encountered. The very things from which the awful devastation of the Big Nuke emerged. And the people, some devolved into near-mindless cultists, some still working at a high level despite being crazed like terminal-stage jolt-walkers, they'd too often found occupying such surviving facilities.

But Mildred had assured him, about half a hundred times so far, that was nonsense. Amélie Mercier, like her father before, did wonderful work here—lifesaving work. Ryan reckoned Mildred would know. He'd learned to respect her opinion when it came to the group's health. If she said Mercier could bring the goods, Mercier could.

"I just wish you'd hurry up," he said.

Mildred started to puff up—like a stepped-on toad frog, J.B. put it—which for some reason always made her deflate in helpless laughter.

But it was Mercier who spoke. "I appreciate your concern," she said, her voice cool. "I am making progress. Dr. Wyeth is a great help. But, please, we must be allowed to concentrate in order to help Krysty."

There was an air of recitation, here, that fascinated Ryan. He wondered if she'd learned to fake some kind of what Mildred called "bedside manner" by dealing with so many sick or wounded Havenites. Mebbe her old man taught her. From what little Ryan had heard the dead whitecoat had been almost as mean an old polecat as Dornan.

For some reason Mercier's quiet speech, however stilted, let the air out of Mildred.

"Ryan," she said, "we know you love Krysty. All of us love her. It's like part of each and every one of us is lying there on that bed up in the house. And I know it's got to be so much worse for you. But you just can't keep jogging our elbows."

He held up his hands, as if holding them at bay. "Fireblast," he said, dropping his hands to his sides. "I just feel helpless. Useless as tits on a boar hog. Sorry about the language."

Mildred sighed again. "You need to find something better to do," she said, "instead of pacing the ville like a panther in a cage, brooding."

"Yeah," he said. "Any suggestions?"

Mildred shook her head. "No clue. Go find J.B. and ask him."

"If you will excuse us, Mr. Cawdor," Mercier said. *That* was the tone he guessed she had been taught to use on barons.

"Yeah, okay," he said again and turned to search for his old friend.

"I GOTTA SAY I'm just as glad to shake that place from my bootheels," Ryan muttered as he paused at the almost physical impact of the heat and sunlight outside. That was another thing the lab had: some kind of climate control that kept it fairly cool and dry. He wondered why Blackwood hadn't arranged something similar for the house. Probably because of cost, and in this case the workroom—lab, he supposed—had priority.

He had to admire a baron who'd sacrifice his own comfort for some greater end.

Ryan wandered at random. The ville proper got its name

from the fact it was built on a flat mound that rose almost thirty feet above the wide Blackwood Bayou that ran alongside it, providing *haven* from all but the mightiest storm surges or tsunamis. Some residents he'd talked to claimed the ville's center was built on the buried ruin of a predark town. He had no idea if that was true or not.

Following Mildred's advice, he kept asking passersby and idlers if they'd seen the Armorer. Some had, but J.B. seemed to have always moved on once he got there.

Haven consisted of maybe a hundred buildings of various sizes. The biggest were a handful of large houses on the outskirts that, like Blackwood House, predated the Megacull and skydark. In some cases by a century or more. The rest were mostly made from planks, with shake roofs. They got progressively smaller and more rickety the farther toward the outskirts you worked. Out in the woods it was mostly shotgun shacks and shanties like the one where they'd found the remains of old Bluie's family and friends strewed like flesh confetti.

There were some pretty impressive postdark structures down by the Blackwood Bayou waterfront, big and permanent. Following his latest lead from a girl in a modest food shop Ryan made his way down the corduroyed ramp road. Warehouses and sizable workshops fronted on the weather warped-plank docks. The bayou here was actually a respectable river, navigable to Haven by shallow-draft seagoing craft such as the Tech-nomads' yachts, and farther upstream for fifty or a hundred miles by flat-bottomed riverboats.

One such, a steam-powered stern-wheeler about the size and length of a predark bus, if much broader abeam, was tied up to the dock now. She had a single soot-blackened stack and the name *Delta Queen* painted on her chipped and peeling prow.

J.B. stood on deck talking about her engines with a red-haired, red-faced woman a little taller than the Armorer and about twice as wide, who smoked a corncob pipe, cussed like a coldheart and turned out to be the owner-captain.

"Catch you later, Nat," J.B. told her as he walked down the gangplank to boom his heels on the wharf. "Safe running upriver."

"Keep yer tail outta traps, you sawed-off smooth talker!" the beefy woman said, waving with one hand and mopping sweat from her big brick-colored face with a greasy handkerchief with the other.

"You really know the way to a woman's heart, J.B.," Ryan commented as they walked back up the crushed-shell footpath to the center of town.

"Yeah," J.B. said with a big grin. "Talk about her engines! You know, they built them a generation back, somewhere upstream. Big parts like the boiler are scavvie, or put together from it. But they're casting up there. Plus making smaller parts out of brass, like they do here. Some good work."

"So it isn't true the whole world's just waiting to run out of salvage and die?"

"Well…" J.B. shrugged. Despite the awful wet heat, he was wearing his leather jacket along with his fedora. "It's just a matter of people doing what they just natural do—make stuff and sell it to each other."

"Why aren't more people doing that, then, instead of scraping by on what they can root out of ville ruins and scratch out of the ground?"

J.B.'s shrug had more amplitude this time. "Reckon mebbe the Tech-nomads got it right—too many people on the bottom are too scared of oldie tech, and change. Too many people up top got them vested interests in what Trader liked to call your status quo. That and just plain inertia."

"Mebbe," Ryan said.

They bought mangos from a stand by the central square

and sat on a broken-down buckboard parked in the shade of a big sycamore. J.B. sat up on the box. Ryan leaned against the bed. Nobody seemed to care or even take notice.

"I just feel at loose ends, J.B.," Ryan said. "Like a hex nut rattling around in an old tin can."

J.B. bit into his fruit. Juices spurted down his chin.

"So Mildred told you to look me up and see if I could distract you."

"Pretty much, yeah."

J.B. laughed. "Well, let's talk about the other night."

"That was bad trouble. The worst. And folks are on edge, between waiting for the Beast to hit again, or the pirates to come to town, or mebbe word of the latest swampie outrage up in the back country to drift in. Still, Haven isn't a bad place to light. Not bad at all."

J.B. cocked an eyebrow at his friend. "I'd call it more than somewhat likely it'd do you no harm to relax for a day or two. Put your feet up. Let your ribs finish healing."

"They're better," Ryan said. "Mostly. But how can I relax when Krysty's… I don't know. Nobody knows. She looks fine. Except for acting dead."

"And worrying yourself to death is going to fix that how?"

Ryan shook his head. He realized the worry had become a sort of addiction, like booze or jolt. He hated nothing worse than the sense of being out of control of himself. And here it was the core thing in his life, mebbe the one good thing, the redeeming thing—his intense love for his redheaded beauty—that was eating away at his self-control like rot at roof beams.

"So what I can't figure out," he said, trying to distract himself, "is why Mildred gets along so well with that skinny ice queen of a healer. They seem, pardon the expression, different as black and white."

He knew Mildred might take offense at that phrase. She

came from a day when humans hated each other on the basis
of the color of the skin. These days, with the world crawling with swampies and stickies and scalies and scabbies and
one-off muties, plus the fears and hatred of the haves and
have-nots, skin color was just another thing in most villes,
like blond hair or a boil on your nose or whether you wore
rope sandals or went barefoot. A descriptor. A way of telling
one broke-tailed, drag-assed shabby survivor in Hell from
another.

But J.B. just laughed again.

"Ryan," he said, "that girl gets homesick for her own time.
In a lot of ways that count, we're as different and strange
to her as so many stickies. She's with somebody now who
speaks her own language. Mebbe not the same as she does,
but a dialect."

"Reckon so," Ryan said, nodding. "But she's got Doc to
talk to."

"Yeah. And you know what happens when those two rub
up against each other. Get along like steel and flint. Make
sparks."

Ryan admitted that was true.

"So what's your take on this place, J.B.?" he asked. "Seems
like it's not a bad place to roost, but I don't know. When a
thing looks to be too good to be true, it is."

"You got that right. But mebbe this place's different."

"How you reckon?"

"Talk, mostly. The way people act. They fear plenty of
things—there's plenty to fear. Walking down the street in
broad daylight—or who overhears what they say—does seem
to be one of them."

"Meaning the baron's yoke lies gently on their shoulders.
And he talks a good line. What do the people say about him?"

"They seem to love him. And his sister. They're what you
call a package deal. He puts his lily-white ass on the line

fighting for them, and he doesn't torture and kill them for fun like his old man and his piece-of-shit sec boss did. Elizabeth works to help the sick even when she's so weak it seems a puff of breath'd blow her over. Fact is, everybody loves the baron and his sister,"

"Begging your pardon, John Barrymore," a familiar voice said, "but I fear that simply is not so!"

Chapter Seventeen

They both turned. Doc ambled toward them. He was in his shirtsleeves, though he carried his ebony swordstick with its concealed blade in one knob-knuckled hand, and wore his inevitable giant LeMat revolver in a covered leather holster at his hip. His eyes were wild and unfocused and his hair stuck out to one side, like a broken bird's wing.

"What are you talking about, Doc?" J.B. said. "You been wandering around the last couple days like a sick dog looking for a place to lie down and die."

Doc joined the two men and hunkered down on his long pipestem legs in the shade of the plane tree. "Sometimes I do become lost in the mists inside my own mind, yes," he said. "But have you known me to be openly delusional, my friends?"

"Yes," they both said.

"Well, all that aside. I have heard many things these past several days. And some I believe that you, as I did, will find most unsettling."

"I'm listening," Ryan said.

"You are correct that our host—host and hostess, actually—are beloved. Widely and deeply. Yet a narrow and surprisingly virulent channel of dissent runs beneath the surface."

"Would you try to speak English" the Armorer asked.

"Believe me, John Barrymore, I am. Indeed, I often feel impelled to say the same of you and your contemporaries—

no matter. There are those in Haven who fear and resent Tobias and Elizabeth Blackwood. Even hate them with fierce passion!"

Ryan shrugged. "How's that news? Nobody alive today stays that way without stepping on somebody's fingers as they grab for the last crumb of food. Goes triple for a baron being a baron."

"But these are not generalized animosities, Ryan. Some people actually blame Baron Blackwood for the Beast's attacks! Or at the very least, believe he knows more about them than he lets on, and therefore allows its depredations to continue through inaction, for some dark reason of his own."

"Forgive me if I'm skeptical," Ryan said.

"How do we know this isn't more random crazy thoughts? You've been acting like you had your skull soup stirred up some these last few days."

Doc smiled thinly. "In this case, my friend, the key word is *acting.* When I act insane, people talk freely when I'm around—as if I am not there. Even before I became a companion of yours I learned the value of pretending to be an even madder hatter than I was during my torture at the hands of the unspeakable Cort Strasser." Doc shuddered. "The sows," he said in a hollow voice. "I still remember the sows..."

"Those sows're all chills, now, along with that bastard Strasser," Ryan said. "Focus now, Doc. Why does anybody blame the baron for the Beast?"

"It seems there was a Beast in the old days, too. The late Dornan ended it, after he killed his own father to supplant him. Some people who blame Tobias now yearn for an iron hand like Dornan's to take control of the ville. They even yearn for his sec boss, Dupree."

"So mebbe the old baron wasn't so bad as Tobias made him out to be to Ryan?" J.B. said.

"I've also heard tell of that," Doc said. "Horrific stories. Dupree would often troll in people apparently at random for torture, to see what was going on. Or more likely, given the long-understood inefficacy of torture for forensic means—"

"Talk plain, Doc!"

Ryan waved a hand at the Armorer. "Let him go. He's on a roll."

"—given that, most likely the torture was meant to elicit names of parties to imaginary conspiracies, spoken in order to make the pain stop. Dupree could then show what a splendid job he was doing, and at the same time emphasize baronial power, by handing those named over to Baron Dornan for the baron's pet method of execution."

"Which was?" Ryan asked.

"He would stake them spread-eagled in this very square, and have a heavily laden wagon driven over their limbs again and again, breaking them multiple times. Perhaps this very wagon, according to some."

J.B. jumped down from the box. Ryan stood away from the wagon's side.

"He would then have the broken limbs threaded through the spokes of a wheel, and leave the victim to expire in unendurable agony before the public's eye. A method comparing very favorably to a Renaissance execution technique called, appropriately enough, 'breaking on the wheel.'"

"Dark night!" J.B. said. "That makes my skin just creep. And you say some people actually want that back?"

"They believe such measures enhanced the safety and fortunes of the citizenry."

"There's always that kind of nonsense goin' on," Ryan said. "Nobody loves everything. There's always dissidents running down the current boss and pining for the old one."

Doc shook his head. "Alas, I fear there is more substance to this talk. Because of who it is doing the talking."

"Who's that?"

Again Doc shook his head. "While I might be able to identify some on sight, I can put no names to any faces. What troubles me is that those who suspect Tobias of complicity in the Beast attacks run the gamut from the lowest social rank to the highest. Historically, that is an explosive mixture."

"Yeah," Ryan said. He jutted his jaw forward. "Likely I wouldn't know who the people were if you did tell me their names. But if there's important people in the ville talking openly with the poor folks that way, I'd say Tobias and his sister have themselves another problem. Could be worse than pirates and the Beast put together."

"You really believe him, Ryan?" J.B. asked. "I mean, I don't know. It still sounds kinda crazy to me. Everybody I talk to just can't get over loving the two Blackwoods."

"Doc tells straight," a voice said from behind them.

Both Ryan and the Armorer jumped. J.B. spun in air like a cat, snatching comically at his hat.

Behind them Jak leaned against the box of the wagon, his arms folded, grinning sarcastically.

"Don't sneak up on a man like that!" J.B. exclaimed. "Good way to find yourself staring up at the sky."

"Didn't!" Jak said. "Been here five minutes."

"You did not see him arrive?" Doc asked sweetly.

The Armorer scowled ferociously. Ryan grinned.

"They both got us," he said. "So, give, Jak. What did you hear?"

A shrug. "Same like Doc. Local boys got arguing, on bayou. Lucky Louie knocked Wet Willy out flatboat for saying baron know where Beast from. Wet Willy got hollerin' about Gotch Eye gone get him. Made so much noise, others stopped laughing and hauled back in."

"You know," J.B. said, "reckon that's as many words as I ever heard you string together before."

"Yeah, and I've got to tell you, J.B.," Ryan said, "you've turned into a real chatterbox."

"So what do we do about this?" J.B. asked, ignoring his friend's comment.

"Such information is the sort of thing a baron might reward most highly," Doc said with a glint in his eye.

"I'm not coming within a longblaster shot of *that* spiderweb," Ryan said. "Selling information like that makes enemies. And it makes barons wonder how a body happens to come into possession of such dangerous facts. I'd rather walk across the Great Salt with my canteen as dry as a bone."

Doc smiled slyly.

"I do believe the cagey old bastard was testing you, Ryan!" J.B. exclaimed.

"If I were doing such a thing, our fearless leader passed with flying colors," Doc said. "As I would have predicted."

"So, what J.B. asked," Jak said.

"Huh?" Ryan said.

"What now?"

Ryan thought a moment, scrubbing his tongue along the inside of his teeth. "What we usually do," he said. "Keep our heads down, eyes open and blasters ready."

"Perhaps, even without trying to parlay these tidings to our advantage," Doc said, "it might after all be prudent as well as considerate to warn Tobias something is afoot."

Ryan cocked a brow at him. "Contradicting yourself, or second thoughts?"

"I encompass worlds, my dear."

"Um. Yeah."

"Tell him what?" J.B. demanded. "That Doc's been wandering the ville spying on his subjects."

"No," Ryan said slowly, as his mind processed the options. "No need for that kind of detail. I think Doc's right, though. I should mention to him, without going into specifics or making a big fuss about some loose talk going around. Nothing else, not angling for any kind of reward."

"You sure that's a good idea?" J.B. asked.

Ryan grinned. "Better be?"

As HE CAME OFF the stairs onto the top floor of the big house Ryan heard a murmuring voice. He froze. It seemed to come from the door to Krysty's room, which he could see stood open.

He soft-footed down the corridor. It was made easier by the fact a runner of dark, floral-figured carpet ran down the hardwood floor. Not that he needed help. He could move like a stalking catamount when he wanted.

He felt no sense of menace. Quickly enough he recognized a soft feminine voice speaking. Still, it was a mystery, and he hated mysteries, especially in the room where his lover lay helpless.

At the edge of the open door he stopped. He realized the speaker was Elizabeth Blackwood. He leaned carefully around the doorjamb.

The baron's sister sat next to Krysty's bed with a large old-looking volume open on her lap. She wore a dress of light-weight off-white linen with her raven hair streaming unbound down her shoulders. Her beautiful wan face was set in concentration.

"'Leaving the main stream,'" she read, "'they now passed into what seemed at first sight like a little landlocked lake. Green turf sloped down to either edge, brown snaky tree-roots gleamed below the surface of the quiet water, while ahead of them the silvery shoulder and foamy tumble of a weir, arm-in-arm with a restless dripping mill wheel—' Oh, Mr. Cawdor! Can I help you?"

"Sorry to intrude," he said. "I was just coming by to check on Krysty. I, uh, I guess she's still the same?"

The slim shoulders rose and fell in a shrug. "Yes. At least she appears to be peacefully asleep. It doesn't look like any coma I've seen."

"No."

Elizabeth folded the book shut. "Amélie believes she is fighting off the effects of the snake poison. Dr. Wyeth says Ms. Wroth has an unusually robust metabolism even for a person of this time and place."

"Robust," Ryan said. "Yeah, that's one way to say it."

When the dark-haired woman continued to look quizzically at him, he went on. "After the Big Nuke, it's said that waves of plague rolled all around the world. Some were gene-engineered, or so I hear. Plenty were just natural, what with all the billions of dead bodies lying around unburied everywhere. Sickness took more than the nukes did. Mildred claims the people who were susceptible to disease died out and didn't pass on their genes. So everybody alive today got triple-tough immune systems."

"We still have disease," Elizabeth said. "Some quite terrible."

"Yeah. That's a fact. Some of those just might be artificial plagues somebody made up in a lab just to be triple mean."

She shuddered. "How could anybody set out deliberately to create something so awful?"

"Some folks're just bad," Ryan replied.

"Do you really think so? I have a hard time believing that. Isn't evil a choice we make? Perhaps the outcome of a chain of choices?"

"Mebbe," he acknowledged. "Then I guess perhaps some folks just choose to be bad." But he'd run across plenty were so deep-dyed bad that it seemed like they had to be born to it. The name Cort Strasser, which had come up once today, returned to mind.

"I fear you may be right, Mr. Cawdor. Would you care to be alone with Ms. Wroth?"

"No. No, you're fine. I can see she's in good hands."

He pointed to the book. "Wind in the Willows?"

Her face brightened. It made her beauty almost unbearably radiant. Like looking at the noonday sun.

"You know it?"

"Read it as a kid. It was a favorite of mine." His father, Baron Titus Cawdor, had kept a well-stocked library at Front Royal, and insisted that his offspring be read to as youngsters, and learn to read as early as they could.

"Really? I hope you don't think it's too childish to read to a grown woman. I mean, if she can even hear me—I hope she can. I feel she can."

For a moment Ryan felt too hollowed out to speak. Me, too, he thought. I talk to her at night.

"It's okay," he said. "She likes it. I'm sure."

Elizabeth smiled.

"I guess I'll head out, leave you two to it," he said.

He started to turn away, then stopped. "Thanks," he said, and walked down the hall.

"THERE'RE SOME PEOPLE in the ville who seem to have a grudge against you," Ryan told the baron a short time later, in Blackwood's study. "Seems some of them have a notion you're somehow to blame for the Beast. I know. But I thought you might need to know that kind of talk's going around."

Blackwood sat at his desk shuffling through documents, apparently ville records and ledgers. Ryan was impressed. Most barons didn't bother with any kind of paperwork, even when they could read. And had paper.

He set the papers down and looked calmly up at Ryan. "Do they say why they feel this way?"

"No. It's just—talk. And I can't put names to any of it.

Thing is, seems like a cross section of ville folk seem to be saying it. And that can actually get around to turning into something."

"I appreciate your concern," the baron said. "And your warning."

"Really, Baron, there's nothing to worry about," said St. Vincent, breezing in with a feather duster. "That kind of loose talk always happens around Haven, or any other ville for that matter. And normally talking is as far as it ever goes. Isn't that right, Master Cawdor?"

"Yeah."

Ryan wasn't sure how he liked the easy brazenness with which the majordomo let on he'd been eavesdropping on their privileged conversation. But he knew enough about ville life to know servants listened in on their masters all the time. It was a plain matter of survival, in their cushy and hard-to-come by jobs if not in terms of their lives. And he had to admit the lean and elegant St. Vincent seemed concerned about taking care of his brother-and-sister bosses.

St. Vincent opened one of the glass fronts to the book cases and began to dust the dark, age-cracked spines of the volumes. "It's most kind of Master Cawdor and his friends to repay your hospitality with such concern, Baron," he said without looking around.

"Yes, St. Vincent," Blackwood said. "Yes, it is. Thank you, Mr. Cawdor."

Ryan shrugged. "Don't want there to be any trouble. Reckoned you should know."

The baron nodded. "Indeed. And how fares Miss Wroth?"

"Same as before, Baron," Ryan said sadly. "She doesn't get worse, but she doesn't get better. It bothers me, I don't mind admitting. Not knowing what's wrong. Nor what to do about it."

"Is Dr. Mercier assisting adequately?"

Not even his intrepid spirit was up to ragging Mildred and Mercier about her any more today. "Yeah. She and Mildred seem to be working on it around the clock."

Blackwood smiled and nodded. "I trust they'll find a cure for her condition soon. Will you and your friends be so kind as to join my sister and me for dinner? I have some guests I'm expecting."

"My friends would string me up if I let them miss out on a meal like that. Not that the chow you feed us regular isn't tasty."

"Splendid! I'll see you at dinner. And now, if you'll excuse me..."

Chapter Eighteen

"The pirates have grown into an intolerable menace," said the tall, gaunt man with the black side whiskers sweeping out from the sides of his dark, beak-nosed face and the spade beard. "Is it true that the latest report from the coast say that the Black Gang has already reassembled in the wake of the hurricane?"

"And the battle our honored guests took part in," Blackwood said, "yes." He broke off a piece of freshly baked bread.

"That's unacceptable, Baron!"

"What would you suggest we do about it, Master Landry?"

Ryan sat forking up a spicy crayfish *étouffée* on rice. He held a chunk of the excellent bread in his other hand. A glass of white wine sat by his elbow.

As before, the fan swooping in deliberate circles above the long table with its spotless white-linen cover did little more than stir heavy, hot air. Even the gesture was welcome after a day spent in the sun.

"Why, we have to take the fight to them, clearly!" Landry exclaimed. "Take the offensive upon the sea."

"What would you suggest we do it with?" Blackwood asked mildly. "By himself, the pirate who styles himself Black Mask has more boats available than we. He's busy making allies as we speak. And his men are experienced at sea fighting, while ours are not."

"Why, seize the necessary ships! From the merchants and fishermen."

"That would put a stop to trade in a hurry, Franc," said Bouvier, Tobias's other influential guest from the ville. Unlike Franc, who was mostly a big farmland owner and also a major local brewer, Ryan understood Bouvier had strong shipping interests.

For a moment Landry champed his thin lips. "What about it? Too much of our wealth goes to outsiders as it is. We should be self-sufficient anyway."

Ryan looked at J.B., across from him with Mildred sitting at his side. Both tucked into their food with their accustomed appetites. Fortunately the baron believed in serving his food plentiful as well as good.

J.B. rolled his eyes. For all that it was dangerous and sporadic, trade was the lifeblood of survival. Lack of it could make Haven slide from relatively secure and prosperous to desperate in a matter of months. The two men hadn't spent their apprenticeships under a man legendarily called the Trader for nothing.

"Do you enjoy the wine, Master Landry?" Elizabeth asked sweetly.

"Oh, yes, Lady Elizabeth. It's most delicious."

"It's an import. This isn't exactly wine country, around here."

His cheeks turned red beneath the furze of his sideburns.

"Clearly that's out of the question," Bouvier said, "to attack Black Mask in his own element."

He was white-haired and red-faced like Barton, who sat at his usual spot at the table's foot, as usual saying nothing. But stouter, and also clearly older. His jowls clashed with the collar of his purple predark shirt where they spread out over it.

"At the same time," Bouvier went on, "it's a scandal how open we lie to attack. We do need to build up our defenses in the worst way."

"And yet," the baron said, "the more labor and resources we devote to building defenses, the less we have to build up the production that gives life and promise of a better future to the ville. To all of us who live in Haven."

Suave St. Vincent leaned over Ryan's shoulder, refilling his glass. "Perhaps our distinguished visitors would care to offer some suggestions as to how we may best secure ourselves here in Haven."

"Excellent notion, St. Vincent," Blackwood said. "If you'd be so kind?"

Ryan looked around at his companions. Doc sat beside him. From the absent smile, the faraway look in his lined eyes, Ryan guessed he wouldn't have much useful to contribute. Nor would Jak, seated next to Mildred so that she could keep an eye on his table manners.

J.B. caught Ryan's eye. Ryan nodded slightly.

"Okay," the Armorer said, waving with his own chunk of bread for emphasis. "You got some squared-away weapons and folks who know how to use them. But the pirates got blasters, too, good predark weapons with loads of ammo. Even a few automatic weapons. Plus they got grenades and RPGs, and *Black Joke* mounts a 105 mm recoilless rifle. They can bring heavy firepower down on you."

"We possess some fairly sophisticated grenades of our own," Blackwood said, "including some that can be launched from crossbows. As you know, black powder, which we make here in the mill, serves quite well for such purposes."

"I've seen your mills," J.B. said. "They're ace."

"We also have clay-jar Claymores we can pack with metal scrap or even pebbles. These can be set on tripwires or command-detonated using battery-powered clackers. Thanks to trade with the Tech-nomads, we have a small stock of rechargeable batteries, as well as solar-powered chargers for them."

"There are an awful lot of pirates, too," Mildred said. "Even though we tried our best to thin them out."

"Black Mask will have replaced his losses by now," Barton said. He sat at the far end of the table, tucking into his second portion of the spicy stew with relish. "For one thing, the storm will have smashed or foundered fishing vessels for miles along the coast. Lot of men are suddenly looking for new livelihoods."

Elizabeth smiled wanly. "In a way I'm not sure I'm grateful for your insight, Master Barton, as keen as it is. It is... unpleasant to be reminded that our enemies are not all just brutal coldhearts ravening for human blood. Some are decent men just trying to find a way to feed their families."

"Wolf come eat you," Jak said around a mouthful of food, "don't care if good wolf, bad wolf. Kill all same."

He winced and protested as Mildred dug him swiftly in the ribs with an elbow. "Hey!"

"Remember," she said sotto voce, "food to your mouth should be a one-way trip."

The raven-haired woman sighed. "Such is the sad reality of our time."

"If it is any consolation, Your Ladyship," Doc said, snapping suddenly back into focus, "it has always been that way. Through history, the exceptions have been but islands in a sea of despair."

"None of which loads any mags," Ryan said. "Baron, you sound as if you're confident you can hold off the pirates. I've seen you fight. There's none better. But there's a limit to what a few fighters can do against a whole horde. No matter how skilled or motivated they are."

"I'm not sure I'd say I feel confident," Blackwood said. "So far the harm the pirates have done us has been limited in human terms because coastal dwellers can just run off into the swamps when attacked. The property loss to pirate theft and vandalism causes hardships to our people, but so far we've been able to furnish them enough to begin rebuilding. Against sporadic raiding there is no defense I can envisage, given their strength and mobility asea—and our own limitations."

"But if they invade..." Mildred said.

"As I'm sure they will," the baron said. "Our greatest strength, then, lies in defense in depth. Invaders will have to run a gauntlet of ambushers—householders and citizens, well-armed, on their own terrain, fighting for their homes. And should they force their way to Haven proper, they'll face the same inspired defense in a built-up area. Which I understand from my historical readings is terrible terrain for an attacker."

"Generally I think historians are talking about considerable more 'building up' than you got here, Baron, if you'll forgive my saying so," Ryan said. "But I think the principle applies, though, yeah. Attacking a ville's always a tough proposition, even one a lot smaller than this."

"Rationally, why should they attack us at all, Tobias?" Elizabeth asked. "We can impose greater costs on them than they're likely to recoup even if they succeed in plundering Haven!"

"But sometimes these guys aren't rational," said J.B., biting off a chunk of bread and chewing it, earning a look of dismay from Mildred as crumbs tumbled down his shirt-front. "A guy like Black Mask gets a bee in his bonnet, he won't reckon profit and loss. Plus Haven's a plum prize."

"Plus he's a pure stoneheart," Ryan said. "It's not like he's going to shed any tears for any blood he doesn't leak himself. More of his dregs you chill, the bigger his piece of the pie."

The baron nodded. "This is why I'd be so much happier if you—all our honored guests—would consent to sign on and help us past the point your companion, Krysty, recovers."

Landry scowled. "You were complaining about limited resources, Baron? Why would it be advisable to add new mouths to feed on an extended basis?"

"Nonsense," Bouvier said, taking a hearty slug of wine. "These people are skilled fighters. They add far more than they could possibly consume. They're worth any number of farmers and laborers pulled from their tasks. No matter how enthusiastic they are, such people remain amateurs."

Ryan didn't bother polling his companions with a look. "All I can say is what I said all along, Baron. We'll stay and do what we can to help you until Krysty's fit to fight again. Then we'll talk long-range."

"And as I have said," Blackwood said with a slightly regretful smile, "that's fair enough."

"Speaking of Krysty," his sister said, "have you any good news for us, Dr. Wyeth?"

Mildred sighed and looked down at her plate, which was empty except for a little sheen of yellow crayfish grease. Ryan already knew her answer. He'd intercepted her the moment she'd stepped into the house.

"Only that she's not getting worse. Amélie says she remains hopeful. She knows a lot. Also, she has a remarkable facility, given that it was put together so many years after skydark."

"Her father was a remarkable man," Blackwood said. "A man of great determination as well as ability—traits his daughter carries on. He was persistent and resourceful enough to find the materials to build the laboratory. And my father supported him without reserve. I've tried to do as well by Lucien Mercier's daughter."

Elizabeth put her napkin on the table in front of her. "Brother, if you and our guests will excuse me, I believe I shall retire."

St. Vincent materialized behind her to help pull out her

chair and assist her to her feet. At a gesture from the majordomo, a female servant appeared at Elizabeth's side. Elizabeth gratefully put an arm over her shoulder for support.

"Elizabeth—" Tobias said.

She waved a hand. "It's nothing," she said. "Just weak. I'll
be fine when I lie down."

She made her way out with the help of her servant. The
baron turned a look of pain and helplessness around the table.

Ryan knew how he felt.

RYAN'S EYE SNAPPED open to the amber gleam of an oil lamp
turned low.

Krysty's dead, son, a voice said in his head. Face it. She's
lost. You're lost. She was the better half of your soul. Now
she's gone forever.

He sat up so violently he almost made the cot fold up on
him. He felt hotter than the air would account for. Wildly he
looked at Krysty. She still lay on her back, covered by a sheet,
her cheeks the color of ivory in the dim light.

Somewhat more cautiously he climbed off the cot. He
licked a finger and held it under her nostrils. He felt the slight
cool pressure of her breath. She was breathing shallowly, as
she had since he had awakened here in Haven. But at least
she still breathed.

But this is how it ends, the voice said. She'll never get
better again. You've lost her. You're lost, little boy. You're
doomed to wander forever alone.

He shook his head. He wasn't a fearless man. Any man
who said he felt no fear was just a flat-out liar. A man who
really didn't feel fear had something wrong inside.

Ryan had felt fear many times, in many forms. He had
always mastered the fear. He had always one way or another
found what it took to do what had to be done. That was what
made him the man he was.

But he'd never felt fear quite like this before. It curdled his guts and turned his joints to jelly. It was a burning pain like cancer in his brain. It seemed to offer no hope, no escape.

"Nuke it," he snarled, keeping his voice low as if there was any danger he'd wake the sleeping woman. As if that wouldn't feel like the best thing that ever happened to him. "I'm not going to give in. I'm not!"

Ryan, he thought he heard a voice say.

"Krysty?" There had been no sound. The woman lay as she had for days now. She obviously hadn't moved. Or spoken.

Ryan, listen to me, the beloved voice said in his skull.

He shook his head. "I'm imagining this."

He felt her soft laughter fall on him like gentle rain. *You still haven't learned better, lover? Believe what you want. You always do anyway.*

"You got that right," Ryan said, folding his arms and feeling like a stupe for holding a conversation with a woman in a coma.

First, you'll never be left alone. Unless you choose to be. I'll always be with you, live or dead, until you tell me you don't want me hanging around anymore.

"That'll be never."

That's a long time, lover.

"You said it first."

Again, he felt more than heard the unvoiced laughter.

Exasperating as always. That's my Ryan. The other thing is—you need to be ready to let go.

He crossed his arms. "That's not going to happen."

You say that now, but there'll be a time someday when you just have to walk away.

"Are you trying to tell me something, here, without coming out and telling me? Are you saying you're not coming out of this?"

Ryan, I don't know. I wish I did. All I can tell you is, I'm fighting, and Gaia fights with me. As to whether this will only end with me dying not even she can say. What I'm saying is, when the time comes—whenever it comes—promise you'll walk on and get on with your life.

"You trying to scare me worse?"

No. Never that. I just want to know you won't chain yourself forever to my lifeless husk.

He inhaled a deep breath, let it slide out in a long exhalation between his teeth. "I'll walk that road when it opens before me," he said. "Till then, I'm sticking."

That's my Ryan. That's the Ryan I know. I love you.

"I love you, too," he said.

And then it was as if he was the only one left awake in the room, as if the person he'd been speaking to had gone back to sleep.

"I'm crazy," he said, shaking his head in disgust.

But the fear was gone. He still felt weak, as if from fever, but he no longer felt as if the fear were tearing him apart from the inside.

He climbed back onto the cot and fell instantly asleep.

HE CAME AWAKE with a strong hand clamped over his mouth and his own hand gripping its wrist. His eye snapped open, but he saw nothing immediately.

He recognized the smell of Jak Lauren. The youth was bathing daily—all it took, it turned out, was for Elizabeth Blackwood to ask him please to do so. But Ryan had been with him long enough to know how he smelled clean or dirty.

The soap had a faint scent of lilac.

"Ryan, me," Jak said.

He nodded, and the pressure came off his mouth.

He let go of the slim but steel-muscled wrist. "Got a risky way of waking a body," he said.

"Why stood aside, out of sight. No time now. People outside. Sneaking up on house!"

Chapter Nineteen

In a heartbeat Ryan was up off the cot and moving toward the window.

"Keep low," Jak warned in a hiss.

Ryan waved a hand at him. "Yeah."

He flattened himself against the wall. There was a risk if he looked that somebody below would see him. As dim as it was, the lantern's light was enough to make it hard for him to see movement in the darkness—and enough to silhouette him for a watcher outside. But he knew that turning the light off was worse. People noticed changes, like lights going out. Especially in a house they were night creeping.

But his luck was in. He saw seven or eight figures, men or youths from the way they moved, stealing across the darkened lawn from the black wall of the trees to the front porch. Dark hoods hid each head. They carried a variety of cudgels—stout sticks, planks of wood, lengths of lead pipe. Ryan saw knives and single-shot blasters tucked into belts.

They weren't coming to deliver fresh eggs.

None looked up. That wasn't any huge windfall. People usually didn't. As long as Ryan didn't do anything to catch their eye, like move fast or turn a lamp up or down, only bad luck would betray him.

"Right. Why didn't you raise the alarm, Jak?"

The teen gave him a look of half-uncomprehending disgust. By his very nature Jak was himself a supreme night hunter. His answer to attack by stealth was counterattack by stealth.

May have a point, Ryan thought. A counterambush—falling by surprise on attackers who believed themselves secure in the advantage of surprise—appealed to Ryan's own dirty-fighting instincts.

"Go rouse the baron and our friends," he said, "quiet-like. Then do what you gotta do." Trying to tell Jak how to ambush the ambushers was like telling him how to breathe.

"You?" Jak asked.

"I'm going to drop in and give these boys a nice warm Southern welcome. Move."

But the teen hesitated, a pale ghost in the dimness. "Krysty."

Ryan pressed his lips together, looking at his lover lying faultless and entirely vulnerable beneath the thin cotton sheet.

"I don't want to fight in here," he said. "Best way to keep her safe's stop them well shy. Right."

He looked around. Jak had already vanished. Ryan nodded.

The window stood open as far as it would go for air. It was covered by a metal-mesh screen. Ryan drew his panga, which he kept honed close-shave sharp. With decisive yet quiet motions he slashed three cuts in the screen and folded it down.

He poked his head out. Though he seethed with rage and desire to throw himself on the foe, he forced himself to move deliberately. A quick check showed him the portico covering the front entrance to the mansion was too far away to jump to. But there were other windows spaced along the third floor. Windows with sills.

That was enough, because it had to be. He grabbed the sill and stuck one leg out. Turning to face into the bedroom, he brought the other leg out, so his bare feet gripped the sill as he crouched. He cast a last longing look at Krysty, then he turned and sprang at the next sill.

He made it effortlessly. He looked around, more out than down. No one had noticed him.

Quickly as he dared Ryan shuffled sideways to the end of the sill nearer the portico. Two more windows. Then he'd be directly over the peaked roof of the porch. He could lower himself to the next sill, and from there quietly to the top of the portico.

He gathered himself, then jumped sideways.

Maybe he misjudged distances in the darkness and with the adrenaline yelling in his veins and hammering at his heart. Maybe the sill was off true, cambered just a smidge outward. Or maybe there was some kind of loose rubble on it, flaked-off paint perhaps, that slid.

The balls of Ryan's feet hit the weathered wood and slipped right off. He fell toward the ground two dozen feet below.

JAK SLIPPED down the stairs to the second floor. He'd checked the baron's room. It was empty. Blackwell had either gotten the word already and acted, or he was just elsewhere. Either way, Jak reckoned he'd done the first part of the job Ryan gave him. He was always going to warn his companions in preference to searching a big creepy old house for an absent baron.

He tapped the door of the room he shared with Doc. It was an arrangement that worked surprisingly well. They didn't have a lick in common. For his own reasons each preferred to keep quiet during downtime. So when they bunked together neither troubled the other with idle chitchat.

"Doc," he said quietly in a voice he knew would carry less far than a whisper. "Jak."

"Yes, yes—"

"Stay ready. Coldhearts come. Don't let reach Krysty!"

"You may depend on me, young man, for—"

The albino teen had moved on, as silent as a ghost in a hallway lit only by starlight trickling through open windows at either end. Doc might not make small talk, but let him get going on one of his speeches and he ran on like a babbling brook.

Next came the door to J.B. and Mildred's room. Jak turned the knob and cracked the door. The pair came instantly awake at the slight sound.

"Trouble," Jak said. "Coldhearts night creep. Ryan says keep quiet and bushwhack."

"And not let them get to Krysty!" J.B. added as Mildred swung off the bed. "Got it."

Jak nodded and shut the door. He descended the next stairs to the ground floor.

Voices came from the front stoop. Grinning like a wolf in the darkness, Jak found the deepest-shadowed corner of the dining hall and slipped into it to await his prey.

This was the night. And this was *his* house.

FRANTICALLY, RYAN grabbed at the sill. His right fingertips slammed the edge and bounced off. His left hooked the very end of the small wooden ledge. Elbow and shoulder wrenched as they took the full force of his falling weight. At the impact his half-healed ribs shot pain like a knife into his lungs.

At once his grip began to slip. He writhed frenziedly, then got his right hand up. Relief flooded him. He was back in the game. The ribs wouldn't distract him. That was only pain.

He looked down. The hooded men were hunched over, straining forward. From the angle of their heads they were all staring fixedly at the front door of the big house, as if their eyes were attached to it by fishhooks on strings.

Ryan slid his hands to the right, pulling himself to the far sill's end. He swung his legs left then right, three times.

The third time he launched himself with all the strength

in his shoulders and arms. He flew sideways through the air. His right hand reached and it caught the final sill, followed an instant later by his left.

Shit, Ryan thought, as he dangled and firmed his grip, this is the easy way to do it.

He glanced down. The peaked porch roof waited right below him. He thought about a drop straight down and decided against it. It wasn't far, but the downward-angled sides of the roof meant too much danger of slipping or twisting an ankle. Plus he doubted he could land silently.

He looked closer. The second-story sill wasn't far below his bare toes. He calculated, swung inward a bit, dropped.

His landing was sure. It was also quiet. As fluid as a mountain lion down a boulder outcrop, Ryan flowed down to hang from the ledge and drop with only the faintest of thumps to the portico roof.

He got a good foothold on either side of the peak. Then drawing his panga in his right hand and his SIG-Sauer P-226 handblaster in his left, he walked bent-over to the end of the roof.

Some of the coldhearts were on the porch now, muttering softly. Four others stood on the grass just short of the steps up.

Ryan leaped toward his prey.

"Get your pants on, John," Mildred said. "Having your naughty bits dangling in the breeze will only distract you."

"Right," the Armorer said. He had started to join her where she stood with her back to the door, and the door opened to a hairline, clad only in boots, shotgun, eyeglasses and fedora. He turned back to the bed, scooped up his pants and sat to pull them on.

Mildred had taken her own advice, after a fashion. She had pulled on a thigh-length T-shirt to give at least the psy-

chological sense of protection to her own tender parts. She
hadn't bothered pulling on underpants. There were advan-
tages to internal plumbing.

She had her .38 ZKR 551 target pistol held barrel-up in
her right hand.

"Somebody's coming," she said. She heard J.B. trying to
stand. "No, I got it. Back me."

Footsteps, she thought. Coming up the stairs.

EVEN BEFORE HIS toes touched the grass of the front lawn
Ryan's panga chunked into the hooded back of the head of a
lean man in a checked flannel shirt hanging untucked over
badly holed blue jeans. The impact shivered up his arm.
His feet struck. He flexed his legs deeply, allowing his own
weight and momentum to yank the blade free.

The intruder melted and his knees struck ground. Then he
turned into a lumpy puddle.

Ryan was already rising, swinging his left hand. He had
aimed his leap to land behind and roughly between the man
whose skull he had split and the shorter man on his left, who
had a big gut and a bum left leg. The second was turning,
holding a wooden ball bat but not swinging it, as though he
wasn't fully aware of the fate that had befallen his companion.

Ryan rapped the magazine end plate at the bottom of the
SIG's grip hard against the man's right temple. As a rule he
didn't care for hitting people with blasters. Most made crappy
clubs, and if you banged them around too much, *clubs* could
be all they ended up being good for. Right now he couldn't
be choosy.

The second man pitched forward, dropping the bat to
clutch at his face but not saying anything, stunned.

Ryan's plan was to tie up as many of the sneak attackers as he could here, outside the house. Whether they were

chilled, incapacitated, run off, or just occupied beating and stomping him to a helpless pulp on the ground, they wouldn't be threatening Krysty. He couldn't say, now or ever, that he didn't care about being chilled. *Survivor* was core to who and what he was. But this time he could say surviving wasn't his number-one priority.

He judged his best bet was to turn himself into a whirlwind of pain and potential death.

"No blasters!" hissed a tall, black-clad figure, its features obscured like those of the other attackers, that hung back not far from the deeper shadows of the trees. Ryan felt relief. He hadn't wanted to shoot because he didn't want the cold-hearts shooting back. Apparently they didn't want to alert their quarry.

For a moment there was only motion: slashing, clubbing, feeling resistance to his strikes, hot blood splashing his face and bare upper torso. Shouts and groans. He kept his attacks moving, kept them fluid, never lingering, trying not to be predictable.

But the numbers caught up to him.

An ax handle caught him across the belly, doubling him over briefly. He threw himself forward, diving beneath and inside the skull-crushing follow-up blow. Coming to his feet, he slashed another man upward across the gut.

A long, bubbling scream erupted inside the house.

Chapter Twenty

As he and his partner stole softly up onto the big house's second floor, Bo Gentry was sulking. It was just luck of the draw they got to lead the way up into the baron's house, and Bo was on fire with excitement. But his dog-dick partner Jean-Paul Dolan, who he never wanted to get teamed with in the first place, insisted he had to go first. He hissed and pissed about it so insistently on the stairs Bo got to fearing he'd rouse the house. And that might bring Baron Blackwood down on them, when their only job was to secure this floor, make sure the outlanders didn't interfere while the strike team moved past to the third floor.

Bo didn't want to piss off Le Patron, and he *surely* didn't want the baron descending on him with those two swords of his like two whole butchers on jolt.

If all went to plan—and Le Patron assured them that it would—they were in no danger of facing their albino overlord, which was doubly good, since they intended him no harm. The point to the mission was to force him to see reason, force him to reveal where the Beast could be found.

All Bo and Jean-Paul had to do was to make sure the outlanders didn't interfere. Along with suitable bludgeons, each man had been provided a rare cartridge blaster, Jean-Paul a Smith & Wesson .357 Magnum revolver, Bo a double-barreled sawed-off shotgun, to intimidate them. Or kill them quickly, of course, if they wouldn't see reason.

The intruders heard a strange tap-tap. They froze, spying

an outlandish figure in the deep gloom at the hall's far end. It was an oldie, tall but stooped, lank hair hanging in his face. He wore a strange single-piece long-sleeved garment that covered him neck to ankles, and he walked with the aid of an ebony cane, on which he leaned heavily.

Jean-Paul glanced back over his shoulder at Bo and grinned. Jean-Paul was much larger, which also figured in Bo's giving in when Jean-Paul wanted to go first.

Standing upright, Jean-Paul swaggered forward. "Give up now, old man, and we won't hurt you. Much."

The old man straightened a few painful degrees, enough to raise his cane without toppling onto his face.

He poked the cane toward Jean-Paul's face. "Show respect to the aged! You shall not pass!"

Jean-Paul laughed. "You have made your choice, old man. Mebbe you can stand up straight when I shove this cane up your withered old ass!"

And he grabbed the tip of the cane and yanked it away.

Except the old man was still holding the head end of the cane. Starlight skittered faintly along a long, thin piece of metal protruding from it.

"*Merde!*" Jean-Paul exclaimed, holding the swordstick-sheath in front of his face in disbelief. *"C'est impossible!"*

"Not at all, dear boy," Doc said. The slender blade in his hand flashed forward like a striking copperhead.

Jean-Paul screamed long and loud as the tip entered his left eye.

CLUMSY ASSES, Jak thought in contempt as footsteps clomped into the foyer. He judged he faced at least four intruders, perhaps six.

Coiled in the darkness like a serpent, he waited. Five men in black hoods walked past on their way to the stairs. They held clubs and machetes. Each spared barely a glance into the dining room as they passed. Clearly, they expected to encounter no one. Or if they did, servants who would be easily cowed.

Jak grinned. He waited a beat, then slipped forward. When he came around the corner, the first two men were trudging up the stairs. They seemed to be trying to keep quiet, but making a bad job of it. Otherwise they acted as if they owned the place.

Noiselessly he lunged at the back of the last man in file. His butterfly knives whipped open in his hands, as quietly as his bare feet glided over the shabby carpet runner.

Jak cocked back both his arms. From somewhere overhead he heard a prolonged shriek. The men ahead of him stopped dead.

Jak was as surprised as they were, but he never broke stride. As the first two assassins came out of their stunned surprise and rabbited up the stairs, he plunged his small but lethal knives into the kidneys of the last man in line.

There's no such thing as "hurt too badly to scream." Jak knew that from much observation, as well as a few unfortunate experiences of his own. But the pain of certain wounds makes the victim inclined to suck in a breath, rather than immediately expel air in a cry of intolerable agony.

As expected, his victim stiffened, sucking in a whistling breath. From overhead the insane screaming continued. No one seemed to notice what had befallen their trail man, as he fell thrashing at Jak's feet.

Jak pulled his knives free and prepared to leap on the next man, who still stood as if terrified to advance in the face of whatever had caused the terrible shrieks from the second floor.

But the howling also fouled Jak's fine-tuned hearing.

He never heard the burly man who rushed in the front door behind him and caught him in a bear hug with arms as thick as legs.

DOC'S BLOOD was up. Leaving his fallen antagonist to thrash and squall and spray the baseboards with blood and aqueous humor, he advanced on the other holding his swordstick *en sixte*.

"Have at you, young rogue!" he shouted lustily. "Surrender now!"

"Filthy old bastard!" the other cried. He raised a short-barreled, double-barreled blaster to point at Doc's midsection. "I chill you in the belly!"

He pulled the trigger. Nothing happened. Likely he had been ordered to approach the house with hammers down for safety. He had forgotten to lift them.

Before the befuddled young man could cock the double-blaster, a door opened to his left. The angry dark face and black handblaster of Mildred Wyeth protruded from the doorway.

"Not on *my* watch, motherfucker!" she shouted. She shoved the muzzle of her .38 into the intruder's soft side and shot him twice.

RYAN WOULD'VE SWORN he wasn't distracted by the horrible cries coming out of the house's second story, and perhaps he just got unlucky. In a fight against multiple enemies, the dregs weren't generally polite enough to line up and attack one at a time.

He got nailed by a trick worthy of him. Whether by unlooked-for cunning or blind-panic luck, an attacker lashed out from behind and nailed Ryan in the balls.

It was one of the top five nut-shots Ryan had taken in his life, and it hit him at the worst possible time: the end of an exhalation. His body now emptied of air, his every cell screaming for oxygen, there was just no room in his spasm-knotted body for breath to fit.

His vision darkened; his head spun. Or perhaps that was just his body corkscrewing down to the soft damp-springy turf and wrapping itself into a reflex knot of agony.

Ryan's peripheral vision was just clear enough to take note of the worn sole of a heavy boot upraised to stomp on his head.

As SHOTS CRASHED somewhere upstairs, the man holding Jak in a bear hug threw back his head and added his own woman-shrill shrieks to the ululations to the cacophony. The sharp bits of metal and jagged glass Jak sewed into his jacket had bitten deep into the unprotected flesh of his attacker's palms and burly bare arms.

His grip slackened, and Jak twisted free. He flattened himself on the carpet as the invader he'd been trying to backstab wheeled and cut loose with a crossbow.

The steel-spring bow twanged, and the bolt hummed above Jak like an angry bumblebee. It struck the former bear-hugger with a sound like a knife stabbing into a ripe watermelon and sank to the feathers out of sight in the fat of his gut. The intruder's screams took on a deeper, more urgent tone, then he fell.

Jak sprang toward the man with the now-useless crossbow. His blades slashed figure eights in the invader's hood-covered face and chest. Hot gore splashed his face.

RYAN HAD NO STRENGTH, but he still kept a few shreds of his presence of mind. He managed to roll his fetal-curled body onto his back and fire his 9 mm blaster twice upward into the leg and groin of the man about to stomp him. The man fell away, screaming.

Blasters boomed. People started shouting all over the place. Ryan had a sense of fighting going on just past the fringes of his vision.

Purposeful movement caught his eye. The tall black-clad figure directing the others had turned to scuttle into the protecting darkness of the trees. Once inside he'd be home free. If he had an ounce of woodcraft—as pretty much every Havenite did—within a few hundred yards he could lose himself in the marshes and bayous where even bloodhounds couldn't track him.

With a total concentration of will Ryan extended his right arm. Trying to sight upside down through a blurry eye, he cranked out four quick shots. The man in black pitched forward. The tail of the coat or cloak he wore billowed like the wings of some giant evil night bird.

But the dark form continued to wriggle forward, dragging itself into the azalea bushes at the edge of the woods. Ryan tried to get off more shots, but his body failed him. He finally managed to suck in a breath. It wasn't deep enough. Head swimming, he slumped, fighting now merely to breathe through the agony that enveloped his midsection.

He was helpless.

Sensing a looming presence, Ryan turned his head and saw a bare foot and shin, both as white as chalk. Looking up, he saw Baron Blackwood standing tall against the stars. His hair, face, and the formerly white underwear that was all he wore were streaked with blood.

"Are you injured, my friend?" the baron asked in his deep voice, plunging a sword tip-first into the ground and kneeling by Ryan's side.

Already Ryan was able to breathe normally again. Mostly.

"Only my pride," he answered, sitting up gingerly. The dew on the grass had soaked through the seat of his jeans.

"Plus the family jewels."

Tobias grinned and reached out a hand to Ryan. They gripped each other forearm to wire-muscled forearm. Blackwood straightened, pulling Ryan to his feet as if he weighed no more than a child.

With effort Ryan managed not to sway.

"That's twice I owe you for saving my hide, Baron," Ryan said.

"There is no debt, Ryan. The prompt, bold actions of you and your friends may well have spelled the difference between survival and calamity for my house."

"Speaking of which, you don't seem to have been caught sleeping yourself."

Blackwood shook his head, casting pink sweat and blood droplets from his white hair. "St. Vincent warned me intruders were approaching the house. You must have spotted them around the same time. I told St. Vincent to rouse you, then I went out the window."

He grinned. Somehow, despite the sweat and blood that turned his pallid face into a canvas painted with pure horror, he managed to make it almost boyish.

"When Elizabeth and I were young, my father used to lock us in our rooms. I learned several ways to climb safely to the ground, including one over the roof and down the back. It came in handy tonight. You?"

"Found my own way down."

Ryan realized several burly male servants and a couple of women, all armed with an assortment of knives, clubs and axes, were moving around him, securing the wounded intruders and making sure the dead ones stayed that way. He put his own weapons away as St. Vincent emerged smiling from the front door. Stepping delicately over a corpse sprawled at the foot of the steps, he approached Blackwood and spoke softly in his ear.

"Thank you," the baron said.

He turned to Ryan. "By some miracle none of our people were seriously hurt. Your friends are well, although young Master Lauren has incurred some minor gashes and bruises."

"Standard for him. What about Krysty?"

"Safe. None of the attackers reached her floor. St. Vincent tells me servants found my sister sitting beside Miss Wroth's bed with a pump shotgun across her lap."

Ryan grunted and nodded. It was all he had in him.

Guerrero walked up the road at the head of a column of sec men. His round bearded face was coated thickly in sweat that reflected orange highlights from the torch a flunky carried at the big-bellied man's side. Ryan got the feeling it wasn't just the heat that made him sweat like that.

"Baron," Guerrero began as soon as he came in range, "I'm so sorry. I—I mean, there was no—"

Tobias held up a slim white hand. "Enough. None of us was adequately prepared for this treachery. We're all safe, and we'll all be more aware in the future."

To the sec boss's credit he neither kept quivering nor groveled. Suddenly all business, he straightened and asked, "How can we serve, Baron?"

"Secure the prisoners." His handsome features hardened. "We want the blackguards healthy enough to hang."

"Yes, sir!" Guerrero turned and began directing his men. He did it in a solid, steady tone, without hollering and blustering.

Despite the majestic way he'd stepped on his pecker tonight, he wasn't the fat clown he appeared to be. Not wholly, anyway, Ryan observed.

"There was a ringleader," Ryan said, sorting through the jumbled memories of the last few minutes. "All in black. I winged him, but he crawled off into the woods."

"See to him, Guerrero," the baron said without looking around. The sec boss gave the necessary commands. A party of armed men with torches immediately set off into the woods.

A wave of dizziness washed over Ryan. His incompletely healed ribs were paining him once again, accompanying a number of other aches. He couldn't prevent himself from swaying. Blackwood gripped his upper arm and guided him to a bench beside the house. Ryan gratefully sat.

His friends drifted out to join him: Jak, then Doc and J.B. Mildred appeared last, having examined Krysty, finding no change in her condition, as well as checking on Elizabeth Blackwood. Ryan gradually collected their accounts of the battle. He told them what had happened to him.

Soon the search party returned in triumph from the woods. The two biggest men carried a long pole, a hastily stripped sapling judging by the stubs of branches, across their shoulders as they walked side by side. Between them they half carried a man in black clothes and hood, with his arms bound behind him and the pole shoved under them, behind his back. He stumbled along on one leg. The boot of the other dragged along the ground behind. He groaned loudly every time something jarred it.

Guerrero stepped up to speak to the squad leader, then he accompanied the party to stand in front of Blackwood.

"We got the ringleader," Guerrero said. "Cawdor shot him in the ass. Fucked up his right hip. Boys couldn't make him walk, so…" He gestured with a broad hand toward their improvised carry pole.

"Excellent," the baron said. Most of the blood had been sponged off him by servants with buckets of well water. He now had a black cloak with scarlet lining wrapped around him. Its tails flapped in a sluggish breeze that had risen. The wind smelled of rain, although the sky overhead remained clear.

"Set him down," Blackwood commanded. The sec men

deposited their captive on the ground in front of him. The bound man slumped, his good leg folded beneath him, the other sticking out to the side. He moaned softly.

"Take the hood off."

Guerrero reached down, loosened a drawstring, then yanked the mask away.

Franc Landry sat staring up at them from a face gray with misery.

Chapter Twenty-One

Rain spattered down from a late-morning sky the color of slate. Ryan, Doc and Jak sheltered beneath the branches of mulberry tree at the west end of the town square. They watched the construction going hastily up in the midst of the grassy plaza.

"An appropriate day for a hanging," Doc said glumly.

"Better cut throats, be done," Jak said. He had an aversion to hanging bordering on the phobic, having found himself on the wrong end of it, once upon a time.

Mildred, expressing disgust with the whole proceedings, had gone off to Amélie Mercier's high-tech lab. She said Mercier claimed to be on the verge of some sort of breakthrough concerning Krysty. Ryan wasn't getting his hopes up.

"I am not sure kindness is the object of the exercise," Doc said. "Although to his credit, Baron Blackwood is at least trying to render the unpleasant process as humane as possible."

Ryan grunted. He wasn't feeling so tender toward the six condemned men, the survivors of the group of upward of a dozen who had attacked the baron's house the night before. He hadn't slept well. His ribs hurt and his balls ached. His head and stomach didn't feel so great, either. He would've been happy to finish off the bastards himself with an ax handle.

J.B. strolled across the plaza toward them. When he got under the densely leafed branches he took of his glasses and cleaned water and condensation from them with a handkerchief.

"Quite a project, constructing a six-holer gallows on short notice," he said. "Fixing the trapdoors up right's a mite tricky."

He cocked his head and gazed at Doc. "You know, we could have used your help tinkering that contraption together. Reckon it's right up your alley as a man of science and all."

Doc shied like a startled horse. "It most emphatically is not, my good man!" he exclaimed. "Capital punishment, especially public executions, is a barbaric ritual. I do not hold with them. Nor have I ever."

"But I thought, what with you coming from a time when they hanged a lot of people…"

Doc glared. "In this, your own time, in which I unfortunately find myself cast away like Robinson Crusoe upon the savage shore, there exist men so debased as to compel innocent savants to perform indecent commerce with barnyard animals. Does that mean you endorse that practice?"

"Easy, Doc," Ryan said in a low voice. He wasn't worried about J.B.'s tender sensibilities, owing to the fact he doubted there were any. He was worried about Doc working himself into a state over memories of things gone like bullets from blasters.

"Well, no," J.B. said, "can't say as I do."

He pushed up his fedora to scratch the right side of his head. "The way I see it, this bunch needs chilling. They aren't being tortured, so what's the problem?"

Doc looked away, shaking his head. "It is the principle. In any event, this all transpires with unseemly speed."

"Ryan heard St. Vincent advising the baron that swift justice'll help stamp down any trouble before it gets going."

"Indeed? And the baron agreed?"

"That St. Vincent seems to have a double load of influence over Blackwood for a servant," Ryan observed. "Even the boss servant."

J.B. shrugged. "He served Tobias and Elizabeth's old man, too."

Ryan squinted at his friend. "How does that recommend him as an adviser?"

"Well, it seems he was always pretty attached to the kids. He may've played some role in bringing Dornan down, too."

"Would that very fact not tend to display a propensity for treachery on St. Vincent's part?" Doc asked.

"Mebbe St. Vincent hated the old bastard," Ryan said. "Plenty other people did, for good reason. He doesn't sound like a barrel of fun to work for."

He shrugged. "Speaking of which, St. Vincent doesn't work for us. So I hardly see as it matters a spent round."

"Heard some talk when I was helping build the gallows," J.B. said. "That sec boss, Guerrero, palavered some with his lieutenants. And that worried-looking tubby guy, Barton."

"Yeah?" Ryan said.

After wakening he'd sat up holding Krysty's unresponsive hand for a while, then he went downstairs, ate a slight breakfast alone, and drifted outside not too long ago. He'd spoken to no one in the house except for exchanging a few words with the woman who served him beignets, with real powdered white sugar, and coffee. "Landry still refusing to talk?"

J.B. nodded. "Nobody else knows jack. Grunt-laborers, the bunch. Don't know what actual evidence there is to tie the baron to the Beast. Landry wouldn't tell them. Just assured them it was true."

"And they accepted that?" Doc asked.

"They were scared, and used to just accepting anything Landry told them. Only one guy claimed he had the straight goods Blackwood knew all about the Beast and was cover-

ing it up. A 'cropper named Luc Corday. He went straight to
Landry with his skinny, and Landry told him not to tell the
others squat."

Jak stood to one side looking bored and disgruntled. The
night's events had prevented him going for a scheduled predawn hunting trip with his local friends. He snorted a laugh.

"'Fraid they go half-cocked, make triple-big mess. Ha!"

"Could be," Ryan said. "Why doesn't Guerrero just ask
Corday what he had?"

J.B. chuckled. "Can't," he said. "Corday was the dude
whose head you split with that panga of yours, kicking off
the dance."

Ryan swore feelingly.

"Triple stupe," Jak stated. "Attack baron on one man's say-
so! Even big-boss type."

"They are irrationally unhinged by the depredations of the
Beast," Doc said. "Such fear can cloud even the thinking of
men who, candidly, have more practice of thinking."

"Turns out the whole mob was Landry's own employ-
ees," J.B. said, "sharecroppers and haulers. Or poor relatives.
Reckon Landry handpicked them for being double scared and
half smart."

"Why attack last night?" Doc asked. "In full knowledge
we were on hand to aid in the house's defense?"

"Heard that before I took off back to bed last night," Ryan
said. "They got to yammering at Guerrero and his sec boys
about how Landry told them the Beast struck again."

"Wild-goose chase," J.B. said. "Sec goons bitched about
that all morning long. None of the captives could say who the
Beast chilled, or where. Nobody else heard a whisper about
any of it."

"So Landry made it up, to get them stirred enough to move
on the baron," Ryan said.

"I warned you," Doc said, "such sentiment has been building for some time."

"So once he got his crew good and riled," J.B. said, "old Landry said they had to act now because Blackwood was about to recruit us outlanders to help him root them out 'cause they were talking against him. Brought up old Baron Dornan and his wagon-wheel executions. *That* scared 'em right into action."

Ryan shook his head. "What lit Landry's fuse? You'd think in his position he'd need to have some sense."

"Even in a ville as apparently orderly as Haven," Doc said, "the Darwinian pressures of hanging onto large amounts of wealth and influence would weed out the utterly foolish."

"Like I said, he isn't telling," J.B. said. "All he'll say is that he did it for Haven, and they never meant to harm Blackwood. His people back him—they all keep insisting the plan was never to hurt the baron, much less depose him. The whole idea was to take him captive and force him either to reveal the Beast's hiding place or to agree to dispose of it himself."

Ryan gave him an arch-browed look of skepticism. "Why in the name of blazing nuke death wouldn't the baron chill the Beast if he knew where to find it?"

"Hey," the Armorer said. "I didn't buy the deal. Just passing on what I heard."

"Triple stupe," Jak repeated.

Ryan grunted. It was that. But it all refused to settle down and lie peacefully in his brain.

"Too many questions," he muttered. "And they're all in a rush to chill the only one who seems to have any answers."

"Don't think they can lean too hard on Landry, if you know what I mean," J.B. said. "He's still got a lot of kin and contacts. They may not be too eager to associate themselves with him just now, but there's a limit to what Blackwood could do to him, even over something like this."

"I doubt the baron is the sort to countenance torture," Doc said.

"No," Ryan said. "He wouldn't let Guerrero's boys do more than cuff the prisoners around a bit. Not that it took more than that to get them all singing like birds. Except for the one who knows something."

He shook his head. "I just can't get it all to hook up and make sense."

Doc laid a hand on Ryan's shoulder. "My friend, if you insist on having all the world's questions answered, and all her loose ends neatly tied, you will merely drive yourself to madness. Trust me on this."

"He's got you there, Ryan," J.B. said. "Doc's made the trip many times."

Instead of rising to the Armorer's bait, Doc only nodded sadly.

A commotion announced the arrival of the baron and his retinue. He wore a tail coat and a high-collared shirt that looked uncomfortable, as if he were doing penance. He carried an umbrella. His sister walked beside him, her black hair done up in a bun. Her severe black dress with white lace collar made her face look almost as pale as her brother's. Or perhaps it was more than that.

They took their places facing the gallows. Ryan sauntered over to join them, his companions trailing him.

"Ryan, friends," the baron said, nodding to them. Elizabeth smiled briefly and halfheartedly.

"Baron. Ma'am," Ryan said. "Kind of surprised to see you here, Lady Elizabeth."

"I feel obliged to face the reality of what we're doing here, Mr. Cawdor," she said. "It appalls me, however necessary."

He was also surprised to see her up and around. The last

he'd heard, the previous night's excitement had dropped her into a relapse. Mercier and Mildred had been buzzing around her like bees at the last bloom of autumn when he'd gone down for his solo breakfast.

Blackwood squeezed his sister's hand. "You speak for me, dear sister," he said gravely.

"You sure it's a good idea to send them off this quick, Baron?" Ryan asked.

Blackwood's greyhound chest expanded and contracted in a mighty sigh. "Candidly, no. But given our unsettled conditions here in the ville I fear justice must be seen to come swiftly and certainly, or the people will lose all regard for it."

"Isn't that how tyranny so often begins, brother?" Elizabeth asked. Ryan tried not to gape. She'd voiced exactly the sentiment that had flashed through his mind, and which he wasn't about to say out loud.

Almost as much to Ryan's surprise her brother nodded. He had his long hair wound into a sausage-like queue at the back of his neck. "It is. All I can do is hope that I'm equal to the temptation to proceed ever faster down the same slippery slope that's claimed so many."

"At least you're willing to try," J.B. said. "Most barons I've seen have already taken that hill at a dead run. If you'll pardon my saying so."

"What about Landry?" Ryan said. "He's the key to the whole thing."

"He's as stubborn as a mule and as tough as an old cypress tree," Blackwood said. "He wouldn't talk if I consented to torture him. I rather be put to the torment myself! My father—"

It was Elizabeth's turn to squeeze his hand. "There, brother. Be calm."

He mastered himself with visible effort. "In any event, it's most vital of all that he be executed along with those he led into criminal folly. I won't have a double standard of justice for the high and low in this ville, and I want the people to see that with their own eyes!"

"What people's eyes see," J.B. murmured, "and what kind of conclusions they draw from it, can be completely different things."

Instead of flashing into anger, like any normal baron would do when contradicted by a mere citizen, and an outlander at that, Tobias Blackwood only nodded gravely. "You speak the truth, Master Dix. Yet all we can do is all that we can do."

FRANC LANDRY HAD to be helped up to his place at the left-hand end of the line of condemned men by two burly executioners. He wasn't the only one. But in his case it was purely because of his leg crippled by Ryan's 9 mm slug. He tried his best to go to his death with back stiff and head high.

Some of his condemned followers thrashed and blubbered and cried out for mercy as they were wrestled into place. A cordon of grim sec men armed with staffs and clubs held back the crowd. Which really meant they held back a couple dozen mourners, relatives of the condemned, who wept and wailed and held out their hands to their doomed kin.

"How this will serve any end but to increase ill-will and dissonance within this ville," Doc said, "escapes me entirely." He wore his frock coat and held his swordstick as if he were attending a royal coronation.

"You're right on that one, Doc," said Mildred, who had emerged from Mercier's lab to join her friends at the last minute, apparently for the same reasons Elizabeth Blackwood was there. Mercier remained at her labors. Ryan reckoned she'd do the same if she was the one sentenced to hang, up until the actual moment they came to walk her to the gallows.

"It's a hard call," Ryan admitted. "But if you're going to be a baron, that's the kind of choice you got to make."

The others piped down. They remembered all too clearly certain choices Ryan had been forced to make, to keep them all together and safe. Some of them had been downright stonehearted. He was a man who did what he had to, and he knew what it cost.

"An irony," Doc remarked as each condemned prisoner was fitted with a black hood. The key difference with the ones they'd used to hide their features the night before was that these lacked eyeholes. "In my day it was always bruited about that the hoods were to spare the condemned from seeing their own demises coming. The truth was, it was to spare the onlookers from looking into their eyes as they died, and seeing their faces twist in final contortions."

"Lots of folks take to executions like a boozer to shine," J.B. said. "The more face contorting, the better."

"Not this bunch," Ryan said. Eventually, several hundred Havenites had gathered in the square. They showed none of the sympathy for the condemned the relatives did, but neither did they show a flake of eagerness as far as Ryan could see. They stood as stiff and uncomfortable in the rain as their baron and his sister.

Doc sighed. "For all its difficulties, this community seems unusually favored, in its rulership and in what it has built for itself," he said. "I fear such an event as this might well mark its high-water mark."

"Much as I hate to," Mildred said, "I'm going to have to agree with you twice in a row. I don't like this at all."

"Makes everybody," Jak said.

AT LAST THE SIX prisoners were hooded, and nooses tied with the traditional thirteen knots fitted around their necks. Those unwilling, or in the ringleader's case unable, to stand in place on the waiting trapdoor, were held upright by sec men.

There was more than one yellow-tinged pool on the traps already.

As Guerrero marched self-importantly to the big lever that would spring all six traps at once, Franc Landry began to speak.

"Fools!" Landry declaimed. His voice rang clear and sharp as a big bronze bell despite the muffling black cloth. "You poor, deluded fools! Baron Tobias knows the truth about the Beast. Don't you see? The Beast is—"

Blackwood nodded. Putting his back into it, Guerrero hauled back on the lever.

Landry was cut off mid-declaration. Six necks broke with a sound like a string of firecrackers going off in a burlap bag.

Chapter Twenty-Two

As Ryan walked away from the scaffold and the six corpses that hung from it, he felt a fleeting contact of warm flesh on his left hand. Something with sharp edges was pressed into his palm.

He whipped around, ready to fight. A kid stood there, ten at most, a sturdy blond boy in sun-faded blue shorts and a shapeless homespun smock, feet bare on the rain-damp grass. The boy smiled, showing a couple of missing front teeth.

"Supposed to give you a message, mister," he piped up. Then he was gone in the crowd that was slowly and quietly dispersing back to its daily routines.

Ryan turned his hand over. There was a stiff piece of card stock wedged in his palm. It had writing on it in a loopy, spidery cursive.

"What you got, Ryan?" J.B. asked.

"Some kid gave me this note," he said, holding it up. "Stuck it right in my hand before I knew he was there."

"If he goes into some honest trade the world'll miss out on a fine pickpocket," the Armorer said. "What's it say?"

Ryan handed it to him. "Read."

J.B. did. "Huh," he said. "Going to go?"

"Why not?" Ryan said.

"I can think of mebbe a thousand reasons offhand."

"Me, too," Ryan admitted. "But if we're starting to attract serious attention, I'd like to get some clue how or why."

J.B. nodded. "I hear you. We got protection as guests and

big pals of the Baron and his sis. But we may be painting
bull's-eyes on our foreheads, too. You going do like it says
and go alone?"

"Fireblast, no," Ryan said with a wolf's grin.

IT WAS A SIZABLE warehouse on the bayou waterfront. Although its planks were warped and weathered, it looked to
be in good repair. Ryan paused to give it a good scoping by
starlight from outside before striding to the orange rectangle
of light cast from within.

Somewhere up the broad bayou a gator bawed.

Ryan stepped through the open door and sidestepped immediately so as not to leave himself silhouetted in the door,
an easy target. Inside he found stacks of wooden crates, casks
and huge glass carboys filled with brown fluid. It smelled
strongly of tanned leather and some unidentifiable spice, as
well as the kerosene lantern hanging from a roof beam in the
middle of the large central storeroom.

"Cawdor? Is that you?" a voice called. A door stood open
in an office walled off from the far riverside corner of the
building, to Ryan's left. The light of a second lantern shone
from it. "Come on in."

He walked to the door. Inside the man he knew from Baron
Tobias Blackwood's dinner table as Al Bouvier sat behind a
desk. He had his booted feet up on a green felt blotter.

The big-bellied man swung down his feet and stood. He
wore a white shirt with big sweat-stain half-moons under the
arms, dark brown pants with suspenders to hold them up. To
his right a glazed window stood open, covered with an expensive scavvied metal-mesh screen to keep out the night bugs,
some big alarming specimens of which were crawling around
on it buzzing their wings in frustration. The window opened
on the river. Though Ryan couldn't see it, he could hear its
slosh and gurgle and smell the tannin-rich black water.

"Take a load off," Bouvier said. He waved at a wooden chair set in front of the desk with a big thick hand.

"Don't mind if I do," Ryan said, and sat.

"Thanks for coming," Bouvier said. He hefted a square-sided glass bottle three-quarters full of dark amber fluid, tipped it side to side to make the liquid swirl.

"Whiskey? It's real bourbon from what they tell me used to be Kentucky. Not shine colored with tobacco spit."

"You pay and pour, sure. Thanks."

Bouvier chuckled as he splashed two fingers into a heavy tumbler. "Here," he said, pushing it toward Ryan. He poured himself a shot.

Ryan studied it a moment. "Not used to drinking the strong stuff from a clean glass."

Bouvier laughed. "Whiskey like this, you clean a glass special if you got to."

The heavyset man picked up his own glass and looked interestedly at Ryan. Without hesitation the one-eyed man raised his glass and took a sip.

"Smooth," he announced.

Bouvier took a sip of his own and sat back grinning. "You're a man who knows his way around good whiskey. Sip instead of slam."

Ryan shrugged. "Good things are few and far between in this life. A wise man learns to appreciate them."

Reckon he really wonders if I was worried he was trying to dose me, he thought.

"I won't step all around the blaster's muzzle, Cawdor," Bouvier said. "I'll get right to the trigger and not waste your time. What did you think of today's little production?"

Somewhere right outside the structure an owl hooted softly. "Seen worse," Ryan said. "Could have lived without watching it anyway."

"And the sentences? You think they were just?"

Ryan shrugged. "Those men put my people and me in harm's way, who'd never done a thing to them. Anyway, I'd already chilled some of them myself. So I'd be a bit crazy to gripe about it."

Bouvier regarded him a moment with shrewd gray eyes. Ryan crossed his legs, sipped his whiskey and remained silent. He thought he had this deal scoped already, but he wanted to hear it confirmed from the man's own mouth.

"Did you think the punishment went far enough?"

"Torture a bad man, you're just as bad as him," Ryan said. "A man needs chilling, chill him clean and have it done."

Bouvier nodded. "Laudable, laudable. Yet what would you say if I told you that it was excessive softness that necessitated that whole unpleasant business in the square today?"

"I'd say I'd need to hear more to know what mark you're shooting at."

"Fair enough! Simply put, Tobias coddles his subjects disgracefully. The inevitable result?" Bouvier slapped his beefy palm on the desk. "They take advantage!"

He leaned forward. His big face, already glossed with sweat, flushed redder and redder as he warmed to his subject. "Tobias talks about the cost of defending us properly. But there are plenty of idle hands in this ville, let me assure you. For one thing, we have wagloads of these backwoods squatters who don't contribute anything to the common good. They should be compelled to give back, rather than continue to take and take. Don't you agree?"

Who aren't forced to live on your pay so you control them, more like, Ryan thought. "I hear that," he said.

"But Tobias won't crack the whip when it's called for. He wants the people to love him. Realists, Mr. Cawdor—men like you and me—realize it's better to be feared than loved."

Ryan raised his tumbler to sip so he wouldn't have to respond. The word "loved" went through his belly like a needle point. He thought about how good it would feel to smash this man's fat face for profaning a word whose true meaning he had no idea of.

"And that's what caused the attack last night," Bouvier said. "Sheer lack of discipline among the people of this ville."

"I thought it was men who let fear of the Beast get so deep in their bones they lost all sense," Ryan said. "That and an ambitious man with more power and wealth than sense or loyalty."

"Huh?"

Bouvier blinked. He didn't seem angry, just a bit lost that the script had been deviated from. Ryan decided he wasn't used to listening to any voice but his own.

"Well, of course, of course," the big man said. "And that poor fool Franc was only able to rouse those sorry dirtbags to suicidal folly because Tobias hadn't seen to it that they feared their baron more than their boss."

"Likely."

Bouvier nodded emphatically, as if he'd just won a major concession in some big business negotiation. "So, just between you and me and the wall, Haven needs a strong baron. Don't get me wrong. Tobias is a fine man. A great warrior. He means well. But he's too nice, and being nice and having good intentions grease the chute to hell."

He dropped his voice low. "Do you see where this is going, Mr. Cawdor?"

"You want to be baron?"

"Me?" Bouvier sounded genuinely surprised. "Oh, no. No, that wouldn't work at all. To be sure, I'm a skilled manager, and I possess many of the attributes necessary for true leadership. But Haven in its current sad state needs a leader type, if you know what I mean. A hero whom the people can rally around!"

I've seen Tobias fight, Ryan thought. He looks like enough

of a hero for me, swinging those two swords of his. He didn't say it. The truth was, he was enjoying the conversation.

"Where do we fit into this?" he asked instead.

"Haven't I made my meaning plain, Mr. Cawdor? I want you to step up and be baron of Haven."

"Mighty kind offer, there, Bouvier." Ryan rose. "But I'm not looking to be the baron of anyplace. Even if I was, if I was the kind of a man who repaid a man's hospitality by stabbing him in the back and throwing him out of his own house, what kind of man would I be?"

Bouvier looked up as if he didn't understand what Ryan was saying. "You mean, you won't do it?"

"You catch on fast, Bouvier. Anyhow, I suspect the way things would really work out is, I'd only be your puppet. And I don't crave having your hand shoved up my ass to work my jaws."

Bouvier's face went purple, then white. "How dare you?"

"Easy."

A sickly grin spread across Bouvier's heavy face. "So you think I'll let you talk to me like that and just walk out of here free and clear? You know a bit too much to be allowed to wander around loose now, don't you think?"

"No," Ryan said, "I don't think. See, a little while back you may have heard an owl hoot. But that was no owl. It was my friends letting me know the coldhearts you had waiting outside to put the hard arm on me if I didn't play along have been taken down and tied up safely. They can all be glad they don't all have second mouths to whistle through. You can, too, if you care about them."

Bouvier laughed, a bit too brassily and loud. "You really expect me to believe that?"

A scratching sound came from the window. "Move your eyes right, Bouvier," Ryan said. "Easy, now. Don't want to make any sudden moves."

Bouvier looked that way and gasped. Jak's ghostly face was leering in at him—over the vented rib and front sight of his Colt Python handblaster, whose muzzle he'd dragged down the screen to get Bouvier's attention.

"But that wall hangs out over the water!" Bouvier exclaimed, almost indignantly.

"My friend Jak there, he climbs like an old wall lizard. See, we been wandering the Deathlands for years, my friends and I. You think this is mebbe the first time some small-time schemer tried to muscle us into backing their little ville power play? Not that it ever makes any kind of sense but bad."

Bouvier looked thunderstruck. "What do you mean?"

"You try to sign us on because you reckon we got strong arms and cold hearts. You say you think I might make a good baron because I'm strong. Well, yeah, I am, and worse, I'm smart. And as hearts run, none run colder than mine when business needs getting done.

"All of which leads up to—if we're so hard and bad and mean, how is it anything but stupe to go out of your way to step on our shadows by threatening us?"

He started to leave. "Wait, Cawdor!" Bouvier called.

Ryan stopped.

"If you tell the baron—" Bouvier said. He had his bluster back. He either had bigger balls than Ryan gave him credit for, or was a bigger stupe.

Ryan cut him off. "Don't sweat that. Blackwood may be out of the usual line of cut from a different kind of metal than your standard-issue baron, but if he gets to smelling sufficient smoke, even he's going to reckon there's a fire. So I just plain don't want to know."

He grinned as an idea struck him. Leaning over the desk, he snagged the half-full whiskey bottle by the neck.

"This'll pay me for my time. If you're half as smart as

you think, you'll call us square. I'm going to walk away now, Bouvier. You'll be happier if you do likewise."

"Please, wait," the hog-sweating merchant cried. But as usual, Ryan was as good as his word.

Once out the warehouse's front door he cut quickly left, once again to get him out of the fatal funnel. Before he walked ten paces upslope J.B. fell in beside him.

"Any trouble?" Ryan asked.

The Armorer grinned. "Not a bit."

Ryan tossed him the bottle, which J.B. caught one-handed. "What's this?"

"Payout," Ryan said. "You won the bet. He really *was* that stupe."

"I TELL YOU, there was nothing I could have done!" the fat man blubbered. "No power on Earth was going to sway him."

"I'm disappointed, Mr. Bouvier," the man who stood in deeper shadow next to one of the big house's outbuildings said. "Really, I expected better of you."

The man didn't raise his voice. He'd long ago learned he seldom had to. Plus, of course, it was useful for these little conspiratorial tête-à-têtes. While they were behind the house, on the far side from the rooms belonging to the baron, Elizabeth, and those ever-so-troublesome guests of theirs, it never paid to take things for granted.

Indeed, his entire career depended on not taking things for granted.

Bouvier shook his head. "You don't understand. He was a raging beast! There's no controlling him."

"Now, somehow I find it in myself to doubt that, Mr. Bouvier. Ryan Cawdor strikes me as a man entirely in control of himself."

"Well, mebbe it was just the, the animal *feel* of the man. He would have snapped my neck like a twig if he could."

"*That* I believe."

He uttered a short sigh. "It appears we have ourselves a problem."

"I'll say! He's got to be gotten rid of. He's dangerous, I tell you! He'll be the ruin of us all."

"Put your mind at rest, Mr. Bouvier. I will attend to the matter. Cleaning up other people's messes is my specialty."

Bouvier worked his mouth in and out several times, making his jowls wobble. Finally he decided the best course was neither bluster nor blithering gratitude.

"Right," he contented himself with saying. He turned and bustled off toward his own holdings on the ville's far side.

Tall and slim and elegant as a riding crop, the other man stood on the lawn watching the broad figure recede into the night. The crickets and the tree frogs sang counterpoint in the ever-present woods.

He heard a soft step on the damp grass behind him.

"So another of your clever schemes amounts to nothing, St. Vincent."

He turned to where the slim woman stood. "Amélie. How convenient of you to arrive at this juncture."

"I listened," she said. "You knew I was in the house, looking in on Elizabeth." She spoke the last word with quiet, venomous intent.

"Oh, indeed. And the outlander woman."

"Her, too."

St. Vincent felt the lines of his face deepen as he looked back to where the night had at last swallowed Bouvier's bulk.

"These continuing tensions are aging me prematurely," he complained. "I know it. Still, this man Cawdor would make a far better horse to ride to unlimited power and wealth than that milksop Tobias. He's a man of decision as well as action. I know it!"

"Tobias's ambitions are all for building up Haven," Mercier said, a note of defensiveness creeping into her quiet voice.

"And I lust to be the power behind a greater throne than Haven can ever encompass." He shook his head, jutting his lean chin with its narrow beard. "Every man has his price. I just have to ascertain what Ryan's is. And I will."

"I fear these newcomers."

St. Vincent laughed. "Don't, my dear. That which you fear in them is the very thing what will bring us what we want."

He turned to her. "And now, I believe there's a certain little task that you should be about performing."

The shoulders rose and fell in a petulant, theatric sigh. "If I must."

He allowed a hint of asperity into his voice. "You agreed to the plan. Now is no time to hang back."

"Tobias must not be hurt," Mercier said. "You promised."

"And so I did." He made fussy shooing gestures with the backs of his fine hands. "Quick, now! Off you go, child."

"STUPES," BOUVIER muttered as he made his way through deep, dark woods.

The flame of the lantern he was carrying was turned up all the way. But it barely made an impression on the bottomless shadows under the trees, or the black branches that seemed to stretch down toward his face like tentacles. It was fortunate that he knew his own way home so well the lantern itself was but a convenience. A luxury almost.

"Fools. Ungrateful bastards."

He was surrounded by mental and moral midgets. He had thought Ryan Cawdor to be of altogether different stuff. Different stature. A man to bestride history's stage and own it.

But a man of action, withal. Not of contemplation or pondering high strategy. That was where a man of Bouvier's unique talents could best serve a vibrant, powerful ville and baron.

Yet somehow he had misjudged his man.

"I made a mistake," he muttered. "Yes, admit it—a mistake! I have to face fact and move on. Now Cawdor will be dealt with. And I'll just have to keep looking for the right man."

He shook his head, feeling regret. Actual regret. A waste, he thought, such a terrible waste.

A soft rustle came from the woods to his left.

He stopped. Inside hot skin, his blood was ice.

He knew every sound that came from these woods, in every season and weather condition. Just as he knew the path that brought him home most directly through the woods surrounding the ville, instead of taking the corduroyed road the long way around. What he had heard didn't belong.

Something was moving softly to his left.

"Who's there?" he demanded, reaching for the butt of the pistol he'd stuck through his waistband when he'd stopped by his office in the Heights to pick up the lantern. "Come out! Show yourself!"

Another rustle came from the brush. Something pale flashed through the edges of his vision, crossing his backtrail, now on his right.

He turned that way. The sound continued, rhythmic, like quiet steps.

Coming toward him.

His hand fell away from the butt of his pistol. All bravado was forgotten. Here was a horror he couldn't fight.

He turned and ran. His legs were short and his weight was large, but he made good time along the winding path, leaping over roots that humped across the path as though to trip him, slipping on fallen and decomposing leaves.

But he couldn't outrun doom.

He had gone no more than thirty yards when he heard it rushing on him. Squealing in terror, he turned.

It was smaller than he expected. A pale creature of wide eyes, fangs and claws, with a wild dark mane of coarse hair.

But when the jaws closed on his face, he felt his own bones crunch like crisp pastry crusts. Claws tore through his shirt, through the fat of his belly, the muscle and the tough membrane of his body wall like a crow's talons through a writhing grub.

The agony as the monster began to dig his living guts right out of him almost made him forget the pain in his bitten face.

Almost.

Chapter Twenty-Three

"Ryan."

He stirred on his cot and tried to burrow deeper into his pillow. Normally he snapped awake as if spring-loaded. Not this time. News of the brutal murder and evisceration of the merchant Bouvier, quite unmistakably by the Beast, had roused the house in the early hours. Ryan had tramped out with the baron, his men, and J.B. and Jak on a fruitless search for the monster. He had only slunk back to bed as false dawn stained the eastern sky above the trees like spilled spoiled milk.

It was the final anvil piled atop days of fatigue amassed through worry, stress, healing, and of course, mortal combat.

"Ryan, get up." It was Mildred's voice. "We have a visitor."

Grumbling, he sat up. He rubbed both hands over his face, reflexively careful not to dislodge the patch that covered his left eye. Running hands back through his long, dense, slightly curly black hair, he blinked his good eye wearily at the intruder.

"Mildred, is that any way to wake a man?"

"You think I'm nuts? I don't want you to come awake and start choking me because you think I'm a stickie or a mutie bear. Be glad I don't do what I normally would, and stand back even farther and chuck pebbles at you."

Her words finally percolated into his befuddled mind. "What do you mean, we have a visitor?"

"Come see for yourself."

"MUTIE!" JAK Lauren stressed between his teeth.

"Is not," Mildred said, biting into a chunk of reasonably fresh papaya. Despite the on-again off-again blockade by Black Gang pirates, the barony had obtained a lot of fruit grown in the Caribbean and Central America through its sea trade. "Just a dwarf."

"What that?" the albino teen asked.

Ryan stood on the porch with Mildred, Jak, J.B. and Doc. The porch roof offered shade from the early-morning sun, already inclined to stick to the skin and burn like boiling sugar. The smell of flowers in the beds along the house front, the ones that had escaped trampling in the other night's battle, was strong and sweet in Ryan's nostrils. Blackwood, his sister, his aide Barton and his sec boss, Guerrero, stood out on the lawn near the gazebo talking to a man dressed in a long linen smock and dungarees.

Or mebbe half-man, Ryan thought. The visitor was a black man, an oldie from his short wiry white hair and beard and the wrinkled face it framed. But he was trim and held himself upright, and his movements were those of somebody in pretty good shape.

He stood about a yard tall.

"A dwarf," Mildred repeated.

"That's a person, but your half-size model."

"Right," Jak said.

Whatever he was, he was speaking in a high-pitched voice, though Ryan couldn't make out the words. Blackwood was nodding gravely. Then he turned to beckon the group on the porch.

"Ryan, friends," he said, "please join us. This gentleman has brought news for you."

"For us?" Mildred echoed. Ryan shrugged and walked forward. The rest trailed after.

As he reached the small group standing out in the Gulf

Coast sun, he saw Amélie Mercier walking up the crushed-shell path from the ville with a servant who'd apparently been sent to fetch her. Like Elizabeth Blackwood, she sensibly carried a parasol.

"Ryan Cawdor," the baron said, indicating the little dude, "this is Achille."

He introduced the rest of Ryan's party. Achille nodded gravely in turn to each.

"Pleased to meet ya!" he said, pumping Ryan's hand enthusiastically. As did at least half the people they'd run into in the ville, he spoke with a Cajun French accent.

"I come bringing important word to Monsieur Cawdor." He dragged the first syllable of Ryan's name out long.

"That's me," Ryan said. "Shoot."

The man blinked at him for a moment. He had large pale amber eyes. Despite some yellowing around the edges, they were as sharp as a bird's.

"My mistress the healer, wise woman, and incomparable seeress has words for your ears, *monsieur.* Others may come, as you will. But she will speak her truths only to you in person."

"Who's your mistress," Ryan asked wryly, "shy of all the excess wordage."

"She is known as Sweet Julie Blind Eyes," Mercier said crisply as she joined the group. "She is a folk healer, held in great esteem by the people of the ville. She lives miles back in the bayous. Hundreds of people make the pilgrimage to visit her each year."

"What's with the 'seeress' part of that really impressive résumé?" Mildred asked.

"She has the sight," Achille announced proudly. "Both far and second."

Mildred cocked a brow at Mercier. "And what do you think of this, Amélie?"

"What there is of science in the Deathlands has recognized for years that certain mutations convey limited powers of telepathy, clairvoyance and precognition," the healer said. "Precognition meaning, glimpsing visions of possible futures, since it is demonstrated that acting with foreknowledge can prevent foreseen events from coming true."

Mildred blinked at her. "Girlfriend, we have *got* to talk."

"Later," Ryan rasped. "Why should I hike way back in the swamp to talk to this blind woman of yours?"

"Because Mistress Sweet Julie, whose eyes see nothing of this world, but see most clearly in the One Behind It, she and she alone can tell you what you must do if you wish your woman Krysty Wroth back."

Ryan drew his head back, stunned by the words. It's no big thing he knows her name, he reminded himself. Given the bayou grapevine, the whole ville and beyond probably knows about Krysty by now.

He looked to the Blackwood siblings. "Is there anything to this woman? Any chance she's likely to know something useful?"

"She is legitimately wise," Elizabeth said, "as well as honest. And her knowledge of herbs and traditional remedies is encyclopedic."

"Our family has consulted her on occasion," her brother said. With visible reluctance he added, "For generations."

"You're the consummate rationalist, Amélie," Mildred said. "What's your take? Might this witch-woman have the goods?"

Mercier shrugged. Like Elizabeth she looked fatigued. There were dark circles beneath both women's eyes. Ryan supposed she'd been working late in her lab.

"*C'est possible,*" she said. "That is one of the things that drew my father here, along with the late baron's offer of employment and full assistance, of course. This environment contains a wealth of plants whose possible pharmacological properties have never been adequately cataloged. Some, undoubtedly, have arisen since the skydark. They form a major portion of my own inquiries."

"So this self-proclaimed seeress—" Doc began.

"May well possess insight that could prove of value to the treatment of Miss Wroth's condition, yes. At least, I believe such a chance exists."

Mercier looked at Ryan. "I must warn you that there is no certainty that she will know a cure, no matter how strongly she believes."

"Only thing I know is certain," Ryan said, his voice sounding to his own ears as if he'd been gargling battery acid, "is one day we'll all find dirt hitting us in the eyes. A chance is good enough for me. Baron?"

"Of course," Blackwood said, rubbing his hands together. "You'll have everything you need, of course. We'll take a small flotilla of flatboats. We'll need a small security contingent accompanying us. Sweet Julie dwells near the regions claimed by the swampies. Although they hold her in superstitious fear, and would not harm her, such forbearance doesn't extend to us."

"Wait," Ryan said. "Us?"

The baron smiled. "I wouldn't miss this for the world," he said.

As BLACKWOOD SAID, Sweet Julie Blind Eyes lived in the backwaters beyond the ville. Ryan and company endured four hours of poling and paddling through molasses-thick humid heat and clouds of crunchy, biting insects. At least the companions didn't have to share any of the propulsion duties, which mostly left them with hands and energy free to slap the mosquitoes.

Sweet Julie Blind Eyes sat awaiting them as they trudged

up the slope from the little uneven pier on the shore of her tiny island. No larger in any direction than Ryan could heave a rock the size of his head, it had grown up out of the confluence of several channels, so that it had at least fifty feet of water on all sides, around the roots of an ancient cypress. Or rather, several trees with boles grown together.

Like a vertical mouth, a crack eight feet high yawned in the compound trunk of the still-living trees, at least twelve feet across. The doomie sat in the opening like a housewife on her stoop, her long skirts of dark brown broadcloth flowing to conceal her legs and whatever she sat on. Her hair, silver-gray rather than white, flowed in vast crinkly waves over the shoulders of a blouse made of patches of many colors, including what had to be predark prints on scavvied fabric. Years seemed to have concentrated her so that she was as skinny yet dense as one of the gnarled roots of her mighty tree home. Although not so twisty. She sat erect, and though the joints were prominent on the hands that methodically crushed herbs in a small mortar and pestle she held on a thick board in her lap, that seemed because she had shrunk around the bones, not because of arthritic deposits.

"You have *got* to be shitting me," Mildred said emphatically but mostly to herself. "Talk about a blatant female-genitalia symbol! If it was a flower, it'd have Georgia O'Keeffe's signature right next to it."

That made no sense Ryan could even imagine. It didn't sound like anything that he needed to know. Or maybe wanted to. He let it slide.

The woman turned blind eyes toward them. Her face was long and as spare as her hands, with knobs for cheekbones and the skin drawn hollow beneath. But her features showed little sign of wrinkling. She had been a looker once, Ryan reckoned. Her eyes were as white as pearls.

"Welcome, Tobias!" she called in a voice that was strong

and clear though cracked by the weight of years. "You've grown strong and confident in step since last you visited my isle."

She turned her parchment-hued face toward Ryan. "And you must be Ryan Cawdor."

"Mutie!" Jak said for the second time today.

The woman's brow wrinkled. "Yes, yes. Weren't you told that part? But I don't need mutie powers to tell me those things, young man. I just use the senses I was given. By sound I recognize young Tobias, his step and breathing. By common sense I know he's brought retainers. By smell I recognize that some of his party have spent their lives elsewhere, eating foods not found in our hospitable swamps, or brought only as luxury imports."

"But how'd you know Ryan, ma'am?" J.B. asked. He sounded a touch uncertain himself.

She laughed, more a pleasant bubbling flow, with perhaps a touch of static, than a crone's cackle. "Lots of people across the Deathlands mention your deeds, youngster. You'd be J. B. Dix. And Mildred Wyeth, a healer and Dr. Theophilus Tanner. Which would make the young man so worried by muties Jak Lauren, once known as the White Wolf along this very coast a ways."

Blackwood raised a brow. "With all respect to my honored guests, *I* never heard of them before they washed up on the fringes of Haven."

"Sweet Julie spreads her nets wide," she said. "News comes to me from everywhere. Through the wind, the water, the very earth beneath us."

"Just heard 'bout us from ville people!" Jak accused.

She laughed again. "Guilty as charged. But I do not lie. I *have* heard of your exploits. Allow an old lady the pleasure of mystifying for its own sake."

"If you don't mind," Ryan said, "why don't we get right to the matter at hand. How can I bring Krysty back?"

"What would you give to have Krysty Wroth, the red-headed beauty, at your side and hale once more?"

"Anything."

"Anything and everything?"

"I wouldn't sacrifice my friends to buy her back," he said. "Short of that, yeah. Anything and everything."

She nodded. "You may have to pay that. What about your own life? Would you swap that, die so Krysty might live?"

"If it comes to that," he said, "yes."

She nodded. "That, too, it might cost you."

"Tell me," he said. After a moment he moistened lips that had gone dry despite air you could practically grab and from which squeeze droplets of water. "Please."

"I do not possess the cure," she said.

Ignoring Mildred's muttered, "Oh for fuck's sake," she went on. "But I know the one who does—Papa Dough, vodoun king of the swampies in this region. He holds the key to Krysty's cure. You must go to him in the darkest depths of the swamp to get the cure."

"But this is madness!" Blackwood exclaimed. "All my men and myself wouldn't be enough to carve our way to the heart of Papa Dough's stronghold and force him to disgorge this knowledge. If we could, we'd have taken his head long ago, and put an end to the evil that afflicts our people!"

"No, Tobias," she said, "not you and the Black Gang together could conquer Papa Dough's kingdom. The cost of trying would be the destruction of all you have worked for. You're wise enough not to follow that path to ruin. Are you sure, though, that your heroic ability with those swords you wear strapped across your fine strong back hasn't clouded your judgment otherwise? It takes two to wage a war, Tobias.

Mebbe talking more and cutting less would spare you and your people much treasure and pain."

"You sure that's true, ma'am?" J.B. asked. "We've seen plenty of villes overrun because they couldn't defend themselves and were attacked through no fault of their own."

"I'm not advising helplessness, young man," she said in a tone that reminded Ryan of his tutors back at Front Royal. "I'm saying there is a time to fight, and a time to talk. It is usually best to leave the former for when the latter fails."

Blackwood shook his head. "The swampies don't seem inclined to negotiate. They only slay and burn."

"Have you tried talking to them, Tobias Blackwood?"

"They are as beasts," he said. "Insensate."

Sweet Julie turned back to Ryan. "Do *you* think you can fight your way to Papa Dough and take what you want from him by force?"

"If that's what it takes to get Krysty back," he said, "I'll do it or die trying. I've been in way too many fights for that to be my first choice, though."

"Quit stringing us along!" Mildred snapped. "Is there any way to get what we need for Krysty without fighting? Or is it possible at all? Are you leading us into a trap?"

"Now, Mildred," J.B. said.

"Don't 'now, Mildred' me, John! Why're we even listening to this, this phony psychic?"

"Because your whitecoat pal Mercier told us it was an ace idea, Mildred," Ryan said. Mildred's jaw shut with an almost audible clack.

"The good healer means well," Sweet Julie said, "even if she allows concern for her friends to overwhelm her manners. She raises sound questions. The answers are, there may be. It may be possible. And no, if I wanted to trap you, there are a thousand less elaborate snares I could set—and you're wise enough to know that in traps as in most things simpler means stronger."

"I'll do it," Ryan said.

"What?" Mildred yelped. "Has your brain gone critical mass on us?"

He shrugged. "I didn't say 'you.' I didn't say 'we.' Said 'I.' I'm going. I won't ask any of the rest of you to go along. You should probably stay behind and help Mercier with her whitecoat stuff, anyway, Mildred."

"No way! No *way* are you leaving the womenfolk behind when you go into danger! Anyway, I'm as fed up as you are, Ryan, cooling my heels watching Krysty not die and not get better without a thing on God's green Earth I can do about it! I'm coming if I have to steal a boat and paddle after you myself."

"There need be no talk of stealing boats, Dr. Wyeth," Blackwood said gravely. "Whatever help I or my ville can spare you, will be yours."

He looked at the Sweet Julie. "Still, I cannot help question the wisdom of this journey. I can see no other ending for it than blood and doom."

"There is none," she answered. "The questions are, whose blood? Whose doom? I can tell you that if the voyage is undertaken, much suffering and loss will be averted."

He shook his head. "I find it hard to see—"

"That thing I foretold, when you came to me ten summers ago as a skinny tadpole," she said. "How did that go, Tobias?"

He bowed his head. "It came to pass as you said it would."

"Why cannot you predict the future for us with some particularity, madam?" Doc asked. "At least give us some hint of what awaits us in the land of the swampies?"

"What can I, an old blind lady who sits in the crack of a tree all day each day mixing potions, tell Ryan Cawdor and companions about fighting and dangers? You will face forbidding country, horrid beasts, hostile muties, and terrifying tests of your character as well as courage. There. What have I told you that you didn't already know?"

"Well," Doc said, "since you put it that way—"

"Besides," she said, "my doom-seeing powers tend not to be rich in specifics, and are nothing I can control, anyway. All I get are occasional glimpses through the great, ever-shifting fog of probability. I have no more to give you than what I have already."

Doc nodded. "Ryan, you know you can count on me."

"Goin'," Jak announced. "Not afraid swamps, beasts, mutie boogers!"

"I'm not used to being Tail-End Charlie on a thing like this," J.B. said, taking off his glasses and cleaning them, "but it shouldn't need saying anyway. You can always count on me, Ryan. Double when Krysty's involved!"

Mildred scowled thunderously. "I already said I was in," she said. "But—but what guarantee do we have that we aren't chasing a will-o'-the-wisp? That we can actually bring Krysty back this way?"

"If you want guarantees, young woman," Sweet Julie said, her voice for the first time snapping with asperity, "you've come to the wrong place."

Chapter Twenty-Four

"Are you completely out of your mind, Ryan?" Mildred demanded as the pirogue slid along the dark water, leaving a wake of lazy ripples that disturbed the tiny pale green plants that covered the surface. "Bringing us on this wild-goose chase up this damned sewer on the word of some crazy old charlatan?"

"You wanted to come along, Mildred," J.B. pointed out. He rode the third of the three small watercraft with Doc. Ryan and Jak were on the lead boat. Mildred was in the middle with two of their six volunteers from Haven, whom she had dubbed Team Heart of Darkness for some reason. The others were doled out by pairs in the other pirogues.

"Yes, I did," Mildred said. "But that doesn't mean I thought it was a good idea."

"Too late turn back," Jak called, grinning. He was standing in the bow, keeping watch. The two Havenites in the boat with him and Ryan, towheaded teenage boys named Cole and Cody who claimed not to be related although they were near identical and inseparable, had quit urging him to sit. He'd shown his customary grace and his own not-inconsiderable experience with water-wags, so they made an exception in his case.

A screw-steamer riverboat, the *Gypsy Tailwind,* had given the eleven adventurers a ride up the Blackwood Bayou half a day, or about eight miles as J.B. reckoned it through use of his microsextant. They'd tied up to a tree along a sandbar to let

Ryan and company pull up the three pirogues the steamboat had been towing and transfer themselves and supplies aboard. The *Tailwind*'s captain, a guy named Mackerel, tooted the steam whistle three times in farewell as the pirogues paddled up a bayou to the northwest. Then he proceeded on his merry way upstream, carrying a load of Caribbean fruit and planks sawn by Haven's combo water and stream-driven sawmill to a ville called Coverton.

A swollen orange sun hung low above the trees. The six Havenites who had come to guide and guard the companions into Papa Dough's domain rowed the pirogues down a bayou so narrow Ryan could practically stretch out his arms and trail his fingers through the long, skinny beards of Spanish moss that dangled from the cypress boughs. Bullfrogs uttered their bass-fiddle moans from the shallows. A nutria sculled past the other way with powerful strokes of its tail, effort fully holding his blunt, buck-toothed, oversize-rat face clear of his own bow wave.

One of the juveniles, who Ryan had been assured had battle experience, provided the propulsion for the small flat-bottomed boat he shared with them. In the next pirogue Mildred sat alongside Rameau, a dignified yet easy-humored black man of about J.B.'s size and stature, who added to the piratical cast of his dark, rakish ax-blade features with a neat beard, a gold ring in one ear, and a red bandanna tied around his long dreadlocks. He bossed the Havenite contingent.

Rowing was Rameau's taller shadow Bluebottle, just as lean as the boss, with big harsh cheekbones and a bronze cast to him that suggested American Indian blood. A seasoned mutie fighter, he was one of a pair of guides Blackwood had insisted on sending along.

The second was Terance, another frontiersman type and guide. A squint-eyed rawboned redhead, he had almost grotesquely huge and powerful hands stuck on the ends of his snake-wiry arms. He occupied the final boat with J.B. and Ferd, who rowed. Ferd was clearly along for muscle. He was about six and a half feet of it, built like a stump, and about as communicative. He had a face like a ham and big tufts of brown hair sprouting from his saucer ears.

"We'd best find us a nice dry place to haul the boats ashore and get settled for the night," Rameau said. "This is no place a body wants to get caught careless by night."

Chevrons and wings of night herons flapped majestically overhead, interspersed with the occasional outsize great blue heron, their spear-beaked heads tucked back against their bodies on their long necks, their legs trailing all stilty behind. Flying higher, the other way, were flocks of pink Roseate spoonbills, heading for their nests in the saline mangal along the coast. Smaller birds flicked and squabbled in the underbrush close by on both sides.

"Whatever you say," Ryan called back. Blackwood had generously placed him in overall command of the expedition. "You know the country. I always try to listen to the man who knows."

Rameau grinned a startlingly bright grin and nodded. "That's the way to enjoy a long life," he said. "Peel your eyes for a suitable landing, generic blond boys! Justify your existence on this Earth."

"So, Ryan, you must love this woman much, to walk into the open jaws of an alligator for her as you do." Rameau's dark eyes glittered in the light of the campfire.

Big bats fluttered around the fringes, feasting on bugs drawn by the dancing light. Overhead Chuck-will's-widows wheeled and cried out, occasionally visible as dark cruciform shapes against the stars, or when the firelight touched their speckled breast feathers. The crickets and the tree frogs sang their nightly songs. Somewhere out there Bluebottle prowled on sentry duty.

Ryan grunted. Then he realized he owed Krysty more than that. "Yes," he said clearly. "Yes, I do."

Rameau nodded sagely. "She must be much woman."

"She is," Mildred said, "though maybe not how you mean."

Rameau laughed, as he often did. "Dear healer lady, you wrong me! I hear about heroic deeds with Tech-nomads. Krysty Wroth must be a woman of great smarts and wisdom, as well as beauty."

"I hear she has big old boobs," Cody announced. Or Cole. Even though he knew it was a failure of a key command skill, Ryan was damned if he could tell one from the next. He wondered about their allegedly respective daddies, and if they were really as unrelated as their mommas apparently assured them they were.

The white-blond kid oofed as Terance, who squatted on his haunches next to him turning several small carcasses that sizzled and crisped on spits over the fire, gave him an elbow in his ribs.

"Hey!" the kid yelped. "What you do that for? *Cochon!*"

"Teach you some respect, boy," the gaunt and somewhat mad-eyed man said. "Call me a name again, and you'll be eating your meat with about four less teeth."

"Insulting the woman of a man like Ryan," Rameau said, "losing teeth should be the least of your fears."

The boy lapsed into sullen silence. His clone, sitting on the other side from Terance, tittered. The boy shot him an evil glance.

"No roughhousing," Rameau said.

"If you don't mind my saying so, Captain Rameau," said Doc, who had hung the appellation on the Havenite, not that Rameau appeared to mind, "I think the real question is, what motivates you and your comrades to accompany us, given that you all seem convinced we march directly to our doom?"

"For glory, of course," Rameau instantly declared, then laughed as if he'd told a wonderful joke.

"Glory's not much use to a body when dirt's hitting your face," observed J.B., squatting across the fire, next to Mildred.

"*Au contraire,* my friend! That is when it is of most use. If you have fame, that is the only thing that distinguishes you from the billions and billions who have lived and died and been instantly forgotten."

"If you say so," the Armorer said. "I mainly value what I can shoot, eat or—" he noticed Mildred giving him a raised eyebrow "—hold on to," he finished lamely.

She patted his thigh. Ryan thought his thin cheeks flushed slightly. Mebbe a trick of the firelight, he thought.

"Baron say I go," Ferd announced in a voice like a boulder rolling down a wooden chute. "I go."

Even his local companions stared at him in surprise. Those were as many words as Ryan had heard him say in the whole journey so far.

"Baron Tobias says he'll pay us!" Cody said.

"And we can count on him in the future for jobs and rewards and stuff!" Cole added.

"Mebbe it's peering down the bore of a gift blaster," J.B. said, "but remember what they say about barons and gratitude."

"Ah, but Tobias is different," Rameau said. "I admit myself that the fact he asked me specifically to go, made it hard to say no." He grinned. "And the promised reward for guiding you into swampie territory didn't hurt, either, eh?"

"I notice you don't say anything about bringing us back alive," Mildred said sourly.

Rameau shrugged expressively. "Baron Tobias asks much

of his people, which we give freely because he gives much to us. But he doesn't ask us to perform miracles, my dear lady!"

"Nutria's done," Terance announced.

"WHAT COULD YOU possibly have been thinking?" Though it never got loud, St. Vincent's voice rose to a squeak of outrage. "Did you deliberately betray me?"

The confounded woman had the audacity to smirk at him, he thought.

"Your way wasn't working," Amélie Mercier said. "So I decided to get the intruders out of the way for a time myself and leave us both an open field once again." She shrugged artlessly. "Perhaps for good."

"So you bribed that wretched long-haired mountebank who lives in a tree to spin a fanciful tale for Tobias and his guests?"

He had his voice under control again. It was his baseline prudence, no more that had kept him alive through two barons—and the bloody transition between them, in which he had played such a key role. Tobias lay asleep three stories up, exhausted. His sister slept like someone well drugged, which she was. He feared no servants overhearing. He had personally chased them all off to their beds in their quarters in the building behind the main house. He had taught them to fear the consequences of crossing him.

If only he could have done as much for Tobias's whitecoat.

"*Mais non.* I decided on the spot to take advantage of what she said. After all, I could as well have ended it all with the proper words. Tobias trusts my judgment on scientific affairs."

"And we know how prudent he is to trust you, eh, my dear?"

"I would never hurt him!"

Then suddenly the veneer of scholarly reserve, and any

hint of civilization, peeled back like lips from a snarling wolf's teeth. "That bitch sister of his is another question! How I wish I dared put her out of the way!"

"Damn fool woman!" St. Vincent exclaimed. "Don't you know Elizabeth is no threat to you that way? Tobias's love for her is purely brotherly."

He was horrified the instant the words were out of his mouth, although he understood well that a bullet would never go back in the blaster. That they were true made the outburst all the more inexcusable, not less. St. Vincent was a man who held a high regard for the truth. It was why he was most economical in giving it away.

But from the woman's sly look, which, though she doubtless thought it concealed, was an open book to such a master of manipulation as St. Vincent, he knew at once his foolish candor wasn't going to be punished after all.

"Even if that's true," Mercier said, "her *condition* obsesses him. He'll never look at me as long as she's around."

"So why not just inject her with air, cause a fatal embolism, and be done with it?" St. Vincent had read extensively; even as a lad he had understood instinctively what potential power that gave him over a population most of which couldn't read, and of those who could, most didn't care to.

"Because Tobias would suspect something was wrong. He's so brilliant. And it would take no genius to figure out I'm the one in charge of her care." She smiled. "Besides, I rely upon your cunning to dispose of Elizabeth. You are the Devil."

The healer, the committed rationalist, spoke the words with simple conviction.

He smiled. "Yes, dear child," he said, "I *am* the Devil, which you would do well to remember should it come into your powerful but unduly focused mind to cross me again."

She left. He stood glaring after her, realizing his pulse was elevated.

Calm yourself, man, he told himself sternly. Just because we're entering the endgame doesn't give you license to get worked up and lose your self-control.

The pieces and plans were in play. The many tentacles he had cast forth were converging. If one failed, another wouldn't.

The outlanders' departure was a setback, but it was only that. Whether or not Ryan Cawdor and his friends joined with him—whether or not they ever came back from Papa Dough's domain—Haven would have a new baron soon. A strong, vigorously ambitious baron.

And St. Vincent would be the true power behind the throne.

"Naive child," he said, shaking his head as he thought again of Amélie Mercier, "do you really believe I'll simply let you sail away safely into exile with Tobias once I supplant him?"

He smiled thinly between his immaculately manicured beard and mustache.

"But then, I suppose you really do." And he took himself off to bed, thinking happy thoughts about the folly of the wise.

SOMEWHERE IN THE MORNING'S black hours, a bloodcurdling scream yanked Ryan from sleep.

All they found of Ferd was his big footprints in damp soil beneath a tree, with a double-size pile of human excrement between them, and some blood splashed at the base of the tree he'd squatted to relieve himself under.

"Where could he possibly have gone?" Mildred demanded. She had her ZKR blaster in her hand and a wild look in her eyes by the light of torches of resin-rich loblolly pine. "He was a huge, powerful man. He couldn't just have vanished."

The nearest water was a good fifty, sixty feet away, Ryan noted. There were no drag marks.

"Here," Jak said, squatting fifteen feet away from the base of the live oak. He brought his torch low to the spongy ground. "Jaguar."

Bluebottle hunkered down beside the albino youth. *"Oui,"* he said. *"Tigre."*

"You have got to be joking," Mildred said. "How could a cat do that? Make a big man disappear?"

Ryan walked over to examine the print. The tracks were round and surprisingly big.

"He was a big boy, that cat," Rameau told Mildred. "Two hundred fifty pounds easily."

"But Ferd was enormous. He must've weighed more than that, easy!"

"The African leopard, a much smaller animal, can carry a dead antelope several times its own weight up into a tree," Doc declared. "And the jaguar has exceedingly powerful jaws."

Jak had stood. First he looked up into the branches, then he prowled around behind the heels of the footprints, swinging his torch a foot above the ground.

"Here how went down," he declared. He raised his torch. "See claw marks?"

The others gathered around, being careful not to get too close and track up the spoor Jak had found. Only Terance remained back by the embers of the fire, guarding the camp and their gear.

As he frowned up at the heavy branch jutting lowest from the oak tree on this side, maybe ten feet off the ground, Ryan saw fresh gouges in the bark. The moist wood underneath was yellow in the torchlight.

"Cat climb down behind while Fred squatted," Jak said. "Jump on back."

Next he brought the torch toward where some fallen oak leaves were mashed into the ground. "Cat kill quick. Bit through skull."

"Through the skull?" J.B. said. "Rad-blast."

"The spotted leopards," Rameau said. "Their jaws can bite through shells of turtles."

"Here cat went ground," Jak said. "Went up tree there." He held the burning splinter near the big bole to show more gouges, vertical this time.

If everybody held their torches up high enough they'd have endangered the leaves if they weren't moist with dew. They craned their necks, half fearful, half expectant of what they'd see.

"Reminds me of that scene from *Predator* when they find the bodies hanging from a tree," Mildred said.

"What's that?" Ryan asked.

She shook her head firmly. "Not worth explaining. Trust me on that."

"Whoa," Cole said. "So it ate him?"

"Hell of a way to die," Ryan said.

"Ah, friend Ryan," Doc said, "can you think of a better way to die than quickly?"

Chapter Twenty-Five

Terance and Bluebottle led them deeper into the endless swamp, through ever more claustrophobic channels that now and again widened unexpectedly into broad calm pools, or gave way to expanses of low grass on either side. The heat grew more intense, more crushing. Humidity thickened the still air until Ryan felt he could hack a path through it with his panga.

At least the sweat they all swam in seemed to make it hard for the mosquitoes and flies to bite them.

"We can take you into lands claimed by those pasty devils," Rameau said. "We cannot take you to the stronghold of Papa Dough himself. You must find your own way there."

He stood in the rear of the lead pirogue, pushing the boat along against the slow current with a long pole. The water in the narrow twisty channel was too shallow for paddling. He and Bluebottle had taken over for the non-twins in the lead craft with Ryan and Jak. Cody and Cole took turns poling the middle boat where today Mildred rode by herself, looking sour and out of sorts with a well-crushed camou boonie hat crammed down on her plaited head. Doc helped J.B. hold down the rear guard while Terance propelled the last boat.

Ryan reckoned Team Heart of Darkness was too afraid to guide them deeper than a certain point in swampie land. He didn't hold it against them. As it was, he thought they were

pretty crazy to accompany the friends this far, no matter what
was promised. Dead men spend no rewards.

"We can handle that," he told Rameau.

"Not there yet," Bluebottle said, crouching in the bow with
a cocked and loaded crossbow on his thighs. "We can take
you a day closer, mebbe."

They came to a drowned grove on the right, where cy-
presses thrust straight up from green-scummed water. A
dozen or so saplings had been chewed off eight or ten inches
above the surface by beavers, so that they resembled so many
miniature impaling stakes. To the left scrub formed an im-
penetrable green screen around the base of more widely
spaced trees.

"We'll take whatever you give us with thanks," Ryan said.

He burned with impatience to help Krysty. Although that
made his first impulse to rage at anything that hinted of setback or delay, Ryan was used to keeping short rein on his
emotions when the rad-storm hit. The sheer pressure of desire
and need, that twisted his guts and crawled beneath his skin
like an army of biting ants, actually distracted him enough it
was fairly easy to do the smart thing not the stupe one. And
especially not do something triple-stupe like alienate their
guides and allies.

If by some mad as Fire Day chance he got the cure for
Krysty, they were going to need help getting back to her.
Alienating their only allies for miles around would strand
them in deep dreck.

"By the Three Kennedys!" Doc exclaimed from the trail
boat. He leaned perilously over the low portside gunwale,
making the pirogue tip and drawing an angry rebuke from
Terance, which he ignored. "What a remarkable specimen of
an immature *Scaphirhynchus albus!*"

J.B. grabbed his Smith & Wesson M-4000 shotgun with

one hand and adjusted his hat on his head with the other. He looked wildly around. "Where?"

"Think you mean to ask 'what,' J.B.," Ryan called. "Once more in English, Doc. And does it mean we go red?"

"What? What?" With his scarecrow body still leaned outward, Doc turned his face to blink uncomprehendingly at his leader. "It's no threat, no, of course not. It is a pallid sturgeon."

"A pallid what?" J.B. palmed his forehead and slumped back on his bench. "A fish. Dark night, you got me going over a fish, Doc?"

"That's what you get for dozing off in the middle of the day, John," Mildred called. Indeed, Ryan had already noticed that when J.B. snapped to, his fedora had been tipped well forward to shield his eyes from the merciless noonday sun.

"I was only resting my eyes, Millie!"

"It is highly unusual," Doc said. "The pallid sturgeon was rare in my time. I cannot help but suspect their population was further depleted by the ravages of the twentieth century. We may hope that like so many wild species, they have made a strong comeback. Also, it is unusual to see them in slow, shallow water such as this. Their usual preference is for more rapid currents."

"Mebbe they use the bayous as a pathway," Rameau said, "just like us."

"Ugly nuke-sucker," Jak said, craning his head to peer over the side.

"It is swimming toward you," Doc said to the others.

Despite himself Ryan stirred himself to look over as the fish passed the lead craft. It was about two feet long, flat, with a snout like a skinny arrowhead. He had to agree with Jak's assessment.

"Were you a big angler, Doc?" Mildred asked.

"Remember, dear lady, ichthyology was a specialty of mine."

"A fish doctor," J.B. said. "No wonder the man's so crazy."

"You people all crazy," Terance drawled.

Cody uttered a yip of surprised pain and slapped a hand to the left side of his neck. He sat on the portside of the middle boat while his counterpart Cole stood in the stern and pushed with his stripped-sapling pole.

"Ouch," he said. "Something—"

Looking back Ryan just glimpsed a tiny sliver of wood sticking out between the boy's fingers. It appeared to be tipped with a tuft of whitish fiber, like cotton.

Like a rag doll, Cody slipped over the gunwale and fell into the water.

"Poison dart!" Ryan yelled. He drew his SIG-Sauer and covered the brushy left bank.

"Cody!" Cole yelled.

Dropping the pole, he turned to dive in after his friend. Moving with a speed that belied her sturdy build, Mildred lunged and grabbed Cole by the back of the waistband of his shapeless dungarees and yanked him bodily back into the boat, which wallowed with big gurgling surges of greenish-brown water.

"Let me go!" he shrieked, flailing wildly with arms and legs. Mildred caught him in a bear hug and held him tight, with her cheek pressed against his bare sun-browned back to keep her face from harm's way.

"Let me go! Mutie rad-suckers! You chilled him! Come fight me! I'll chill you all!"

As J.B. and Doc went belly-down in the boat, pointing their blasters across the gunwale at the left bank, Terance leaned out, reaching with his setting pole. He managed to snag Cody, floating facedown with arms spread wide, with the tip inside one leg, and wheel him back against the boat.

Then, hunkering to make himself a less perfect target, the rangy red-haired frontiersman reached out to haul the boy in.

Cody's head lolled limply on his neck when his head and shoulders were pulled up out of the water. His tongue protruded from his mouth. His eyes had rolled so far up in his head only the whites were visible.

Terance tested the pulse in his neck with a finger, then flicked a fingernail against one wide-open eyeball.

"Chilled," he said.

"Poisoned dart indeed," Doc said, turning his head to examine the boy. His big knobby hands kept his LeMat leveled toward the bushes where the projectile had come from. "Perhaps by a venom derived from some local variant of curare."

"I don't think anything like curare grows along the Gulf Coast, or anywhere in the U.S.," Mildred said.

"Much has changed in the last century, would you not say?"

"Keep us moving!" Rameau cried. He had a single-shot caplock pistol in his hand that was half as long as his arm. Though its lock plate was less ornately engraved than the ones Barton carried, Ryan noticed, it was a solid, serviceable-looking piece that had clearly been made by a Deathlands blastersmith.

Terance wrestled the limp body the rest of the way aboard, grabbing an arm and pushing himself starboard with his legs to counterbalance the weight and keep the narrow pirogue from flipping over. Keeping low, Doc slithered forward to examine the boy. Terance got to his knees and began pushing the boat along again with the pole, this time with only the strength of his arms and back.

Doc grunted sorrowfully and shook his head. "The boy is dead indeed," he called. "The poison acts with remarkable swiftness."

Cole's furious struggles subsided. He melted into Mildred's embrace and began to sob heartbrokenly.

Ryan lay on his belly on one of the lead pirogue's crosswise benches. The sun-warmed plank seemed to scorch his skin through his shirt. He had his 9 mm blaster shoved all the way out in both hands. The far bank was a dozen feet away. At this range his sniper rifle would be more an encumbrance than a useful weapon.

But he saw no motion at all in the brush.

Beside him Rameau grunted. "Triple stupe am I! I should have seen."

"What?" Ryan asked.

"Note—no little birds, hopping about inside the bushes there. They fled when the ambusher crept forward and haven't yet returned."

Ryan looked at Jak, who crouched beside him with his Python in hand. Jak's face twisted in disgust.

"Had eyes skinned right," he confessed. "Sorry." Apologies were even rarer from Jak than complete sentences.

"I can't blame you," Ryan said. "A man can't look all ways at once. Only a mutie got eyes in the back of his head."

"Speaking of muties," Rameau said, "see why we hate them, the swampies? They strike like cowards, and flee."

"Long gone now," Bluebottle agreed. He had a flintlock longblaster aimed toward the scrub despite his words.

"With all respect, Rameau," Ryan said, "if you were my enemy and came armed into my land, I'd chill you any way I could."

"We're still in Haven," Bluebottle said.

Ryan shrugged. "That wouldn't stop me, either, if I thought you were coming to visit with bad intent."

Rameau sighed. "Ah, my friend. You suspect these beasts' breasts harbor human hearts, their misshapen heads human thoughts. I fear you will learn differently, and all too soon. I only hope you survive the lesson."

"We've had a lot of hard lessons," Mildred called from the next boat. "Including from other types of swampies."

Left without propulsion or steering, the pirogue had begun to drift backward with the current, which fortunately was anything but swift. Terance had steered the pointed prow of his own boat up to contact the other's hull, and now expertly if laboriously drove both craft up the stream.

"We survived them all so far," Mildred finished.

"Cole," Rameau called, "snap out of it. You must get back to your duty, eh?"

The youth glared at him rebelliously.

"We all mourn your friend Cody," Rameau said. "But you'll find no vengeance here. Only death. Now you must man up and pole your boat."

"Mebbe the ambusher moved on, mebbe he didn't," Ryan said. "We don't want to hang out in the chill zone long enough for him to fetch a bunch more of his buddies with blowguns, do we?"

"I'm going to let you go," Mildred told Cole. "If you make a wrong move, boy, I'll fetch you one upside the head so hard you'll feel it yesterday. Do you understand me?"

"I'm fine," he said sullenly.

She released him and sat back, watching him like a chicken on an anthill.

Ryan saw him measure his chances at a leap in the water, then Cole glanced over his shoulder at Mildred's face. What he saw in her dark eyes made him turn back, recover the pole, which fortunately he'd dropped athwart the boat instead of overboard, and get cautiously back to his feet to resume his duties.

"Good boy," Rameau called. Then, quietly he said to Ryan,

"He'll be trouble later. He and Cody grew up like this." He held up two dark fingers pressed hard together.

"Man's got to learn how to bury his dead," Ryan said back, as softly, "and then walk on."

Then the full implication of what he'd said struck him like a giant icicle through the belly.

But Krysty wasn't chilled yet, he reminded himself fiercely. He had to hold tight to that.

THE SHADOWS GREW long over the swamp. The flying insects came out in redoubled force. Barn swallows with gorgeous blue-black backs, the males with scarlet throats and golden breasts, came out to eat them, barnstorming crazily up the bayou, inches over the water, then pulling up and wheeling around for another run. Like fighter planes in an old war vid, Ryan thought.

The big birds were commencing to flap overhead in ranks, back to their nests. Rameau had his crew looking for a likely campsite for the night. The need to be moving on, to get at last to the long-awaited cure for Krysty's mysterious condition, burned ever more fiercely in Ryan's belly. But he knew, practically, that if his guides were unwilling to push on after dark, it would be certain death for him and his friends to do so.

"Eyes skinned!" Jak called. "Gator!"

"*Merde!*" exclaimed Bluebottle, who was poling the lead craft. "He is some gator, that."

And so he was. It was making straight toward the pirogue from a place where the land widened out into waist-high weeds on both sides, around what looked like a broad pool. The creature looked like a giant spear moving through the water, with a huge knobbly head with bulbous eyes.

Ryan picked up his Steyr, worked the action enough to confirm the gleam of a cartridge in the receiver, slammed it home and locked it up. The alligator was a monster, a good fourteen feet long. If he had to chill the thing, 9 mm slugs were likely to bounce off his armored hide, especially that flat skull.

The behemoth never so much as glanced their way. He cruised on past downstream, driving himself hard with side-to-side strokes of his mighty tail. His wake was so strong it rocked the pirogues.

"He runs like he has Job on his tail," Bluebottle said reverently.

"Job?" Doc called from the rearmost craft. The gator passed it without slowing. "Why would a gigantic armored saurian fear an Old Testament prophet?"

Rameau snorted laughter. "No prophet, this Job," he said. "That's Cajun French talk for the Devil."

Bluebottle continued poling them into the pool. It was big, fifty yards wide by about eighty long. The surface was placid. In the gathering gloom of evening it looked as serene and unthreatening as a scene could look, even with the bugs griping at every exposed inch of skin.

"Bottom dropping fast," Bluebottle muttered. He laid the pole carefully along the boat's long axis, then sat in the stern and picked up a pair of paddles. "Too deep to pole."

Shifting carefully to midships, he socketed the paddles into eyes set in either side of the boat and began to scull it across the pond. In the trailing craft Cole did likewise. Still in shallower water Terance continued to stand and shove with his pole.

The lead watercraft had picked up speed. They were already well out, almost to the middle of the pool.

"What that?" Jak said, pointing left.

About thirty feet to port and abeam of the boat Mildred shared with Cole, the water had begun to bubble and froth furiously, as if it were coming quickly to a boil.

From the midst of the roiling water arose dark humped mass. Before the water weeds and murky water had sluiced away enough for Ryan to catch any notion what it might be, something startlingly long whipped up and out of the water in a horizontal line of spray.

Somebody shrieked shrilly in intolerable agony.

"Gotch Eye!" Bluebottle shouted, voice vibrating fear. "It's Gotch Eye! High John de Conquer, save us!"

Chapter Twenty-Six

Instinctively, Ryan turned toward the sound of the screaming, which went on and on like a line unreeling. He saw Terance standing in the stern of the last boat. His head was back, his mouth wide open, venting that wrenching sound at ultimate volume. Something resembling a tree root as thick as his arm, was wound about his waist. He had dropped his pole to clutch at it with both hands. Lesser tendrils, no thicker than a rubber hose, waved from the rootlike tentacle. They seemed to branch into even smaller filaments.

It wasn't fear that made Terance scream like that. The guide was a hard man. If he hadn't mastered his fears long since, he would have either died or gone into some more placid line of work than waging an endless war of treachery and ambush with a merciless foe like the swampies. It was the sound of a man in all-consuming agony.

Ryan saw a red line along Terance's contorted cheek that practically glowed. As he watched, a skinny tendril whipped one of the guide's bare forearms. It left a crimson weal on the leathery skin.

Another tentacle lashed out of the water toward the center boat. "Get down!" Ryan yelled. "Don't let it touch you!"

A third tentacle erupted right beside his own boat. As it reared higher than he stood, Ryan whipped out his panga by sheer reflex. The tentacle lashed toward him.

He struck. The heavy, sharp blade bit through the tentacle and severed it without hitting bone. Six feet of the tip, writhing like an eel, flew over the boat to splash into the water on the starboard side.

The tiniest little hair of a tendril brushed Ryan's left cheek. The pain hit him like a sledgehammer to the face. Blue-white lightning shot through his skull, and he dropped straight into the bilge as if poleaxed.

He heard shouts join the screams. By a wrench of sheer willpower he forced himself back up on his arms in time to see Terance yanked bodily out of the flatboat and through the air by the slimy green-brown mottled tentacle. He soared a brief arc and was pulled beneath the water with a giant splash.

Ryan saw the creature clearly now. Where the boiling had taken place as the thing surfaced now floated a patch of bubbles about the size of the boat, ranging in size from tiny froth to pearlescent globes the size of his head. A mass of something that looked like seaweed, but with an unpleasant greenish-black sheen, floated in a wide circle.

From the midst of the vileness rose a single eyeball the size of a predark soccer ball. Horrifyingly, it resembled an immense, detached human eye, white with red veins, a murky iris of brown and green and a great staring black pupil.

The pirogue rocked side to side in a tumult of splashing. The left side of Ryan's face convulsed irregularly. The pain remained intense, but it was no longer overpowering, something Ryan could handle.

He fumbled out his SIG-Sauer, tried to sight through the spasms. He got the terrible giant eye lined up like a pumpkin resting on the front-sight post. But as he squeezed off three quick shots, another wave threatened to swamp the boat, causing it to heel over. The shots went high.

"It is trying to upset our boats!" he heard Doc shout from the third boat.

A tentacle lashed at Ryan's craft, and he rolled to the side. He couldn't see what Bluebottle or Jak did to dodge, but because neither screamed in pain he reckoned they got clear. Or were hit so badly the corrosive poison had stunned them.

"Don't let it touch you!" he roared. "Not even the tiny hairs!"

The tentacle whipped back as if it had touched something hot. The end was missing, leaving a stub that gouted greenish-black ichor. Bluebottle crowed in triumph. Ryan remembered he carried a tomahawk with a forged-steel head, which he called his *casse-tête,* or head breaker. He'd probably chopped through the tentacle with it.

Ryan rolled back onto his belly. As he tried again to line up a shot from a platform rolling wildly on waves thrown up by Gotch Eye's thrashing, a human form erupted from the midst of the dark patch.

It was the head and shoulders of Terance. He was barely recognizable. The blue-black seaweed-like stuff draped him like a blanket. Steam and a sizzling sound rose where the wet leaflike clusters clung to his features, which seemed to be melting in front of Ryan's eye. Lips like a melting wax mouth spread apart to emit a scream that made the man's earlier shrieks sound like cries of joy.

Blasters bellowed. J.B.'s shotgun roared three times in quick succession. The left side of Terance's melting head blew off in a spray of brain and blood and chunks of "seaweed." The screaming stopped. The guide sank back into the churning mat as if dissolving.

This time as Ryan lined up his shot, a tentacle whipped at him again. He only just caught the quick movement from the corner of his eye, yanked his hand back in the boat and ducked his face behind the gunwale just in time. The tentacle slammed against the plank hull. None of the terrible tendrils touched his skin.

"The bastard mutie knows what a blaster is!" he yelled. With a sick shock he realized that not only was the monster trying to upset the boats and pitch more occupants into the water for the seaweed-stuff to digest alive, it was also trying to spoil their aim.

He tried popping up and snap-firing. He got off two shots to no visible effect, then dropped back down as a tentacle slashed the air above his head. Thing was bastard fast, too.

How do we beat the nuke-sucker? he wondered.

He heard the muffled booms of feet move inside the boat. The pirogue rocked to something other than surging water and bashing appendages. Ryan looked around to see Jak stand upright, his legs braced wide. His white hair flew as he reared back an arm, then it whipped forward. No sooner had it reached the end of its motion and a glittering knife spun end-over-end from his snow-white hand, than he plucked another from his other hand and cocked the arm back to throw once more.

Ryan looked back at Gotch Eye in time to see a splash of murky water right next to the giant orb that named it. Then the knife struck the lower left-hand side of the monster eyeball. It hit wrong and glanced off, vanishing among the mounded bubbles.

Jak's third throwing knife pierced straight into the middle of the great staring pupil.

A weird whistling filled the air, ten times as loud as the sounds Terance made when he was being melted alive by the creature's acid. The tentacles beat with mindless fury, spewing water fifteen feet in the air. The great eye, oozing clear green fluid from the knife wound, drew hastily beneath the surface with an immense sucking sound. The seaweed mass seemed to be sucked toward the center and down with it.

The odd cluster of bubbles took longer to retract. Ryan heard the stubby shotgun barrel beneath the main barrel of Doc's huge LeMat handblaster roar. A foot-wide cluster of bubbles exploded. The stench they released threatened to yank Ryan's stomach inside out.

J.B. fired his M-4000 as fast as he could cycle the action. Bubbles popped rapidly. The stench grew almost overwhelming.

Wailing filled the moisture-saturated afternoon air. The water boiled almost as violently as it had right before the monster appeared. Two huge tentacles lashed at the sky directly above the churning mass as if in supplication, then the intact bubbles vanished beneath the water, too.

The pond's surface rhythmically smoothed itself. A stinking polychromatic sheen where the monster had been was all that remained in view.

Ryan popped the partially expended magazine from the butt of his SIG-Sauer and fished for a full one. If the horror came back, he didn't intend his slide to lock open after just a couple shots.

"Anybody hurt?" he called.

"We're all fit to fight," J.B. said, "but Rameau got his arm stung."

Ryan looked back. The Havenite boss sat in the second flatboat with his face not much darker than Jak's and his eyes dilated. He'd clearly gotten stung far worse than Ryan had.

And Ryan's face still felt as if the whole left side was on fire. The affected area hadn't gotten numb at all. He could feel the scar tissue that ran down that side of his face flexing stiffly as muscles twitched.

"We've got to get to shore soon," he said. "Anybody know how to treat this shit?"

"It seems a lot like jellyfish venom," Mildred said. She was examining Rameau's stung arm and not looking too pleased with what she saw. "You're supposed to scrub that with sand."

"We have passed some sandy banks. Surely we can find another," Doc said.

"If we can't, maybe grass will do," Mildred said. "Or, I don't know, dry cloth. I know you're not supposed to use water. Damn! I just remembered—you're supposed to do things opposite if it's a Man o' War sting. How do we know what that bastard had?"

"We don't," Ryan said. "So we fake it. What's next?"

"Then rinse with vinegar. Um, any mild acid will do, I guess. Do we have anything like that?"

Ryan knew his companions didn't. Rameau was busy grinding his teeth together to keep from howling like a stickie on fire. Ryan looked back at Bluebottle, who shook his head. He wasn't looking too healthy, either. He probably was just shaken, the one-eyed man thought. No surprise there.

"We may have to skate on that," Ryan said. "Anything else?"

"Um, apply ammonia."

"And where do we get that?"

Mildred looked uncomfortable. She was scrubbing at Rameau's wound.

"From urine, my friends," Doc said. "It is the most readily available source."

"Ace on the line," Ryan said. "Anything else?"

"Apply aloe vera. Sometimes I have that in our med supplies. We're out now."

"We have the aloe vera," Bluebottle said. "We carry healing kits."

"Luck, for once. Okay. Keep your eyes peeled for a place to land and camp for the night."

Ryan dug through his pack for a spare pair of socks and dabbed at the slime the tendril had left on his face with the worst holed one. Then he pitched it overboard.

"Littering, Ryan," Mildred said.

"What?"

"Never mind." She shook her head. Rameau had kind of sunk down into the boat. He looked bad.

"What the hell was that thing?" Mildred demanded. "It was like a…a cross between an octopus, a jellyfish and kelp. And—and a person! That eye was structured exactly like a human eye!"

"Mutie," Jak said laconically.

"Perhaps," Doc called. "And perhaps not. When I was held, a helpless captive out of time, I overheard my captors talking about a project to create an artificial life form that could be used to explore some unimaginably alien world."

"You think what they came up with was *that?*" Ryan said.

"I cannot know. But those words did come rather forcibly back to me now."

"*That*'s a planet I never hope to see," Mildred said fervently.

"Think it's dead?" Cole asked.

"All I know is it'll be a bastard while before the rad-sucker fucks with us again," Ryan said. "I'll settle for that."

Mildred looked at Rameau, who had begun shivering in uncontrollable reaction.

"Got to treat this now," she said. She stood uncertainly amidships and began to fiddle with the fly of her camou pants. "Everybody turn your heads. Cole, honey, you just concentrate on keeping us moving."

"Why?" Jak asked.

"No vinegar," Mildred said. "So, here goes the next step of the treatment. You understand?"

After a moment Ryan said, "Oh, for nuke's sake. Everybody look away while Mildred drops her pants. The woman's being all proper again."

"How about that facial wound, Ryan?" she called sweetly.

"It's fine!"

"THANK YOU for giving poor Terance the coup de grâce, my friend," Rameau said through chattering teeth to J.B. "It was all that could be done."

They had built a yellow dancing fire from driftwood in the middle of a space they'd cleared in an expanse of waist-high grass. Overhead a few clouds slid like gray rafts across a sea of stars. For various reasons nobody felt like camping back among the trees. They wanted a wide field of fire around them this night.

The usual swamp smells of decay and decomposition seemed thicker and more cloying than usual.

The Armorer shrugged. "Glad I stopped his suffering," he said, "but I can't claim credit. Fact is, I was aiming for that rad-blasted eye."

The aloe had helped. Ryan's face still felt as if a razor was cutting his skin, over and over, but the terrible venom prickling had stopped. Still, given that Rameau had gotten it worse than he had, the man had to be bastard tough to talk at all.

"Poor Terance," Mildred said. "I'll see that face in my nightmares the rest of my life."

After a moment she added, "He'll have plenty of company."

J.B. patted her shoulder. "Well, I don't have to worry about you dreaming about any handsome dudes," he said with a chuckle.

Mildred's face turned a sort of greenish pale in the yellow firelight. She immediately stood and stomped off.

"What?" J.B. looked thunderstruck. From Ryan's angles the lenses of his specs were blank yellow circles. "I was just trying to lighten the mood! What'd I do?"

"For a man as smart as you are about so many things," Ryan growled, "you can be a real stupe sometimes. Don't you know anything about women?"

J.B. turned to look into the darkness after Mildred. He

took off his hat and scratched the thinning spot on top of his head.

"Guess not, Ryan. What do I do now?"

"Get up and go after her!"

The wiry Armorer scrambled to his feet and trotted after the angry healer. Shaking his head, Ryan turned back to the fire.

"We're in enemy territory now," Rameau said. "They should be careful."

"They'll be fine," Ryan said. "They're all grown up. They can take care of themselves."

He threw another chunk of driftwood onto the fire. Sparks trailed up toward the stars.

Rameau dropped his pointy-bearded chin to his clavicle. "I hope we can all say that. It is a hard road we walk." He shook his head. "But we knew that when we set out upon it. If there's blame, it falls on our own heads."

"Yeah, well, I wondered why the baron sent two guides with us," Ryan said. "Reckon I see the sense of it now."

THE MORNING DAWNED bright, but there was a yellow cast to the eastern sky and dark blue clouds piled up away off to the southeast.

"Storm buildin' out over Gulf," Bluebottle said.

They ate a breakfast of cold frog legs and fish they'd roasted the night before. Rameau's right arm wasn't working well, and Mildred tied it up in a sling for him. Given how Ryan's face still felt it was a wonder he was functioning even today. The pain of the sting hadn't kept him from sleeping soundly. Hardly anything ever did. But this day he felt as if somebody had split his cheek open with Bluebottle's *casse-tête* and poured salt in.

Mildred had rubbed more aloe juice onto the wound,

which helped. The bone still throbbed with every beat of his heart.

Mildred was moving around quite happily this morning. It had been more effort than usual for the companions to ignore the sounds she and J.B. made reconciling after their spat.

The previous evening they had drawn the flatboats onto the low shore and done the best they could to get the grass to stand back up where they had dragged them, to make it less obvious they were there. The grass was green, water-fat and resilient, which helped. Ryan didn't think it'd fool anybody raised in these bayous for more than the time it took a cartridge to light off when you dropped the hammer, but all they could do was the best they could.

He shouldered his pack and his rifle and stood. The others did the same. Without making an issue of it, the much bigger Bluebottle helped haul Rameau to his feet. The man looked past Ryan. His anthracite eyes went wide.

A pair of beings, as much like barrels as men, with exaggerated broad features, hair like steel wool and skins the color of chalk, stood between the party and their boats. One carried a spear with a leaf-shaped steel head, the other a chunk of hardwood that looked as if it might have started out as an oar and become a bladed club. They wore necklaces of gator teeth and fingerbones. The one with the spear has a shiny brass ring through his wide, flat nose.

Quickly, Ryan looked left and right.

Swampies rose out of the grass on every side.

Chapter Twenty-Seven

"Surrounded," Jak said.

"You monsters!" Cole shrieked. "You chilled Cody! Die!"

He ripped his big-bladed knife from the beaded buckskin sheath at his belt and threw himself toward the nearest muties, the ones blocking the way to the boats. So fast did the boy move in his tearful vengeance frenzy that Ryan, for all his steel-trap reflexes, couldn't move fast enough to stop him.

The swampie he attacked was a head shorter than the boy's five-six. But like all his mutant brothers—at least in this part of the bayou—he was wide and massively muscled beneath layers of fat. His yellow eyes went wide as the boy lunged for him, raising the knife high over his white-blond-haired head to stab.

One-handed, the mutie rammed his spear forward. Ryan heard a wet sound and a soft grunt escaped the boy's mouth, cutting short another cry for bloody vengeance.

Then the spear tip poked right out the back of the blue plaid shirt the youth was wearing.

Cole sucked in a long, shuddering breath, then he began to scream in the terrible agony of a gut wound.

Behind him Ryan sensed blasters come up, heard safeties click off, flint cocked back from frizzen and hammer raised from capped steel nipple. The swampies, who surrounded the small party completely, aimed spears, clubs and crossbows.

There were at least twenty of the short, squat muties

ranged around the humans. And swampies were tough to kill. Supposedly they had double sets of all their internal organs. Beyond that, their thick rolls of fat over muscle provided a decent natural armor. The companions had encountered many different types of swampies during their travels, and they all shared a variation of that trait.

"Stop!" Ryan said, stepping forward and holding out his empty hands to the sides. He didn't shout. He just pitched his voice to carry, and gave it an edge like a trumpet blast.

Under the circumstances, shouting could act like spraying gasoline on a bonfire. Using his best voice of command froze everybody in place. At least for a moment.

Given the numbers and the way the swampies had them dead to rights, it could have been oldies and kids surrounding Ryan and his companions, and it still would turn to massacre if blood ever broke.

Cole kept screaming. The swampie yanked the spear out. The boy fell to the blood-stained grass, folded himself into a knot of agony and began to writhe and howl.

"We mean no harm here!" Ryan said. "We come to see Papa Dough. *I* came to see Papa Dough. I need to ask his help."

That caused a deep bass murmur among the swampies.

"If you come in peace to my father," said a voice deep and resonant as a bull fiddle, "why does the young'un attack us?"

Ryan turned. A young-looking swampie with a frizz of black hair and beard had stepped forward behind him and to the left. He was no taller than five feet but even wider than his fellows, shoulder and gut. Flesh beads of ritual scarification around his slightly protuberant but clear green eyes indicated high rank. He wore a crimson-dyed leather loincloth and carried an elaborately carved but altogether lethal-looking war club.

"I am Jon Dough," the young swampie said. He carried

himself with dignity beyond his years, and his speech and manner suggested a level of intelligence Ryan didn't usually associate with the muties. Like many of the folk Ryan had encountered here, he spoke with a strong Cajun accent. "I speak for my father."

"The boy's best friend was killed yesterday by a blow dart from an ambush," Ryan said. Cole's cries had subsided to desperate groans and mewling. "He blamed you swampies. Grief and vengeance hunger made him crazy."

"It was our people who shot his friend," the swampie acknowledged. "Your kind haven't earned welcome here in our lands."

Ryan shook his head. "My friends and I have nothing to do with your disputes with Haven. I come here in sore need. My woman lies poisoned and helpless back in the ville. A wise woman told me my only hope to save her was held by Papa Dough. I come here to ask his help."

"What do you offer?"

"That's between me and him."

"You are brave, if not very smart."

"I'm sorry," Bluebottle said under his breath. "I never had a clue these cannies was sneaking up on us."

"Cannies?" Jon Dough said. He was quickly going hotter than nuke-red. "You lie. You kill us, tear up our crops, burn our huts. Why do you insult us, too?"

"But—"

"Shut up!" Ryan snapped. "Everybody, back away from the trigger."

"They killed my boy," Rameau said mournfully.

"He rushed them. He couldn't expect different. And he sure as nuke-shit didn't pause to think about how he was putting the rest of us right on the chopping block of an old fashioned hog-butchering, now, did he? Anyway, that bullet's left the blaster. We need to talk!"

"If you mean us no ill will," Jon Dough said, "you surely will not object if we kill the two who invade from Haven with swampie blood staining their hands?"

"I do object, Jon Dough. They're my people. I stand and fall with them."

Jon Dough shrugged. "Then why shouldn't we just chill you all?"

"If I may interject here, Monsieur Dough," Doc said, "you obviously had compelling reason not to chill us out of hand. Clearly you could have. You surrounded us with such craft that not even the animal-keen senses of young Jak Lauren detected your presence."

"Mebbe we wanted to hear what the hell made you think you could just waltz into our land," the swampie boss said. "Or mebbe we just wanted to fuck with you, eh?"

"Hear me," Ryan said. "This business is between me and your father. We're in your power here. We pose no threat to him, any more than we do you."

The young swampie looked mulish. Clearly he felt Ryan was somehow challenging his own authority.

"Let's cut straight to the point," Ryan declared. "If I have to eat a big, steaming pile of Papa Dough's own shit to save my woman, that's what I'll do."

He ignored the multiple gasp from his friends behind him. "You would so debase yourself over this woman?" Jon Dough asked in surprise.

"I'd never let myself fail Krysty through weakness of my own. Even squeamishness. Nor out of pride. If that makes me less a man, so be it."

Jon Dough pursed his huge, pale lips.

"And anyway," Ryan said, "if your father wants to, he can always chill us."

"Way to argue our case, Ryan," Mildred muttered.

But Jon Dough nodded his head. "I'm not big on sentiment

where you mannies are concerned, but you impress me, stilt man. You got big brass ones, if nothing else. So I'll take you to my father, and he'll decide your fate. *Bon.* It'll be entertaining, if nothing else."

Ryan nodded at the writhing Haven boy, who'd begun to gobble half-intelligible pleas for his mother. "What about him?"

"Have you the healing lore to cure him?" Jon Dough asked.

"Not a chance," Mildred said. "Not without major antibiotics and quick surgery in a sterile environment. None of which I happen to have packed in my ruck. You?"

Jon Dough shook his head. "Even if we would, there's nothing we could do to save him with such a wound. Nor even the blind woman who sent you here."

"You know of Sweet Julie?" Doc asked.

"The very animals of the forest know her."

Ryan looked over his shoulder to Rameau. "He's your man," Ryan said. "What's your call?"

Rameau moistened his lips with a bloodless tongue. "Mercy," he croaked.

"Oh, God." Mildred sighed. She knew what "mercy" meant in the Deathlands.

The swampie who stood beside the one who'd speared Cole stepped forward. He raised his club. When he brought it down the youth's tow-haired head came apart like a melon struck with an ax.

"Make the mannies ready," Jon Dough commanded. "We march."

The party was quickly relieved of its gear and weapons. Not gently, but without any overt cruelty. To Ryan the process suggested plucking a chicken, which he found both reassuring and somewhat unnerving.

They were blindfolded with items of their own clothing.

"Don't try to work them off," Jon Dough said as Ryan's good eye was covered. "If they so much as slip without you warning us, we chill you on the spot."

FOR ONCE Mildred's relatively short legs proved no handicap on a forced march. She towered over their captors, and their leg-to-height ratio made her look like a giraffe. The swampies set a steady pace, but even for her it was no more than that at which she might've walked to the library in med school.

Of course, that didn't account for the humid heat or the marshy spots that tried to suck the boots clean off her feet, nor the obstructions that crossed their path, humped roots or fallen logs. The swampies warned of obstacles in their deep voices. Evidently the idea of tormenting their captives by watching them trip and fall or slam their shins held little appeal to them. Or they were merely so practical they didn't want to waste marching time on frivolous diversions.

The prisoners' hands weren't bound, which let them scramble more easily over the larger blockages. They weren't allowed to carry their packs. The swampies were sturdy and as strong as mules, and didn't seem to mind the added burden. Mildred suspected they didn't want to risk losing any of the precious booty if a prisoner bolted and was shot down into some gator-infested bayou where even the swampies didn't dare try to retrieve it.

She became acutely aware of nonvisual sensory inputs. For the most part the sense of feel brought discomfort: humid heat, the sweat that tickled its way into every cranny and fold of her body, the chafing in her hinder parts. As for sound, the swampies discouraged their prisoners from talking, even during rare rest and water breaks. They themselves spoke seldom, in a sort of subterranean mutter. Given the extremely slangy French Creole they normally used, she wouldn't have been able to follow the conversation if she heard it clearly.

She found herself concentrating on the birdcalls and chirps and trills, which came from all sides from the woods and brush and the egrets and herons wading in the sluggish dark-stained waters. Also she learned to recognize when the swampies guided Doc, who walked immediately in front of her—J.B. came next, a comforting warmth even if she couldn't physically sense his nearness—over some obstacle lying in the path of what to them had to have been his freakishly long legs. They took great care over what they had to assume was an addled oldie.

It struck her, during a brief halt as the swampies helped their blindfolded captives negotiate a fallen cypress one at a time, that they were being unusually solicitous for the welfare of their enemies. This kid Jon Dough takes his responsibility to deliver us to his Daddy in prime shape pretty seriously, she realized.

That epiphany didn't comfort her as much as it might've. She couldn't help recalling that in her own time it was customary to nurse the convicted into the best possible health just to execute them.

By where the sunlight stung the skin of her face, she sensed they generally marched northwest as the sun mounted up the sky, rolled over the top and headed down the home stretch to its nightly resting place.

In what she judged midafternoon her blindfold began to slip. A gleam of light invaded the lower half of her right eye. Although even the vagrant and insignificant shine of sunlight, probably still filtered by a layer of cloth, dazzled her dark-accustomed retina, it lifted her spirits.

Briefly. Then she remembered what the swampies had told them about fooling with the blindfolds. Or even if they simply slipped.

She cursed the unknown mutie who had adjusted and retightened the knotted T-shirt at the last drink and pee break—in-and-out water stop, as she'd come to think of them. Swampies were capable of remarkable dexterity with the unwieldy-looking sausage fingers they had, to judge by their handicrafts. Just my luck to draw the one with five thumbs per hand, she thought bitterly.

For a time she marched in a rapidly rising fever of fearful anticipation. The sweat rolling down her face and her sides redoubled in volume and velocity. She grew sick to her stomach.

I'm chilled if I do and chilled if I don't, she thought. What do I do?

Then it was as if another voice in her mind said, Wait, girlfriend. Remember what they actually told you.

It was *that* voice, the voice in her head that usually assured her that she couldn't possibly make whatever she was doing anything but a fearful mess. Which made it a triple-pisser that she realized with something of a shock that it was right.

Jon Dough had said if the blinders slipped without the captives warning their captors they'd be killed out of hand. That implied if they *did* warn the swampies they'd be fine. Didn't it? Didn't it?

What if they misinterpret the situation? she thought. What if they blame me anyway? What if they lied?

The panic was rising rapidly over her head like floodwaters. She recognized the fact. And one of the first lessons her new, unasked-for life in the Deathlands had taught her was that panic equaled death. Once you let yourself lose presence of mind, you lost your chance at life.

She forced herself to take a deep breath and hold it for half a dozen heartbeats before letting it out deliberately as she could. Another and another, ignoring the way her body demanded she breathe faster and pump more oxygen to her trudging, increasingly fatigue-poisoned muscles.

Take a chill pill, girlfriend, she told herself, using the

phrase in the sense she'd grown up with—since its modern meaning would be "suicide capsule." Nobody promised you'd live forever!

She caught herself just on the cusp of laughing out loud. Given when your birthday was, you made a good start at that already! Mildred summoned saliva into her mouth, swallowed so her voice wouldn't crack into unintelligibility.

"All right," she said aloud. "A little help here. The blindfold's slipping and I'm sure as hell not gonna mess with it!"

She heard a swampie voice call halt from right nearby, an oboe honk. She stopped. In a moment, strong, disproportionately large hands were tugging at her, urging her to squat so her captors could adjust the blindfold. *Or cut my throat,* she thought.

But the hands, working with brusque efficiency, just rearranged the cloth knotted around her head, and retied it more tightly. Then she was prodded back to her feet and the march resumed.

Relief flooded her. *Don't get giddy, girl,* her inner voice warned. *We don't know what's waiting at the end of this day. Our last meal could still be a cold cut or a hot stake.*

EVEN THROUGH the blindfold she could sense that day was ending when suddenly the nature of sounds changed around them. The wild noises of bush and woods and bayou didn't stop, only seemed to retreat a ways. And inhumanly deep voices began to mutter excitedly around them.

We've reached a ville, Mildred guessed.

They were led by twists and turns deeper into what she estimated was a sizable settlement. She could somehow tell there were walls nearby, reflecting the sounds of their passage and tamping the slight, soggy breeze that came up as the sun started to go down. Then hands gripped her elbows, forcing her to stop.

Hands fumbled at the back of her head. Mildred's heart raced. The blinders were coming off. This was it.

The cloth came away. Torches burned to left and right on bamboo holders taller than Doc. Sitting in front of her on a giant ornate and gaudy cane chair—topped, yes, by the grinning skull of a big alligator—sat an immense swampie with a head like an albino jack-o'-lantern. Mystic designs had been daubed on the expansive canvas of his belly in ochre, green, vermillion. Strings of golden beads, flowers and rattlesnake skulls hung from the area where his head sat upon ax-handle-wide shoulders in lieu of a neck. For a scepter he held a mirror-shiny ebony walking stick with a highly polished silver head not too different from Doc's swordstick. Its elegant simplicity was almost incongruous next to the emphatic—not to say *barbaric*—display of throne and occupant.

Lips like papaya quarters split back from teeth the size and general shape of the tablet erasers Mildred had used in school. Laughter emerged from the mound of chalk-pale flesh in a rolling-thunder boom.

"Welcome to Papa Dough's Damn Fine Domain!" the bizarre apparition exclaimed.

Chapter Twenty-Eight

Ryan stepped forward. "I'm Ryan Cawdor. I've brought these people here. If any offense has been committed, it's on my head."

The walking-stick scepter lolled to one side. Papa Dough put the other elbow on the arm of his chair and leaned his cheek against his palm.

"You don't really want to deny me my moment of showmanship, here, do you?" he said.

Ryan took a sharp breath. "Reckon not," he said, stepping back and nodding.

"Good, good. I like guests who mind their manners."

He waved the walking stick. A mutie who was comically short and wide even for a swampie, so that he looked more toad than humanoid, waddled forth to proclaim the might and terrors of Papa Dough, Vodoun King of the Southern Swamps.

"'The earth trembles when he walks. When he frowns, catamounts piss and gators flee. When he laughs, the stars giggle along. When he farts, birds on the wing die as far away as Mobile.'"

He went on for a time in this vein, in a voice like a cannonball rolling in a rain barrel. Papa Dough slumped deeper and deeper into his amazing throne, which made him look as if his skeleton was dissolving inside the unbelievable mass of his fat. At last he stretched a tubby arm and tapped the cane on the herald's shoulder.

"All right, all right, Crapaud. That's enough. I'm awesome. Blah, blah. We know."

The toadlike mutie looked as if he were about to cry. "But I was just warming up, *M'sieur!*"

"Scuttle."

He scuttled.

"Okay. Despotic display, done. What's on your alleged mind, skinny bones?"

"My woman, Krysty Wroth, lies helpless—"

Papa Dough waved a vast hand. "Yeah, yeah. I know why you're here. I'm just fucking with you."

"How do you know?"

"Julie. We send messages back and forth all the time." His face darkened. "That's how I know how this war started—with a cynical lie. But she didn't dare speak truth in Haven. It would've got her chilled. And we swampies, when we are attacked, we fight."

Jon Dough bustled up. "Have I done well, Father?" he asked.

"Yeah. You did. You got the stilties well-tenderized. And this one matches up with what Sweet Julie said—he'll listen to reason, if for no other reason than he's a survivor. He knows well that if he's not reasonable, all of his friends are chills."

The younger Dough bowed—no easy feat, given his basically globular shape—and withdrew. His father clapped hands the size of a big man's butt cheeks.

"Bring chairs for my guests," Papa Dough ordered, "and let the feasting begin!"

He looked at Ryan with his huge bulbous eyes. "Hope you-all brought your appetites, boy. I make a mean crawfish and sausage *filé* gumbo!"

"THIS REALLY IS GOOD, Your Majesty," Doc said, scooping up more gumbo and rice with a wooden spoon. "Truly excellent."

"Yeah," Mildred said. "You weren't kidding. You made this yourself?"

"Well," Papa Dough said, visibly pleased, "given the demands of my office, my role consists primarily of supervision. It *is* my recipe, though."

"He sits on his ass in the shade while everybody else does the work," his son said, chewing a hearty bite of tough-crusted, tasty bread.

Papa Dough smirked. "Rank hath its privileges, boy. And always remember, it'll be your fat ass sitting in the shade one day."

Ryan accepted a refill of his heavy fired-clay bowl, forcing himself to smile at the swampie girl who twinkled at him as she served him. He would've thought he looked as unappealing to her as her coconut-with-a-lemon-on-top shape looked to him. But apparently things didn't work that way.

"Please don't take this wrong, Papa Dough," he said, "but how did you happen to wind up talking like that?"

"Mannie tutors, of course," he said. "My daddy, bless his soul, didn't think it was fit for the true people to be ruled by an ignorant hick."

Doc's bushy brows rose. "But you war with the people of Haven! How could your father enlist tutors from among, um, standard humans?"

"Haven's our neighbor to the south," the king said. "There are other directions, remember? And while we tend to try to keep contacts with the stilties minimal to avoid unfortunate misunderstandings, we maintain friendly relations with various trading partners."

He scowled. "We're friendly to those who treat us as friends. If you come as an enemy, we'll be waiting for you!" He slapped a thigh to jiggling.

"We got a sample of that when our ship wrecked down near the coast," Ryan said.

"The people who attacked your party have been punished severely," Papa Dough said. "The ones that mad thing Tobias left alive."

"But why?" Mildred asked.

"Isn't it obvious? We're not predators. We're not wreckers. You were obviously not from our enemies in Haven. And anyway, only a triple-stupe nukehead fucks with Technomads!"

LATER THEY SIPPED RUM and listened to the music-and-language tutor to Papa Dough's daughter Jane play a Spanish guitar and sing. The tutor was a pretty young Caribbean Spanish woman who wore an orange flower in her long black hair. She sang softly, to allow the king to converse with his prisoners, who somewhere in the course of the evening, seemed to have changed into guests.

Of course Ryan well remembered the old joke: Good night, I'll probably kill you in the morning.

"It was Dornan, of course," Papa Dough said, enfolding a mighty brass goblet of rum in one hand. "And that vicious bastard Dupree. They decided what they needed to really consolidate power in the ville was an outlander enemy. So they sent a couple secret raiding parties into my father's domain, committed the usual atrocities. My people retaliated. And the war was on."

"Dornan was a pig," Rameau said woozily. He had taken on a double load of rum, which probably helped a little with his stung arm. He had adjusted to receiving hospitality from recent mortal foes a lot more readily than Bluebottle, who sat aside looking vaguely scandalized at the whole thing. It hadn't stopped him tucking into the king's gumbo with a will.

"When the Beast returned," Papa Dough said, "they needed an excuse to intensify the war, distract the people even more. So they cooked up the idea of telling their subjects we were cannies."

Outrage made his huge face scary, especially in the light of the dwindling fire. "That's just gross. I don't mean to be racist here, but even if we were going to eat people, why on Earth would we eat you? I mean, you don't even have any meat on your bones. And it's stringy."

In the sudden silence that followed the monarch's outburst, especially among the normal humans, J.B. said, "Tobias keeps up the lie? He strikes me as a good man, I have to say."

Papa Dough turned the full force of his scowl on the Armorer. J.B. looked back mildly.

The swampie King sighed and his brutal features softened. "Don't expect me to see it," he growled. "But he and his sister were raised to believe that lie. They might've questioned it a little harder, especially after Tobias killed his father to keep the old baron from chilling Elizabeth."

He set his cup down. "So, down to business. You've proved you had courage getting here and facing down my boy. You showed you were a leader by cooling everybody down when that poor fool kid went jolt-walker on my people. You've passed the tests with flying colors. So far."

"Tests," Ryan repeated dryly.

Papa Dough shrugged. The rippling fat aftershocks continued for several seconds after. "You're on a quest to save your beautiful princess, allowing for your standards of beauty. You got to pass tests. It's standard. Anyway, you're here. And you're not a bad type, for a stilter!"

He leaned forward conspiratorially. His gut squeezed out to either side. "So here's the deal—to get what you want, you must promise to bring me what I ask for."

"What?" Ryan said.

Papa Dough held up a big finger. "Tut-tut. You don't get to ask that. You have to say yes. You have to mean yes. You have to swear to bring me what I demand. No fingers crossed, no takebacks, no welshing!"

Ryan looked around at his friends. All he got back was different shades of unaccustomed helplessness. My decision, he thought, and mine alone. So what's new about that?

"I agree," he said.

"No horseshit?"

"No horseshit."

"Cross your heart three times and hope to die if you lie!"

Ryan raised his right hand to his breastbone and made an *X* with his thumb, three times. "If I lie or cheat you, may I wind up staring at the sky."

Papa Dough nodded, grinning hugely.

"Can he ask now?" Mildred said tentatively.

"Huh? Oh, sure."

He rose ponderously to his feet. "Ryan Cawdor," he declaimed in his best ceremonial bass-drum boom, "what I want you to bring me is...peace."

"Say what?" Ryan asked.

"Peace. Peace with the Havenites. An end to the age-old war!"

"How in the name of glowing night shit am I supposed to do that?"

"You're the one on a quest, son. Not my problem."

"If anyone can do it, Ryan." J.B. said, "you can."

"But do I have to do it before I help Krysty? Fireblast, we're days out of Haven! If I have to go back, find a way to stop the war, then drag ass all the way back—"

"Deep breaths, boy. You're hyperventilating. Remember—you swore, cross your heart, hope to die. You're good for it. Only..."

Ryan lowered his head and gave him a blue-laser glare. "Only?"

"The kicker is, I don't have the secret. Not personally.

You're going to have to get it from our own witch-woman, Maman Fucton."

"Maman what?"

"My consort. Mad as Fire Day. And you must please her."

He laid his hand on Ryan's shoulder, which was only possible because Ryan was still sitting.

"It's the only way, boy. She holds the secret to your woman's recovery. I shit you not. But I don't envy you. This is your hardest test of all!"

Chapter Twenty-Nine

Dressed only in his camou pants, Ryan stood tall in the dawn-light. The grass was dew-wet beneath and on his bare feet. His only armament was his panga in a sheath at his waist.

His friends stood behind him, including a taciturn Blue-bottle. Rameau was still passed out, and no one had had the heart to rouse him. Ryan couldn't help noticing that the swampies hadn't seen fit to trust any of the others with their weapons. And they were well surrounded by a fence of spears, even if those didn't happen to be pointed at them at the moment.

"Remember, boy," Papa Dough said, "you'll have to fight even to reach Maman Fucton. Then you must penetrate her moist, capacious, mossy cave and please her."

Ryan tried not to wince at that description.

"Now," the swampie monarch said, holding up a gourd to Ryan's face, "drink the drink." He wore a circlet of red berries and a ceremonial robe of black fur that showed the faintly darker shadows of rosettes. Ryan guessed it was the skin of a black jaguar.

"What is it?" he asked, accepting the gourd. Its fluted surface was smooth and hard, mottled green and pale yellow.

"Necessary. Drink it fast. It goes down easier that way."

Still giving the short, wide monarch the fish eye, Ryan raised the gourd to his lips. He decided to hold his breath, in case that helped, and chugged the contents.

It didn't help. Probably nothing would, including a complete surgical excision of all his taste buds. The flavor affronted his very being.

But he drained it to the ultimate drop. For Krysty.

"Gah!" he said, doubling over as the vile stuff hit his gut like a mule kick. "It tastes like distilled ass, sweat and sulfur!"

"That's how you know it's strong medicine," Papa Dough assured him.

Ryan straightened. He looked at him suspiciously as he handed back the gourd. "What medicine?"

"You got to be electric to face Maman Fucton, boy. Trust me on that! Now, run. Your woman waits and daylight's a-wastin'!"

Ryan ran.

HE FIRST REALIZED something was wrong when the green monkeys started hooting his progress from the trees as he dodged among their wavy boles. He was pretty sure monkeys didn't live hereabouts. Even green ones. With pink feather crests, like cockatiels.

Bands of color tracked across the sky like a malfunking vid screen: lemon yellow, sour-apple green, purple, pink, tangerine. Pretty much the colors you'd see glowing on a tomato gone seriously around the bend.

Dosed, he knew. He wasn't much surprised. For reasons of his own Papa Dough was choosing to treat this whole fandango as a weird backwoods ritual. And Ryan had been through plenty of those before. Luci drinks or smokes or other forms of mind alterants were standard operating procedure.

His path was clear at least. Then again the way it was behaving made the old Irish toast he'd heard somewhere, someplace—possibly on a different planet, at least from the one

he was seeing now—of "may the road rise up to meet you,"
look like the perilous and nauseating idea it actually was.

Ahead of him rose a hill. It probably really did look like
a huge breast. Papa Dough had told him to find and steer
for such. A deeply buried part of his rational mind begged
to doubt it actually had a crown of brush shaped like a huge
dark-green nipple, though.

He saw the cave entrance, oval and surprisingly narrow,
with moss and brush tufts sprouting from rock all around it,
awaiting fifty yards ahead. Then he came into a clearing car-
peted with grass and yellow and purple and polka-dot wild-
flowers and stopped.

The guardian of Maman Fucton's cavern stood waiting for
him.

He was like a dozen swampies rolled into one. He had to
have stood nearly eight feet tall and about as broad. His hair
was golden and smoothed back. His skin was gold, too, but
from the way it sparkled in the morning sun it suggested he'd
been painted or dusted with actual gold powder. He wore only
a green-dyed leather loincloth.

At least Ryan hoped the leather was dyed. From the smell
that washed over him from the creature, there was plenty
room to doubt.

"So, I don't reckon there's any way I can convince you to
step aside and let me pass?"

In response the monster beat a glittery gold man-boobed
chest as wide as Ryan stood tall with fists bigger than Ryan's
own head. He leaned forward perilously, given a gut that suggested he'd swallowed an oldie Volkswagen Beetle wag for
breakfast, and roared. Thirty feet away the reek of his hot
breath suggested something that came out of a dragon. And
not necessarily its front end, either.

Casually, Ryan strolled to his left. How agile can the nuke-
sucker be? he thought. The creature flexed its legs, which

were like tubers, the same width from thigh to where they sort of spilled over the tops of splay-footed, crack-nailed feet. He turned in place to keep facing him.

Ryan darted right.

He had no awareness of the monster backhanding him. He was just suddenly flying backward into the air. He had just come to terms with the fact, more or less, when a shaggy-barked tree trunk hit him square in the back. He fell like a sack of grain into some bushes that broke his fall. Some of it.

"Fireblast!" he croaked. Brush crackled as he pushed himself up on hands and knees. He coughed, then spit, and was relieved to see no red in the spittle that gleamed on the grass. "You're quicker than you look. Guess you'd have to be."

He picked himself up. The gigantic golden swampie stood waiting for him. His orange-size bug eyes glared, his nostrils flared.

"So I get the notion that, if I hit you and you find out about it, I'm in deep shit."

He drew his panga. "So we do it this way, big boy."

Despite the way the drug he'd drunk tugged at the edges of his vision and twisted the world into fantastic shapes and vomitous colors around him, Ryan's tactical mind was sharp and racing. He hoped that wasn't another illusion.

He circled counterclockwise around the giant. The creature had to weigh half a ton, he judged. It was bastard tough killing a normal swampie who barely came up to Ryan's armpit. If they had doubled organs, this thing might well have *four* sets. Plus wads of fat and muscle sheathing its body, and a thick round skull, that he wasn't sure 9 mm round from his SIG-Sauer handblaster would even pierce. If he'd had the piece along. He judged it likely he could drive his panga with all his strength and weight into that immense gut and not even force the tip to the tough membrane of the body wall.

But structurally, he knew, any humanoid creature had its weak points. He'd have to attack one of those. And he'd have to make it stick.

He reversed to orbit clockwise, slowly closing with the creature. The swampie clenched and unclenched his hands. Just the joints working made sounds like walnuts cracking.

He ever gets those meathooks on me, Ryan thought, all he'll have to do is squeeze and I'll crumble like a dry leaf.

He feinted left again. The monster committed his weight to his right. Ryan changed course to dart straight toward the behemoth swampie, transferring his panga to his left hand. Ducking under the startling swift swipe of an arm, he hit the ground just to the mutie's left in a forward roll. He struck for the tendons at the back of the chubby left knee. Severing those would bring anything bipedal crashing down. Nor was that spot armored by either muscle or fat. If he could immobilize the creature, he'd have a lot better chance of chilling it.

Somehow he now knew that he had to defeat the monster. He couldn't merely dodge past it. Not that he'd managed that so far.

The giant swampie swatted backward with his left hand. It caught Ryan's wrist a glancing blow, numbing it. The panga flew out of his hand. The mutie's backswing continued to clip the side of Ryan's head.

Yellow sparks shot from temple to temple. Ryan was knocked sideways. He hit on his right shoulder and rolled over and over before fetching up stunned on his back.

The sun shone hot on his upturned face as his vision spun, then a cloud blotted the sun. Vaguely the one-eyed man realized the cloud was shaped a lot like a colossal bare foot. Upraised to stamp his head flat like a June bug. A *lot* like that.

He snapped out of his mental fog at once. The swampie stood astride him, his funk almost suffocating.

But there was another spot that wasn't armored, and on any male mammal was particularly vulnerable.

Ryan brought his knees to his chest and kicked with all his strength, straight up. He felt something big and dangly and soft squash beneath his bare heels.

The mutie emitted a shrill squeal through cavernous nostrils. He doubled forward, clutching at his wounded parts.

Ryan scooted butt-forward along the grass, which was helpfully slick with morning dew. He grabbed the rear flap of the stained leather loincloth, trying not to think about how soggy it was. Much less with what. The garment began to slide down the vast doughy buttocks as Ryan yanked himself to his feet by means of it.

However many lungs he had, the giant mutie was having no success getting air into any of them. He was trying to inhale in short gulps, each one of which sounded like a stepped-on frog dying. Ryan yanked the loincloth down to the mutie's thick ankles. Then, bending, he grabbed hold of a forward-angled lower leg. Hauling upward with all his power, he threw his weight sideways against the exposed buttocks.

The gigantic mutie toppled forward with the majesty of a falling building, ending in a thunderous face-plant into the sod.

The behemoth moaned. Leaving it no time to recover, Ryan yanked the loincloth the rest of the way free, then jumped onto the mutie's back as if he were scaling a spongy boulder.

The mutie had managed to drag in some breath. He let it out in a roar of rage, pushing himself off the ground with a seismic surge of his muscles. But Ryan dropped to his knees between the giant's golden shoulder blades, whipped the loincloth over his head and under his chin. Then he began to pull back with all his strength.

Don't roll, he silently begged the creature. For Krysty's sake, don't roll!

The loincloth's reek was exquisitely foul, like a cesspit a skunk had drowned in. The previous week. It made Ryan's head swim and his stomach try to crawl right up his esophagus and out his mouth to escape. He bit down hard and clenched every fiber of every muscle he possessed.

One thing the immensely powerful and durable mutie wasn't was smart. One arm pushed his blubbery upper body off the ground while the other groped blindly and ineffectually over his shoulder for Ryan. He wasn't flexible, either. Fat and muscle bound his joints, restricting their motion.

Then belatedly the mutie hit on the right answer. His arm flexed, then he reared upward and heaved his weight right, to roll onto Ryan and crush him beneath his bulk.

Ryan hung on as long as he could, strangling the mutie. At the last instant he leaped free and rolled. He wound up on his own belly this time, breathing like a steam engine with the throttle stuck wide open. He expected to be smashed into a pink rug at any instant.

But after he managed to pull in a lungful of air, smelling as sweet as honey after the horrible stench of the mutie and his ooze-drenched loincloth, he raised his face from the grass and looked around.

His foe lay on his back, arms and legs splayed. His eyes were closed and his tongue lolled from his open mouth like a giant dead slug. His chest quivered to continued breathing, but barely.

"Nuke-sucking bastard," Ryan muttered, climbing painfully to his feet and casting around for his panga.

His eye lit on his panga, lying a few feet away in the grass. He went and picked it up. Then he stood straddling the great upturned face with the long blade held point down in both fists, high over his head. He reckoned stabbing through its eye into its brain for a sure chill. Whatever organ arrangements swampies had, they definitely didn't have two of those.

He sucked in three deep breaths to strengthen his own arms, which trembled with exertion and complete adrenaline overload, then he stretched up on his toes to strike.

The eyes opened. Up close they were golden, huge and somehow innocent.

"*Pwease,*" the monster croaked. Instead of the boulder splitting roar of before, it now spoke in a child's voice.

Ryan froze. It was so completely unexpected.

"Unca," it said, high and thin. "You win. Pwease, no kill." Tears as big as Ryan's thumbs welled up over its thick lids and rolled down its vast cheeks.

Ryan crushed the hilt in his hands so hard the panga shook.

The vision of a beautiful woman, scarcely higher than his waist, nude and lush and inviting appeared in front of him. "Do it," her voice commanded in his head. "Do it, or you fail the test."

Still Ryan failed to strike home and end it.

"Pwease."

Trader's face appeared, lean and scarred and grizzled, hanging in air right in Ryan's own. "Do it," he rasped. "'Member how I taught you, Ryan. Chill your enemies, today and tomorrow. Chill them fast and chill them good."

"Yeah," Ryan wheezed. "That's right!" But he still didn't strike.

Another face appeared. Its splendor blanketed both Trader's disembodied vision and the full-bodied image of the naked golden woman.

"Krysty?"

"Ryan," she whispered. "Lover, do me proud."

She vanished. All he could see was that fat face, eyes pleading, lips blubbering, crying like a frightened child.

Ryan took another deep, shuddering breath. He tossed the knife away.

"He's no threat anymore," he said to the naked woman and his long-gone mentor, "and one of Trader's first rules was, no chilling for chilling's sake. If that doesn't suit you, then fuck you. I won't kill him to amuse you, fail the test or not."

Then the sick feeling hit him like an avalanche. He dropped to his knees, vomiting so hard he fell onto all fours.

After everything he'd eaten ever, and probably at least one lung, came up, Ryan took a breath.

The beautiful woman's outline glittered, wavered. Changed. It widened to become at least as wide as it was tall: still nude and female, with wild hair the color and texture of moss, breasts like watermelons with aureoles like brown plates. She was vined around and around with garlands of orchids. Dozens of fat little infants played in the dirt at her feet or peered cautiously past her short, elephant legs.

"That's my front yard you're puking up in, boy," she said mildly. Her voice, though soft and fluid, was a full octave deeper than his.

He raised his head and blinked at her through nausea-induced tears. "It's not…like I got…much choice."

She laughed musically. If by "music" you meant a stand-up bass. "You got spirit on you, boy. Maman Fucton likes that. Can you stand?"

He could. Barely. She didn't move to help him.

His body felt like one huge bruise. The good news was, he hardly noticed the itching and ache of his stung cheek anymore. The bad news was, it was because the rest of him hurt worse.

Sudden knowledge turned his head to lead. Much too heavy for the boiled celery stalk his neck had become. His chin dropped to his collarbone.

"So I failed the test," he said.

"Au contraire, cher. You passed with colors flying."

"How do you reckon that?"

"It's my test, for starters. Look upon the one whose life you spared."

He turned his head. No giant warrior lay there like a beached whale. Instead it was a swampie child, young and slim. By comparison. He was unconscious, with tear trails shining on his cheeks. He showed no sign of golden coloration, only the usual swampie near-albino.

"It was the drug," she said. "You and he fought in the dreamworld, the World behind the World. You prevailed."

"Against a kid!"

"In the dreamworld, he was as you saw. Had you lost, you would have died, sure as pointing the bone." She shrugged. "It was really you against whom you fought, and you whom you mastered."

"And if I'd chilled him?"

"You would've wandered in the luci-dream until your body starved and you died. And Krysty Wroth would meet a terrible fate."

"Why did you put me through this?"

"What reason has your kind given us to do nice things for you?"

"But I'm not part of whatever's been done to your people. Krysty sure isn't."

"I wanted you to prove you could show mercy to a despised enemy," she said. "Specifically, one of my children."

"That's your own child I fought?"

"It is a harsh world we inhabit. I think you've noticed. He volunteered for the task. He was proud."

It still made no sense. It occurred to him it didn't have to.

"So," he said. "When do we start?"

"Start what?"

"Papa Dough said to save Krysty I had to please you. So, uh, how do you like it?"

"Like what? Oh. *Oh.*" She laughed uproariously. It made her huge breasts jiggle on her huge belly, and the tiny toddlers around her feet to scatter like quail.

"You poor boy. That fat rascal put bad ideas in your head. You cannot please me that way, *cher*. You got to sport one like a stallion to scratch Maman Fucton where she itch. And I mean that just exactly."

Feeling stung, Ryan opened his mouth to defend his impugned manhood, then he shut his mouth. He realized that any argument that started out along the track of "my dick is, too, big enough!" meant he'd already lost big time.

"I could, uh, you know—"

She laughed again. "Poor boy. Don't you know I'm tryin' to let you down easy? You're just not my type."

He dropped to his knees. "How am I supposed to please you, then?"

"But, you already have! You have proved your complete love and devotion to your woman, and thereby given her an anchor to return to the waking world! She can come back now. It's so romantic. It makes me happy."

"But what—?"

"Wait one." She turned and vanished into her cave. He took advantage to catch up on breathing. It was too confusing to think, so he gratefully gave up trying.

Maman Fucton waddled out into the sunlight again. "Come here and hold out your hand, boy."

Numbly, he obeyed. She pressed a vegetable-fiber packet of herbs into his hand. It smelled pleasantly of mint and lilacs. She raised her arms over her head, exposing impressive arm bushes. Her smell was like that of fresh earth, not at all offensive.

"By the power of High John the Conqueror, and St. Excelsior, and Mama Yemana!" she declared. "Bless these fruits of Gaia's bounty, and let them help to reclaim Gaia's child, to the extent they shall be required!"

He looked at the packet in his hand. He looked at Maman Fucton. "That's it?"

"That's it." She made shooing motions with her hands. "Now, go. Go! Chop-chop! You and your friends must set off before noon, to redeem your promise to Papa Dough and save your woman from peril."

"From peril? What peril?"

"Papa Dough will tell you as you make ready. He has more truths to tell you, which you must urgently listen to. You are ready to hear them now."

"But—"

"No buts! You must arrive back in Haven tomorrow morning before the sun clears the horizon."

"Tomorrow morning? We're the better part of a week out of Haven. It's impossible to get back by then."

She smiled. "After what you have experienced here, you think to tell *me* what is possible and impossible? Now hurry. The daylight, you waste it!"

Chapter Thirty

The sound of an explosion roused Amélie Mercier instantly from her fitful sleep on the cot in her lab. She sat up, grimacing in irritation. The thin sheet fell from her slim nude body. She knew precisely what that noise meant, knew what was happening.

"The fool," she said aloud. "He has introduced chaos into the system. He outsmarts himself at last."

She rose and dressed hurriedly, then headed out the door for the big house.

Another blast greeted her. A ball of smoke rolled up a sky milky with predawn light from the direction of the waterfront. She heard a clatter of shots, and screams.

She set out at a brisk pace up the walk to the big house.

MERCIER STOOD OVER the supine body of Elizabeth Blackwood and watched the drug she'd injected take its effect.

The illness was hereditary. Baronial records suggested it skipped generations. Her father's exhaustive notes, combined with Mercier's own researches—and observations—suggested that what was involved wasn't purely a mutation. Rather, the shadowy predark technology of nanotechnology was almost certainly involved. Lucien Mercier's lab journals contained snippets of information, gleaned from old government buildings by scavvies, that hinted of research programs designed to create supersoldiers: fast, strong, and nearly unkillable.

In her unnatural sleep, Elizabeth began to toss her raven-haired head from side to side, clutch the sheets and moan. The process normally took some minutes. Mercier knew that somehow, presumably through the agency of nanotechnological assemblers in her system, Elizabeth's body would absorb the sheet that covered her body as well as unusual quantities of air, to bulk out her muscle mass and strengthen her bones and sinews for the transition.

This was what Amélie's father had been brought to Haven for, on such generous terms, when she was but a small child who had lost her mother under mysterious circumstances. It was to learn the true nature of the Curse of the Blackwoods, and save the baron's daughter, about Amélie's own age, from transforming into a humanoid predator that lusted uncontrollably for blood and human flesh. So far the best Lucien's research, and his daughter's, had been able to achieve was a means of temporarily controlling the change. And it came at the cost of severe physical debilitation.

There were, simply, times when the Beast had to be allowed to run free to kill and ravage. Only that restored Elizabeth Blackwood from the brink of death. This was the terrible secret burden the siblings carried, the shared cancer that ate at their souls—because they truly loved and care for their people, felt genuine anguish for the suffering the Beast caused. Mercier couldn't understand such expansive sympathy herself. But she had learned to recognize the symptoms.

Another thunderous crack was barely muffled by distance. Mercier recognized the report of a high-explosive warhead. The ville had no such weapons. It signified the pirates had found a way to evade Tobias's sec force and attack the ville directly.

Diverging urgencies warred within her. She felt a twisting need to return to her facility, to do her best to safeguard it from the raiders. Yet there was something she had determined to do here first.

Left to its own devices the curse acted in accordance with biological cycles that the best efforts of two generations of Mercier whitecoats had been unable fully to analyze. Extreme physical and emotional stress tended to trigger it, she knew. That was why, sooner or later, it always overpowered the suppressant drugs. When Elizabeth's reduced state began to threaten her life, the curse kicked in.

"Listen to me, Elizabeth," Mercier said with low-voiced intensity. Changes had begun to take place, seen as a writhing as if ants crawled beneath the woman's skin. "You are in danger. Your brother is endangered."

Mercier had administered a counteragent to the suppressant, along with a small quantity of amphetamine, to accelerate Elizabeth's heart rate and blood pressure and help fool the curse assemblers into believing their host was in mortal peril. Already the change had suppressed Elizabeth's rational mental processes. But in her current state, early in the transition, one could still speak to her midbrain, her emotions, and her deepest fears, buried in her reptile brain.

"The red-haired outlander woman in the room down the hall poses a deadly threat to your brother and to you. She has been sent by enemies to seduce him, so that he will throw you aside and be easier to bring down. She's *evil,* Elizabeth. She will come between you and Tobias. She means to destroy you both!"

Elizabeth's head whipped from side to side on the pillow. Some of her hairs had already begun to bond with the pillowcase and subsume its substance. Her features had, just at perceptibility's edge, begun to lengthen as the bones of her face literally restructured themselves into a protruding muzzle for more efficient biting.

But she heard. Fear was obvious on her increasingly strange face. Fear and rage.

Mercier sucked in a short breath, clipped lower lip in upper teeth. She dared not remain here. When the Beast took full control, the only warm-blooded creature on Earth it wouldn't attack on sight was Tobias.

It is enough, Mercier decided. When the Beast awakes, its first act will be to eliminate the menace of Krysty Wroth.

The woman turned, unlocked the door and went out. She closed the door but didn't lock it again.

Despite the rattle of gunfire, now faintly visible in the still corridor half filled with early dawn light, she felt triumph, and the satisfaction of a job well done.

That should do it for at least one of the bitches, Mercier thought as she walked with her customary brisk precision down the hall. With luck, it may even eliminate both barriers that stand between me and achieving my long-sought happiness with Tobias!

Mercier went down the stairs and out the front door. She could hear screams and shouts as well as pops of single shots. Snarls of full-automatic fire answered them. Black smoke rolled into the sky from the direction of Blackwood Bayou. It stung the mucous membranes of her nose, throat and eyes.

Mercier returned to her lab. Fighting hadn't yet reached it. Once inside its familiar sanctuary, she bolted the heavy metal door, then set out with cold-blooded efficiency to make certain preparations for what to do should the door successfully be forced.

Amélie Mercier considered herself a realist. She found it inconceivable to face potential disaster without proper plans.

IN THE PLANK-FENCED backyard of a blacksmith shop not far from the waterfront, Baron Tobias Blackwood squatted on the hard-packed earth with a dozen men clustered around him. He had his broadswords strapped across his back and held one of the ville's few advanced weapons, a fully automatic M-16 A-2, muzzle-up by its foregrip. His ruby eyes were bleak, his handsome sharp features streaked like marble with soot.

"That's the *Black Joke* herself, tied up at our own wharf as pretty as you please," he said. "She seems to have towed a number of smaller boats along behind her, packed with Black Gang pirates and their allies. Reports indicate there may be as many as two hundred of them."

Guerrero shook his head. "How could they get to the river? The mouth is blocked by chains and traps and sentries."

"They weren't supposed to get through at all," Barton said grimly. The baron's stout aide was dressed in shirtsleeves and dark trousers tucked into heavy boots. He had four single-shot handblasters stuffed through the belt, and carried a cutlass whose blade was already red-stained. "But they're here, so we have to deal with them."

"The way the bayous twine together, there are ways to get into one of them and slip to our bayou upstream of our obstacles unobserved," said a squint-eyed straw-haired man named Baker, who knew the country between the ville and the coast well. "We can't watch every nook and cranny of the coast. Once they got in and found their way to the river, they powered up it faster than even our swamp telegraph could spread warning."

"But to do that they'd have to know the way," Barton said hoarsely. "They'd need guides."

Blackwood sighed. He had already confronted the disagreeable truth in his mind.

"We're betrayed, whether by a spy in Haven or unfortunate locals captured by the pirates and forced to guide them past our watchers. That's for later. As Barton says, we need to deal with—"

From the edge of his eye he saw movement.

Even against the tumult of blasts, shots, screams and roaring flames, a loud human voice could carry a remarkable distance, attracting attention even against a background of furious noise. His companions, all sec men, ville leaders or sec men known to the baron as steady types, didn't chatter or permit their voices to rise.

So the two lean, dark men in baggy, filthy blouses of unbleached linen and ragged trousers who prowled into the yard clearly weren't expecting company. They were plainly two of Black Mask's island allies, with machetes in their belts and smokeless-powder blasters in their hands.

Blackwood's moon-white right hand tossed the black rifle in the air. The quick motion caught the intruders' attention. They turned, their eyes and mouths going wide, and tried to swing their weapons to bear.

Blackwood caught the pistol grip. As if the rifle was an outsize handblaster, he stuck it out to arm's length. He shot the intruder to his right first, then the one to his left, both through the chest. Both men collapsed to the ground, neither able to fire his blaster.

A jerk of Guerrero's broad thumb sent a couple of sec men to slit the throats of the pirates, who thrashed and moaned on the dirt.

"—deal with the situation we face," the baron continued as if nothing had interrupted. "We must move now. Those shots would have been heard. I'll lead the resistance here. Barton, you take four men as escorts and raise the farmers and ville folk north of town. When you bring them, send scouts and try to take the marauders in the flank."

Barton looked shocked. "Baron, my place is at your—"

Blackwood stopped him with a wolf grin. "Old friend, isn't your place where I send you? This is how you'll best serve me and Haven. Now go, and remember no one is expendable except the invaders!"

He could feel the others' spirits rise. This would be a long day and a bad one, no mistake. The enemy had twentieth-century weapons and apparently vast stocks of ammo. But Haven held the advantage of terrain, of men and women fighting for homes and children. It was up to him to ensure the coldhearts paid the greater price, and his people the lesser.

As the others checked the loads in their blasters a thought panged him. *Elizabeth.*

But I've done what I could for my dear sister, he thought, set guards at the house and a pair on her door. Beyond that, well, I have things to fight for, as well.

Besides, he thought, she should be perfectly safe in her bedroom.

St. Vincent's heart sang, though he made himself walk up the stairs to the third story with his accustomed stiff-backed yet elegant dignity. Opportunity presented itself; he'd decided to leap. He knew better than to trust the pirates and their notorious leader. But then, he didn't have to. What was important was that surely the pirates would solve the Tobias problem. Or at least severely weaken the foolish young baron's grip.

In the former case, provided Cawdor returned from the swampie realms—and if he were truly worthy, in an evolutionary sense, would he not do so?—he'd be far less squeamish about taking over a ville without a baron. Should Tobias, on the other hand, somehow survive the onslaught of the Black Gang, well, arrangements could be made.

In any event Black Mask's stoneheart pirates were out for loot and plunder. Once they'd sated their base desires they'd leave, regardless of their shadowy leader's agenda. Leaving the field clear for strong men, men of decision, who could guarantee a grateful populace no such calamity would ever befall again.

In the meantime, St. Vincent perceived a second golden chance: at last to ingratiate himself with the object of his long desire. Naturally he was stooping on it like a hawk on a hare.

Two sec men armed with muskets and cutlasses stood guard at the door to Elizabeth's room. Their eyes were wide and their faces stiff with terror and resolve. How thoughtful of Tobias to deploy them here as he sallied forth to fight the invaders.

St. Vincent merely nodded at the two of them, walked up to the door and rapped with the backs of his knuckles. "Elizabeth? It's me, St. Vincent. I need to talk to you."

Neither peasant lump of a sentry objected when he opened the door to Lady Blackwood's chambers. After all, he was the majordomo. He had the run of the house. If St. Vincent had business in the lady's bedroom, that was his business.

Especially for a brace of bumpkins who'd never seen the inside of the house before, nor ever expected to.

His knock got no answer. He knew Elizabeth neared the end of her cycle, when her body would need renewal and rebel against the restraints and ravages of Mercier's drug. But she still had strength enough to awake and to escape to safety, with the noble help of St. Vincent, and a long-laid plan for getting out of the ville secretly and in a hurry. He would ensure she was well aware of who had actually saved her while her precious brother was gallivanting off about his self-absorbed derring-do.

Not far from town, but not easy to find, a farmhouse waited. He and Elizabeth would be safe and comfortable there until the pirate threat, like a hurricane, inevitably blew over. During which time a hand as masterful as St. Vincent's could surely cultivate the seeds of gratitude into most delicious blooms.

He opened the door. "Elizabeth—"

The honeyed flow of words stopped in his throat as if they'd turned to stone and stuck there. There were hints of Elizabeth Blackwood visible in the grotesque elongated shape that crouched on the cratered ruins of the bed. The skin was the same pallid ivory. The perfect features were drawn forward into something resembling a snout, but the structure of those fine cheekbones remained the same. The mane of black hair that hung down her back seemed little changed, if perhaps somehow coarser.

The shriveled dugs and skinny, wiry haunches certainly didn't suggest the form of his long-time and secret beloved, which in his official capacity he had contrived to glimpse nude on sundry delightful occasions. And when the eyes, those distinctive violet eyes, turned and briefly locked on his, there was nothing remotely human about them.

"Elizabeth," he said, "wait—"

The creature sprang. As opened jaws and outspread talons flashed toward him, he cried out the last coherent utterance of his life. *"Not the face!"*

Chapter Thirty-One

"Sorry, boys," said the captain of the *Pocket Rocket*. The dumpy forty-foot wooden riverboat had picked up Ryan and friends not long after their swampie captors had removed their blindfolds. "That smoke there's rising from the Haven docks. Means trouble."

Mock Murphy had a shock of light brown hair and a face that seemed to consist entirely of seams. As it had throughout their brief relationship, a corncob pipe protruded from a corner of his razor-slit mouth.

"You can bring us down to the ville without going all the way to the main docks, if you're worried about the fire," Ryan said.

A boom hard-edged with high-frequency harmonics rolled up the river toward them. A flight of startled cormorants rose squawking from a sandbar.

Murphy shook his head. "That there's artillery. I'm not goin' nowhere near that."

Ryan winced. The reluctant river captain was right, and the one-eyed man had an uncomfortable feeling as to who sported artillery like that along this stretch of coast.

Frustration boiled his guts. He had thought Maman Fucton's prediction of how long it would take the party to return to Haven was either a poor joke or delusion. But no sooner had he returned to Papa Dough's ville, none too steady on his pins, than the swampies marched the outlanders to their own boats, which had apparently been brought to Dough's ville by water, blindfolded them once more, and set out. Shortcuts braiding the waterways of the river and bayou system had to have allowed them to make their way to Blackwood Bayou in half a day.

When the blindfolds had been removed their pirogues were already tied to a trio of cypress trees on the banks of the main channel, and the sun was getting low in the western sky. Jon Dough and a few companions bade them farewell and melted into the dense brush. The companions and their two surviving Havenites were left none the wiser how the boats had been propelled.

Within fifteen minutes they heard a horn, and *Pocket Rocket*'s sharply raked prow chugged around the river bend. They'd flagged it down and quickly negotiated passage to Haven dockside. Which turned out not to be all that far, for a powered craft riding with the current.

Despite the travelers' impatience, Murphy followed his standard practice of anchoring for the night, far enough out in the channel that nothing could leap aboard from an overhanging bough. The party slept on deck, crowding for shelter under a tattered canvas awning when a rain squall passed through sometime after midnight. When the sky had just begun to lighten predawn, Murphy and his two silent black crewmen cast off and got under way again.

Now Haven lay no more than a mile away. Krysty was scarcely farther. Ryan could feel her presence burning like a beacon.

"What's going on?" Mildred asked. She had gone back to sleep curled up on a coil of rope astern when the little wood-plank vessel resumed the trip. Now she padded forward, stretching and yawning.

"It appears the Black Gang has found a way to bypass Tobias's defenses, and fall upon Haven by water," Doc said.

Ryan stifled a groan. "Thanks for helping make our case for us, Doc."

"Don't rag on the old wrinklie," Murphy said. "Worked that out on my lonesome."

He looked Ryan in the eye. "End of the line, folks. I can set you and your boats loose on the stream here. Me, I'd recommend you stay aboard as I put about and chug back up Blackwood Bayou as fast as *Rocket*'s mill will carry her out of harm's way."

"You can't do this," Ryan said. "You made a deal."

"Tobias will pay," Rameau said.

Bluebottle stood unspeaking behind him. The big raw-boned guide had said nothing since they had surrendered to the swampies. He only hung around looking as if he had heard and seen blasphemies.

The Havenite boss was almost back in fighting trim, thanks to swampie herbal remedies. The Gotch Eye sting still hurt, he admitted, but he no longer felt weak or feverish, and had full use of his arm, which was about to come in handy in the fight for Haven. If only they could get to Haven.

"He'll pay if he's still baron," Murphy said. "But wait. I just remembered. Chills got no use for jack. Back upstream we go."

He started to turn to give the orders, then froze as he felt something hard and cool and uncompromising touch his neck.

"Okay, he's behind me now, isn't he? The mutie wolf-boy with that outsize handblaster of his."

"*Albino*," Jak said, cocking the Python. The captain seemed to shrivel even as he raised hands over his head.

"Sorry to play it this way," J.B. said, picking up his M-4000 scattergun from the hatch cover where he'd set it to cover Murphy's crew. They seemed disinclined to resist. "You don't leave us much choice. We've got a friend in Haven, and we need to get there triple quick."

"The captain is certainly correct that we dare not simply steam up to the Haven docks, with the pirates there in force," Doc said.

"Then we'll have to get as close as we can and hustle overland bastard fast," Ryan said.

He turned, wincing, as another sharp explosion rapped out from downriver.

"That's *Black Joke*'s recoilless, sure enough," J.B. said.

Ryan's guts twisted. *Krysty!* he silently screamed.

"KRYSTY." THE WORD rang in her mind.

Krysty Wroth slept. She knew that much.

At some deep layer of her mind she remembered a storm. And a snake, a sudden pain, a sense of invasion as venom suffused outward from the bite. Then instead of the expected agony, a wave of dizziness, a wave that became a spiral, and carried her with it down and down...

Now—when was now? Where was now? And was that her lover's voice that called her name?

Krysty, a different voice said in her dream.

"Gaia?" It wasn't the voice of her body that spoke, but it was her voice.

I am that which you choose to personalize by that name, yes. As your subconscious is processing vast forces at work into a voice you appear to hear, and words you believe you understand.

"Why are you speaking to me?"

You are healed. Your body has long since healed itself from the Dream Snake's bite. You have been kept unconscious through treachery. You sleep now under the influence of a drug.

It was true that Krysty could sense no lingering trace of poison or other damage in her body. Even though she had a strange sense, as if inhabiting a stranger's house.

You must move instantly. Otherwise no power of mine can save you.

When her eyes opened, she was falling to a hardwood floor covered by a crocheted rug from a height of less than a foot.

Something landed with great violence and a muffled impact just above her on the bed. Krysty hit the rug and rolled to the left, away from the danger.

She saw a creature crouching on the four-poster. It was perhaps the size of a very large dog. Its slenderness and general shape suggested a tailless cat, but it was hairless except for a lionlike mane of midnight hair. And the muzzle suggested a wolf or dog, although it was much shorter than either's.

The monster turned and squalled at her, then leaped. It reached with hands humanlike, but sprouting curving black claws that glistened with what Krysty thought was fresh blood.

By reflex Krysty pulled up both legs and kicked out. Her bare feet struck the creature in its pale belly, beneath washboard ribs. The pouncing horror gasped as air was forced out of it. Then it was flung clean over the bed by the force of Krysty's kick.

Krysty realized the power of the Earth Mother had charged through her body, giving her incredible strength.

Screeching furiously, the creature launched itself over the bed at her. Frantically, Krysty dodged. Her prehensile hair wound itself into a tight scarlet cap, mirroring her own agitation.

She flung herself toward the door. The creature struck where she had lain, just beside a bedside table where a kerosene lantern burned low. Gray light streamed through the open window, providing more illumination. Neither gave much.

The monster recovered from a skid across polished hard-wood and slashed at her with its talons. Krysty threw herself onto the bed and rolled across it.

The creature seemed taken by surprise by the speed and strength that its prey's muscles gave her. Krysty judged it was both stronger and faster than she was, although some-what lighter. She had escaped damage at its claws or needle fangs so far because it kept underestimating her.

She feared it would learn fast.

Krysty rolled off the bed, turned, grabbed it by the wooden frame and hurled the whole several-hundred-pound mass in the creature's face as it sprang at her again.

She hoped to crush it against the wall. Somehow it man-aged to push itself down in time not to get smashed by the massive frame. But the monster failed to reappear at once. It was injured or stunned.

Krysty bolted to the door. The scrape of nails on polished wood made her swerve aside.

A claw lashed out and raked Krysty's left shoulder. The monster slammed into the door. Solid oak panels cracked on impact. The creature slid to the floor, gathered itself, then launched itself like a quarrel from a crossbow.

Krysty pulled a chest of drawers down between them. Agile as a monkey, the creature scrambled over it and leaped at her again, at her face.

The titian-haired beauty got her hands up in time to grab the monster's upper arms. It tried to kick her and eviscer-ate her with its long-clawed toes. Controlling its upper body with her grip on its arms, Krysty twisted her hips. She tried to throw the creature away from her, but it got its feet on the floor and dug its claws into slick hardwood.

For a moment Krysty wrestled with the horror, strength against strength. Its breath stank of blood and ripped viscera.

To Krysty's shock, she realized the eyes, though slanted, were violet, and she thought she saw a trace of humanity there.

Shock made her concentration blink. Fangs snapped for her face, but she yanked her head back in time. The jaws clashed shut just short of the tip of her slightly snubbed nose.

The creature seemed to smile at her.

With a whoomp the pool of kerosene spreading from the lamp that had been smashed by Krysty ignited. The woman had been too preoccupied even to notice the smell of spilled fuel. Garish yellow light filled the bedroom, as yellow and blue flames chased each other up the mattress's underside. Smoke began to pool and bubble on the ceiling.

That distracted the monster. Krysty pushed its straining arms upward. Lowering her head, she thrust her shoulder against the monster's breastbone, above a pair of curiously shrunken dugs. She put a foot against the wall behind her to brace and pushed with all her Gaia-granted strength.

Smoke clawed at her eyes, her throat and laboring lungs. She ignored it. There was nothing but the dire need to channel every ounce of strength the Earth Mother had granted her.

Usually Gaia's strength lasted a short time, and drained her. She would pay for this later with bone-deep aches and total weakness. But first she had to survive long enough for there to *be* a later.

Step by straining step, Krysty forced the monster back. It tried to snap at her nape, but her shoulder was locked beneath its chin. It was stronger than she was, even with her great strength. But she had gotten lower, and the simple advantage in center of gravity was making the difference.

Her hair lashed at the monster's cheeks and blazing violet eyes to distract it.

Krysty heard the flames crackle, felt the heat on the top of her head. Smoke began to claw its way down her nasal passages and throat to her lungs. If they fought here too much longer, the smoke would incapacitate them, and then the flames would have their way.

The smoke took on a sudden acrid foulness as the monster's mane ignited. It whipped its head around.

Krysty let go with her right hand, cocking it back in a fist. The monster's left arm began to whip toward her. Krysty's straight right deflected the slash in passing, her fist catching the side of the narrow thrusting face as it turned back toward her. She felt and heard bone crack.

The creature squealed, and Krysty felt the tension go out of its muscles. She had stunned it, if only momentarily.

Seizing her advantage, Krysty flexed her knees. Then with every ounce of the strength that seemed to flow up from the Earth itself, through the foundations of the big house, through its wooden planks and beams that had once been living trees, and up into her body through the bare soles of her feet, she picked up the monster and flung it hard against the door.

The back of its head struck the frame so hard the wood cracked again. The monster collapsed in a tangle at the foot of the white-painted door, as if all its joints had come apart at the same time, and left it a jumble of dissociated bones in a pale skin bag.

At once it began to change. The sharp feral features seemed to soften and spread. The muscles like bunches of wire and steel cable began to bunch and shift inside the smooth pale skin.

Suddenly the Gaia strength fled Krysty. She dropped with a painful jar to her hands and knees, panting and trying not to throw up in a sudden wave of nausea. She breathed in huge shuddering gasps, not yet gripped by the usual total weakness.

The air was clean and cool down here near the floor. That helped.

Krysty raised her head. What had been a monster was

melting and reforming into a shape like that of a young woman. Already the face was almost human. A lovely face, she saw. The horrific snarling visage of moments before had been a cruel parody.

She saw her backpack standing in the corner, by what had been the foot of the bed. She forced herself to her feet.

She picked up the bag and shouldered into the straps. The flames had begun to spread, already eating through the ceiling. She had to get out of here now, but her way out was blocked by the unconscious…young woman. Krysty could tell that she was still breathing. But barely.

Krysty faced a choice. She owed the young woman nothing, as far as she could see. She had been trying her level best to mutilate and kill Krysty, mere hammering heartbeats before.

But had her mind and character changed as well as her form? How culpable was the person taking shape before Krysty's emerald eyes of the terrible acts and intentions of the monster she had been?

Strength was flowing back into Krysty's muscles. Oddly, she was regaining her normal power. Apparently payback for the supercharge would come later.

"Thank you for looking out for me, Mother Gaia," she said. "I hope what I'm about to do isn't triple stupe."

She went to the door, stopped, slung the woman across her shoulders, pack and all, in a fireman's carry. The woman was noticeably lighter than the monster was. Her limbs were slimy. Krysty realized there was a pool of some kind of liquid on the floor where she had lain.

Her lips skinned back from her teeth in a grimace of disgust. Something was going on here she didn't understand. She felt no overwhelming urge to learn the details. Only to get away from this place now.

For the first time she became aware of the sounds of gunshots, muffled by distance. A substantial battle was raging not far away. That, and the increasingly hot, vigorous and smoky fire threatening to choke her with the stink of burning feathers and kerosene, were excellent reasons to move.

Out in the hallway she saw the remains of what a quick tally of heads and limbs suggested were three dead men. For some reason the only one whose features were untouched had a remarkably well-manicured mustache and pointed beard, and in the staring wide gray eyes the most concentrated look of horror Krysty had ever seen on a human face.

Despite her burden, Krysty went quickly down the two flights of stairs. She encountered no living person inside the big house. Instinctively she shied away from the front door. Casting around, she soon found herself in a large, spotless kitchen, which had a back door.

She left the woman, still completely unconscious and now completely human, on the lawn well clear of the house. She could smell gunsmoke now, hear shouts as well as shooting. A serious explosion made her wince as it assailed her ears.

Leaving a beautiful naked woman lying out in the open in the midst of a battle wasn't the kindest thing to do, but it *was* kinder than leaving the mysterious shapeshifter to burn alive. And there was a limit to how much even Krysty Wroth's big heart bled for someone who had just tried to rip her limb from limb.

Wearing only a gossamer nightgown and unwilling to linger long enough to root in her pack and do something about, she slipped into the woods.

Chapter Thirty-Two

As soon as Amélie Mercier heard the ringing impact of something heavy and metal on the steel door of her laboratory, she knew her fate was sealed.

She closed her laboratory notebook, placed it in an insulated safe beneath the desk and locked it. The safe itself was bolted to the concrete floor. The pirates wouldn't easily dislodge it. She hoped it would survive their depredations and the...necessary consequences.

She had already made preparations. Now certain final details had to be attended to. She carried them out punctiliously, her whole being focused on following proper procedures. Procedure, detail—those defined a well-ordered life.

Finished, she sat in her scavenged swivel chair facing the door and waited.

At last whatever massive metal object the raiders had found to use as a battering ram got the better of her door. It crumpled, tore away from the hinges. Light only just beginning to show a golden color poured in.

It was followed by men with rough voices and pawing hands, whose breath and bodies stank. Mercier didn't resist them. She knew it would do no good, might only enrage them at worst. In any event she was no fighter. She lived by and for the mind.

Although if she had had the chance, perhaps her heart could have won a place in her existence. But that would never come to pass now.

They stripped her naked. She felt light-headed. They mauled and slobbered on her small, firm breasts, licked her neck, even her face, with their disgusting, reeking, viscous slobber. She bore it all with detached calm.

Nor did she give them the pleasure of showing fear or resistance, or anything at all, when they bore her down on her back on the cool concrete floor. She lay limply passive as they pulled her legs apart.

The others chanted and cheered as the first man prepared to rape her.

No one noticed when her right hand groped out, beneath her desk, and found an igniter. Clicked it.

She had the last gratification of seeing her potential rapist's eyes bulge from his filthy face as the flames enveloped him. Then the explosive combination of pure oxygen from the concentration machines, and the acetylene gas took over, shattering the lab's interior and everything inside in a yellow flash.

Amélie Mercier felt an instant of searing dragon's breath. Then nothing.

"THAT SMOKE," Jak said, pausing as he led the group through the woods toward Blackwood's house. He had learned the trails and paths around the ville hunting with his local friends. "Not like."

Ryan frowned at the white and brown smoke. It was coming from about the direction Jak told him the big house lay.

"Krysty," he said. Slinging his Steyr, which he had been carrying in his hand, he started to run.

"Hey," J.B. called, "you're heading into a battle, remember?"

"I'm heading toward Krysty!"

AT THE EDGE of a little clearing, with knee-high grass and flowers and dense brush on the far side, Jak stopped short. He held up an urgent hand. "Someone coming."

The two companions had run half the distance to the big house, close enough for Ryan to see the smoke streaming from the high-peaked roof of the big white building. And not from the chimney pots. His being rebelled against stopping now, with his lover trapped in a burning building. But if Jak told you to stop in the woods, you stopped. Or the odds were you were on the fast track to the last train west.

Then the albino teen sniffed and said, "Oh."

The brush stirred across the little clearing. Jak straightened. Instead of aiming his Colt Python, he pointed its vented barrel at the ground. Ryan frowned. This wasn't Jak's usual behavior.

A figure stepped from the brush. Ryan had an instant impression of ivory skin, contrasting with scarlet hair that stirred though there was no breath of breeze in the clearing. A very familiar voice was cursing a backpack for hanging up on the brush.

It wasn't possible.

"Krysty?" he said tentatively, as if afraid she was an illusion that would vanish into air.

She looked at him with hot green eyes. "Ryan," she said, "where the hell have you been?"

Then they were in each other's arms, their mouths joining in a long and searching kiss.

They didn't break free until the others joined them. "Sorry to intrude on you young lovers," Mildred said, "but we've got a situation here."

"A spontaneous remission, by the Three Kennedys!" Doc exclaimed. "So our journey into swampie land and the sacrifices our companions made were in vain."

"What's he talking about, lover?" Krysty asked.

"You got bitten by a snake. You went into a coma. We had to go stop a war with some swampies to bring you out of it. Or so we were told."

He looked at the others. "Not so sure it wasn't necessary. Maman Fucton told me my just being there might provide kind of a lifeline to bring Krysty back. Thought it was just a metaphor at the time."

He teetered on the brink of saying why she said she told him that, then he didn't. There were some things a man just didn't have to talk about. Also the thought of talking about how Maman Fucton said his love and devotion were the key to Krysty's pulling out of her deathlike trance put a knot in his tongue.

"What about that herbal packet Maman—that is, the swampie shamaness gave you to heal Krysty, Ryan?"

Ryan frowned a moment, then laughed. "Reckon she gave it to me so I'd feel I got something for my pains. Something happened there, and I believe it helped Krysty pull out. As to what, I'll never know. And I'm fine with that."

"And what will you do with the packet now?" Mildred said.

He shrugged. "Hang on to it, I guess. Who knows what it might come in handy for."

"So where to now, Ryan?" J.B. asked. He nodded toward the sounds of shots. "That isn't our battle now. Especially given what we know."

"I don't know as it isn't our battle," Ryan said. "These people did right by us. Mostly. Anyway, I made my deal with Papa Dough. I aim to carry it through, Black Gang or no Black Gang."

"That's fair," J.B. acknowledged.

"Ryan, the most amazing thing happened to me," Krysty said.

"Not now, Krys—"

"Mother Gaia wakened me just as I was attacked by some sort of horrible creature. I knocked it out and it turned into a young woman with long black hair!"

Ryan pursed his cheeks and let a lot of air slide out his mouth. "We got a lot to fill each other in on. But we also better get a move on, if we want there to be anybody left to help against the pirates."

"You can go ahead and start," she said, laying her pack down in the grass and opening it up. "*I'm* going to get out of this nightgown and put some clothes on as we talk."

"IS IT A GOOD SIGN or a bad sign when the shooting and shouting starts to die down like this?" Mildred asked.

"Depends on who it means won, Mildred," J.B. said.

Giving wide berth to the burning house, which they feared would prove a beacon for trouble, they had worked their way close to the main square. Now they crouched in an alley that ran between structures of brick and planks from the local mill. An empty wagon and some crazily stacked crates and barrels offered concealment from casual observation.

Mildred's heart hammered in her chest. She was acutely aware that even now they might be surrounded by bloodthirsty enemies. So what else was new? she asked herself, trying to drain the tension.

It didn't work.

"That fearful cannon has remained silent for some minutes," Doc said.

"Recoilless blaster takes a spell to reload," J.B. said.

At a sign from Ryan, Jak prowled ahead. A handful of moments later he was back, looking agitated.

"Square full pirates," he reported.

"Very well," Doc said. "The cessation of combat appears to be a bad thing, then."

"Still our fight, Ryan?" J.B. asked.

"Still our fight." Mildred knew the Armorer wasn't being timid. Only practical.

"What's our move?"

"Let's get a better look at the situation," Ryan said.

Jak led them into a side yard. There was a chicken coop but no chickens, and a little garden, a couple of chairs on a swaybacked porch. Mildred could detect no signs of life anywhere in the building or immediate environs. Any occupants had either fled the fighting or joined it.

They crouched by a fence that allowed them to look through knotholes at the plaza, still a block or two away.

Before she should squelch it a groan escaped Mildred. "They've got Tobias."

EVEN KNOWING what he did, it angered Ryan to see the baron in such a state. Naked from the waist up, he staggered under the weight of a huge timber beam, which had been tied across his broad shoulders with thick ropes and his arms lashed to it. He looked badly beaten. His long white hair hung lank in a face that was a mask of bruise and blood. Blood streaked his body. Laughing pirates prodded him along with the muzzles of longblasters.

"This isn't good," he said. "Mebbe he didn't play entirely straight with us about his sister, but he doesn't deserve this. We've got to try to do something. Doc, you pair with Jak. Mildred and J.B., you're the other team. Krysty, you're with me."

"Always, lover."

"We're north of the square. J.B., Mildred, try finding a position on the west side near this end. Doc and Jak, you take up position on the north side."

"If we sneak around to east and south," J.B. said, "we'd be firing them up from the rear, sitting clean astride their route of retreat. That throws a good scare into folks. Does a lot to even out triple-bad odds."

But Ryan shook his head. "Two reasons. First, it'd take too bastard long. Second, when those coldhearts break and run, do you want to be sitting right smack between them and their ride out of town?"

J.B. chuckled. "Right, Ryan. I hear you."

"Infiltrate as far forward as you safely can, find some good firing positions. Teammates watch each other's backs. Standard stuff. Wait for me to shoot my longblaster."

"What about you and Krysty?" J.B. asked.

Ryan showed his teeth in a grin. "I been lugging this fancy sniper rifle all over the Deathlands. Time to do me some sniping."

"WE'RE NOT seriously thinking of taking on this pirate horde all by ourselves, are we?" Mildred asked as she and J.B. slipped through a deserted hardware store.

"We'll see."

"It's nuts! There's a hundred of them out there." She gestured through a front window. "They'll roll right over us!"

"They're pirates, Millie. Not looking to get shot. They're out for loot and a good old time. Hit them hard and right, they'll just scatter."

"What if they don't? Besides, even if Ryan needs to pay off the debt to the swampies, can't we just wait until the pirates pull out and talk to whoever's left in charge of the ville then?"

"Might not be so eager to listen to us if we didn't help when the chips were down. Anyway, I'm so sure this fight's done. These Haven folks are tough. I think they may muster a counterattack here before long."

"Aren't we staking our lives on a lot of ifs?"

J.B. gave her a quick tight smile. "Haven't we always?"

Jak hunkered down next to a wag piled high with cargo covered in waxed canvas. It was one of a line of similarly laden wags parked with tongues down along the west side of the square. That was one of the things about the ville: people could leave their goods out like that and not have to worry about them getting stolen. The kids he'd run with since coming here all took that sort of thing for granted, which struck him as being strange.

Well, they left their stuff out safely until *now.*

He glanced over at Doc, crouched behind the next wag in line with his big handblaster in hand. Jak felt a slight resentment being saddled with Doc, but he had to admit the old man handled himself pretty well in a fight. He didn't make too much noise creepy-crawling, either—by the standards of people who weren't Jak Lauren.

He'd learned to make allowances.

They had a narrow path between buildings handy, so they could pull back if they needed to run. That was always important to Jak—knowing you had a way out.

With a hunter's patience he settled down to watch events over his front sight, and wait for Ryan's shot to start the party.

Most of Haven's buildings stood a single story high. For some reason several of the rare two-story structures clustered just half a block back from the square's northwest corner, around one that actually sprouted a third story. It was barely more than a little square room with a roof and big windows looking all four directions. Ryan reckoned it was likely a watch tower.

It was an ideal spot for a sniper. So Ryan moved on. He picked a second-story roof one building west of the three-story tower. Once he opened up, any pirates better off than double stupe and blind in both eyes would just naturally reckon he was shooting from the highest point around, and open up on the little blocky watchtower with everything they had. There was even an off chance there'd be line-of-sight between the structure and the *Black Joke*'s bow-mounted recoilless blaster. Ryan wanted no part of that.

As he wriggled forward on belly and elbows across the rooftop, Krysty said from behind him, "Lover?"

"Yeah?" He glanced back. He wasn't any more worried than she clearly was about pirates overhearing. The cold-hearts were raising a powerful hullabaloo out there, laughing, shouting, jeering at their prize captive. Ryan suspected casks of imported rum had been discovered and used to fuel the general good feelings among the marauders.

Krysty was dressed in a gray checked man's shirt and jeans, and she carried her little Smith & Wesson 640 snubby in her hand. Even former Olympic shooter Mildred, a wizard with a handblaster, would have had her work cut out for her hitting anything she aimed at with that piece at this range. But Krysty wasn't there to shoot at pirates down in the square. She was there to shoot pirates trying to climb on the roof and blast Ryan in the back while his eye was glued to his scope.

"Would you *really* have screwed that swampie magic woman to save me?"

Ryan's stomach did a slow roll, and not just because of the unwelcome visual image her words brought to mind. This was one of those questions any man feared from his partner.

As he usually did where Krysty was concerned, when in doubt he fell back on honesty. "Yeah. Made up my mind I was going to get you back whatever it took."

She smiled like the sun breaking free of the clouds that had stolen in from the sea to cover the ville.

She caressed his calf and briefly laid her cheek against it. "I'm a lucky woman. I love you, Ryan."

"Um. Love you, too."

She pulled away and was all business again. She had his back, and no coldheart was getting past her. Well shy of the lip of the roof, Ryan reared up to peer down at the square.

"Fireblast!" he said. He sat up and got his legs around in front of him so he could bring up the rifle and prop his elbows inside his thighs. The rifle thus steadied, he peered through the scope to confirm his startling initial impression.

"It's Black Mask himself down there!"

Chapter Thirty-Three

Ryan clicked off the longblaster's safety, sucked in a breath and started to let it go as he sighted in on the black-cowled head of the surprisingly slight figure in its black frock coat and pants. Then, "Damn," he said.

A body blurred by being off the focal point obstructed his vision. He looked up over the top of the scope. A phalanx of six burly black-clad pirates, with black shades and black bandannas tied around shaved heads, had taken up position in a semicircle behind the pirate chieftain.

"Sec goons in my line of fire."

"Should we move?"

He gave his head a quick shake. "No time. Now, shush. I need to hear what I can."

MILDRED COULD HEAR quite well. She and J.B. were crouched, barely breathing, a yard behind open windows in the storefront, behind and to Black Mask's left. They didn't have a shot at him, either, thanks to his bulky bodyguard.

"So Baron Blackwood," the pirate boss said. They could tell he was speaking because of the way his hood slightly muffled his words. "You have no idea how long I've waited for this moment."

Blackwood had been bashed by rifle butts to his knees on the trampled grass of the north end of the square. His head hung so that his hair hid his face. The light rain had resumed. The drops made tiny explosions on the beam across his back.

"But then, you've no idea who I really am." Black Mask's voice sounded more cultured than Mildred expected. It was dry and rasping, and cut like a thin whip.

Blackwood's head jerked up. He showed a look of puzzlement mixed with disbelief. Unless that's my imagination, Mildred told herself. Not easy to see his expression beneath all that blood and bruising.

"Yes," Black Mask said. "I believe a light is beginning to dawn."

Deliberately he reached up, unfastened his hood and pulled it off.

SIXTY YARDS from where J.B. and Mildred were concealed, Jak could see the face revealed when the mask came off. "Triple ugly," he muttered softly.

It was a normal enough middle-aged dude face, triangular, fairly thin. But something had clawed the right side of it all to shit. Then it had gotten bastard infected. That whole side was furrows of scar tissue like a plowed field.

ALL MILDRED COULD SEE was the back of Black Mask's head. His hair was dark, curly, cropped short. It seemed to be dusted with gray.

But Blackwood reacted as if he'd been shot. "Dupree!" he exclaimed.

"Dupree," she repeated softly. "That's—"

"Baron Dornan's old sec boss," J.B. finished softly.

"But I thought he was—"

"Chilled? Blackwood thought so, too." J.B. held a finger over his lips and turned his attention forward again.

The pirate mob cheered and jeered. The diminutive Dupree stood with hands on hips, soaking in the moment.

"You thought I died, didn't you, you treacherous whelp? The one decent thing I ever did in a long and nasty life was to help Dornan try to kill that bitch-pup sister of yours. Too bad his reward for a good deed was you chilling him with his own sword. And that sister of yours ripped my face open and left me looking like this! The Beast of Blackwood left me looking like this!"

He raised his head and turned it this way and that. "Are you getting an earful, you Havenite pieces of shit?" he shouted. "I know you're out there, cowering in your holes like mice. Yes. It's the truth. The mass of fucking scars on the front of my head bears witness. Elizabeth Blackwood is the Beast! And her brother's been covering for her all along!"

Blackwood was sitting bolt upright despite the weight of the beam on his back. His expression was like a thousand miles of badlands. Rain ran down his face like long pent-up tears.

"They used you. The Blackwoods used you. For sport. Like cattle!"

"That's not true!" Blackwood shouted. "Elizabeth has no control over her sickness. We tried our best to stop it. Tried to...at least to keep the damage down."

"I bet that makes a huge difference to the families of those your sister ripped limb from limb. 'Oh, I feel so much better about the Beast eating my baby girl Michelle's guts like a string of sausage, now that I know it's really that lovely Elizabeth Blackwood.'"

"So now you pose as liberator of Haven?" Blackwood challenged.

"Oh, no! What do I care for the people of Haven? You, and Elizabeth the Beast had that right. They *are* cattle. They were never fit to lick dog shit off Baron Dornan's boots. They let this happen to me. How they must've celebrated, thinking that bastard Dupree had finally been chilled!"

He laughed. "Well, you all fucked up. Dupree didn't die.

Dupree didn't forget, either. No, Tobias, you hypocritical bleached turd, I'm going to loot this town of every scrap, every scavvied thing that might possibly be of value. Then I'm going to burn it down. To the nuke-dusted ground! All your precious people will be sold into slavery, and the weak ones chilled. After my boys have had a chance to play with all the prettier women."

The pirates shook grubby fists in the air and roared approval. *That* they understood. Dupree turned left and right, making rising motions with his turned-up hands to encourage them.

"I'm going to tear down everything you tried to build here, Tobias, you ungrateful prick. Before you die, in long and excruciating agony, you will know the supreme taste of ultimate failure. And, oh— What have we here?"

He turned. A party of men appeared from Mildred and J.B.'s right carrying a limp female figure dressed in a sodden white silk gown. She appeared to be unconscious. Raven's-wing hair trailed on the dirt of the street beneath her.

"Elizabeth?" Mildred said. "Oh, shit."

She looked back in time to see, clearly, Blackwood mouthing the word "Elizabeth."

So she was the Beast, Mildred thought. Maybe she deserved to die. She didn't deserve what these monsters would do.

"What good luck!" Dupree crowed. "Here she comes now, the Beast herself. Not looking so formidable, is she?"

Dupree stiffened. "Wait! What does this mean, anyway? I gave explicit orders that the big house was not to be touched until I said so!"

"It was already on fire when we got there," one of the men accompanying Elizabeth said defensively. "She was lying out on the lawn and some servants were dressing her. They ran off, so we thought we'd bring her to you."

"Oh. Right." Dupree seemed to bounce up and down on his toes. "Right! Excellent idea. I think I'm going to rape your sister before your red rat eyes, Tobias. I'm going to take my time. And then a hundred or so of my closest friends—" he waved around at the ragged mob, who howled in excited anticipation "—will take their turns pleasuring her. Whatever's left, you'll get to watch me torture to death, before I crucify you in the middle of this square and burn your squalid little ville around you! How do you like that, young Baron Tobias?"

Then, his voice faltering, he said, "Tobias?"

"Dark night!" J.B. exclaimed softly. "He's *changing.*"

Rage knotted Blackwood's face. But mere muscular tension couldn't account for the bizarre crawling that was taking place beneath his fine alabaster skin. Before Mildred's shocked eyes his features altered. His jaws stretched into a blunt, fanged muzzle. His eyes retreated behind massive protective brows.

His ropes appeared to be melting into the very skin of his arms. As if they were being absorbed by them. The arms themselves sank into the surface of the heavy wooden beam to which they were tied, as if drawing substance from them.

"Blind norad!" Dupree shrieked. "He's a beast, too! Chill him! *Chill him!*"

Most of the pirates hooted and cheered. They couldn't see the monstrous transformation taking place as Blackwood's muscles writhed and rearranged themselves on a skeleton that was, impossibly, itself shifting structure. They thought this was a new sadistic game their boss was playing with his victim.

But one of the black-clad cadre guarding the former Black Mask understood perfectly well what was happening. He raised a pump scattergun toward the monstrous white face snarling from beneath the wooden beam.

The pirate's shaved head exploded in a shower of chunks and dark spray.

"WHY CHILL THE SEC MAN, not the boss?" Krysty asked, risking a glance at the scene below as the ejected empty spun free and Ryan jacked a fresh cartridge into the chamber.

"Got no clear shot at Dupree," Ryan said. "Anyway, I reckon this is between Blackwood and Dupree. If the nukesucker looks like he's winning, I'll chill him though."

He sighted and fired again. Another black-clad bodyguard fell.

"Eyes peeled," he warned Krysty as he racked the bolt. "They'll come running to the sounds of my shots like a dinner bell."

THE PIRATES HAD BEEN firing blasters in the air off and on, as coldhearts who aren't very smart will in times of exceptional high spirits or in a state of drunkenness. At first they didn't realize there was anything different about the shots echoing across the square.

Then Blackwood broke the massive beam across his back.

Mildred gasped as he flung the heavy halves away. One struck a pirate in the back and just folded him in two the wrong way. His spine snapping sounded like a handblaster going off. Before anyone could react the Beast Tobias had sprung forward and grabbed Dupree with his clawed hands.

The white monster, which looked more lion than wolf, hoisted the former sec boss and current pirate king over his head into the air. Face up to the rain, Dupree howled and thrashed, to no avail.

With a ripple of monstrous muscles, Blackwood bent his

old enemy backward slowly, slowly, until Dupree's spine snapped, too. Mildred winced as she heard the distinct pops of multiple vertebrae giving way.

Then, tossing his prey in the air like a housecat with a mouse, Blackwood caught the still-shrieking Dupree and twisted his head off his shoulders. A great gout of blood covered the baron face to feet with the dying pulse of his enemy's heart. He brandished the horror-struck head in the air and roared.

Mildred saw a bullet strike his side. He barely reacted. She sighted the ZKR on the head of the nearest black-leathered bodyguard, then fired. The coldheart crumpled. She felt the sideblast of J.B.'s shotgun as he pumped rounds at the pirates. From across the square Jak and Doc opened up, as well, their weapons cracking and booming respectively.

The pirates wavered. As she emptied her cylinder and fumbled in a pocket for a speed-loader, Mildred knew her lifespan was now measured in minutes if not seconds. Even as Blackwood flung himself into the mob, tearing men apart and tossing pieces aside in a way that could only remind her of a whipper-snipper she saw there were just too many of the bastards, too well armed.

"Been a good run, Mildred," J.B. said, stuffing fresh green-hulled shells into his tubular magazine. He saw how hopeless their situation was, too. Of course he would.

Mildred shot a face that appeared at the window in front of the temporarily helpless Armorer. It twisted away.

"Really good, John. Have I told you how much joy you've given me?"

And that was when hundreds of infuriated Havenites, rallied by Barton from north of town, poured into the square, shouting and shooting with vengeful glee.

BARTON WINCED as a fresh set of ear-punishing explosions rippled off to the east. White flashes lit the black cloud of smoke that rose from the direction of the bayou.

"I wish they hadn't done that," he said. Meaning, that the victorious Havenites hadn't put the torch to Dupree's flagship *Black Joke.* "Aside from the fact we could use the supplies and any information aboard her, we'll be lucky if half the warehouses the pirates failed to set on fire don't burn down now."

"People can feel some pretty high spirits after a victory like today's," Ryan said.

He and his companions stood on the front lawn of Blackwood's house, now trampled from its former manicured elegance to sorry muck. The rain, the servants' vigorous but not very effectual bucket-brigade efforts, and the ancient house's intrinsic toughness had slowed the conflagration's progress. But even as more folks freed from the battle turned up to help fight the blaze, the great house was doomed.

But this day's victory had been major. When the forces Barton had whipped up scythed into them, the pirates, already demoralized by coming suddenly under fire when they thought they had everything sewn up—not to mention getting shredded to pieces by the Beast Tobias—had turned and run right off. Few even tried to make it back to the boats. They just headed due south into the swamps, hoping to make their way to the coast, where they ran smack into a couple hundred angry Havenites swarming up from the Gulf, eager for payback from years of torment and plunder at the Black Gang's hands, which they were, so far as Ryan knew, busily wreaking even now.

Ryan put his arm around Krysty, who snuggled close and beamed at him. "Sometimes you got to just know what victory is," he said.

Barton's big shoulders slumped. The man was plainly spent, physically and emotionally.

"You're the seasoned fighting man," he said, "so I suppose I should pay attention. I hardly know what to think just now. Where could Tobias and Elizabeth be?"

"Coming yonder up the path," Doc said, pointing with his swordstick. He stood under the gazebo, staying dry. Or at least not getting any wetter. The way he'd been staring into space, rocking on his heels and humming "The Battle Hymn of the Republic," Ryan was surprised he was connected enough to the here-and-now to notice.

Half naked, barefoot and looking as if he'd showered in gore and forgotten to towel off, Blackwood carried his sister's limp form step by torturous step. Men ran to help him, but he shrugged them off. Instead he walked straight to the porch of blazing house.

"Be careful, Baron!" Barton yelped. "It isn't safe there. The whole house is about to come down!"

Blackwood smiled gently and nodded. "Yes, my good and faithful friend. I know."

He looked down at his sister, who clung to his chest like a feeble child. "It's the last chance, Elizabeth, dear. Are you sure this is how you want it?"

She nodded.

The baron of Haven looked up. His eyes were blood-colored pools of sadness.

"My sister and I are guilty of many crimes. I make no excuses. We have tried to atone by our actions, but I know now that was never possible."

"Baron, what are you saying?" Barton cried.

"That the Curse of the Beast must end here. It is carried in our very Blackwood genes, altered somehow by heedless science before the days of skydark. I name you baron now, Barton. I know you'll do better at it than I, if for no other reason than that you have no ravening monster lurking within, awaiting only the moment to escape.

"And farewell to you, Ryan Cawdor, Dr. Tanner, Jak Lauren. Mildred Wyeth and J. B. Dix. Good friends and heroic ones. And Krysty Wroth—I apologize for my sister's actions and wish only you could have known each other under better circumstances."

"Me, too, Baron," Krysty said. "But wait, there's no need—"

Sadly, he nodded. "Yes, there is need."

Without more words he turned. Yellow flames now belched out the front door. Pausing only to kiss his sister on the cheek, he carried her unflinching straight into them.

Overcome with fatigue, Mildred twigged a beat late. She uttered a scream and tried to throw herself forward in a belated effort to stop them. J.B. caught her from behind and held her despite her sobbing struggles.

The greedy flames instantly swallowed Tobias and Elizabeth Blackwood. As if on cue, the whole mighty structure fell in at once upon them with a vast crashing and groaning. The heat that welled from the collapsing house drove everybody scrambling back.

A fountain of yellow sparks shot skyward toward the clouds, oblivious to the now pouring rain, like souls ascending to the heavens.

Epilogue

"You know, Ryan," J.B. said, standing with his foot up on a locker behind the bowsprit of the vessel now doing business as *Fallen Angel.* Above and behind him her triangular mainsail snapped and boomed in a stiff easterly breeze. "I kinda wonder, didn't poor Tobias know all of us got monsters inside, just waiting to get out?"

He paused a moment and shrugged. "Granted, not all of us got monsters that actually turn into lions and munch pirates when they break free."

"Philosophy, John," Mildred said from behind him, "isn't your strongest suit."

Behind them the crew out of Haven moved briskly about their seamanly duties in the clean-smelling early morning air. They were all pleased at their handsome new vessel, a fifty-foot schooner, although there were still some nasty cleaning duties left over from the previous owners.

They wouldn't be needing her anymore. Scarcely had the flotilla of pirate boats towed behind the *Black Joke* vanished up a masked and little known inlet into the system of interlinked waterways than Havenite coast dwellers rowed out and fell upon the skeleton crews left on board the larger ships, hungry for retribution. As seasoned seafolk themselves, the Havenites made sure to damage the vessels as little as humanly possible.

The crews, not so much.

Krysty put her arms around Ryan's waist from behind.

"Wouldn't it've been lovely if we could have stayed, lover?" she asked.

He patted her hands. "Yeah, mebbe."

A shift in the wind carried a fine mist of salty spray into his face. In the heat of the Gulf morning, even with the sun just peeking mischievously at them from dead ahead, it was welcome coolness. He smiled.

"Well, couldn't we at least have taken Barton's offer of employment on a trial basis? With the swampie war ended and the pirate situation dialed way down, Haven's a pretty stable ville. They should be back on their feet in a year or two."

Barton, once a baron's chief aide-de-camp, now baron in his own right, had agreed at once to the terms brought by Ryan from Papa Dough, pending face-to-face negotiations in a few weeks' time to shake the details into place. Barton had never believed in the war. But he had been a genuinely loyal servant of the ruling family, especially its final generation.

And that, Ryan knew, was the point where the metal seriously commenced to scrape.

"You seriously believe he meant it?" J.B. said. "After we burned down the house, not to mention his favorite baron and his sister."

"But Barton seemed like a good man."

Behind, Jak uttered a caw of laughter. "So Tobias! How that work out?"

"Baron Tobias was indeed a good man," Doc said deliberately. "A flawed man, it is true. But in this wicked age of this wicked world, where is the man who is not?"

"Baron turn into monster," Jak said. "Some flaw!"

"Admittedly, some flaws are of greater magnitude than others."

"I agree with Doc," Ryan said. "Tobias was a good man. But in the end trying to do good in two different directions tore him apart."

"And what moral instruction do you draw from Tobias's dilemma, my dear Ryan?" Doc asked.

Ryan shrugged. "World's a complicated place, for sure."

"When you're thinking of a good man being bent this way and that like a length of bailing wire," J.B. said, "you might also consider the old saw about barons and gratitude."

"Why, John Barrymore!' Doc exclaimed. "You *are* a philosopher!"

"Dark night!" the Armorer said. He brushed at his scuffed leather jacket. "Don't let on. People might fear it's catching."

"Elizabeth was a good woman, too," Krysty said.

"Powerful judgment," Ryan said, "allowing as your only interaction with her involved her being a ravening monster thirsting for your blood, and all."

"I can't pretend I sensed anything from that creature but rage and hate and fear," Krysty said. "But I talked to people of the ville about her. About the life she tried to live, as opposed to that which was pressed on her. The evil wasn't of her choosing. It was a hateful gift of predark science."

"She could've stopped it, though," Ryan said.

"How?" Krysty asked.

"She could have chosen suicide, instead of continuing to change shape every now and then and go kill people—then in between work hard to make up for what the Beast did."

Krysty sighed. "You're right. The world isn't simple."

"Still," Mildred said, "it would be good not to be constantly driven from pillar to post, We don't even have to put down roots. Just…rest."

"We all feel that way, Mildred," Krysty said. "But J.B.'s right. Haven wasn't an option after everything that happened. Not really."

"Least they let us ride boat where it go," Jak said.

"They owed us that much, sure," J.B. said.

Ryan turned around to face his friends. "Listen up,

people," he said. "I want it, too. What you all want. An end to constant running and gunning. Peace. Sanctuary. I promise one day we'll find it—*home*."

"Cross your heart and hope to die?" Mildred asked playfully.

Ryan did the deed with his thumb. "Cross my heart and hope to die!"

And, laughing, they sailed away up the golden trail of light on water, into the rising sun, toward a dream that receded as perpetually as the horizon.

* * * * *